What would happen if Greek extremists blackmailed Britain into returning the Elgin Marbles – particularly if the blackmail involved the Queen, and dark secrets about her uncle, the Duke of Windsor's past?

A drawing by Raphael is sent anonymously by post from the 'Apollo Brigade' to Edward Andover, Surveyor of the Queen's Pictures. This is followed by two other pictures, all looted by the Nazis from various countries during the war. Andover soon finds himself not only preventing secrets from the Queen's family past being made public but fighting a demand for the return to Greece of the Elgin Marbles, a demand which turns to violence and murder, as the identity of the Apollo Brigade becomes known and they engage Andover in a desperate fight for survival . . .

'Inventive, pacy, political thriller. Keeps sleep at bay' *Guardian*

'Intelligent action in a realistic thriller' *Mail on Sunday*

Peter Watson was for many years a journalist on the staffs of *The Sunday Times*, *The Times* and *Observer*. In 1982, after disguising himself as an art dealer, he exposed a gang of art smugglers who were stealing old-master paintings in Italy and selling them in New York and London. His account of the adventure, *Double Dealer* ('Enthralling' *Time* magazine), won a Gold Dagger Award from the Crime Writers' Association and the BBC TV film of the book was nominated for an Emmy.

Since then Peter Watson has exposed several other art-world scandals – the trade in fake art deco vases, the smuggling of Etruscan pottery out of Italy and the gold lining stolen from Tutankhamun's tomb. He has written for a number of magazines, including *The New York Times*, *Connoisseur* and *Spectator*, and his collecting column is syndicated around the world.

Peter Watson is also the author of the international bestselling thrillers, *Crusade* and *Landscape of Lies*:

'Classy entertainment' *Evening Standard*

'Non-stop action, an incredible vortex of fights and frauds' *Guardian*

'*Crusade*'s real edge is that it could be next week's news' *Daily Mail*

Stones of Treason

Peter Watson

HEADLINE

First published in 1991
by Hutchinson, a division of The Random Century Group Ltd

First published in paperback in 1992
by HEADLINE BOOK PUBLISHING PLC

10 9 8 7 6 5 4 3 2 1

ISBN 0 7472 3742 5

Printed and bound in Great Britain by
HarperCollins Manufacturing, Glasgow

HEADLINE BOOK PUBLISHING PLC
Headline House
79 Great Titchfield Street
London W1P 7FN

Author's Note

In the spring of 1945,
in the immediate aftermath of
the Second World War,
Anthony Blunt – then Surveyor of
the King's Pictures –
was dispatched to Hesse in Germany
on secret business
on behalf of King George VI.
In 1979 in the House of Commons
Prime Minister Margaret Thatcher revealed
that Blunt was a self-confessed
Soviet spy, and that
MI5 had known of his spying since 1964.

So much is fact – but this is a novel.
The action takes place in 1996.

For
Robert Ducas

Contents

WEEK ONE

The Missing Masterpiece

1

Wednesday

Edward Andover knew that it was mildly eccentric in someone with his station in life but the fact was he preferred a bicycle for getting around London. Strictly speaking, it was probably beneath him to be seen pedalling along the Mall, books and files wedged untidily into the basket on the handlebars, his left thumb constantly tweaking the bell at tourists who straggled into the road. The black and yellow headphones of his Walkman didn't help either. They were clamped to his head like the strings of a bonnet, as he soaked up that morning's helping of Basie or Bruckner. The Surveyer of the Queen's Pictures, as Edward had now been for five glorious months, spent most of his waking hours in the elevated company of Hans Holbein, Leonardo da Vinci and Sir Peter Paul Rubens. A bicycle simply didn't fit.

None the less, on that Wednesday when it all began, Edward arrived at St James's Palace on his bike and there was good reason. It wasn't far from his grace-and-favour flat in Kensington Palace, it was a brisk July morning with the sunlight as bright as butter and, if you had the passion for pasta that Edward did, it was about the right amount of exercise. It wasn't arduous enough to bring on a heart attack – and might just keep one at bay.

He turned off the Mall into Marlborough Road. Half-way along he free-wheeled to a stop in the small courtyard of St James's Palace and dismounted. Edward wheeled his bicycle towards a shiny black door set into the wall of the palace and half hidden within a cloister. He spent his life in grand buildings. He could not fail to, for the Royal Collection was divided among magnificent households: Buckingham Palace, Windsor Castle, Hampton Court, Balmoral Castle, Sandringham and Kensington Palace. St James's Palace, however, was his favourite, and not just because his office was here. He relished the fact that St James's was in among the traffic of London, rather than set back behind some huge royal retaining wall. He liked the fact that he could pop out to Christie's, or his club, or across the road to Hardy's to

3

have his fishing rod repaired, or to buy some flies. The London Library was five minutes up the road and so was Paxton & Whitfield, where he could pick up some fresh Parmesan. At Balmoral the driveway alone was two miles long, and the village a mile beyond that, so it took all morning to cash a cheque.

Edward knocked on the black door. He sensed movement behind a spy-hole set into the woodwork, then heard a rattle as a bolt was slid back. The door opened and a uniformed security guard smiled at him. Edward needed no pass; his face was his pass.

Edward Andover was a tall, rather lanky man of thirty-five with a nose that had a prominent bridge to it. He had broken it playing the saxophone in his school jazz band: the drummer, a small Welsh boy with more enthusiasm than skill, had lost control of his sticks during a performance of a Jelly Roll Morton number and one had hit Edward slap in the face. He took comfort in the fact that he had once found a nose just like his own in one of Leonardo da Vinci's sketchbooks. Edward's eyes, brown as country eggs, were set off by tufts of pale blond hair, which sprouted energetically from the crown of his head but failed to cover his brow.

He signed in and parked his bicycle in a small inner courtyard where the fire-buckets were stored in a red row. He slipped off his headphones and took the books and files from the basket on the handlebars. A door across the courtyard opened into a corridor with windows along one side: his office lay that way. Through the windows he could see a small square lawn. Beyond that was a wall, with roses, and beyond the wall there was another lawn. He knew all about that second lawn though he had never been there: it was the Queen Mother's garden. Clarence House, the Queen Mother's official home, rose beyond the wall and the gardens; it was built of a faded yellow stone which Edward hated. Left to him, he would have blown up Clarence House and started again.

Reaching the end of the corridor, he turned into a large hall with a wide pale-oak staircase. A view of an English castle, one of the Royal Collection's many Canalettos, hung above a dead fireplace. Here another uniformed security guard sat at a desk. Edward moved across and signed for his mail. Ever since the letter-bomb scares of the 1970s the mail for the entire royal household was screened. Today there were about fifteen envelopes –

average. He picked them up and mounted the staircase. His office was on the first floor.

'Dr Andover . . . this is for you as well.'

Edward looked back down at the guard. The man's fingertips were resting on a parcel, which leaned against the legs of the desk.

Frowning, Edward stepped back, bent, and felt the parcel with the fingers of one hand. The packet must have been a couple of inches thick, and nearly square, each side almost a yard long. The wrapping was brown waterproof paper held in place by a strong white string. His name and the palace address had been written in bold black capitals with a felt-tip pen. He lifted the parcel. It was light – very light. Instinctively, he felt there was a picture inside. The size was right, the weight was right, if there was no frame. But who would send a picture through the post? It could damage so easily. And why? The Royal Collection was still added to, though Her Majesty, bless her, was no Charles I when it came to connoisseurship. But sending paintings, valuable or otherwise, through the post was unheard of.

He looked at the security guard and shrugged. Carrying his books, his Walkman and the rest of his mail in one hand, Edward grasped the package in the other. He turned and mounted the stairs a second time.

His office was entered through that of his secretary, Wilma Winnington-Brown. Wilma was a handsome woman, almost as tall as Edward and with a near-identical nose. A widow of long standing, whose late husband had been a colonel in the Blues and Royals, she had his pension to supplement her modest stipend from the royal household and always looked as spick and span as a palace guard. Bossy in the extreme, she was referred to throughout St James's Palace as 'The General'.

She was on the phone as he entered but flashed him a smile as bright as a broadside. Her perfume clogged the room. Edward smiled back and went through to his own office. It looked out on to Cleveland Row. This was a small square which, in The General's terminology, governed the approaches to Clarence House and Lancaster House. For almost all the time Cleveland Row was deserted. No cars were allowed to park there any more and, unless you were one of the very few privileged to lunch with the Queen Mother, the road led nowhere.

Edward adored his office. Its chief feature, as you could not help noticing, was its sloping floor. At some stage in the past – two hundred years ago perhaps, or three hundred, but in any case before the age of foundations – the palace building had settled. The broad oak floorboards, now almost white with age and scrubbing, had sagged and bulged and warped but they hadn't given way. The room had character.

The wall opposite the windows was lined with books and auction catalogues but on the wall away from The General's office, opposite Edward's desk, hung one of the perks of his job. At the moment it was a white chalk drawing by Veronese, a few delicate lines on blue paper. Edward had the pick of the Royal Collection if he wanted it. Whenever he was researching a picture he could, with Her Majesty's permission, which she almost invariably gave, remove that picture for study. He would hang it opposite his desk for weeks on end.

He placed his mail on his desk and set down the Walkman. He laid the parcel on a table which he used for conferences and then began to replace on the shelves the books he had taken home the night before. As he was doing this, Wilma came in. She put a cup of coffee on the desk next to the unopened mail.

'Two messages – and may I say you look a bit peaky this morning, Edward. You weren't up too late last night reading, I hope? You must look after yourself.' Few generals – few secretaries, come to that – were as maternal as Wilma Winnington-Brown. One of her children was an unmarried daughter of twenty-eight and she lived in hope.

'What are the messages? And, if you must know, I had dinner at the National Maritime Museum last night. The food there is enough to make anyone seasick. And it was all over by ten-fifteen.' He saw The General smile contentedly before adding: 'Then I went down to the Albatross Club and listened to the Louisiana Big Band till half past two. I'm not "peaky", General, I'm shattered. Now – messages, woman, messages.'

She grimaced, then smiled. She liked to think she was more of an adjutant than a secretary. 'I've put your sweetener in your coffee – just one, so don't add any more behind my back. Now . . . message number one is from Chetwode at Sandringham. They had a bad cloudburst last evening and a skylight wasn't properly fastened. The rain got in and fell across one of the Watteaus. Chetwode would like instructions.'

Edward picked up his coffee and sipped it.

'Message number two: Geneviève Chombert called from the Louvre. They would like to move your lecture next week from Tuesday to Wednesday – do you mind? Seems one of the other speakers can't make Wednesday and she wants you to swap. I said you'd let them know before lunch – don't forget it's an hour later over there. Oh – and yes: don't forget also, message three, that I'd like to leave a little early tonight – the son's birthday.'

It always amused Edward how The General referred to her offspring as 'the son' and 'the daughter', as though they were nothing to do with her. He replaced the coffee-cup on his desk and smiled. 'I'll do a deal with you. You may leave at four provided you get some new batteries for me on the way back from lunch. Scarlatti was definitely slowing down as I came along the Mall.'

'It's beneath me but I'll do it,' she said, turning back to her own office. 'I'm a secretary, you know, not your mother-in-law.'

Grinning, Edward walked across to the table and stood over the parcel he had placed there. The morning shadows cast by the window-frames reached across the waterproof paper, dividing the packet into squares, like the strips on a canvas by Mondrian. Edward didn't recognize the handwriting on the paper but then he had no idea who would send him such an object. Even now the curiosity he felt about the contents of the packet was outweighed by a sense of intrusion: his was a fairly peaceable, almost routine, existence, well away from the limelights of the world. He liked it that way. Telemann's oboe sonatas contained more than enough excitement for him. Also, just now he was overburdened with work. Sir James Hillier, Director of the Royal Collection and Edward's boss, was in hospital, recovering from a back operation. For the time being that left Edward with more than his usual quota of duties.

With a sigh he took up a pair of scissors, reached for the package and cut through the string. As he had thought, when he reached the object inside the wrapping it proved to be a picture. However, as he turned the thing over and round, so that he could look at it the proper way up, his pulse throbbed in his temples. This was a very good picture indeed. It was a drawing, in black pencil and chalk on faded yellow paper, and mounted on card. It showed a woman and two children, two chubby babies, the whole formed into a pyramid-type structure.

On the left was a sleeping infant while at the right another was pointing at the first.

Edward examined the drawing from all angles. It appeared as though, at some stage in the past, it had been folded: fold lines were visible and divided the composition roughly into six rectangles. The clothing was well drawn and so were the fingers. Obviously it represented the Virgin and the infant Jesus and the other child was probably the infant St John. That much was clear, but beyond that the picture looked Italian, either late fifteenth or early sixteenth century.

But why had it been sent to him?

He had been so intent on the picture, so carried away by its beauty, that he had forgotten to look for any covering note. He bent down and searched amid the wrappings on the floor. Sure enough, there was an envelope: his name was typed on the outside. He straightened up, placed the picture back on the table and tore open the envelope. Inside was a single sheet of paper, plain, with no heading. Two lines were typed on the sheet, laid out like verse. The message, however, was prosaic. It read:

THERE ARE MORE WHERE THIS CAME FROM.
YOU'LL BE HEARING FROM US AGAIN. THE APOLLO BRIGADE.

Mystified, Edward turned the paper over but there were no other marks and certainly no signature or name of any kind. He examined the envelope again: nothing, just his name, typed. He reached down a second time for the wrapping-paper and found the postmark. It was smudged but might have read 'London N1' or 'N7'. It was dated a couple of days before and hadn't even been registered. Part of him was exasperated at what appeared to be some sort of game. He reread the lines. 'There are more where this came from.' Did that mean the picture was a forgery? That drawings like the one on the table could be turned out in any number? But he was sure the picture was not a forgery, not a modern one anyway. Then he realized why he wasn't more exasperated. Whatever game was being played, it was fairly serious. The picture was too good.

Yet that didn't help. Why him?

On top of one of the filing cabinets next to his desk was a small wooden easel. He reached for it now and set it down on the table. He arranged the drawing on it so that it could be viewed from his desk. The second line of the message said he would be hearing again, so presumably the mystery would be cleared up in due course. He had things to do and had better get on.

He spent the rest of the morning at his desk. He arranged for a local restorer at Norwich Museum to go across to Sandringham and report back to him on the damage to the Watteau. He called Geneviève Chombert in Paris and confirmed that he could deliver his lecture – on baroque pictures in the Royal Collection – as easily on Wednesday next week as on Tuesday. All the time he was on the phone, he scarcely took his eyes off the drawing on the easel.

He set to work polishing his lecture for Paris. He had a good library here in his office and got up from time to time to consult a book. On one of these occasions, as he passed the drawing, he picked it up again and inspected it closely. Then he took down another book from the shelves, flipped through the pages and stopped at a particular illustration. He examined it closely, comparing it with the drawing on the table. Then he read what was written in the book below the illustration. As he did so, he moved back to his desk and shouted to Wilma: 'Get me Michael Arran, please!'

Arran was on the line in seconds. The Director of the National Gallery was a busy man but Edward Andover was both a friend and a powerful figure in the museum world. At least twenty of the main attractions in the National Gallery in Trafalgar Square were loans from the Royal Collection.

'Are you busy for lunch, Michael?'

'I'm afraid I am, Edward. But I should be back by three, and I'm in the gallery all afternoon after that. Is it something urgent?'

'I don't know.' Edward explained about the package.

'Odd, I agree,' said Arran. 'But I'm not sure why you need my help.'

'Not you personally, Michael. I need the expertise of your staff. This is an odd business, as you say, but I'm beginning to believe that "odd" is not a big enough word to describe it.'

'What do you mean?'

'This isn't just any picture, Michael. I've done a bit of checking and I've compared it with similar drawings in the books I have here. But I can't be certain – that's why I need your help. However, I've a very good idea that this drawing sitting on my desk, this piece of faded paper, sent unregistered and unprotected through the mail, is an original – by Raphael. It must be worth millions.'

The diode display on Edward's telephone answering machine stared up at him out of the gloom. The figure '3', square and squat, cast a green glow over the top of his desk. He had worked late, trying to complete his lecture – but had failed. It needed another half-day's work, he reckoned. Even so, he hadn't reached his flat in Kensington Palace until after eight, by which time the light was going.

He loosened his tie and went to the bar, or the lacquered tray with bottles on it that he called a bar. He mixed himself a whisky and soda, and raised the glass to his lips. He surveyed the flat. The wallpaper, the curtains and quite a bit of the furniture came with the job but the pictures were his own. There was a lovely watercolour of Ely Cathedral by William Callow – brown, yellow and peach. A view of the Nile by Edward Lear – vivid blue and gold inks. Over the door to the bedroom was placed a small oil by Edward Molyneux, showing two roses in a glass. The water was depicted meticulously and the petals were a gorgeous tangerine. On his desk was a photograph of him driving a 1934 Bugatti at Silverstone. Old racers were Edward's one extravagance.

On the floor by his desk was a pile of papers two feet high: his filing cabinet. He could never bring himself to throw anything away – certainly not paper. There was another pile, of old letters and bank statements, on the bottom row of the bookshelves by the window. A third was crammed into an old briefcase half hidden underneath the desk. If this room wasn't untidy, it was definitely cluttered. He pressed the switch on the answering machine.

After a few clicks, and a pause, a voice said: 'This is Father, Edward. Sorry to miss you. Barbra sends her love. Please call us when you can. Hope you are well. Bye!' Edward was an only child. His father, a successful architect, lived at Stanford in California, where he lectured at the university and had developed a new bridge that was supposed to withstand earthquakes. Edward's mother was dead and Barbra was his father's second wife, an American. The three rarely met: even a telephone call was unusual, though Edward did miss his father. The pair were touring the Western Isles in Scotland and would be in London soon.

The second message was already beginning as he took another swig of scotch. 'It's Samantha. You *did* promise to take me to that big jazz concert, at the Albert Hall. Can you bear it? Arabella, my friend from school, wants to come. Don't worry if you've changed your mind, or forgotten – we'll just stick pins into your effigy at school. That's it. Bye?'

Sammy was Edward's godchild – a gangling blonde of sixteen, with a huge appetite for new experiences. Edward smiled, thinking of her. The trip to the Albert Hall would be hilarious. He drank more whisky and waited for the third message.

'Hi, it's Nancy. Where *are* you? Don't answer that if it will make me jealous. I'm in Hackness – Yorkshire in case you're not sure. Some great tombs by Matthew Noble, but you probably know all that – it's hard trying to teach you anything. It's hard even trying to talk to you in person. This is the third message in a row that I've had to leave on your goddam machine. Where *are* you, Woodie? Is anyone else listening to this with you? If they are, switch off now.' After a few seconds' silence, during which Edward sank some more of his whisky, Nancy's voice was heard again, more of a whisper this time. 'Woodie, I've just had a bath and haven't got dressed again, not yet. All I'm wearing is the telephone. If you were here . . . I've thought of something I *could* teach you. So long.'

Slowly, Edward tapped his teeth with the rim of the whisky glass. An image of Nancy Tucker, lying on a bed, danced before him. Nancy was a Californian living in London. They had first met when Edward was giving a lecture at the Courtauld Institute of Art, where she was a graduate student studying the history of sculpture. Now in her late twenties, Nancy had grown up on the beaches near San Francisco and still had the straw-coloured hair and brick-brown complexion of her teens. At twenty, however, she had discovered art, suddenly turned serious and swapped the beach and the surf for the seminars of a college back east. She had graduated top of her class and been rewarded with a scholarship to study in London.

Nancy had proved full of surprises. Edward drained his glass and thought back to their first time together. The first surprise had come when *she* had asked *him* out. They had gone to a movie – he kept finding himself using Americanisms now – and

11

afterwards she had surprised him again by hauling him off to the nearest McDonald's for a 'Big Mac' hamburger. She insisted on paying, confessing to Edward that, despite her Fendi hand-bags, her intimate knowledge of the greatest sculptors of the world, despite the fact that she had a secret supply of Iranian caviare and that one day she would inherit one-thirty-fourth of the Vosné-Romanée slopes in Burgundy, she was a 'junk food junkie'.

On their first night, Edward had watched, amazed and amused, as Nancy had carried the tray to their table. She wore good-quality, simple clothes – straight, plain dresses that half hid the details of her figure but totally revealed her shape. Her skin was so good that she only wore tights – or 'hose' as she called them – on the coldest of days. She had a ballerina's neck that helped to take her height to five foot eleven.

She had set down the tray on the table, and handed him a plastic knife and fork.

'I wonder if they know their flatware is Regency?' he said with a grin, holding up the handle of the fork.

'Don't be such a snob, Woodie.' Her brother was an Edward, too. She missed him, she said, and, since he was known as 'Woodie', she had given Edward the same honour. She waved some chips on her fork in his direction. 'Fast food made America great. It tastes just as good as Yorkshire pudding, or kedgeree.'

'I *hate* Yorkshire pudding, and I've never had kedgeree.'

Nancy hadn't replied. She couldn't: she had some hot fries in her mouth and was busy fanning air at her lips with her fingers.

Eventually, Edward had said, 'I thought the movie was a bit over the top. The American imagination at its worst.'

She had flashed him a glare, to see if he was serious or joking. 'Booshi!' she said with her mouth full. Edward took this to mean 'Bullshit!', a favourite word of hers. She cooled the fries in her mouth with a swallowing of iced Coke.

Edward shuddered but grinned. 'I mean it. Sentimental, mawkish, optimistic beyond reason.'

The film had featured a nurse in a mental hospital who had got through to an autistic patient who had witnessed a politically sensitive crime.

'People need happy endings.'

'Americans certainly seem to, more than most.'

'How would you like ketchup on your collar?'

'Is that your argument?'

'It was an *entertainment*. Don't take it so seriously. It's already grossed two hundred million.'

' "Gross" is the right word.'

Nancy had licked her fingers then and Edward, sitting in his flat in the gloom, now reflected that whatever she did, however American Nancy Tucker was, 'gross' was the last word to describe *her*. She had a natural grace, a wholesomeness that he found enchanting and endlessly self-renewing.

However, Nancy had not been over-impressed by his attachment to the royal household. Nancy was a republican and thought all royal families should be abolished. Not executed or deliberately humiliated or impoverished, but simply overlooked and turfed out of any official role in a modern state. Only when Edward had explained that his chief job at the Royal Collection would be to produce a catalogue of the Queen's baroque holdings and the sculpture did she concede that his work was fit for a full-blooded male.

Outside McDonald's, the night had smelled damp and the clouds above were dark and heavy with rain that was yet to fall. 'Jazz?' he had said. It was still early, barely eleven, and he felt it was time he repaid some of Nancy's hospitality.

That was when she had swung another surprise on him. 'No,' she had breathed. 'There's something I'm longing to say.' She had looked him in the eye, then kissed his cheek and held her lips close to his ear. 'All night long, I've wanted to say: "Take me back to the palace." '

'You don't want royal families, but you're happy in their palaces, eh?' But he had taken her back all the same and they had made love on that very first evening. Edward still cherished the discoveries he made later that night. Nancy's brown back and the sweep of flesh on her thighs were like the slopes of a desert, driven smooth by the wind. Her shoulders, her long, long neck, the deep groove of her spine moved in and out of the shadows like a wild animal glimpsed in the bush.

But there was one more surprise to come. After that first date, Edward didn't see Nancy again for nearly two weeks. She had gone away – she was just beginning her survey of sculpture in British churches – and didn't tell him, or anyone probably, where she was. After ten or eleven days she had called him, proposed a movie and, when they met, was as warm, as high-spirited, as irreverent as on their first meeting. When Edward had asked where she had been, she was vague, but the pattern was set. When they were together, Nancy was so full of affection that Edward found himself wondering whether she had been denied it as a child. She also had the strongest sexual appetite of any woman he had known. But the unpredictability was galling. The fact was, Edward missed Nancy but he was growing a little weary of her comings and goings.

The fact that they kept missing each other on the phone was typical of Nancy too. She knew Edward's movements yet seemed, almost deliberately, to call when she knew he wouldn't be in.

He sighed and dialled the number of the hotel where he knew she was staying. But of course she was out at dinner. He smiled. She'd be lost if there wasn't a McDonald's nearby.

2

Thursday

At the very top of the National Gallery, in Trafalgar Square, there is a studio which every artist would envy. An enormous double-glazed skylight floods the room with what feels like a waterfall of light. Even on a dull day it is as if you are up among the clouds, and the daylight in the studio is never less than shimmering.

This is where the nation's collection is cleaned, revarnished, revitalised. Even to reach the studio, where four or five enormous easels stand about like blind totems on a Pacific atoll, is something of an adventure. Access is by means of one of the largest, and certainly one of the slowest, lifts in the world. When the great Venetian masters – Bellini, Titian, Tintoretto and Veronese – carried out their commissions for the Doges and cardinals and wealthy merchants of the 'serene republic', they were instructed to fill the most sumptuous and the most enormous buildings. Their canvases – great banquet scenes, which decorated the refectories of the monasteries, or vast battle formations, which occupied the political buildings of state – were often over twenty feet long, and almost as high. These days, when they are transported to the studio at the top of the National, the lift has to be big enough to take them, and gentle enough so that when it starts or stops there are no jerks, no sudden movements of any kind to dislodge the precious paint.

Edward Andover now stood beneath the great skylight, trying to hear what Michael Arran was saying, above the sound of hailstones as hard as teeth clattering on to the glass. No bicycle for Edward today, no Telemann or Teagarden over the earphones. He patted his hair into place as he listened. Edward was a bit self-conscious about his receding hairline.

'I *said*,' groaned Arran, pointing to the skylight to explain the need to repeat himself, 'I *said* that Martin is on his way. We won't keep you long.' Arran was a small, fussy man.

Edward had brought the picture to the National the previous

afternoon. If it was indeed a Raphael it was much too valuable to be entrusted to a messenger.

Edward's main field was baroque art, Arran's was German and Dutch painting, so they had called in Martin Ramsay, Keeper of Italian Painting at the National. Yesterday afternoon, Ramsay had stared hard at the drawing, removed his spectacles, put them back on, pushed them up over his forehead, whispered, 'Good Lord!', and then looked at Edward. 'May I keep this overnight? There's a piece of research I'd like to do.' They had arranged to meet here today after lunch. Ramsay had said, mysteriously, that the studio was the best place 'from a security point of view'.

Edward had turned this phrase over in his mind on the way up in the lift. What on earth could Ramsay mean? Was he being melodramatic? Was the picture at risk in some way? Edward turned now to Arran, to ask his view. For a moment the clatter on the skylight had eased.

As he did so, however, the lift doors slid open and Ramsay came into the room, followed by a security guard. He looked around at the three or four restorers working in the studio, then turned to Arran. 'With your permission, director, I think we should send everyone downstairs.'

Arran bridled. 'Come on, Martin. What – '

'I mean it.'

Arran could see that he did. He turned and waved his arms at the restorers, shepherding them to the lift. Slowly they complied. They were in the middle of things and didn't want to leave brushes and pigments just lying around. But at length the last one disappeared inside the lift, the guard closed the doors and the odd-shaped box began its slow journey downwards.

'This had better be good – '

'It is,' Ramsay cut in. 'I don't see how it helps Dr Andover's mystery, but what I have is very good. I can guarantee that.' He walked over to an easel and placed the drawing on it. The others followed and he turned to face them. 'There's no doubt it's a Raphael,' he said.

'You mean it's a known picture, in all the books?' Arran looked surprised.

'Not *all* the books, Michael. But enough, yes.' Ramsay turned the picture over and pointed to a mark. 'See that: "1774E"? I thought I recognized it last night, but I've now confirmed it. It's an acquisition number – for the Uffizi Gallery, in Florence.'

Edward gasped. 'It's a Uffizi picture . . . ? You mean it's stolen?'

Ramsay's eyes were aglow. 'Oh, it's stolen all right. Only this is a rather special theft.' The hail roared afresh above them. 'This picture wasn't stolen last week, or last month, or last year for that matter. That's why I didn't want anyone else to hear this. Not for the moment anyway. It might embarrass Her Majesty.'

The others stared at him. The glass panes above them threatened to crack under the barrage of hail.

'This is Raphael's *Madonna of the Veil*. It was looted from Florence in the early 1940s. By the Nazis.'

'Hi! This is your Sowerby correspondent. In other words, I'm still in Yorkshire. Looked at the Joseph Wilton statue of Archbishop Tillotson today, so the research is proceeding. By the way, Yorkshire pudding isn't *so* bad – certainly beats kedgeree. Not that I wanted to talk about food, Woodie. What *do* I want to talk about? You're right . . . call me. So long.'

Edward grinned to himself, stopped the machine and reset it. Nancy had the best telephone manner of anyone he knew. Very sexy. He followed his routine: poured himself a whisky, admired the framed piece of Arabic calligraphy which hung next to his bookshelves, and dialled the number Nancy had left.

'You save my life!' she cried when she heard Edward's voice. 'I was just going to have my *third* bar of chocolate. God, it's so *boring* up here in the evenings. In California you could at least walk on the beach. If you walked on the beach in Yorkshire, even at this time of the year, your spit would freeze.'

'You're being gross again.'

'I *feel* gross. I've had two enormous bars of chocolate.'

'I thought you felt . . . in your message you said you wanted to talk about – '

'That was *hours* ago, Woodie. I made do with chocolate.' She laughed. 'It's nice to hear your voice, though. What's happening at the Court of St James?'

'As it happens, quite a bit.' He told her what had happened at the National Gallery that afternoon.

'Now *that's* what I call a mystery. Why "Apollo Brigade", do you think?'

'Search me. Apollo was the classical Greek god of the arts –

17

but I don't need to tell you that. As to brigade . . . it sounds military.'

'Maybe it has something to do with Nazis. Maybe that's the military link.'

'Maybe, maybe, maybe.'

'So what are you going to do?'

'Refer it upstairs. The Surveyor of the Queen's Pictures is part of the Lord Chamberlain's department. He was out today but I'm seeing him tomorrow. Talking of which . . . when am I going to see you?'

'The train takes about three hours.'

'I could be with you for a late dinner tomorrow. We'd have the weekend.'

'Beats bars of chocolate. But are you sure you want to come? It's a tiny room, with a tiny bed – '

'Change to something larger.'

'Is that an order?'

'We might as well be comfortable.'

'It's not very sophisticated here.'

'Perfect.'

'And it's much colder than in London.'

'Are you trying to put me off?'

There was a pause. Then Nancy said, softly, 'No, Woodie, no. I'm not trying to put you off. I wish you were here already.'

3

Friday

Edward had been surprised when, as soon as the Lord Chamberlain heard what he had to say, he invoked still higher authority. 'This is one for Mordaunt, I think.'

In fact, Edward was more than surprised. Francis Mordaunt was the Queen's personal equerry or private secretary. The Queen's equerry was *the* power figure at Buckingham Palace. Nothing of consequence happened without his say-so and nothing at all happened without his knowledge. He saw Her Majesty virtually every day, and that was, roughly speaking, about sixty days a year more than the Duke of Edinburgh.

Mordaunt could not see Edward immediately. It emerged that the equerry was out of the country for the entire day. The Queen was to visit Berlin later in the year and he was checking the arrangements. He would be back later that evening, however, and Edward received a further unpleasant surprise when he was phoned during the afternoon by one of the equerry's three secretaries. Edward was summoned to a meeting with Mordaunt the next morning, at ten o'clock.

'On a Saturday?' Edward was flummoxed. Weekend meetings were unheard of in the royal household.

'Sir Francis insists. He is most anxious to see you.'

Edward cursed. His brand-new plans to spend the weekend in Yorkshire with Nancy had exploded in his face.

'But there's no way I can get out of it,' he grumbled to her over the phone. 'Hillier's away, in hospital, and I know Mordaunt has a lot of the sergeant-major about him.'

'If you're meeting him at ten, why not come up here afterwards? We'd have one night?'

Edward was pleased Nancy was so keen and arranged to phone her again as soon as his meeting with Mordaunt was over. That evening, being stranded unexpectedly in London, he polished off his Louvre lecture so that, before his rendezvous with Mordaunt at Buckingham Palace he could call in at his own office, to make photocopies of his typescript. He wanted one or two colleagues to read his lecture before he delivered it.

It was when he called in at St James's Palace, to use the photocopying machine, that he discovered there was another package in his post that morning. A second picture had been delivered.

4

Saturday

Edward had only once before been to the equerry's private lair in Buckingham Palace itself, and that was shortly after he had been appointed Surveyor, when he had been invited in for a glass of sherry.

From the side entrance to the palace in Buckingham Gate he was led up a flight of stairs by a middle-aged woman wearing a woollen two-piece suit. Uniforms were kept to a minimum inside the building. The wide staircase had a skylight at the top and opened into a spacious corridor leading to the formal stairwell which, on one side, gave on to the grand balcony overlooking the Mall. This was the place where the royal family assembled after coronations, weddings and Trooping the Colour. The other side of the stairwell led to a smaller balcony and reached a narrow corridor that, had it not been so well lit by natural light from above, might have reminded Edward of the House of Commons. Sofas – blue satin with gold ormolu beading – lined one side of the corridor, while a series of panelled doors led off the other side. The carpet, thick and spongey, was a deep blue; the pictures on the walls were portraits, eighteenth-century English; although, in museum terms, they were second-rate, they were still good. The Royal Collection was *very* large.

Two-thirds of the way along the corridor, a door was open. Edward was shown in. The office, cluttered with secretaries on weekdays, was empty just now but an inner doorway was also open and through it Edward could see Francis Mordaunt on a sofa reading a newspaper.

'In here!' Mordaunt shouted, folding the paper and springing to his feet. He thanked the woman, who retreated into the corridor and closed the door behind her. Mordaunt made sure that the door was shut, then turned, shook Edward's hand and, in the same movement, led him towards the sofa. 'No coffee, I'm afraid. Saturday. Water?'

'Thanks, no.'

The room was bright. It had a round bay-window overlooking the gardens, the pond and the top half of the Hilton Hotel. Inside, it was festooned with photographs. Francis Mordaunt – *Sir* Francis, of course, knights bachelor being as numerous in the palace these days as royal mistresses were in more interesting times – came of a good West Country family, with aunts and uncles, nieces and nephews, godchildren and pets, all of which were represented somewhere in this room. It was also immaculately tidy. No piles of papers rising like Hong Kong tenement buildings. But then Mordaunt did have three secretaries.

He sat on the sofa next to Edward. Mordaunt was a slight man and today he was dressed casually. He was wearing a blazer, a white shirt with no tie, a pair of pale-grey flannels and brown handmade brogues. The darkness of the blazer made him look pale as well as slight. On a first encounter, you might be tempted into thinking that the equerry had no presence.

Edward knew that to be mistaken. Mordaunt's grey eyes could go very cold if he was crossed. His tenacity was legendary, and his earlier training as a diplomat meant he could see all angles to a problem at the same time, usually before everyone else. He had been equerry for nearly two decades.

'Now,' said Mordaunt, taking a handkerchief from his pocket and polishing his spectacles. 'I'm told you have been sent a picture anonymously, which may have been stolen by the Nazis in the Second World War.'

'Another arrived this morning.'

The polishing stopped, but only for a moment. 'Tell me everything, from the beginning.'

Edward repeated his narrative, bringing Mordaunt right up to date with that morning's arrival. 'It was wrapped in the same paper as the other one, with the same writing. This second picture looks to me like a Canaletto. It's a view of Venice . . . canals, palazzos, the usual mix.'

'And was this looted by the Nazis too?'

Edward shook his head. 'I don't know. There hasn't been time to check.'

'Was there a note this time?'

'Yes. I've got it here.' He reached into his jacket, took out an envelope and passed it to Mordaunt. As before there was just his name typed on the outside and as before the sheet inside contained two lines:

THIS SHOULD SETTLE OUR CREDENTIALS.
AS YOU CAN SEE, THEY WERE NOT DESTROYED. THE APOLLO BRIGADE.

'I'll keep this, if I may,' said Mordaunt, folding the paper, sliding it back into its envelope and slipping it into his blazer pocket.

There was no point in Edward contradicting him. 'Have you any idea what this is all about? Or what the "Apollo Brigade" is?'

Instead of answering, Mordaunt asked a question himself. 'How many people know about all this? You, the Lord Chamberlain, Arran at the National Gallery, this Ramsay chap. Your secretary –?'

Edward shook his head. 'She's seen the Raphael, but she's not aware of its significance.' He eyed the equerry. 'Come to that, neither am I.'

Mordaunt still didn't bite. 'How soon can you confirm that this second picture is Nazi loot?'

'As soon as I can contact Martin Ramsay. He has a book, a dossier really, issued by the Italian and German governments in the 1970s. It lists all the major works of art which both governments agree were looted in the war and are still missing.'

'Can you do that over the weekend?'

'I can try, if it's that urgent.'

'It's that urgent,' hissed Mordaunt.

'I've got Arran's home phone number and he'll have Ramsay's. Look, Francis, isn't this a matter for Scotland Yard –?'

'You haven't alerted them, have you?' Mordaunt looked startled.

'No. Not yet.'

'Thank God for that! This is a Palace matter, Edward, and must remain within the household, at least for the time being. Until I say otherwise. You are to tell no one what you have told me. *No one*. When you contact this . . . Ramsay, don't even mention the second picture. Think up some excuse, about the first picture maybe. Try to get the dossier out of him without giving any more away. Leave everything else to me. I'm going to assume for the moment that this second picture *was* looted in the war. But the minute you find out for certain I want you to let me know. What are your plans for the weekend?'

Edward hesitated. The force of Mordaunt's reaction when he

23

had mentioned Scotland Yard had unsettled him. There hadn't been a chance before to say that he had also told Nancy about the pictures. Now he wasn't sure that he could bring himself to do it. 'I'm going to Yorkshire, to visit friends. I was going last night.'

Mordaunt bit his lip. 'No. At least . . . what I mean is: seeing Ramsay must come first.'

Edward began to protest but Mordaunt cut him short. 'I'm sorry but I shall be cancelling *my* plans too. If you can find Ramsay quickly – fine. Have your weekend. But whatever happens I shall definitely need you at your desk first thing on Monday, at nine. Just in case.'

'Just in case of what, Francis? You're making no sense.'

Mordaunt looked away, got up and went to stand by the window. 'You don't need to know yet, Edward. So I can't say. I'm sorry, but you'll have to take my word for it that this is a Palace matter – and very important.' He stood for a moment, still gazing across the gardens. In the distance the sound of an ambulance carried on the air.

Suddenly Mordaunt broke his reflective mood and turned back to Edward. 'Now, off you go and chase down this Ramsay character.' As Edward got to his feet, he added, 'And don't forget to keep the two pictures locked up safely. We don't want to lose them. Can you find your own way back to Buckingham Gate?'

Edward nodded and waved a feeble farewell. Mordaunt was by now seated at his desk, his blazer unbuttoned and his hand on the telephone. 'Will you close the door behind you, please.'

Edward drew the door shut gently. One of the many little things he had grown to like about the inside of Buckingham Palace, which was not his favourite building from the outside, was the solid doors, which slotted into place as crisply as the breach in a shotgun.

As Mordaunt's door clicked shut, Edward could hear the equerry already speaking into the phone. 'Windsor switchboard? Francis Mordaunt here. I wish to be connected with Her Majesty. Find her, wherever she is. Tell her it's me and that the matter is urgent.'

5

Sunday

When Edward did, finally, contact Ramsay, he was in despair and very angry. Mordaunt's request – Mordaunt's *diktat* – had ruined his weekend. Ramsay, it turned out, had spent Saturday in, of all places, Yorkshire. But Edward had been unable to reach him and so had himself been confined to London.

Nancy had been surprisingly forgiving, when he had phoned her with the news. 'I'm a lousy Yank, don't forget,' she had said with a chuckle. 'For us, work *always* comes first. Mordaunt is sure as hell acting like royalty himself.'

'And why won't he tell *me* anything?' Edward had fumed. 'What *is* it about these pictures?'

'I'm not a great Canaletto fan, are you, Woodie?' asked Nancy. 'His people are just cartoons.'

'They don't move you, I agree. But put a Canaletto in a room, a view of Venice or the Thames, for example, and you get a wonderful feeling of space.' Edward sighed. 'That was clever, getting me on to art. I'm coming off the boil.'

'Call me tomorrow,' said Nancy softly. 'After you find this Ramsay guy. The phone is better than nothing.'

No sooner had he put the phone down on Nancy than it rang. He snatched at it; was it Ramsay at last?

'Can you hear me, Edward?' No, it was his father.

'Yes, Dad. Fine. Where are you?'

'Overbister.'

'Over where?'

His father chuckled. 'It's in the Orkneys. We've been looking at rare birds. I'm staying with Roddy Dunne and Marjorie – you remember: he's number two at the RAF base up here, at Sanday. But we'll be in London on Wednesday – I'm looking at a Ferrari GTO you might like to see.'

Almost the only thing Edward and his father had in common was their love of cars.

'What year?'

'Nineteen sixty-two.'

'Jesus!' Edward need no reminding that 1962 GTOs were as rare as Orkney birds and far more expensive.

'Coxwold Cars, Eaton Mews West. Wednesday at twelve. We can have lunch afterwards.'

'I shall be in Paris, Dad. A conference at the Louvre.'

'Damn! We're going back to California next morning.'

'I'm sorry.'

'Yes, I am too.' The phone went dead.

Edward sighed. His father thought he didn't like Barbra. It wasn't true, but what was true was that, since he had met Barbra, Edward's father had changed. He was trying to stave off old age and Edward found it embarrassing. The old man may well have thought the conference story a lie. Oh well. Edward cheered himself up by ordering the tickets for Sammy's trip to the Albert Hall. He ordered four. Nancy could come too.

It was late on Sunday morning before Ramsay answered his phone and early afternoon before he could meet Edward in his office at the National Gallery. As instructed by Mordaunt, Edward didn't mention the Canaletto but instead pretended that others in the royal household wanted to see for themselves that the Raphael was indeed included in the list of Nazi looted pictures before deciding what to do.

'What's going to happen to it, Edward?' Ramsay asked.

Edward shrugged, as casually as he could. 'It will be returned, of course – eventually. Some sort of diplomatic ceremony, I assume. You won't say anything just yet, will you? There are inquiries to be made, and the Palace would like to make any announcement. You wouldn't wish to embarrass us.'

'Of course not. Don't worry. You lend us too many pictures. But I'll be interested to know what's behind it all.'

'You'll know as soon as I do, I promise.'

Ramsay said that Edward could borrow the book on looted pictures and he dropped it into the basket attached to the handlebars of his bike.

He rode off down Pall Mall, but as soon as he was out of sight of Ramsay and the National Gallery he pulled over to the side of the road, by the Reform Club, and opened the book. On page 83 a view of Venice stared up at him. It had been looted from

Parma in 1940 and had been painted by Antonio Canale, better known as Canaletto.

That afternoon he tracked Mordaunt down at Windsor and confirmed the news. The equerry thanked him, warned him again not to discuss the matter, and rang off. Edward then called Nancy.

She was out but phoned back in the evening. When she asked how he had got on, Edward didn't know how to reply. 'Mordaunt keeps swearing me to secrecy. You'd better forget anything I've told you.'

'I don't want to talk about all that, anyway. Guess what I did today?'

'You haven't been at the chocolate again?'

'That's none of your goddam business. No, I saw the collection of death masks at Milton Rudby.'

'Grisly.'

'No! *Fascinating*. We should revive the practice – they're much more immediate, more faithful, than portraits.'

'I'd like a portrait of you, Nancy. I'm forgetting what you look like. When are you coming back?'

'Another week up here, perhaps. Maybe we can do next weekend what we didn't do this weekend.'

'Yes. Let's hope no more pictures turn up.'

'What pictures? See – I've already forgotten. So long.'

WEEK TWO
The Apollo Brigade

6

Monday

Edward was at his desk, as instructed, by nine o'clock. The weekend had been a washout but there was Paris to look forward to. He had already booked one dinner, at L'Ambroisie in the Place des Vosges where they did the best ravioli in the world, Italy not excepted. He spent part of the morning discussing his lecture with colleagues. Every time the phone rang he expected it to be Mordaunt but, by the time he went out for lunch, the equerry still hadn't called.

Edward was lunching with Thierry Dinant, a distinguished Belgian scholar from the Royal Museum in Brussels. Dinant had called Hillier about a week before but, on finding that the Director of the Royal Collection was in hospital, had invited Edward to Overton's instead.

Edward made his way there shortly after one. Dinant's choice could not have been more convenient. The Belgian was tall and rather stern-looking, with thick glasses. He spoke perfect English. He was already seated at the table and greeted Edward warmly.

'Monday's not the ideal day for fish, I know. But I can never resist the whitebait here. I hope you don't mind.'

Edward shook his head. 'You seem more of a regular here than I am – and my office is across the road.' He smiled.

'I have been travelling a lot recently, it's true, and to England as much as anywhere. I'll tell you why in a minute – but let's order first.'

Dinant caught the waiter's eye and for a while he was engrossed in ordering the food. Edward was half amused and half comforted by the seriousness with which he did this. When he had finished, Dinant sat back on the banquette seating and looked at Edward.

'How bad is Hillier?'

'I'm not sure. He's had an operation for two slipped discs. It's a tricky business. Some people recover quickly – and completely. Some don't. With him it's too early to tell.'

'I'll deal with you, then.'

'What on earth do you mean?'

'I said I would explain why I have been travelling so much. For the last three years, besides my duties at the Royal Museum in Brussels, I have been head of something known as the Rubens Research Project. As you know, Rubens had a vast output and a large studio. Towards the end of his life he had gout. These facts taken together mean that there are inevitably certain pictures attributed to him that are nothing of the kind. It's the task of the Rubens Research Project to separate the wheat from the chaff.'

The waiter brought the wine and Dinant tried it.

'Over the past months, I've been inspecting so-called Rubenses in – oh, Madrid, Milan, Melbourne, Moscow. Pleasant work but hard. I've also looked at the pictures in your Royal Collection.'

At this, Edward flashed him a look. That must have been agreed with Hillier, for this was the first Edward had heard of it. What was coming?

Dinant, who had been leaning forward, now sat back as the whitebait arrived. He squeezed lemon over them.

'You . . . or should I say Her Majesty has a picture entitled *The Three Marys at the Sepulchre*. I'm sorry to say that my colleagues and I do not think this is by the master.' He swallowed some whitebait.

Edward had guessed what Dinant was going to say moments before he said it. He toyed with his food. How should he respond?

Dinant spoke again. 'I'm telling you this out of courtesy, of course. Our research report will not be published until next year. You may like to alert Her Majesty in advance and perhaps alter your own attribution in anticipation. I'm sure that some newspaper will make play with the idea that a Rubens in the Royal Collection is a fake.'

Dinant showed no emotion as he said all this and he could not have guessed what was going on inside Edward's head. All Edward said now was, 'What is your evidence, Thierry?'

Dinant pulled down the corners of his mouth. 'The picture is not mentioned in the letters. The minor figures, which in a real Rubens would have been painted by assistants, do not fit with the style of any known assistant, and the provenance is the same as one or two other pictures which we believe are fake.'

Edward didn't reply immediately but sipped some wine.

Dinant was right about one thing: if the papers got hold of this they would have a field day. A fake in the Royal Collection! However, that wasn't what concerned him most.

'Hillier is not going to like it.'

Dinant lowered his eyes. 'I know. But I can't help that. They are not his pictures. They couldn't be sold anyway. We are not hurting anyone's pocket.'

'Yes – I see that. That's not what I meant.'

'What did you mean, then?'

'It calls his scholarship into question. He is certain the *Three Marys* is a genuine Rubens.'

'He *is*? I'm surprised. There must be – what? – two thousand pictures in the Royal Collection. He can't be expected to know everything intimately.'

'No . . . I agree with that. You're a good scholar, Thierry, but there are certain things you don't know.'

'You mean there's something else about this picture that I don't know?'

'In a manner of speaking – yes.' Edward leaned back as the waiter brought their main courses and then fussed around, serving spinach, potatoes, hollandaise sauce.

'Go on,' urged Dinant as soon as the waiter had left. 'Explain what you mean. What don't I know about this picture?'

Edward wiped his lips with his napkin. 'You don't know that a month ago I sent Hillier a memo concerning the *Three Marys*. In that memo I said that I thought the picture was not by Rubens. For exactly the same reasons as you. He replied just before he went into hospital. He said I was wrong and implied, more or less, that I didn't know what I was talking about. Now you say the same thing as I do. He's not going to like it one bit. I haven't been at the Palace very long and already I'm having a run-in with my boss. Your research isn't going to help, either. In fact, it's going to make the situation a whole lot worse.'

7

Tuesday

Psychologically, and to an extent administratively, Buckingham Palace is divided into four. There are the royal apartments, at the north end of the building, which almost no one except the royal family and their personal servants ever sees. There is the administrative area on the west side, where Mordaunt and others have their offices. There are the great rooms of state: the ballrooms, banqueting halls, reception rooms for investitures, and so on. These are located in the centre of the palace, on the east side, looking out on to the Mall. Finally, there is a very small area with a very special function. Edward wasn't aware of this when he was summoned, by Mordaunt, on the following Tuesday. It was again a glorious morning, so he walked over from St James's, arriving, as he had been asked, just before noon. He was due at Heathrow at five, for his flight to the Louvre conference. There should be plenty of time.

This time, one of Mordaunt's three secretaries came to meet him at the Buckingham Gate entrance. She led the way deep into the palace, at ground-floor level. They passed a billiard room – for staff – with three tables; several kitchens, a shoe-repair shop, a laundry where green velvet uniforms, with gold piping, hung in rows. They walked until they were, Edward judged, right under the royal apartments. He was shown up a staircase and into a room with an easy chair, and offered coffee. There was one other person in the room, a man a couple of years Edward's junior who, to judge from his haircut, shoes and general demeanour, was a policeman in plain clothes. Had Mordaunt gone back on himself and brought in Scotland Yard? Now, perhaps, the mystery would be explained. The man nodded at Edward but said nothing. He was reading a paperback.

Edward sat back in the easy chair and sipped his coffee. He had nothing to read as they waited.

He was getting used to waiting. There had been no word from Mordaunt yesterday after lunch. He had waited until six, growing

34

steadily more tetchy. However, on his arrival at St James's Palace this morning, The General told him immediately that he was summoned to BP. 'You look worried, Edward,' she added. 'And you've worn the same tie two days running. Am I allowed to know what's going on?'

Edward shook his head. '*I* don't know what's going on, General. I'll tell you as soon as I find out anything. *If* I'm allowed to.'

She sniffed. 'You're as bad as the son. He has his secrets too.'

Though Wilma always succeeded in cheering Edward, his sense of well-being had soon been lost as he walked from one palace to the other. Edward had been slightly miffed by his treatment from the equerry. He hated being kept in the dark. But at least things should be cleared up now. The whole business had obviously been moving behind the scenes. He looked across at the policeman. He seemed a bit young to be of senior rank. At the same time, where Edward now sat was obviously some sort of anteroom: perhaps Mordaunt and the policeman's superior were in the next room, discussing the affair.

No sooner had he thought this than the inner door opened and Mordaunt appeared. 'Come in, Andover,' he said. 'Bring your coffee with you.'

Mordaunt beckoned Edward forward. 'Do you know Mr Lockwood?'

As he stepped into the room, Edward took a large breath and tried not to let his jaw hang open. As he shook hands with the Prime Minister, he said, 'We met once, at the Royal Academy dinner.'

The Prime Minister nodded but said nothing. In the newspapers it was often said of William Lockwood that he bore a marked resemblance to the late Herbert von Karajan, the German conductor. He was small, with wiry, iron-coloured hair, an intense gaze and deep creases in his cheeks.

Slightly dazed by the sudden turn of events, Edward found himself a seat next to a window. He could see now that they were in a sort of sitting-room with french windows at the far end, opening on to a balcony and, beyond that, a bed of roses. Rather late in the day, he took in the fact that, this being Tuesday, the Prime Minister must have just finished his weekly audience with the Queen. So this was where it took place.

Amazingly, the Prime Minister appeared to be waiting for

Mordaunt, who had slipped back into the anteroom and was speaking in subdued tones to the policeman who, Edward now realized, was a bodyguard. The equerry came back in, closing the door behind him. 'I was just checking with Webber, sir,' he said to Lockwood. 'I understand you are due at the New Zealand High Commission at one-fifteen. We may need all the time in between but we'll try not to make you late.'

Lockwood moved his gaze from Mordaunt to Edward. He looked serious. 'Now what *is* all this? Her Majesty asked me to stay on – and so I have. But – '

'In fact, sir,' interrupted Mordaunt, 'it will be better if Dr Andover speaks first. It's always better from the horse's mouth.' The equerry looked across at Edward. 'Edward, tell the Prime Minister about the paintings you have been sent.'

Edward did as requested. How many more times was he going to have to tell his story, he thought to himself, without finding out what the damn mystery was all about? At least he had a new snippet to add to what Mordaunt already knew. 'A third picture arrived this morning,' he ended. 'This one is a Poussin sepia drawing. It's signed and was stolen – by the Nazis again – in Piacenza. I know because Ramsay loaned me his catalogue.'

'Any message?' asked Mordaunt.

'The usual two lines. Shall I read them?'

The equerry nodded.

' "Three should put it beyond doubt. If you are convinced, cancel the royal film première on Thursday. Then you'll hear from us again. The Apollo Brigade." '

Mordaunt stared at the paper in Edward's hand. 'Show me that,' he said, stretching forward.

'Cancel the première?' said Lockwood. 'That sounds like an order, like blackmail. What *is* this?'

'Hold on!' Mordaunt put an urgency into his voice without speaking loudly. 'Hold on. There's quite a bit to come.' The equerry glanced briefly at the third message, folded it and slipped it into his pocket. He looked at Lockwood. 'Most of what Dr Andover has just told you, he outlined to me last Saturday. I admit that, unless you are privy to certain information, Edward's narrative is thoroughly odd. But I can assure you that if you know what Her Majesty knows, and what I know, these developments are very sinister . . .' He let the last word hang on the air.

Mordaunt crossed his legs. He had the Prime Minister's full attention.

'Let me give you some background, sir. You may read all the documents if you wish, but that would take more time than you can probably spare. The background will lead you to a conclusion before I can finish the story.' He removed his spectacles. 'This all starts with one of Dr Andover's most illustrious – and extraordinary – predecessors. I mean Anthony Blunt, who was Surveyor of the Royal Collection for more than a quarter of a century, from 1945 to 1972. As the world now knows, Blunt was a Soviet agent, a Russian spy from at least the mid-thirties until, probably, the early sixties. For a period of twenty years, while he was employed at the Palace, Blunt was also in the pay of Moscow. Now, in 1945, right after the end of the war and before it was ever suspected that he was anything other than he appeared to be, Blunt was sent by King George VI on an errand of the greatest secrecy and the utmost importance.'

Lockwood leaned forward. 'Blunt! They sent *Blunt*?'

Mordaunt nodded. 'The errand concerned, among other things, the relationship of the King's elder brother – Edward VIII, the man who abdicated and became the Duke of Windsor – and Adolf Hitler. As you may recall, sir, the Duke was, alas, something of a fan of Hitler's. The errand I refer to concerned a number of paintings and documents which, at the end of the war, were in the possession of the Hesse family, at Kornberg, near Frankfurt. The documents detailed exactly the agreements the Duke had reached with Hitler over Edward's role in Britain should the Nazis ever conquer these islands. Needless to say, those papers were very embarrassing to the royal family, but the paintings . . . the paintings were the most damaging of all.

'The Hesses were – are – related to the British royal family, both being descendants of the Kaiser and of Queen Victoria. Prince Philip of Hesse ranked fifty-third in the Nazi hierarchy – he was actually imprisoned after the war – and in the 1930s had married Mussoloni's daughter. From about 1938 onwards, he acquainted himself with the paintings of Italy and arranged a number of "gifts", to Hitler and Goering.

'A little later he arranged other "gifts". These were also paintings, but this time the recipient, or intended recipient, was none other than his relative, Edward, Duke of Windsor.'

Lockwood shifted in his chair. 'The Duke *accepted* Nazi loot?'

'Remember, this was the time when he was being shunned by the British establishment. He had been left out of his father's will. He wanted a proper job – felt it was his due – but instead got the Governorship of the Bahamas. I say this not to excuse him, but to explain. Obviously he couldn't bring the pictures to Britain, or the Bahamas, so they were kept in store for him with his relatives, who just happened to be the Nazis in charge of confiscation.'

'How *many* pictures were there?'

'We're not sure. But let me get on. Blunt was, as I say, above suspicion at that stage and, as the Surveyor of the King's Pictures, he was the natural person to send. He was accompanied by Sir Owen Morehead, the royal librarian, who was charged with recovery of any incriminating documents. They were both dispatched to Kornberg and other Hesse residences further south, in Darmstadt, to retrieve the material. They found everything easily enough – after all, the King's relatives had got word to him during the war. But whereas Morehead came straight back with the documents, Blunt stayed on in Germany with the paintings and a few other papers relating to them. When he did get back, a couple of days after Morehead, he said that he had destroyed the incriminating pictures and their related documentation. Among his other duties, Blunt was a member of the Monuments, Fine Arts and Archives Commission, whose official job it was to track down looted art. Blunt said that Germany was crawling with these types and that, in the chaos of the times, and not knowing who knew what, he judged it safer to destroy the pictures than do anything else with them. It had taken him a while, he said, to find somewhere safe, out of harm's way, where he could burn everything. *He* said there were more than thirty paintings.'

'You mean he just burned *all* of them?'

'We thought so. I was not at the Palace then and of course such action seems extreme to us now. But it may not have seemed extraordinary at all at the time. The Palace was frightened of anything – *anything* – getting out, and in a certain light Blunt's action could be seen as effective and patriotic. However wonderful the art might be, the fate of the royal family, in the aftermath of war, was far more important.' Mordaunt uncrossed and recrossed his legs. 'It therefore appeared, at the time, that he had completed his task successfully. Everyone at the Palace relaxed. In retrospect, however, and especially after the disclosure that he was a Russian agent, doubts about his activities in Germany arose.

'It was then assumed, here in the Palace, and never denied by Blunt, that after he had collected the paintings and the documents in Germany he did not destroy them as he said. Instead, as an active Soviet agent, in possession of highly sensitive British documents, he would have been failing in his duty if he did not take very different action – action whereby he could embarrass the Palace if ever he wanted to. Accordingly, the Palace has always assumed that Blunt went from Kornberg and Darmstadt to Switzerland. That would account for his delay in coming back. Somewhere in Switzerland, he would have hidden the paintings in a discreet bank. I have to tell you that, ever since Blunt died, some of us here at BP, and one or two senior figures in the security services, who know all about this, have suspected that the royal family might find itself embarrassed all over again by Anthony Blunt. The threat of blackmail, as you correctly identified it, sir, has always been there. Now, it seems, it is out in the open.'

'But why would the Russians play this card now?' Lockwood looked hard at the equerry. 'I take it you *do* mean that the Russians are behind this. But I don't – '

'No. We don't believe this is the Russians, sir.'

'What! Who then?'

'There's still quite a bit of the story to come.' Mordaunt moistened his lips with the tip of his tongue. Edward thought, incongruously, that the equerry had a nose like Jack Teagarden's. 'As a spy,' Mordaunt went on, 'Blunt was nothing if not careful. That's why he wormed his way so deeply into the establishment, and so successfully. In the . . . profession he had chosen, it was prudent not to trust anyone – and certainly not his Russian masters. In the post-war world anything could happen. So, after he made that journey, from Kornberg and Darmstadt to Switzerland, the chances are that he didn't tell the Soviets where he had hidden the pictures. He may have told them *what* he had but not where they were hidden. You'll recall that when Blunt's secret career was made public it came at the end of a long period of speculation about a "fourth" or "fifth" man in the Burgess–Philby–Maclean business. The government's hand was forced – the security forces were fighting among themselves and leaking more and more details to the papers – and, if Blunt had tried to use the pictures as blackmail then, to stop his role being revealed, it would never have worked. Someone else would have leaked it. True, the royal family would have been involved in an almighty scandal, but at that stage it would have done Blunt himself no good.'

Lockwood turned to look at Edward. 'I hope *you're* not a spy, Dr Andover.'

Edward felt uncomfortable, but just smiled.

Mordaunt continued. 'So Blunt held his peace in 1979. There were even those who thought that, because he had kept quiet, maybe he had told the truth in 1945 and really destroyed the paintings. The pictures which Dr Andover has received have demolished that hope.'

'But who has them now? If this isn't the Russians, who is it?'

'As I say, we don't think it is the Russians, not official Russia anyway. Given the aid we are committed to and the fact that the Queen is to visit the country next year – the first time a monarch has gone to Russia since before the assassination of the Tsar – it doesn't make sense. It might be a freelance Russian who *was* in the KGB – but how would he have found out about the bank?'

'How would *anyone* find out about the bank?'

Mordaunt wiped his lips again. 'Good point, but consider this. Blunt was a terrible snob, very petulant, arrogant. He hated what happened to him in 1979: he was vilified and reviled by those whose approval he craved, he was attacked in Parliament and the press, he was stripped of his knighthood. If you talk to people who knew him, you'll also find that he was one of those types who could not forgive, who bore grudges for a very long time, for ever. Now, assume that he felt all that in the last years of his life – '

'But he had been a spy!' Lockwood was growing exasperated.

'Yes. But his secret had been kept by the *establishment*, from 1964 to 1979 – fifteen years. The establishment had *connived* in the cover-up. He had every right to expect the secret would be kept until his death.'

'He had *no* rights!'

'Not to us, I agree. But you have to see this from his point of view if you are to understand what may now be happening, or about to happen.'

Lockwood was silent.

'If he did bear a grudge then, in the three years between his exposure and his death, he could have made certain arrangements.'

'Such as?'

'He was homosexual. He had several lovers. Maybe, on his death, he left some of them the number and address of his bank account in Switzerland, plus an indication of what was there. Maybe he wanted these friends to blackmail the Palace. That way he could damage the country a final time, from beyond the grave and long after we could get back at him.'

Lockwood stared hard at Mordaunt, and swallowed. 'But this is 1996. He died thirteen years ago.'

'Whoever is doing this is careful. They had to work out all the details of what went on, cross-check Blunt's story with others. More and more has emerged about the Duke's early role in the last few years, but only since his official biography was published in 1990. Some of the documents were kept secret for fifty years – till 1989 at the earliest. Some 1945 documents were declassified only last year.'

Lockwood bit his lower lip. 'And you think they want money? The "Apollo Brigade" sounds political.'

Mordaunt glanced at Edward. 'I looked up "Apollo" over the weekend. Among other things, he was a classical god who had a homosexual affair with another classical god. For Apollo Brigade, read Homosexual Brigade.'

The equerry adjusted one of his gold cufflinks. 'These blackmailers have been sending these paintings to establish their credentials. They have sent us three pictures – "free of charge", in effect – to convince us that they have the rest of the "collection". They sent them to Dr Andover knowing he is too new and too young to be aware of their significance but knowing also he had the expertise to check them out, and to be able to confirm to me, and to Her Majesty, that these are the originals and not mere copies. If these are the originals, which they are, it follows that this Apollo Brigade also has the incriminating documents that go with the paintings. By roping in Dr Andover, the blackmailers, who must have known Hillier was ill, spread the knowledge of this thing. That puts extra pressure on Her Majesty, and on me.'

Too right, thought Edward. The mystery had at last been solved. And how. Wilma would explode like a mortar shell when she was told. Nancy would . . . he wouldn't be able to tell Nancy.

'Having established beyond doubt that they have the pictures,' Mordaunt went on, 'the blackmailers have now asked us to signal to them, by cancelling the royal film première on Thursday, that we can read between the lines, that we understand what they have and what its significance is. Presumably, after we do that, *if* we do it, we shall hear from them again, with their demands. That is why we – Her Majesty and I – thought it appropriate to bring you in now.'

The Prime Minister bit his lip but said nothing. He was thinking.

Mordaunt went on, 'Obviously, this must be kept secret. A leak could be very damaging. A major scandal.'

Lockwood glanced at his watch. Edward did the same: 12.45.

The Prime Minister pursed his lips. 'How long have I been in politics? Forty-two years in Parliament, anyway. I've seen some things . . . But the Crown being blackmailed . . .' He shook his head, then looked hard at the equerry. 'I take it you don't want to call the blackmailers' bluff?'

Mordaunt looked uncomfortable. 'This is the difficult part, sir. Under normal circumstances, Her Majesty would take the view that blackmailers should on no account be treated with. She is also conscious that, under the law, all people – all families – should be treated alike. What we are suggesting does, I realize, sound like special pleading. At the same time, the Crown *is* special, it *is* different. In a sense, this blackmail attempt is aimed at all of us, the entire country. If any of this leaked out – '

'The events *are* fifty years old – '

'Do you think that matters?' Mordaunt's eyes flashed behind his spectacles. 'Think of the esteem the royal family is held in in this country, Mr Lockwood. And not just this country – held worldwide. Everybody envies Britain her monarchy. I don't mean Her Majesty only, but the institution, as a focus for national feeling, a force for stability, an emotional centre that we can all share and take part in. Is it worth risking that?'

'The Duke of Windsor abdicated. He was out of the way – '

'You think *that* matters? He was still part of the royal family. Her Majesty's father went to great lengths, extreme lengths, to stop all this leaking out in the 1940s. He was right to do so then and the Queen has no intention of letting this new version leak out now.' Mordaunt paused and gathered himself before going on. 'I think you should read the documents *we* have, sir. The

Queen's uncle was not going to be Hitler's stooge all by himself . . . A dozen famous families were willing to throw in their lot with him.'

The Prime Minister stroked one of the creases in his cheek. 'Maybe it would be a good thing to have that out in the open.'

The equerry leaned towards Lockwood. Edward noticed that Mordaunt's eyes had gone very hard. He said, 'You can't know how detailed the documents are, sir. The Duke was to be King, the Duchess – Mrs Simpson – was to be Queen, Churchill was to be exiled in deepest Germany. The real King, George VI, was to be forced to abdicate and kept under house arrest outside Berlin. Our very own Queen would of course never have been Queen. The details are overwhelming, sir. They even list the people who were willing to throw away any resistance to Hitler and become members of the Windsors' – the Nazi King's – Cabinet of stooges. You would be surprised who had agreed to hold office. The Duke thought he was more popular than his brother and that his return to the throne would be acclaimed. He was a fool but he had the support of some of the most famous families in the country. Even today, fifty years afterwards, it would shake Britain to know how high – and how wide – the treachery went.'

Lockwood was not Prime Minister for nothing and Mordaunt didn't intimidate him. 'So! . . . why not let these fine, these noble, these *distinguished* families sweat it out? What's it to me?'

'Because . . . sir . . .' For a moment Mordaunt stuck his tongue in his cheek, considering his delivery. 'Because . . . two of those families are represented in your Cabinet.'

There was a silence for perhaps thirty seconds. Long enough for a flight of geese to flap by overhead and vanish out of earshot.

Edward watched as the Prime Minister stopped stroking his cheek and pressed his fingers to his lips. By law, Lockwood had to call an election in the next few months, before February. He had a majority over all other parties in the Commons of thirty-four and was trailing in the opinion polls.

At length, the Prime Minister looked at his watch again and said quietly, 'Go on.'

'I'll be as brief as I can,' said Mordaunt, his tone brisker, now that his point had been made. 'All of this *has* to be kept secret. Our interests, and yours, coincide. We have tried to think it through here at the Palace and our reasoning is as follows. The crucial point in any blackmail attempt is the handover of the money. That is the one chance of making physical contact with the criminals. The government – Scotland Yard, the security services, whatever – must have expertise in this sort of thing. So that is where we need your help.'

The Prime Minister stood up. He walked towards the french windows and looked out at the roses. As Edward watched Lockwood's compact frame, he heard one of his shoes creak. The Prime Minister's hands were clasped behind his back. He stared out of the window, turned away from the others, for minutes on end.

Edward looked from Lockwood to Mordaunt. The equerry's performance had been clinical but, in its way, impressive. No wonder Mordaunt had kept him in the dark at the weekend. Edward turned his gaze back to the Prime Minister. He didn't envy Lockwood his decision. It must be distasteful to cover up for a weak man who was willing to be a traitor. But, with an election fast approaching, could Lockwood risk it being known that two members of his Cabinet had had fathers who . . . ?

The Prime Minister had turned. He took a few steps forward. With one hand he gripped the back of the chair. 'If these people want money, why don't they sell the paintings on the black market?'

'Because the paintings are too well known. No dealer or collector with the money would touch them. Am I right, Edward?'

Edward nodded. He addressed the Prime Minister. 'There is a booklet, sir, which details a lot of what the Nazis looted.'

Lockwood grunted. He seemed to have made up his mind. 'I shall cancel my lunch,' he said. 'I shall stay here and read your file. If you are right, Sir Francis, this whole business could get very messy. My bodyguard has the scrambler phone: ask him to bring it in. And maybe you could organize some sandwiches and water. Better make it fizzy water. That file sounds as though it may take some digesting.'

William Lockwood marched into the Cabinet Room at 10 Downing Street and sat at the first available chair. The light was going – sunshine never reached the Cabinet Room; indeed, sunshine and security rarely mix. Overhead, one jet after another growled home into Heathrow. This wasn't a meeting of the full Cabinet – far from it. Indeed, not all the others present were ministers or even MPs. In Lockwood's view the meeting was too sensitive for a full Cabinet. Mordaunt had asked for the Prime Minister to involve only Privy Councillors, but Lockwood wasn't having that. With an election so close he had his own future to think of. There were not only parliamentary elections due; these days the leader of the party was elected too, if there *was* a rival. That contest took place every October. Since the contest that had dramatically ousted Thatcher, the leadership ballot was taken as seriously as a general election.

Opposite him in the Cabinet Room sat the Home Secretary, Tom Lessor, a tall, lugubrious man with a crimson birthmark on one side of his face. On his left was Jocelyn Hatfield, Chief Whip, a small figure whose jacket sleeves were too long for his arms. Next to the Prime Minister was Eric Slocombe, his political adviser, and beyond him was Bernard Midwinter, the Downing Street press officer. On Lockwood's left, the last to sit down, was Sir Evelyn Allen, Cabinet Secretary. He wore a bright lemon tie with his grey flannel suit; it was the only splash of colour in the entire room. The double doors were closed and the six men left alone. Lockwood had a thick blue file with him but, for the moment, it remained closed. 'This will have to be an official committee, I suppose,' he said, 'but I want to stress that it is a secret committee, and must remain so.' He half turned to Allen. 'Let the minutes show that.'

Allen nodded, scribbling notes.

Lockwood looked at the faces ranged around the table. 'You are scarcely going to believe what I have to tell you. It has taken quite a while for me to get used to it myself.' He patted the blue folder. 'But this is a Buckingham Palace file. It confirms the basic details.'

The mention of Buckingham Palace caused several of the others to look up.

The Prime Minister raised his voice. 'We are confronted with a most unusual problem. Unique, I'd say. How serious it is, politically . . . well, to be frank it is too soon to tell. But it could be . . . catastrophic. Terminal, from our point of view. I would therefore be grateful for the thoughts and comments of those in this room, both now, when you have heard what I have to say, and tomorrow, when you have slept on it.'

Lockwood got up and paced about the room. As he did so, he recounted the entire saga, from Anthony Blunt's initial visit to

Germany in 1945 to the three paintings Edward had received. It took the Prime Minister all of half an hour. Allen scribbled the whole way through.

When Lockwood had finished, he stood with his back to the window, sucking the end of his spectacles. No one else spoke. 'As of now,' he said at length, looking at Allen, who was still busy committing these secrets to paper, 'only the six people in this room, plus Her Majesty, Her Majesty's equerry and Her Majesty's Surveyor of Paintings, are aware of the threat. Apart, of course, from this "Apollo Brigade", whoever and whatever that might be.

'I am sure I need not underline the delicacy of the affair. This country has often criticized other governments who have dealt with blackmailers or kidnappers. We are about to do just that. At the same time, the royal family is undoubtedly something special in this country, far more beloved than any politician.' Lockwood smiled grimly. 'Myself included.

'Nor do I need to remind anyone in this room that the government faces an election very soon. This is not the time for us to take undue risks with our popularity. During the afternoon I've read the Palace's own file on this matter, so that I now know which members of the government come from families implicated in the Windsor business.'

'Who, Bill?' It was Hatfield.

Lockwood shook his head. 'It made frightening reading, I can tell you. However, there's no need for anyone else in this room to know their names. It should be enough for me to reassure you that no one around this table is involved. But the two people concerned *do* have important jobs – meaning that the publicity could be damaging, politically. Given an election around the corner and our current standing in the polls, it could mean . . .' He tailed off. 'It therefore goes without saying that this "Apollo Brigade" has to be dealt with. We can't just call their bluff.

'We have a little time. It is now Tuesday; the blackmailers won't be in touch until Thursday at the earliest. For now, I will give you my thinking and you can respond. Then we can all sleep on it and reconvene tomorrow when we shall need some decisions.' He put on his spectacles. 'There is now no question in my own mind that we should do what we can to protect the royal family. A royal scandal, even an old one, is worth avoiding if at all possible and this new factor about the looted Nazi pictures is pretty unpleasant. The Italians, the Dutch, the Norwegians, the French, the Austrians, the Poles, the Czechs and the Greeks all lost works of art to the Nazis, many of which have never been recovered.'

'The Americans too,' said Lessor. He had an American wife.

Lockwood nodded. 'The Americans too. As I now know from the Palace file, the Americans spent a small fortune at the end of the war trying to find some of these masterpieces. None of those nations is going to be best pleased by revelations that many of them were bribes for the Duke of Windsor. More immediately, of course, the interests of the country and of the party coincide. If the government didn't offer help, if the story got out, and then the Palace let it be known that we had stood to one side . . . well, I think we could kiss goodbye to forming the next government. I can't at the moment see how aiding the Queen will actually help us back into power, since we can't breathe a word of all this. But that's politics.

'Now, I'm not bringing this matter to Cabinet – not yet anyway. There are twenty-one people in the Cabinet and it leaks like a Panamanian oil tanker. That's why this committee was formed. At first, I'd like your immediate reactions – your gut feelings about all this. Tom, let's start with you.'

Tom Lessor was from Shropshire and was as monarchist as they come. 'Surely there is no problem, Prime Minister? Legally or morally, I mean. Blackmail of the Crown is treason.'

Lockwood smiled. 'When was someone last prosecuted for treason?'

'I don't know, Bill, but don't laugh. You'd have the sympathy of the country if this ever got out.'

'Joss?'

Hatfield was a QC, in Lockwood's view a superb pragmatist who had no real convictions of his own. He simply liked to be on the winning side. The Chief Whip had the habit of cocking his chin, as if the collar of his shirt was irritating him. He did this now. 'The key issue is security. Will the story leak? If it doesn't leak, it doesn't much matter what we do, politically, I mean. If it does leak, then of course we must be seen to support the Palace. As you rightly say, with an election so close, we daren't do anything else.'

'Morally?'

'Ask the Archbishop of Canterbury.'

Lockwood smiled again and looked at Midwinter. 'Will it leak?'

Midwinter was a Cardiff redhead with a redhead's temper and a jaw which jutted out like the map of South Wales. Temper-losing was Midwinter's most valuable political asset, earning him few friends but lots of respect in what had once been Fleet Street. 'If I may put it indelicately, Prime Minister, the Palace has you – us – over a barrel. The story won't leak from this committee. However . . . if you – we – don't help the Palace, and it all goes sour, as it's almost bound to if they have to pay up, then they will drop us in it. And they'd be right to, of course, from their point of view.'

'Eric?'

Eric Slocombe had a pencil-thin moustache, a feature which the Prime Minister's wife, Sally, loathed with a passion. She said it made him look like an unsuccessful bookie. He also had a toupee which didn't quite match his real hair. But Slocombe's political acumen was as sharp as shrapnel and he didn't gamble in politics unless he could control the odds. Lockwood, though he would have preferred a more physically prepossessing adviser, well appreciated Slocombe's gifts.

'Well,' said Slocombe. He was one of those people who, when he talked, remained entirely immobile save for his lips. 'The political problem, the immediate political problem, has been over-looked so far. It is not the Queen, it is not the press, and it's not the public – at least, not directly. It is George Keld.' He turned to the Prime Minister. 'Mishandle this one, Bill, and Keld will have you in the Tower faster than you can cry "Canaletto". We've got to keep all this away from Keld.'

Lockwood nodded and smiled grimly. Keld was Secretary of State for Defence, the Prime Minister's chief political rival within the party and, to many people, his heir apparent. Lockwood was sixty-nine, Keld twelve years younger, so age was on his side. He was the only person who came within sight of rivalling Lock-wood in the party's annual leadership election. If he stood. He was a very hard-line Defence Secretary.

Lockwood walked across the room and put his hand on Slo-combe's shoulder and squeezed it. 'Thank you, Eric, realistic as ever. And thank you all for your advice. We'll reconvene here tomorrow morning, when we've all slept on it. Tom, overnight what I want from you are the names of Scotland Yard's top blackmail detectives. Maybe the Yard have a list of prime suspects, or tell-tell signs that might reveal who we are dealing with. There must be blackmailers already in jail, some of whom might have heard about this "Apollo Brigade". But don't tell anyone *why*. Not yet. Better alert O'Day at MI6, too.'

Lessor nodded.

The Prime Minister looked at Allen. 'At some stage, we're going to need an operations room of some sort. Not yet – not till the blackmailers make contact and we know exactly who and what we are dealing with . . . but be thinking about it, will you? And again, don't let on what you are planning *for*, even to people within the building.' He raised his voice slightly and said, 'I don't want to overstate things but it could be that the jobs of everyone in this room depend on this little problem. We don't want it to blow up in our faces. We'll meet here again tomorrow, at nine-fifteen. I don't need to remind you to come in the back way.'

He glanced at his watch. Suddenly, to the others in the room he looked preoccupied. In a different tone, he said, 'I must visit my grandson in Great Ormond Street hospital. The little blighter keeps having blackouts.' There was a pause, but then Lockwood resumed in his original tone. 'After that, I have to get changed. Dinner at the Danish Embassy. If only our royals were as innocuous as theirs.'

'This way, sir,' said the usher, showing Edward into a room filled with two round tables and gold-backed chairs with red velvet cushions. 'I'll tell Sir Francis you have arrived.'

Edward didn't sit. The chairs looked as though they had been made for a troupe of circus dwarfs. Also, he preferred to pace angrily about the room. Not for the first time, he was miffed with the equerry. Edward half understood that, in the circumstances, he couldn't attend the conference in Paris. But he had worked hard on his lecture and had been looking forward to the jaunt. That was only one thing. He wasn't happy either that he couldn't tell Wilma anything. Again, he understood why – but Wilma was probably the best security risk in the entire country and it would have made his life considerably easier to tell her what was happening. As it was, she was already sulking, banging things on tables and blowing cigarette smoke into his face.

Then there had been the phone call. The first message on the machine when he had arrived home that evening, after getting an earful in the office from Geneviève Chombert who was justifiably angry that he had let her down at the last moment, was from Nancy.

'Hi! Remember me? This is your fast-food freak of a friend. Where *are* you, Woodie? Being alone in bed is bad enough, but being alone on the phone . . . I *hate* it. So long.'

That had been frustrating enough but what had really curdled Edward's blood was the next message. 'This is Sir Francis Mordaunt's secretary at BP. I have an urgent message. He would like you to go to the royal box dining-room at Covent Garden Opera House, at eight-thirty tonight. The front-of-house staff will be expecting you and will show you where to go.' No 'please' or 'thank you', no apology for disturbing his evening – not that he had anything planned, but that wasn't the point.

Mordaunt's imperious summons had really got to him. As Edward waited, or was kept waiting, he could hear the music in the auditorium. It was Offenbach's *Tales of Hoffmann*, the Barcarole, to be precise. He loved it and, despite himself, felt his anger slipping away. That almost made him angry all over again.

The door opened and Sir Francis came in. He was dressed rather foppishly, in a black velvet bow-tie, with velvet pumps that had his initials extravagantly embroidered on them in gold thread. He waved Edward to a seat. In the auditorium the Barcarole swelled to fill the entire opera house.

'Lockwood has formed a committee to cope with this "Apollo Brigade",' he said without any preamble. 'The Home Secretary, the Chief Whip, the Cabinet Secretary and a few others. We wanted only Privy Councillors involved, but Lockwood's worried about the political side so he's got his own staff on the committee. As a result of *that*, Her Majesty and I think the Palace should be represented, and the Prime Minister has agreed.' Mordaunt paused, picking up a knife that was laid where he was sitting. He stabbed the tablecloth. 'We'd like you to take it on.' For a moment he just looked at Edward, then scored a pattern in the tablecloth. 'It's tidy and the best solution from a security standpoint. Obviously, the Queen herself cannot attend this sort of committee . . . I've got a lot on anyway but also my face is too well known. If I spend much time in Downing Street, then sooner or later someone's going to ask why. I could send the Lord Chamberlain, but why involve more people than we have to? I hope you agree.'

Edward's instincts about the chairs had been right. They were uncomfortable and weak – he felt as if he was about to fall off. But that was also because he was slightly giddy now. If he joined this illustrious committee, how often would it meet? What would happen to the Royal Collection? Hillier was already away sick. At the same time, Edward realised that he didn't have much choice. One simply didn't turn down requests from the Palace.

'Hillier's in hospital, as you know. My secretary can hold the fort for a few days – but she'll have to be told.'

Mordaunt started to object but Edward found himself talking the equerry down. 'If she doesn't know, she can't field all the questions she'll be asked. With Hillier already off, if I am suddenly unavailable as well it could look very odd.'

Mordaunt played with the knife again. He scored the tablecloth again. He glared at Edward, who had never been on the receiving end of the equerry's famous frozen stare. It certainly was terrifying. 'Very well.'

Edward nodded.

Outside, the Barcarole was ending. Mordaunt stood up. 'There's an interval now. You'd better be gone when the others get here. The committee meets at Ten Downing Street at nine-fifteen tomorrow morning. Nine-fifteen prompt. Let's talk as soon as it's over.'

Edward could hear people starting to leave their seats. As he went through the doorway of the dining-room, the back of the royal box was just being opened by one of Covent Garden's bewigged flunkeys. Edward didn't wait to see who Mordaunt's fellow guests were; he quickly found the stairs to the lobby.

Outside, it was a warm night, though as he looked up the sky again threatened rain. He walked down Floral Street and turned into Covent Garden piazza, where a troupe of amateur acrobats was entertaining the crowd. One of the troupe was continually left out of everything, made fun of, the patsy or fool, there to be picked on by the other performers and laughed at by the spectators. Edward stood and watched for a while, thinking about his few minutes in the Opera House. How many deals had been done in that room? he wondered. It must have seen more famous faces, and more powerful personalities, than many more obvious venues. He had always wondered where the 'corridors of power' were actually located: now he had been allowed a glimpse of one of them.

Tomorrow he would get more than a glimpse. Tomorrow, Wednesday. He would be here after all and could see his father and Barbra. It would probably be embarrassing but he would do it all the same. His father always stayed at the Stafford: he would call the hotel when he got home. The old man would take it as proof that the conference story had been a lie all along. Well, it couldn't be helped.

His mind came back to the evening's events. Why, Edward wondered, as he moved off down King Street, had Mordaunt chosen not to sit on the committee himself? He was busy, yes, but this matter was surely so important, so vital, that it took precedence over everything else.

Edward had reached Leicester Square before he had an answer – or, rather, before he could admit to himself that he had been manoeuvred into a trap. It was, he had to concede, a classic piece of diplomacy, at which Mordaunt excelled. If the Prime Minister's committee succeeded, then everyone connected with the negotiations would get a pat on the back, from Lockwood to Mordaunt to Edward. However, if it failed, Mordaunt would be in the clear. He could move the blame to Lockwood – and Edward. Like that acrobat in the piazza, Edward was the patsy.

8

Wednesday

The policeman stopped and knocked lightly on the shiny mahogany doors in front of him. He opened one and leaned through. Edward heard him say, 'Dr Andover, sir', and he was then shown through immediately into the Cabinet Room. As Edward was introduced, a steward brought in a tray of coffee. He set it on the table and retreated, closing the double doors behind him. Evelyn Allen made sure they were properly latched and sat down. He was the last to do so.

Edward had been disappointed, minutes before, to have been brought into Number Ten the back way. He had been looking forward to stepping through that famous portal, but instead had been driven in an official car to a small, anonymous door just off Horse Guards Parade, and then led through a warren of corridors that made St James's Palace look like a well-thought-out barracks. He had arrived two minutes early for the meeting but even so all the others were already in the room. The Prime Minister wasted no time in getting started.

Lockwood turned to the Home Secretary. 'Facts first,' he said. 'Then we'll come to the second thoughts any of you might have had overnight. Tom?'

Lessor took a pen from his pocket and played with it. 'O'Day at MI6 is standing by, but our man at the Yard is Chief Inspector Robert Leith. Technically, he's number three in the Serious Crimes Squad. Fifty-one, very bright – he's put fifteen blackmailers inside in the last four years.' Lessor held up a sheet of paper. 'There are forty-one blackmailers currently residing as guests of Her Majesty; these are their names and – er – addresses. As to *modus operandi*, any characteristics that might betray who we are up against . . . I'm told there is no list but that Leith will be a help when and if he's brought in. The bad news, however, is that blackmailers are not ordinary criminals. Most of them have never committed a crime before and rarely do so again. They take to blackmail because they stumble across some sensitive information – as seems to have happened in this case.' Lessor nodded, meaning he had finished.

Lockwood sucked the earpiece of his spectacles. 'Anyone else? Overnight thoughts?'

Hatfield put a finger inside the collar of his shirt and stretched his neck. 'I've had one thought,' he said. 'At some point, presumably, they are going to ask for money. Is the price negotiable? There must be some haggling, I suppose – or am I mistaken?' He looked at the Home Secretary. 'Scotland Yard will know.'

Lessor nodded, meaning he would check it out.

Lockwood swivelled in his chair, looking at each of the others in turn. 'Anyone else? . . . Anyone else had any relevant thoughts at all during the night?'

Midwinter leaned forward. 'Are you convinced by Mordaunt's arguments, Bill? I mean, you *do* expect this "Brigade" to ask for money, rather than something political?'

'I'm not sure what I think,' replied Lockwood. He looked at Edward. 'I take it that story about Apollo being a homosexual, like Blunt, was accurate?'

'Yes, sir,' said Edward.

The Prime Minister looked at Midwinter again. 'All we can do is wait – and try to be prepared.'

'Then I have one other question.' Midwinter returned Lockwood's stare. 'What about the cash, Bill?'

'Well, if it ever comes to that, the Queen will pay – '

'Yes, yes . . . I was assuming that. But . . . I am also assuming the demand is going to be pretty steep. No doubt Her Majesty has the money, in some form or other, but if . . . if she has suddenly to convert assets into liquid cash . . . well, can it be done quickly and might it be a security weakness?'

Lockwood nodded. 'Who knows what the Queen is worth? . . . But I take your point, Bernard. This "Brigade" might just ask for a massive amount of money – a hundred million pounds, for instance. That would raise a few eyebrows.' He made a note on a pad in front of him. 'Thank you. Anyone else?'

The Cabinet Secretary coughed. It was the first sound he had made at either meeting and all eyes turned to him. 'As you asked, Prime Minister, I have given some thought to an operations room. That, however, raised a subsidiary point. Assuming that contact is made with the blackmailers, and assuming that the handover of the money is the best occasion we shall have for . . .

catching these people, then the best group to deal with it would be Unit 15 from SAS.'

Lockwood nodded. 'Yes – that's right. That doesn't give us any problems, does it?'

Th Cabinet Secretary hesitated and Slocombe answered for him. 'SAS comes under defence. Under Keld. He would have to know. He'd find out if we didn't tell him.'

There was silence in the room. Somewhere else in the building a door banged shut. 'Ssso,' said Lockwood, at length. 'Either we bring in Keld – or we don't use Unit 15.'

'But why *not* bring in Keld?' Lessor loathed party in-fighting.

Slocombe steepled his fingers. 'Instinct,' he said in a low voice. 'The hard lessons of a hundred little victories and as many – almost as many – defeats.'

Lockwood nodded. He picked up the note he had written on a pad and slipped it into a pocket. 'I agree. We leave George Keld out of this one. If that means we can't use Unit 15, then we don't use Unit 15. Scotland Yard have the Special Patrol Group, which guards embassies and diplomats; there's the outfit that guards Heathrow. Tom, this is one for you.'

'I'll have a decision by tonight. And put them on standby.'

'Good. Now, before we disband, I remind you once again that this committee and its proceedings are secret, very secret. No notes, no cryptic asides to your wives or mistresses, no enigmatic paragraphs in your diaries tonight. Is that clear?' His cold stare raked the room. One by one the others nodded acquiescence.

'Hmm. Now, Dr Andover, fix a meeting at the Palace, will you? You came in here the back way just now, is that right?'

'Yes.'

'Well . . . you'd better find a back way for me – into the Palace, I mean. If I keep going in by the front door, some of our nosy friends in the press might think I've come to resign.'

When Edward arrived at Barry Coxwold's small mews shop-cum-garage, the owner came forward to greet him. Edward knew him vaguely, from car meets and auctions. It did not matter that he couldn't afford one of Barry's cars. Edward was an enthusiast, a fast driver of his own much cheaper and much restored classic car, and therefore one of the fraternity.

'Edward!' Coxwold exclaimed, pumping his hand. 'Who shall I introduce you to first? Age – or beauty?'

Edward grinned, stepped over to Barbra and kissed her on both cheeks. She was dressed in a navy blazer and very pale, very expensive, blue jeans. She had her own head-hunting agency in Stanford and obviously did very well.

'Edward, elegant as ever.' She had a deep, expensive voice, clotted with the best Bloody Marys money could buy. 'Such lovely blond hair.'

'What there is of it. You look wonderful, Barbra.' And she did. She looked barely forty-five, let alone the fifty-four Edward knew her to be.

He turned to his father. They shook hands, then embraced. In many ways, Edward's father had adjusted well to life in California. Edward had loved his mother, Elisabeth, but she had been a homely soul. Edward's father had been upset by her death but liberated too. He had left for America a year later, by which time Edward was at university, and had never looked back, either personally or professionally. The one thing . . . the one thing that Edward couldn't stomach in his father now, though, was that he dyed his hair. It was brown, verging on red in the wrong light. In California it might be normal – and acceptable – but to his son, who had known him as the original, mousy-haired architect, it was absurd.

'What do you think?' said his father. He meant the car, not his hair.

Edward walked around the machine, its bodywork gleaming with that unmistakable Ferrari red, the black and yellow badge shining on its nose, the chrome wheels looking as though they had never been anywhere near a real road. 'I think you must be doing very well, to be able to afford this.' He grinned at Barry Coxwold. 'You too.'

Coxwold said, 'I'll leave you alone with her, for a bit. She grows on you.' He retreated to his office.

Barbra, Edward and his father stood looking down at the car.

'What's the horsepower?' said Edward.

'Three thousand.'

'Oh *my*!' whispered Barbra.

Edward's father walked around to the far side of the car and peered into the driver's footwell. When he stood up, he said, 'What happened to Paris?'

Edward blushed. 'Problems at work.' He never mentioned the Palace if he could avoid it.

'How often do you see the Queen in your job, Edward?' Barbra was not so coy.

'I've been there five months – and we haven't met yet.'

'Not once?'

'Not once.'

Barbra looked disappointed.

'And that American woman, Nora . . . the icecream heiress . . . do you still see her?' Edward's father had got into the car now, and was testing its 'feel'.

'Not Nora – Nancy. She's fine. Yes, I still see her.'

'What's her second name?'

'Tucker.'

'Ever hear of Tucker's icecreams, Barbra? Edward's girl comes from San Francisco.'

Barbra looked at Edward and shook her head. 'Can't say I have. But then I don't care for icecream. Are you going to be long, darling? I'm hungry and I'm sure Edward is. You know how he adores pasta. Let's go to Mimmo d'Ischia.'

'Lunch, lunch, lunch. How you keep your figure and eat so much I'll never know. Now, Edward, the price on this car is two million, two hundred and fifty thousand dollars. Should I buy it or should I buy a picture? Barbra wants a Schnabel.'

'No contest, Dad,' Edward replied at once. 'I'm an art historian, for pity's sake. I love pictures more than I love anything. It's obvious. If that's the choice – buy the car.'

Edward sipped the tea and wiped his lips with a napkin. He smiled inwardly. The tea was Ceylonese. So *that* was what was used at Buckingham Palace. It was just the kind of snippet the tabloid papers would pay a small fortune for. One of Mordaunt's secretaries was pouring. Apart from her, there were two more people in his office: Lockwood and with him Sir Evelyn Allen, Cabinet Secretary.

As soon as they all had their cups, and the secretary had left, Lockwood began. 'Sir Francis, Evelyn here has begun plans to ensure that this . . . problem will be dealt with. It isn't easy. Even a secure headquarters, or operations room, is difficult. Number Ten is too public, Scotland Yard is too leaky . . . Still, we'll have to manage somehow. The Home Secretary is having his people draw up a shortlist of men – detectives, security people – who are specialists in blackmail. For the moment, I think that's all we can do until this Brigade makes contact. I do, however, have one – rather delicate – question.'

'Thank you, Mr Lockwood, for your assistance so far. Very reassuring. What is your question?'

'Money.' Lockwood smiled a shade sheepishly. 'As of now, we can't be certain what the Brigade's demands are going to be. But if it is money, as you seem to think . . . well, I know it may seem like treason for me even to utter this but . . . since Her Majesty *is* Queen, the blackmailers may be tempted to ask for a lot of money – a very great deal indeed. What I'm asking is two things really. Is there a limit to how much she would pay to prevent this scandal breaking? And do you have . . . can the Palace get a large amount of money quickly?'

There was a pause, into which Lockwood added, 'Normally, I wouldn't dream of – '

'No, no. That's quite all right, Mr Lockwood. I understand. But I can't answer your first question. I simply don't know if there's a limit above which Her Majesty won't go. And I'm not sure she does, either. We'll just have to wait and see what demands are made. As to your second question, what sort of sums do you think we are talking about?'

Lockwood shrugged and looked at the Cabinet Secretary.

Allen said, 'I understand that the world record for a ransom is seven and a half million pounds.'

Mordaunt scribbled the figure on a piece of paper. He used an immaculate, slender, silver propelling pencil.

'I'm not sure that anyone would ask for much more than that,' added Lockwood. 'Assuming they ask for small denominations – say twenty-pound notes – and used bills, they probably couldn't carry much more. Seven and a half million in twenty-pound notes would fill something like a hundred average briefcases. Say fifteen suitcases.'

Mordaunt nodded. 'Let me offer this. There will be no problem with liquidity up to, say, twenty million pounds. After that, if it is necessary to pay and if Her Majesty *decides* to pay, we may need some time.'

Lockwood nodded. 'In that case,' he said, 'I think we are as ready as we can be, save for the headquarters headache.' He fixed Mordaunt with his gaze. 'Perhaps Her Majesty could catch a chill this afternoon and could cancel all engagements tomorrow?'

'We'll do it,' replied the equerry. 'Of course we will. There might be some comment, though. You won't have heard yet but Princess Margaret, who is in Mustique, has contracted some mysterious illness and is confined to her bed. If the Queen also goes down . . . well, you see what I'm saying.'

'An unfortunate coincidence, I agree. But these things happen.' Lockwood looked at Allen. 'It's not as big a problem as finding secure headquarters – '

'May I say something?'

The Prime Minister looked irritated for a moment, and Mordaunt surprised. They all looked at Edward.

'How many people would be needed in this "operations HQ"?'

Lockwood looked at Allen again. The Cabinet Secretary formed his mouth into a pout. 'Two or three to begin with. More later, depending on what happens.'

'We have a restorer's studio in St James's Palace,' countered Edward. 'It's large and central. We have two full-time restorers on the household staff but one is at Balmoral and the other is at Windsor at the moment, and they will stay there as long as I tell them to. We often have specialist restorers working on particular problems – but in any case no one else ever goes into the studio. No one would notice if your policemen or security people were to move in there. All they would need to do is to wear white coats. Then they would look the part.'

The irritation had gone from Lockwood's eyes. He turned to Allen. 'How does that sound?'

'Dr Andover is right. It's central, discreet. And safer and easier to have police or intelligence people come to the palace than to have Andover and others frequenting somewhere they might be noticed.'

'And we've had to tell Andover's secretary.' Mordaunt reimposed his presence on the room. 'She's first-rate and no security risk at all. She could help with routine.'

Lockwood stroked the crease in his cheek. 'Thank you, Dr Andover. I will leave you and Evelyn to sort out the details.' He turned back to Mordaunt. 'I wouldn't tell your press office the real reason Her Majesty is cancelling tomorrow's engagements.'

'Don't worry, Mr Lockwood, our security is good here. I shall send for Her Majesty's doctor and tell him she has diplomatic flu. She's had that before, more than once, and he won't ask for details. Speaking of illness, Prime Minister, may I enquire how your grandson is?'

Lockwood flashed a glance at Mordaunt. 'I wish I knew, Sir Francis, I wish I knew. I'm told there's to be a brain scan – tomorrow, perhaps. Maybe we'll learn more then. It's surprising how much these doctors don't know . . . and worrying . . . but thank you for asking.'

They all stood up. 'They made a formidable pair, the Duke of Windsor and Sir Anthony Blunt.' The Prime Minister looked at the equerry. 'I wonder which of them did the country more damage.'

'Hello, machine. What a friend you are. Always there, always ready to listen, no complaints. Except for the sex angle, you're perfect. I'd quite miss you if I was ever unlucky enough to speak to your master in person. Tell him I'm in Belton – that's Lincolnshire. Sculptures by the Stantons, John Bacon and others. Ask your master if he knew that Bacon invented a secret material for carving very ornate bits on monuments – and that even today no one knows exactly what the material is made of. Incidentally, near the church with the Bacon sculpture is a place called Belton House. *Weird*! An entire exhibition devoted to the Duke of Windsor, with what they claim is the only portrait of him as Edward VIII. Your namesake, Woodie – but there the likeness ends. I hope. What a sad man! He obviously regretted abdicating all his life – you only have to see the photographs of him later on to understand that. I hope you are getting all these messages, Woodie. They're costing me a fortune. So long.'

Edward pressed the button to reset the answering machine and tugged off his bow-tie. Tonight there had been a dinner at Christie's to mark the imminent sale of what they called their 'important impressionist' pictures. The dinner had been the usual mix of mega-rich property tycoons, minor royalty and bony widows from Palm Beach, awash in diamonds and liver spots and held together by face-lifts. Plus three or four academics, like himself, to add respectability and authority to the evening. Edward had only gone because Nancy was still away. Otherwise he would have preferred a Big Mac in her company.

He poured himself the day's last scotch (and, as it happened, the first). That crack of Nancy's about the Duke of Windsor . . . bit of a coincidence. He swallowed some Dewar's. Her information about John Bacon wasn't new, not to him anyway. But he hadn't known about the exhibition at Belton House. He was just about to take another drink when a thought struck him. Nancy had gone away just a day or two before the first parcel had arrived at St James's Palace. Was Nancy's reference to the Duke of Windsor *really* a coincidence? She couldn't be mixed up in all this, surely? Was that why she had gone away just now? Another thought struck him: was that why he had been chosen as an intermediary?

9

Thursday

From *The Times* of London, Court & Social Page:

THE QUEEN HAS A CHILL
Official engagements cancelled
Princess Margaret also indisposed

The Queen is suffering from a slight chill, Buckingham Palace announced yesterday. There is no cause for alarm, said a spokesman. Professor Alastair Senior, the physician royal, had attended Her Majesty and recommended that she remain in bed for 48 hours.

As a result of the Queen's illness, three official engagements for today have been cancelled:

11.15 am:	The opening of an old people's home at Enfield;
1.00 pm:	A lunch for the mayors of five Pennine towns, at Buckingham Palace;
8.15 pm:	The royal première for *Picasso*, Mr Ken O'Farrell's film of the great painter, starring Karlheinz Tutov, at the Odeon, Leicester Square.

KENSINGTON PALACE: Princess Margaret, who is on holiday in Mustique, is confined to bed with what is believed to be mild food poisoning. She has been attended by the medical staff of the Royal Bridgetown Hospital, Barbados.

The red phone warbled. Edward snatched at it – but then forced himself to act slowly, more casually. He looked across at the two other men in the room, who lifted their earpieces. Edward counted to three and picked up the receiver.

'Edward?' It was The General's voice.

'Yes?'

'I have Pieter van Zuylen for you. From the Rijksmuseum.'

'Very well.' Edward relaxed, nodded to the other two men, and they set down their earpieces. This wasn't what they were waiting for.

As Edward chatted with the director of Holland's venerable national gallery, his eyes roamed the room. It had been a natural enough suggestion of his that the operational headquarters be sited in St James's Palace but, he had soon realized, he was only digging himself in deeper.

He had been introduced to the other two men in the room over a light – a very light – breakfast at Mordaunt's house in Chester Square (the equerry 'lived out'). For security's sake he had dispatched his housekeeper somewhere and cooked the breakfast himself, if one could call brewing coffee and warming croissants cooking.

Bob Leith was the Scotland Yard man, a small Welsh terrier with dark hair that was thinning and through which could be glimpsed the rolling countryside of his scalp. He came with the Home Secretary's stamp of approval as the Yard's top operations man in the Serious Crimes Squad. 'I'm told he has handled more blackmail cases than there are fake Utrillos,' Mordaunt had confided to Edward just before Leith arrived. Edward supposed that was the equerry's idea of a joke.

Kennedy O'Day was altogether different. Tall, bony and sandy-haired – those were the characteristics one noticed at first. From a distance, he was handsome, striking even. Close to, one took in the broken veins on his cheeks (drink?) and disconcerting wisps of hair abandoned on the bridge of his nose. Was it vanity or eccentricity that prevented him taking a razor to them? Intense blue eyes and small teeth with gaps in between made his a hard face, too. Where O'Day came from, what department of Whitehall (or the moon) he inhabited, had not been formally explained to Edward. It was not hard to guess, though, for he had arrived for breakfast with a diagram of St James's Palace, showing the telephone points, and during breakfast he had taken a call from someone who was clearly his assistant and had apparently been at work in the palace during the night. This ensured, he said, that Edward's calls could be put through to the studio.

O'Day had also double-checked Wilma Winnington-Brown's background. 'No money troubles, lives within her means, devoted to her children and the memory of her dead husband, who was a British observer in Vietnam. Likes gin and sherry, and puffs away like the original Royal Scot.'

'I could have told you all that,' Edward had replied, rather tetchily.

O'Day's lips had widened into an alarming grin. The gaps in his teeth made his mouth resemble a small piano keyboard. 'And has she told you that she once killed a man who tried to rape her? Brained him with an alabaster lamp that was handy.' The grin spread over O'Day's face again as he enjoyed the effect this information had on Edward.

Not that Edward was surprised for very long (the women in his life were full of surprises, he reflected). He could well imagine Wilma dispatching a rapist. In a way, it endeared her more to him.

Breakfast over, O'Day, Leith and Edward had transferred to St James's Palace, one at a time. Inside the studio, Edward had moved a huge canvas by Canaletto so that anyone casually looking in would find the view blocked. The back of the canvas faced the door so that it would not be immediately obvious that precious little restoration was going on. During the night a bank of phones had been installed, each with two earpieces on long leads. Whenever an instrument rang, all three men could listen in.

At length, Edward put down the phone on van Zuylen. He prayed for something to happen. The Canaletto had been a talking point to begin with but it only highlighted the fact that the three of them had little in common. Edward had asked Leith early on for instructions when the call finally came through. The chief inspector had told him to act as naturally as possible.

'Shouldn't I try to keep the conversation going? So you can trace the call?'

Leith had pulled a face. 'If you can. That's what everyone thinks. If they are any good, the blackmailers will know it too. If they are even half-way professional, they will do all the talking, then ring off very quickly. We'll try to trace the call – of course we will. But don't expect miracles. I'll be listening for clues – but mainly to get some idea of the characters we are dealing with. In blackmail, if this is regular blackmail, our best chance is always the handover of the money.'

They had lapsed into silence again and Edward had returned

to his own preoccupations. He was specifically worried by something else, something which showed how corrupting this affair was already becoming. This was a short exchange he had had with Mordaunt before the others had arrived for breakfast. It had occurred to Edward that even if the blackmail was successful, then, even after paying out the sum that the blackmailers demanded, the Palace would still be left with a looted Raphael, a looted Poussin, a looted Canaletto and God knows what else on its hands. How would they explain that? Edward had wondered and had asked Mordaunt what they would do.

'Well, we can't return them to their rightful owners, can we?' the equerry had replied, rather primly. 'Too many awkward questions might be asked – how we came across them and so forth. The whole story might even leak out. No, I think the safest course would be to destroy them.'

Edward's phone rang again, shaking him from his distasteful reverie.

Leith and O'Day reached for their earpieces. By the second ring they were both ready and Edward picked up the receiver.

'Yes?'

'Edward? An overseas call. I think so, anyway.' Wilma spoke in a confidential tone. 'He won't give me his name but says you are expecting to hear from him. He says it's about some Old Master pictures.'

This was it!

Edward looked across to the others and they both nodded. 'Yes, that's right, Wilma. This is the call we are waiting for. Put him through, please.'

Suddenly a voice was saying, 'Edward Andover? Edward Andover?' It sounded foreign and assured. It also sounded just round the corner.

'Yes . . . yes. This is Andover. What can I do for you?'

The other voice chuckled. 'You can do quite a lot for me, Dr Andover, oh yes. And I can do a great deal for you . . . for the Queen anyway. I take it you are familiar with the background to . . . this telephone call?'

Edward nodded at the phone. 'Yes . . . yes, I am.' Leith had pressed a button to alert his deputy so he could try to trace the call.

'The first thing is to discuss the way we shall communicate. At the end of each conversation I shall give you a time and a location for the next call. I assume you are taping all this so I shall never repeat anything. Is that clear?'

'Yes . . . No! what do you mean, location?'

'Where are you now, Dr Andover?'

Edward paused. Fatally. 'In my office, of course.'

'Hmm. I doubt it. It doesn't matter. Are you in central London?'

'Yes.'

'That had better be true. I'll show you what I mean by giving you an example. I shall call again in an hour from now – but not on this number.'

'What –?'

'*Listen!* I shall call you, *you*, Andover, in precisely sixty minutes – at the public phone booths just inside the entrance to the British Museum.'

'What on earth –?'

But the line had gone dead.

Edward held the receiver in his hand for a moment, looking at it. Then, gently, he replaced it. He looked across again at Leith.

The policeman shrugged. 'Your conversation took sixty-five seconds. We need about twice that. This way our friend buys time: that means safety for him. Also, it wrong-foots you by putting you in unfamiliar territory. He's hoping that might slow you down – mentally, I mean.'

'What can be done about it?'

'Nothing. We play along. Forget tracing the call, Dr Andover. Ten to one, it's coming from abroad, and from a public booth. These days you can dial direct to almost anywhere from almost anywhere else. He'll use a different phone next time, too. He'll use a different phone every time. Calling from a public booth also makes our friend harder to trace.'

'Did you get any sense of the man behind the voice? It seemed an assured, confident voice to me. Well educated perhaps.'

Leith shrugged again and stood up. 'We ought to go. Give ourselves plenty of time. Then we needn't use the siren and draw attention to ourselves.'

Edward stood up also but O'Day interjected, 'Sir Francis is on the phone.' He had called the equerry as soon as he'd heard the blackmailer's voice. 'He wants a word with you.'

Edward took the receiver. 'Francis.'

'What's he like? What sort of man is he?'

'He hardly spoke a hundred words!'

'But you must have *some* idea.'

Edward thought, glancing across to Leith as he did so. 'Young . . . thirties, maybe. Educated, maybe . . . Self-confident.'

'British?'

'Nnno, and not African, not oriental. Spanish? Portuguese? I'm guessing.'

'Hmm. O'Day says he will have a mobile phone with him at the museum. If you need my advice, just ask. But keep in touch, fast.'

It was only after Mordaunt had rung off and Edward was getting into Leith's unmarked car that it occurred to him that the equerry, if he really wanted to stay on top of things, could have come to the British Museum himself. Edward dwelt on this thought as the car swept up the Mall and around Trafalgar Square. In Charing Cross Road, a disturbing idea wormed its way into his thoughts. He had told no one about his suspicions of Nancy, though it had subsequently occurred to him that *she* had asked him out, *she* had made all the running. Now he found himself wondering about Mordaunt. Apart from the Queen herself, Mordaunt was the only person privy to the Blunt file and the only person to know how much liquid cash the Crown had. Was *that* why Edward was making the negotiation and not the equerry? He hardly dared think it through: were Mordaunt and Nancy in it together?

The entrance to the British Museum was thronged with people. Crocodiles of Japanese mingled with groups of Americans, Germans and Dutch.

On the way there, Leith had been in touch again with Mordaunt on the car phone. They had discussed whether the security people at the museum should be involved. It had its advantages and Leith would not have to tell them everything. On the other hand, the presence of O'Day and Edward might cause one or two awkward questions to be asked. They had therefore decided to 'freelance', as Leith put it, at least to begin with.

Edward followed Leith across the lobby of the museum, his mind in turmoil. He examined his watch: twelve minutes to go.

By the bookstall there was a row of three phones, two of them occupied. Leith said, 'The blackmailers will have thought this through. They know there are three phones here and they will have all the numbers. We just have to keep one booth occupied, and the phone inside it free. There are three of us so we can take turns to use the booth. That way we won't draw attention to ourselves. But the minute it rings, Andover, you pick it up.'

'Shouldn't we split up? We might be being watched.'

Leith looked from O'Day to Edward. 'Our friend didn't insist you come alone. That's unusual, but I can't quite work out what it means. I'd rather stay within earshot, anyway. In case I can help.'

They waited, forming a small queue all by themselves. From time to time, Edward scanned the crowd for anyone who might be watching them. No one stood out.

He pulled back the cuff of his jacket and checked his watch. A minute to go. O'Day was punching the buttons on his mobile phone. 'Shit!' he said suddenly. 'This bugger won't work in here. I'll have to go outside.'

'Fat lot of use that will be,' growled Leith. 'How are you – ?'

The phone rang.

Edward jumped – he didn't know how nervous he was. Quickly he regained his composure. Or tried to. The others gathered round and, as the phone rang a second time, he reached for the receiver and put it to his ear.

'Andover.'

'Well done. The arrangements seem to have worked out.'

What should Edward say? Should he take the lead? No, he thought that would be demeaning. He was non-committal. 'I can hear you very well.'

'Good. Unlucky for you, all this, eh? It's not as if you were royal yourself.'

Edward said nothing. The other man seemed unhurried – or maybe that was an act. Either way, he was behaving as if he had no fear the police might trace the call. He was composed and, as Leith had said, Edward was unnerved and made uncomfortable by the location – and by the idea that perhaps the voice's accomplice was watching, somewhere in the lobby. It was also hard to be relaxed when you were standing in a clammy booth.

It was as if the other man could read his thoughts. 'I can picture where you are,' he said. 'The three booths near the bookshop . . . I've made scores of calls from there in the last months, while I was working on this matter.'

Edward was determined *not* to ask the other man how much money he wanted – it was certainly too demeaning. At the same time, he did wish the voice would make its claim. The uncertainty was exhausting.

'I *love* the treasures of the British Museum, Dr Andover, don't you? Goya's drawing of the Duke of Wellington, the Rosetta Stone, all those cuneiform tablets and ancient mummies.'

'I didn't anticipate discussing archaeology with a blackmailer!' Edward knew he was being too sharp but maybe it would help unseat the other man. He might be an aficionado of the British Museum but he was still a criminal.

'Surprised, eh? You're in for quite a few surprises, Dr Andover, I can guarantee you that. And most of them in the next few minutes. However, yes – let us get down to business. We have been polite with each other for long enough.' There was a pause. Then: 'You've had enough time to consider what I have. You must also know what it's worth. How much do *you* think it's worth, Dr Andover? Five million pounds? Fifteen? Fifty?'

Edward scribbled these amounts on to the back of his cheque book and passed it to Leith. He wasn't sure how to reply. But something was called for. 'You yourself said it: I'm not a royal. I'm the intermediary – '

'What is the Queen worth, do you think? A billion certainly, these days. *Four* billion, I read somewhere. And what's the Royal Collection worth, Dr Andover? You must have some idea of that?'

Edward, horrified, said nothing.

'Say a hundred million pounds each for the Raphael and the Michelangelo. Fifty million each for the Holbeins, five million each for the Canalettos. Not to mention the Bellinis, the Duccio, the Rubenses, the Raphael cartoons, the Dürers and all those Van Dycks . . . I reckon the collection alone must be worth a billion pounds – but the exact amount doesn't matter. You see my point? Her Majesty *can* afford fifty million pounds. She could raise the money, if she wanted to, by selling just one picture.'

Edward shuddered, thinking of the outcry there would be if even one drawing were to be sold from the Royal Collection.

'My demands, however, are for much less than fifty million,

and for far more. I told you there would be some surprises, Dr Andover. Here's one: I don't want any money at all.'

Edward frowned. He hadn't heard right, surely? Leith and O'Day were looking at him. He had heard wrongly . . . He *must* have.

'I can understand if you are . . . confused, Dr Andover. No one ever heard of a blackmailer asking for no money, eh?'

Edward didn't speak. There was nothing he could say. This was not how it should be, not at all.

The other man was speaking again. 'No money and nothing are two very different things, of course. This conversation isn't just a waste of time.' The voice laughed, but it was a cackle, harsh and self-satisfied at the same time. 'Are you listening, Dr Andover? You had better be paying attention now, because we are at last in Prime Time. The Queen, Sir Francis Mordaunt, any other bigwigs you may have brought in, will want you to recall all of this exchange. Exactly.'

Edward stared at Leith as he listened to the voice. But he said nothing.

'Our terms, the Apollo Brigade's terms, are a simple exchange. Very simple indeed. When you hear it you won't be surprised. In fact, you'll see the simplicity of it all. The beauty, the sheer political beauty of it all.'

'What do you mean, the *political* beauty -?'

At this, Leith moved closer to Edward. He seemed to grow in size.

'Aha! You picked up on that . . . Well done, Dr Andover . . . Three rooms from your phone booth, barely a hundred yards from where you are standing, there are ninety-three pieces of stone. Carvings in high and low relief. Metopes is the technical Greek word for some of them but they are much better known as the Elgin Marbles – '

'What –?'

'They . . . *they* are to go back to Greece. Back to Athens and the Parthenon. Where they belong. You have a month.'

Edward's mind was reeling, switchbacking this way and that. This proposal . . . it was a joke, surely? It wasn't in the script, no one had warned him it might follow this path, or anything like it. The voice was so . . . self-confident, so *relaxed*. And, he realised now, its accent was Greek.

He recovered slightly. 'That's impossible. The Queen would never – '

'It's not impossible at all, Dr Andover, but in any case that's not for you to decide. You will relay these . . . proposals to Her Majesty and you will add the following: in just over a month from now the Olympic Games begin in Atlanta, Georgia, in America. The Centenary Olympics, the games which should by rights have gone to Athens. Greece, as you know, is not taking part in the Atlanta Games, as a protest. We are holding our own Olympic Festival – just the original sports of boxing, wrestling, running, chariot races, javelin and discus, but it is a festival too: music, theatre, all the arts. People forget, but the original temple of Olympia, Dr Andover, was decorated with sculptures, showing the triumphs of Hercules and Apollo. Think of the publicity for the festival, when the Marbles are returned, think how the Atlanta Games will be overshadowed, think how the world, the International Olympic Committee, will regret its choice of America – brash, money-grabbing America. Greece will have its pride back, and the Marbles. People will flock to Greece to see these things. We shall have turned defeat into a magnificent victory.

'We have two demands. There are a lot of Marbles and they are heavy and precious. So we appreciate they cannot simply be put in a suitcase aboard an airliner. In the first place, therefore, we want your government to announce its *intention* of returning the Marbles. Once such an announcement is made, at the highest level, a government could never go back on its word. Second, we expect the return to begin in three weeks. Allow another week for shipping and unloading and the Marbles will arrive on the eve of the Olympic Festival. Atlanta – America – will be gloriously upstaged.'

Edward could scarcely keep up with all this. The man was . . . well, it was no normal blackmail, if there was such a thing. 'You know you can't – '

'Dr Andover! You're a nice man, I'm told. I like you. I think, from what I know of you. I like the sound of your voice, anyway. But you are an *intermediary*. Repeat what I say to your superiors – the Queen, Mordaunt, Lockwood, whoever. I shall call again in two days. I will speak only with you. Give me your reply at that time. The Apollo Brigade will then proceed accordingly. But no more talk now.' The phone went dead.

Dumbly, Edward waited, hanging on to the phone, as if the voice might come back. The others were staring at him.

Eventually he replaced the receiver and stepped out of the booth. 'Well?' said O'Day. Leith just stood there.

Edward repeated the conversation.

Leith whistled.

O'Day looked grim. 'The *Duke* of Windsor, *Sir* Anthony Blunt – and now *Lord* Elgin. Only in Britain do we give titles to such *tits!*'

The flat used by Prime Ministers at the top of 10 Downing Street is surprisingly modest. There is a sitting-room decorated in blue and yellow chintzes, a small study with an eighteenth-century walnut desk and prints by William Nicholson, a compact kitchen and two bedrooms with yellow watered silk on the walls. It is well insulated from the bustle below and normally very quiet; and the phones don't ring – they have lights which flash on and off.

The flat was anything but quiet at the moment, however. Though it was late, the sitting-room was crowded and Lockwood was shouting. The Prime Minister was standing, a bottle of whisky in one hand and his unravelled bow-tie in the other. He had removed the latter as he helped the others in the room to a nightcap. It had gone midnight. After the episode at the British Museum, O'Day had not been able to get in to see Lockwood until five in the afternoon and then only for a few minutes. Lockwood had exploded at the news and then instructed O'Day to 'hang on'. The Prime Minister had had to go straight into a meeting of the Northern Ireland Committee and then to a dinner for the Foreign Secretary of Vietnam, who was on an official visit. There had just been time, however, for him to instruct O'Day to call this late-night conference in the flat. The others of the *ad hoc* secret committee were arrayed around Lockwood in the sitting-room. Edward was also there. Lockwood's wife, Sally, was with their daughter's family – there was still no word from the hospital – so the Prime Minister felt free to shout without disturbing anyone other than the security guards.

'I'm seeing the Queen in the morning. And that smarmy equ – ' He remembered Edward was there and looked over to him. 'I'm seeing Mordaunt. He says nothing's changed – but of

72

course it has! Money is money – but these bloody Marbles! That's political.' He slopped whisky into Slocombe's glass. 'I've a good mind to tell him – and Her blessed Majesty – what to do with their precious mystery. Let it all come out so that everyone can see what a little shit the Duke of Windsor really was. Bah!' He had moved away from the political secretary but now he turned back again. 'What do you say, Eric, do we let the royals roast?'

The political adviser pursed his lips. 'There's something I'm still in the dark about, Bill. How do we get from Blunt nicking these paintings at the end of the war to this "Apollo Brigade"? It's all Greek to me.'

Lockwood shifted on his feet. 'Mordaunt gave me his theory this afternoon, over the phone. The Hesses are related to our own royals *and* to the Greek royals. The Duke of Edinburgh, Prince Philip of Athens as he was, has a sister married to a Hesse. Mordaunt concedes that the Blunt 1945 adventure was known about in royal circles and must have reached the Greek side. After that – who knows? Blunt was a bastard. He may have had the idea himself, and approached the Greeks, or they may have approached him. He was a world authority on Poussin, the seventeenth-century French painter, whose works often referred to classical Greece. So Blunt often had to go to Greece for his research. Who knows who he met there? It's well known – now – that Blunt liked all sorts of lovers.'

The Prime Minister stopped for breath. He looked angry again. 'This affair is so . . . God, Blunt was a *shit*!' He groaned. 'You see why I'm pissed off, Eric. How often do I swear like this? So . . . earn your wages . . . Shall we let their Britannic Majesties face the music?'

Slocombe smacked his lips and grimaced as he swallowed. It looked as if he didn't like whisky. 'I wouldn't advise it, Bill.'

'Don't you turn on me now.'

'I'm not! You know that. May I have some water with this, by the way? It's too grown-up for me when it's neat.'

Lockwood nodded at Allen, who got up and disappeared into the kitchen.

'So! What's your advice this time?' The Prime Minister said it belligerently, standing over Slocombe.

'Don't let your feelings about Windsor cloud your judgement. In this case Mordaunt's right. The game has changed but the way we play it hasn't. Remember, the Elgin Marbles don't belong to the royal family or the Crown, they belong to the nation – in effect, the government of the day.'

'I see all that. But even so we can still keep our distance – '

'Hear me! If any of this story leaks out, it *all* will. Think, Prime Minister, how things have changed. The most important way they have changed is that a non-financial demand has been made. We couldn't know before that they were going to do that. But the Elgin Marbles are not just art objects – they are a political symbol these days. For that reason alone the government can't help but be involved.'

'Yes, yes, yes, Eric, but – '

'*But* . . . having said we would help to begin with, as you and the Chief Whip so rightly argued, here's what will happen now, in my judgement, if we pull out.' He paused as Allen came back with the water. Slocombe held up his glass for the whisky to be topped up. No one else spoke. 'The Palace will leak *its* version of the story: that we were unwilling to help out the royal family when it was being blackmailed *politically*. We will be made to appear as callous and uncaring. There will be a fresh scandal in the press about the Duke of Windsor and Nazi loot and all those fancy families who were willing to join him, but who in this room can say it won't be overshadowed by a major rift – now, in the late twentieth-century, a few months before a general election – between HM and HMG? You see my point, Bill?'

'Reluctantly. Very reluctantly.'

'True enough, the royal family won't gain many friends for this fresh evidence of the Duke's Nazi links and sympathies, but we stand to lose far more. Think how the opposition will exploit any rift between us and the royals? Think how Keld would use any of your mistakes against you in a leadership contest. That's October – even closer than a general election. This business could do us more damage than anything else. To many people in this country – most, I would say – the monarchy is far more important than a bunch of Greek relics.'

He gulped at his whisky and water. His face contracted as if he was in pain but it was his way of savouring the taste. 'In theory, most people are against dealing with blackmailers but ask anyone at Scotland Yard and they will tell you that almost everyone who is *actually* blackmailed considers payment and most actually *do* pay up. Deep, deep down most people have a terrible sympathy with the victims of blackmail – which is quite separate from what they feel about blackmail and blackmailers in theory. We *all* have secrets, skeletons in our closets. So don't imagine this is an ordinary terrorist crime, like hostage-taking on aeroplanes. This is a *political* manoeuvre but one with a difference.'

'So! You are suggesting we give in?' Lockwood drained his glass and slumped into a chair.

'I think we are probably left with no choice, Prime Minister – but I am not advocating we do nothing.' He paused but no one else joined in. 'I believe this case is more dangerous than anyone else here in this room appears to think. *Politically* dangerous, I mean. I've already outlined what I think are the dangers if we don't support the Palace. I think the dangers are just as great if we give back the Marbles.'

The Prime Minister made a sound, somewhere between a grunt and a scream of pain.

In response, Slocombe lowered his voice, so they all had to lean forward to hear him. 'If the Marbles go back to Greece, the Palace keeps its secret. The Crown will be held in exactly the high esteem as it is now. The government, however, will have made a grand gesture that will earn it some kudos among a handful of intellectuals and worthies in this world but, again in my judgement, to most people of Britain, we risk becoming known as the government who "gave away" the Elgin Marbles, who disposed of our heritage. We shall be seen as wimps, weak at the knees and wet behind the ears. It is not as great a danger to the party as the other course but, in a close-run election, it could be decisive. In a close-run election, *anything* is decisive.'

Midwinter broke in. 'Come on, Eric. You can't just present us with cul-de-sacs in either direction.'

Slocombe was drinking more whisky. He wiped his mouth with the back of his hand. 'I know, I know. I suggest two things. We have almost a month before this Olympic Festival, as they are calling it. Now, if we were to conduct ourselves during that time *as if* we intended to fulfil the bargain, that might persuade the blackmailers they have the upper hand. As a result they might relax and that might help us to find them. But in any case we can do things over and above the bargain. For instance, we could have it leaked that we were thinking of returning the Marbles. We would deny it officially of course, but the source of the leak would be credible – a worthy backbencher you could promise promotion to in the next administration – and so the rumours would not go away completely. The blackmailers would believe them.

'Then a few days after that, we could close the Duveen Galleries at the British Museum, saying at first that they were due for renovation. A few days later we would arrange for the Marbles to be moved from the museum. Again, the official explanation might be that they were being restored, or protected while the gallery is being refurbished. But that of course would renew speculation about our intentions. Either way, the aim would be to ensure that the blackmailers *believed* we were keeping our side of the bargain. In fact, we would just be buying time.'

'Let me get this straight. You are saying we should give the *appearance* of co-operation . . . but all the time trying to find out who the blackmailers are?'

'Yes – and put that way it doesn't sound so cock-eyed, does it? This problem is only a few hours old. The more you think about it, the more obvious it becomes that we can't refuse to co-operate with the Palace and we can't just give in. We have to play this like the police play any blackmail – pretend to go along with it but all the while trying to track down the buggers.'

'But . . .' Lockwood stood up again and placed the whisky on the mantelshelf. 'If we make that sort of announcement, even as a leak, or if we close the British Museum, even part of it . . . well, pandemonium will break out.'

'Very probably, Bill. We'll have to weather it.'

'You're sure we shouldn't just call their bluff?'

'Yes, I *am* sure. This is a classic political problem. Either course has its dangers, grave dangers. Judgement is called for. You're good at that, Bill, or used to be.'

'But . . . but how are we going to start?' The Prime Minister turned to O'Day. 'Commander? What do *you* think of Eric's plan?'

'It's not my place to comment on the political aspects, sir,' said O'Day pompously. 'Operationally . . . it doesn't look as though we are going to get very far via the telephones . . . there'll be precious little chance to trace these calls, so far as I can see – and very little point if they use a different phone every time.'

'The other operational difficulty', said Leith, interjecting, 'is that there is now not going to be any handover of money. The blackmailers don't have to show themselves – ever. Have you thought of that?'

Lockwood let out a growl. 'Terrific! Eric here tells me we've got to play for time – and you operational people tell me we've nothing to play *with*. Brilliant!'

'I can think of two ways forward, sir.'

There was a moment's silence as all eyes turned to Edward.

'Ah! Dr Andover. For those of you who don't know, the Queen's Surveyor of Pictures had a good idea about an operational headquarters room.' The Prime Minister smiled at Edward. 'What is it this time?'

'Well, sir, the paintings that were sent to me had N7 postmarks. I've checked in the phone book and there are three Greek Orthodox churches in the N7 postal district – obviously that's a Greek area of London. The police there could be asked if they've heard any unusual rumours, or if strange or prominent Greeks have moved into the area recently.'

Lockwood turned to O'Day. 'Well, commander?'

'We can try, sir, but I doubt it will turn up anything. Most blackmailers are not habitual criminals so I doubt if the local police will know anything. But . . . well, we can try. Then there's our own computer, in my department. We'll try that, too.'

'Yes, try,' Lockwood said, sharply. Then he looked at Edward again. 'And what was your other idea, Dr Andover?'

'I take Inspector Leith's point that there will now be no hand-over of money, but I can't believe that this Brigade would go to all this trouble and get no credit for themselves if they succeed. It's not in human nature. They must have *some* plan to boast about their achievements or take credit. I'm guessing now, but they must belong to one or other groups in Greece who campaign for the return of the Marbles. These lists could be checked. Who knows – maybe some of the names are in N7?' Edward sipped his whisky.

The Prime Minister eyed him. 'You must be a good researcher, Dr Andover. You think like a detective.' He turned to O'Day. 'You have people in Athens, commander?'

O'Day nodded.

'Dr Andover has given us a start, I think.'

'Yes, sir.'

'Leith, you will handle the North London investigations.'

'Yes, sir.'

'Thank you for your help, Dr Andover. To be frank, I'm far from sure that these lines of inquiry will lead anywhere but I agree that we must pursue them. We must pursue *any* possibility. Has anyone else got any ideas or suggestions?'

No one spoke.

'Very well. We will pursue the strategy suggested by Eric. Starting with Dr Andover's ideas. I think that from now on and for security's sake, this committee will meet here, in this flat, every day – at midnight. Arrive singly, by the back door. I want everyone present at all times and I want everyone to *worry* about this problem at every opportunity. We've got a little time before the blackmailers call again and it would be good to have made some progress by then. Now, thank you all – and goodnight.'

Going down the stairs, Edward received some friendly smiles from the others on the committee and he ought to have been more pleased than he was. In fact, he was confused and worried. He had been wrong to harbour any suspicions about Mordaunt – but what about Nancy? Nancy's flat was in N7.

Edward reached home at about one-thirty. For days now, it hadn't even occurred to him to go to the Albatross. He now dreaded what he would find on the answering machine. It wasn't only Wilma Winnington-Brown and Barbra, who had given him such a good going over at lunch the previous day, who thought he should settle down. He half thought so himself. And he half thought that Nancy was the one he should do it with. He unlocked the door to his flat and instinctively looked across at the green diode glow of the message counter on his answering machine. He closed the door and switched on the light. He considered having another whisky before facing Nancy's message but it was late and he dismissed the idea.

He approached the machine. A green figure 1 stared up at him. He pressed the button.

'Darling machine. This is His Master's Vice, speaking from Normanton, near Pontefract, home of Rysbrack's wonderful monument. Tell your master that, after days of marble nudes, granite nudes, limestone nudes and bronze nudes, I'm looking forward to some old-fashioned *fffflesh*! So long.' The line went dead and Edward stood over the machine, staring at it as it clicked and whirred and rearranged itself, ready to receive the next message.

Abandoning his resolve, he poured a scotch and splashed soda on to it. Then he crossed the room to the bookshelves. He took down Margaret Whinney's *Sculpture in Britain 1530–1830,* and turned to the index. He found the entry on Rysbrack. It didn't take him long to find what he was looking for – the sculptor's monument at Normanton. He read the entire entry. Sipping his whisky, he read it again. The entry confirmed something that had itched at the back of his mind. It was exactly as Nancy had said – except for one thing. Michael Rysbrack's monument was not at Normanton in Yorkshire but at Normanton – same spelling – in Leicestershire. Was Nancy confused? No, she might be American and unfamiliar with Britain but she was very bright and you don't confuse Yorkshire with Leicestershire when you are supposed to be telephoning from one of those places. Edward swallowed the rest of his scotch in one gulp. Nancy had lied.

10

Friday

Next morning when Edward reached the office, Wilma followed him through and closed the door behind her. 'You look *terrible*, Edward. You're not getting enough sleep. Now, I've got some pills – '

'No!' Edward was perturbed and angry about Nancy and he shouted more than he meant to. More gently, he added: 'No. I hate pills, sleeping pills especially.' He put his Walkman on his desk.

'What did you have for breakfast, then?'

'Oh . . . coffee . . . nothing really.'

'I'll make you some soup. I know where I can lay my hands on a packet.'

'Don't *fuss*, Wilma.' He smiled but she just glared back.

'Now . . . what messages?'

'I'm going to make you some soup whether you like it or not.' Wilma got this in very quickly, before adding, 'O'Day has been here already. It seems – '

'Later, Wilma! In a minute. We still have to look after the collection. Let's deal with our real jobs first. What news?'

'That's the last thing I thought you'd want to do at the moment, with all this other nonsense on your plate.' She turned and waved at a pile of papers on her own desk. 'I've opened your official-looking letters – and read them. Three things you should know about. The Canadian National Gallery in Ottawa are holding an exhibition of Poussin and want to borrow our *Capriccio*. The exhibition is the year after next. Second, you've been invited to Bucharest by the Romanian royal family. Now they have been restored to office, they are thinking of rebuilding a royal collection and would like advice.'

Edward bit his thumbnail. 'If this other "nonsense", as you call it, goes sour and hits the papers, they may not think we have much to teach them.' He rubbed his chin where he had missed a tuft of beard shaving. 'What was the third thing?'

'Sir James Hillier's secretary called. He'd like to see you.'

'Oh dear, that's all we need.' Edward realised he was being unreasonable. Now that the director was beginning to recover from his operation, it was only natural that he should wish to take up the reins of his post. But such a lot had happened . . .

'Very well. I don't know when I shall be able to see him just yet – but don't let me forget. Also, don't forget to phone Balmoral. We need a condition report on the *Capriccio* – tell them Ottawa is interested.' The Ottawa request was fortuitous: it would keep the restorer busy and out of the office for a couple of weeks at least.

'Now is that all? If it is, we can get back to O'Day. What did he want, so bright and early?'

'He said I was to tell you Leith had drawn a blank, during the night, in North London. The police there know nothing. There's nothing on the MI6 computer either. But they are still waiting to hear from his people in Athens.'

'He made a special journey, just to say that?'

'Not only that. I am to give you this – ' and she held up a key. 'The studio is now locked. He said you would find out why when you arrived.'

Edward took the key. 'Commander O'Day is a bit like a bulldozer. A bulldozer in a china shop. It's a good job Hillier *isn't* around. The noise level would definitely be higher.' He grinned and put the key in his pocket.

'Edward . . .' Wilma lowered her voice to a whisper, or as close to a whisper as her vocal cords would allow. 'Edward, these Marbles . . . are they *so* important? I mean, I know they must be for this brigade to do what they are doing, but . . .'

'Yes, they *are* important, Wilma. They're important because the Parthenon is one of the oldest and most beautiful buildings in western history. They're also important because Britain has an enormous amount – ninety-three pieces – and if they were returned they would transform the Parthenon and make it without doubt the most interesting building from classical antiquity. They're important because they were exported with a permit from the Turks when they ruled Greece – and that means the Greeks have never recognized its legitimacy. And they're important because, if the Marbles did go back, if Britain acknowledged that the Greeks do have a case, a precedent would be set. All sorts of countries might then claim back all sorts of objects if the

81

Elgin Marbles were returned. Once this news gets out . . . well, if you think things have been hectic lately, it's going to get far worse.'

'In that case, I *will* bring you some soup.'

Edward was already on his way out of the office. He waved his arm without turning. He went down the stairs, past the security guard, the dead fireplace and the Canaletto. He then had to climb a narrow flight of stairs on the opposite side of the hall and walk along a balcony that opened on to a small court-yard. This had a small bronze by Adriaan de Vries in the centre. Sculpture brought his mind back to Nancy. Why had she lied? Why? Was she with another man? He almost prayed that she was. Otherwise . . . otherwise she was part of this . . . Apollo Brigade.

He arrived at the studio, inserted the key in the lock and turned it. Just inside the door, he found a burly, thick-necked man – an army type with fingers the size of sausages and freckles as big as snowflakes. The man, who was sitting on a chair, or rather *around* the chair, and reading a paperback, stood up and barred the way. 'Yes?' he barked belligerently.

'I'm Andover. Can't you see I have a key?'

O'Day stuck his head from behind the big Canaletto that barred the view. 'Frank, meet Dr Andover. Dr Andover, meet Frank from our security section. We need security now. Come here and you'll see why.'

Frank didn't smile exactly. But he nodded at Edward and moved out of his way.

Edward stepped forward. He noticed that O'Day had taken it upon himself to rearrange three large canvases – the Canaletto, a Van Dyck family portrait and a huge Paulus Potter 'Bull' – into a rectangle against one wall, so that they formed a room-within-a-room. Inside this 'canvas room' was the desk, the bank of phones, chairs for O'Day, Leith – who nodded – and another person whom Edward had not seen before. She was sitting at the desk with her back to Edward and tapping at a keyboard in front of her. Beyond that was a computer screen.

'Tawsy, stop tinkling the ivories and say hello to Edward And-over.'

The woman abandoned the keyboard and swivelled on her seat. She was wearing a restorer's white coat. They all looked like a convention of chemists.

'Victoria Tatton, Edward Andover. Edward Andover, vice versa.'

Edward and Victoria shook hands.

'Now, although Tawsy here could easily be Miss Whitehall, or Miss Horse Guards Parade, her IQ is the right shape too. Higher, in fact, than my golf handicap. She comes from something called the Hard Languages Unit – HLU. She speaks Serbo-Croat, Hungarian, Bulgarian, Greek, of course, and Turkish, though that's not *very* hard – '

'And I can speak for myself, too. Hello, Edward.' She smiled. She was small, with pale skin, close-cropped, dark-brown hair, a wide mouth and brown eyes that looked defensive.

'Hello. What are the other hard languages?'

'Japanese, Chinese, some of the Bantu tongues.'

O'Day interjected again. 'She has other talents too. She flies, she plays snooker, she shoots, she fences and she also speaks computerese. That's also why she's here. Lockwood knows, by the way, and approves. She has full clearance.'

Victoria smiled at Edward again. 'I wish I could paint, though. Do you?' When she smiled two creases appeared in her cheeks, giving her a sardonic expression. Edward was reminded of the women in the paintings of Georges de la Tour.

'No, I don't paint any more,' he said. 'I wasn't good enough. That's why I became an art historian.'

Victoria went on to reply but O'Day got in first. 'Come on, back to the screen. This is linked to the department's main-frame computer. I'll explain as we go.'

Victoria turned again to the keyboard. Edward could now see that there were columns of names on the screen.

'I've done some work and some thinking since last night's midnight committee,' said O'Day. 'As your secretary may have told you, we drew a blank in North London. The police say the Greeks are a pretty law-abiding bunch and they've heard nothing untoward. That doesn't mean much, of course, but it does mean that we can't count on an early break in that area.

'We haven't heard back from Athens yet, but let me explain what we're doing here. See if you can spot any holes in my reasoning.'

He perched himself on the edge of the desk, next to the computer screen. Edward noticed that his shirt cuffs were frayed.

Did he live alone? It was hard to tell. O'Day was obviously practised at being a closed book. No doubt it went with the job.

'We have to assume, given the timing of all this, that the Blunt pictures and the documents were discovered – oh, at any time since Blunt died in 1983. I've heard Mordaunt's theory and, although we can't be sure, it seems plausible enough that he left all the material to someone who he knew would make trouble at some stage. Mordaunt may be right, too, about how the Greeks became involved. Either way, someone acquired a whole bunch of paintings in a Swiss bank. My guess is that they were left there: Swiss banks after all are made for discreet security. And moving bulky paintings around might attract interest.

'Now, if I'm right, it follows that at some stage recently, in the months before they first made contact with us, there would have been a lot of traffic between Greece and Switzerland. Further- more, that traffic would have involved Greeks who feel strongly about the Marbles.' He looked at Victoria Tatton. 'I'm conscious here of the kinds of records we can get at easily, such as passen- ger manifests.' He turned back to the others. 'If our people in Athens do come up with a list of people – politicos, journalists, academics – who feel strongly about the Marbles . . . then we might – might – find one or more of those names on a Swissair or Olympic passenger manifest. Both airlines fly between Athens and Zurich and Athens and Geneva. It might mean nothing, it might mean that the person in question is mad about skiing, or collects cuckoo clocks, or has a secret bank account his wife knows nothing about. But it might mean we have a starting point.'

O'Day paused. His piano grin put in an appearance. 'You see what I'm saying. It's a long shot. Very probably out of range. But it's the only thing I can think of that will help us come up with a name that might be a target.' He tapped his teeth with a fingernail. 'It also divides up our talents here in this room. Tawsy here can play with the computer and try to hack into the Swissair and Olympic passenger lists over the past . . . oh, year, let's say. Leith can chivvy away at our people in Athens. And you, Dr Andover, can do the same with academics. You are the best placed of any of us for that. I know archaeology is not your main field but you must know whose advice to ask. Yes?'

Edward nodded slowly, thinking. 'Yes . . . but there are two problems we need to face. In the first place, the main authority will almost certainly be at the British Museum itself. I presume I shouldn't go there for my answers?'

'You presume correctly. Next question.'

'I need some sort of cover story . . . I can't ring people up and give them the real reason I want the information. What do I say?'

O'Day sucked his teeth. He was the only man Edward had ever met who could whistle breathing in. 'Hmm. We also want to distance it from the Palace and the government. Do you hold any other positions apart from being on the royal household? Are you on any committees, advisory bodies, that sort of thing?'

'Well . . . I'm on the editorial board of the *Burlington Magazine*, that's a scholarly journal for art historians, and I'm a trustee of the Courtauld Institute – that's part of London University . . . Hold on! The university has its own Institute of Archaeology – it's at the north end of Gordon Square, opposite where the Courtauld used to be. Its library takes all the archaeology journals in the world. Why don't I spend some time there? They are bound to have the Greek journals and very probably there's a special section on the Parthenon in Athens. Yes!' Edward was excited now. 'I may be able to find out what we want without talking to anyone at all. That would be even safer.'

O'Day got down from his perch on the desk. 'What time will this library close?'

'At a guess, five.'

'So you'll be back here no later than half past. Use an official car, to be on the safe side.' O'Day straightened his tie. 'Okay . . . let's arrange our next confab for six. I have to get back to the department . . . Other things are going wrong besides this show. Let's hope we have *something* for tonight's midnight committee. Six all right for everybody?' He looked at each of the others. 'I know you can't guarantee results but I always find that a deadline helps to concentrate the mind.'

Leith and Victoria Tatton both nodded. Edward hurried down by the back stairs to where the cars were waiting. A moment later Wilma Winnington-Brown knocked on the studio door. She had brought his soup.

It was just after eleven-thirty when Edward arrived in Gordon Square. He had the driver drop him some way from the entrance to the Institute of Archaeology – otherwise it might look odd, a scholar arriving in a chauffeur-driven car. He told the driver to collect him from the same spot just after five and then he marched across the square to the glass doors of the Institute of Archaeology.

The library, he knew, was on the first floor. He didn't bother with the lift but climbed the stairs. He had been here once or twice before on research errands to flesh out the classical background for some Renaissance piece in the Royal Collection. Edward nodded to the librarian, a shaggy-haired man in jeans, and turned left inside the door, towards where he knew the card index was. He knew there was not much point in looking up 'Elgin', not here. Whether an archaeologist was for or against the return of the Elgin Marbles to Greece – and he knew that many of them *did* wish to see the stones go back – none of them referred to the Elgin Marbles as the Elgin Marbles. They were metopes, sculptures or reliefs from the Parthenon or Acropolis in Athens. Accordingly, he found the card index marked 'GLO–GYN' and pulled it out. The cards on 'GREECE – ATHENS – PARTHENON' were depressingly numerous and Edward pulled out the entire drawer and sat himself at a table. Slowly he worked his way through the cards. This was a professional library, one of the best in the world in its field, so there were a number of cards typed up in the Greek alphabet. Edward knew enough to be able to decipher them but it wasn't easy and it slowed him down.

He made notes as he went along. At the end of about three hours he had seven names of authors who appeared to be Greek and had written articles specifically on the Parthenon sculptures, published in Greek, German, British or American journals in the previous ten years. This was an arbitrary cut-off but Edward had decided he needed to set some limit. The kidnappers were clearly passionate about their case, fanatical even. But ten years was a long time to burn a political candle. Edward also had the titles of three conferences that had been held on the Parthenon. Now he had to find the published proceedings of those conferences: each would contain a series of articles which might provide further names. Once he had found them and returned to his seat, it took him another hour to go through the books and the exercise gave him four names – but two overlapped with those he already had. That made nine names in all.

It was half past three: an hour and a half left. Edward could not think of any way of fishing out more names, but there *was* time for him to read some of the articles. If one of these names *was* part of the Apollo Brigade, reading an article they had written might give him some idea of the characters they were dealing with. Edward's task was helped here, because he found that four of the articles had appeared in the same periodical, the *Journal of Classical Greece*. He found the journal on the shelves and took down the relevant volumes. The articles, all published in English, despite the fact that the editorial offices were at the University of Thessaloniki, were in general extremely scholarly. There was nothing that was overtly polemical. At the same time, it could not have escaped anyone's attention that, among these archaeologists at least, the Parthenon reliefs were – archaeologically speaking – part and parcel of the Parthenon in Athens. It was implicit in everything that was written that Athens was where the sculptures belonged. In that sense, *all* the nine names probably shared the aims of the Apollo Brigade.

Edward read the articles very closely, searching for clues in the text. Suddenly a buzzer sounded and it was five to five: time to return the books and leave. He collected his things together. As Edward approached the counter where the books were returned, he saw a face he knew. It was Harry Irving, Professor of Sculpture at the Royal College of Art. Edward's heart sank. It wasn't that Harry was a security risk: he was a 'telly don', among other things, and was notoriously long-winded. Irving might keep Edward talking too long, or he might walk out of the building with Edward and see him get into the official car. That was best avoided if possible.

There was, however, no way of avoiding the encounter and Edward prepared himself.

Irving saw him. His face showed a number of emotions: surprise, an anxious frown as Irving tried to work out in advance what Edward might be up to, then the famous television smile designed to put everyone at ease and in their place. 'I'm glad these places close at five, eh? Otherwise I could go on all night. Lynne wouldn't like that.'

Lynne, Edward knew, was Irving's wife. 'How *is* Lynne?' Edward asked. That should keep the conversation away from work, at least to begin with.

'Set to murder me. Three children are like an army platoon to feed and like a critical mass so far as trouble is concerned. All activity turns immediately into an explosion. What brings you here? Bit off your patch isn't it?'

'Not at all!' Edward was ready and he gave Irving a smile that was almost as wide as his own. 'Just because I haven't bumped into you before doesn't make me a stranger here. There are lots of drawings at Windsor, drawings of classical sculpture. I'm trying to make sense of them.' He smiled again, as they reached the ground-floor lobby. 'You know how it is with catalogues. It will take years.' And that should stop Irving prying: make it sound as boring as possible. 'And you? You're even further from home than I am. What are you up to?' Irving would surely prefer talking about himself.

The other man held up a file. 'I'm one of the editors of the *Journal of Sculpture*. Among other things I send out books for review . . . I've been reading other journals, looking for good reviewers.' He put on a sombre expression. 'Tedious, of course. Unpaid work.'

Edward smiled again. Nobody was paid much for editing academic journals: they did it for prestige. 'Never mind, Harry. TV makes up for all that. When are you on next?'

Irving grew serious. 'I've got a series in the summer. Industrial monuments in Britain. An interesting moment in the history of sculpture, as I hope to show. Mind you, there's not the money in TV that there was. I remember the first – '

Edward wasn't really listening. This had gone on for long enough. They had reached the pavement outside the Institute. The day was overcast now, and blustery. He had to get rid of Irving.

'Which way are you headed?'

'What? Oh, Euston Square tube.'

'You go ahead, then, Harry. I seem to have left a pen upstairs – I must go and get it. A gift from my goddaughter. Then I want to buy some books in Dillon's, so I must hurry. Give my regards to Lynne.' He moved back inside the Institute – you had to behave like that with people like Irving. They were as stately as the royals.

He knew that behind the lifts were the lavatories. That occupied a couple of minutes, by which time the editor of the *Journal of Sculpture* was out of sight. The official car was already waiting at the southern end of the square and Edward hurried across. What with the delay caused by Irving, and the traffic in Gower

Street, not to mention an accident in Trafalgar Square, it was eight minutes to six before the dark-green car slid to a halt in the courtyard at St James's. When he reached the studio, the others were already there. O'Day and Leith were standing over Victoria Tatton, who was still working at the computer.

'We've started without you,' growled O'Day. 'At least on the technical bits. Tawsy has managed to hack into both the Swissair and Olympic records. I was about to ask the inspector what he has come up with. Bob?'

'Not a great deal, as yet, but the embassy have promised more for tomorrow. There is apparently a handful of Greek MPs who are very vociferous about the Marbles – here are their names.' And he handed a piece of paper to O'Day, who inspected it. 'There's a well-known television presenter who made a programme about the Marbles and about Elgin – here is his name. There are two books, though the author of one is dead. Then there's a bunch of Greek sculptors who have protested *en masse* to the British Embassy – here is a list of signatories. But that's it. As I say, more tomorrow.'

O'Day looked at Edward. 'What about you?'

Edward opened his briefcase and stepped closer to the others. He handed over his list of nine names. 'In the time available, I can't claim it's an exhaustive list. But I consulted the main journals.'

O'Day took the list from Edward and scanned it. 'Hmm,' he said. 'One of your academics, Andover, has the same name as one of the politicians – but different initials. Phanodikos. Brothers? Father and son? Maybe they work together, as a team.'

Edward's pulse began to race. Were they on to something?

O'Day was speaking again. 'Okay, you two . . . slip out and get yourselves something to eat. Tawsy and I will check these names. We've got – what? – nearly two dozen. Still, it shouldn't take much more than half an hour . . . sixty minutes at the most. We can decide our next move when you come back. Depending on what we find.'

Edward was grateful for the break and led the way up St James's Street. After a few hundred yards, he turned into his club. At that stage in the evening it was the best bet for food. They climbed the stairs to the first floor and found a corner to themselves. Edward ordered sandwiches, a beer for Leith and a whisky and soda for himself.

'Tell me about O'Day,' said Edward, refusing the other man's offer of a cigarette.

'I don't know much. MI6 lives in a world of its own . . . O'Day is from Belfast and made his name over there, cleaning up all that mess. He got the top job when his predecessor, Martin Abbotsbury, committed suicide – though that was hushed up, of course. Very bright, unmarried – and I don't mean he's gay. He's married to the job. Unusually, he *didn't* come up through Oxford or Cambridge, or any university. Not overgood with people but generally regarded as fair, which in that never-never world counts for a lot. The PM respects him, I'm told. That's it. I don't know what his favourite colour is, or where he gets his suits made, or if his cufflinks are real gold. I *do* know he is a keen military historian, reads everything about the Nazi high command. And that he likes Guinness. Will that do? Can I eat this sandwich now?'

'Have you worked with him before?'

'Yes, but don't ask on what. I can't tell you.'

'How come you work with MI6?'

'I was once in the Special Patrol Group – watching embassies and so on. There's a lot of contact.'

'Do you do a lot of secret stuff?'

'I can't answer that, either. Not really.' A pause. 'Yes.'

Edward changed the subject. 'Once we get a name, or names . . . what then?'

Leith tapped ash into the tray. 'Depends on who he is, or she is. Locate that person, trail them, see who their contacts are. Then, once we are sure we've covered everyone . . .' He bit into his sandwich.

Edward stared at the Welshman. 'What do you mean?' Suddenly he was very disturbed. 'What did that gesture mean?'

'Obvious, surely?'

Edward didn't speak. He couldn't.

'Oh, come on, Andover. You're taking this academic ivory tower nonsense too far. You've got a brain – Lockwood seems to think so, anyway. Use it – think things through. None of this is ever going to come to trial – how can it? The Queen's not going into court, as a witness, is she? Why do you think I'm involved? Or O'Day?'

Edward found his voice. 'I was told you were – are – a policeman.'

'Yes. So?'

Edward's mind raced. He was shocked but at the same time he instinctively knew that Leith was telling the truth. He – Edward – *hadn't* thought it through. Perhaps, unconsciously, he had avoided doing so. This brigade, whoever they were, were playing a serious game. Deadly. What Leith said – insinuated – made sense. Except that sense was hardly the word for it.

Leith squashed out his cigarette. 'I can see that you hadn't thought it through.' He softened his voice. 'Don't worry about that part. You won't have to be there. These things are never spelled out, you know – how could they be? The Crown and the government have to be protected. But all the others – O'Day, me, Mordaunt – we know what's expected.'

'And Victoria Tatton?'

Leith nodded. He said, more gently still, 'But don't worry about it. As I say, no one expects you to be there, or anywhere near.' He drank some beer. 'That part is going to be easy, compared with finding these people. That depends on how much time we have to play with and *that* depends on how well Lockwood succeeds in his diversionary tactics.'

'How is that going?' Edward was grateful for a change of subject. Sort of.

'You'll have to ask O'Day for details, but from what I hear they're roping in Owen Cutler.'

'The MP?'

Leith nodded.

'I wonder how it will work?'

'Not our problem.'

Edward was intrigued by the policeman's mind: he could work on a case like this and yet have no curiosity about aspects which did not immediately concern him. And apparently had no moral scruples about . . . the other business.

'What do you know about Victoria Tatton?'

Now Leith grinned. 'Not bad, is she? She's like mountain snow, though – very bright but very cold. Some people like them like that.'

'What's her background?'

'You tell me. I don't know much about Miss Tatton – it *is* miss, by the way. I do know she lives on a houseboat on the Thames, at Chelsea, because I dropped her off there once when we worked on another project abroad and travelled in together from

Heathrow. But she's fanatical about her privacy. She never social-izes, doesn't drink, lunches God-knows-where, never carries a shopping bag. Either she's got no sins at all, or she's so sinful she needs to keep them under lock and key all the time.'

'And MI6 and Scotland Yard, of course, prefer the latter.'

Leith grinned. As he did so, a high-pitched whine suddenly cascaded from his breast pocket. Others in the club looked irri-tably across at the source of the intrusion. Without looking down, Leith reached up and switched off his bleeper. 'O'Day demands our presence.' He guzzled the rest of his beer. 'Come on.'

On their way back to the studio, they passed Wilma Winning-ton-Brown, who was just leaving for home. She came up to Edward. 'Hillier's secretary has been on the phone again. They're getting quite tetchy. Can you see him tomorrow? It might be diplomatic.'

Edward nodded. 'I'll try.'

'Any progress?'

'I can't tell you.' Then he whispered, 'Not really.'

'Will you be staying late?'

'I don't know. Why?'

'I bought a thermos flask. It's on my desk. The soup's in it. Don't go hungry.'

Edward looked after her as she rushed off. Maybe he should marry Wilma.

He hurried after Leith into the studio.

'No good,' O'Day was shouting. 'No bloody good at all. Not a name, not one.'

Edward closed the door.

'It was a long shot, anyway,' Leith said to O'Day.

'Ye-es, but you hope, don't you. You always hope.' He worried at his teeth with a fingernail. 'Lockwood is not going to be happy. Not one bit.'

'Maybe they drove or went by train? Maybe they went from London?' Edward looked at Victoria Tatton as he said this. He smiled vaguely but she didn't seem to notice. Mountain snow.

O'Day was shaking his head. 'Of course, they wouldn't have needed to fly direct – but we can't check every flight on every airline in Europe. And why shouldn't they fly direct? They weren't doing anything wrong, not then. They wouldn't drive or take the train. This was too urgent, too exciting! They'd be in a hurry.'

He grabbed a chair and sat on it. 'So, we need some other approach. We can't go to the Prime Minister tonight with nothing. I've enough broken blood vessels as it is.'

Leith shook his head. 'Bricks without straw, sir, you're trying to make bricks without straw. This is a blackmail case. It's in the nature of the beast – '

'I know all that.'

Leith was silent.

O'Day looked at Edward.

Edward shook his head.

The MI6 man looked at Victoria Tatton. She pushed back her chair from the computer terminal and carefully put back a strand of hair that had fallen down over her face. 'If the pictures have been kept in a bank, maybe someone who works there is involved. Can we get a list of bank employees and check if there is any overlap with the list of names we have?'

'Well, at least someone is using their grey matter to see things in black and white. I don't think we can get the names of every bank employee in Switzerland – that would include the whole population except for the ski instructors. But perhaps we could restrict it to Greek employees . . .' He reached for a phone that was connected directly with his office.

'Clemmy? Yes, look, I want a call to Berne. Tony Riley, that's right. As soon as.' He sat back and looked at the others. 'This will show how good our service is. I should be able to get in touch with anyone in the field in thirty minutes. Fifteen if we are in the middle of something.' He raised his voice. 'But don't you lot relax. Keep thinking while we are waiting.'

They didn't get the chance. Within seconds the phone was flashing: very impressive.

Except that it wasn't the call O'Day was waiting for. It was for Edward and it was Sir James Hillier, calling from his bed.

'Edward? It's James.'

'I'm pleased to hear you, sir. And to know you are on the mend.'

'You might act like you mean it, my boy. This is the third time I've had to call you today.'

'I . . . I'm sorry. I was planning to drop by and see you tomorrow. Bring you abreast of all that's been happening.'

'See that you do. They've moved me from the hospital – I'm at Windsor and not dead yet, far from it.' The line went dead.

Edward replaced the receiver. What was he going to say to Hillier? The old man wouldn't like it if he thought he was being kept out of something when his deputy was in it up to his ears.

The phone flashed again.

It was Riley, in Berne. O'Day explained what he wanted – the names of any Greeks employed in banks in Switzerland. Whoever Riley was, he appeared not to be thrown by this demand, nor by the urgency. 'I need to hear from you', O'Day was saying, 'by this time tomorrow and I know it's Saturday. Without fail and I mean that in both senses. The service is on the line here.' He put down the receiver and rubbed his face with his hand.

Edward spoke to O'Day. 'Is there anything else we can usefully do tonight? I have some catching up, with my other job, I mean.'

O'Day groaned. 'When we see Lockwood at midnight, what are we going to tell him? Nothing. We are twenty-four hours down the line and no further forward. If you worked for me, Andover, I could order you to sit here all night and worry at this problem until something did shake loose, until one of us had a brainwave. But you don't so I can't. I *do* believe, however, that you only make progress by worrying at something.' He rubbed his face with his hand again. 'All right. You can stand down for the time being. I shall expect you all at the midnight committee. You too, Tawsy.'

They began to disperse. However, as Edward left the studio and turned towards his office, Victoria Tatton said softly, 'May I come?'

'I'm just going to my office, to collect – '

'There must be *some* paintings here from the Royal Collection. This is a palace, after all. I'd love to see them.'

Edward looked at her and then nodded. 'We'd better go this way, then.' He led her along the balcony overlooking the court-yard. He pointed out the de Vries bronze. 'This has been here for ever. It's been growing here. No one ever really paid any attention to it – but then a few months ago someone paid seven million pounds for another de Vries at Sotheby's. Now we're having it restored.' They worked their way back to Edward's office, inspecting along the way a Gentile da Fabriano, a Hogarth and the Canaletto by the dead fireplace. While he retrieved things from his desk, Victoria stood in front of the Veronese drawing. 'When I see all this,' she said quietly, 'I know I was right to stick to computers and languages. I would never have been good enough.'

Edward smiled. 'From what Inspector Leith tells me, you live like an artist. On a houseboat, I mean.'

'You were talking about me?' She turned to eye him.

'Only in the nicest way.'

'I wonder. What did he say?'

'That you are fanatical about your privacy. I hope I haven't intruded.'

She didn't reply but looked at the Veronese again.

Edward collected his things and locked his desk. Victoria dragged herself away from the drawing as he locked the office. Outside, she stood by her official car as he prepared to bicycle. He put his papers in the basket fastened to the handlebars. When he had finished, she handed him a scrap of paper on which she had just scribbled her address.

'Ever been on a houseboat?'

'No.'

'It's not a palace.'

'They used to have royal barges on the Thames in Tudor times. But I thought you were fanatical about your privacy?'

Now she smiled and the creases reappeared in her cheeks. 'I'm fanatical about three things . . . four things, really. Pictures, pasta, rare books – and not mixing those three with married men like Bob Leith.'

The Prime Minister's flat, 'above the shop', was not only the most comfortable part of Downing Street, it was also the most exclusive. Although nine hundred and ninety-nine people out of a thousand in Britain had never been to the official Number Ten, it *was* visited by many of the country's leading lights. The flat, on the other hand, was not.

Since he had been Prime Minister, William Lockwood had found that, when he wished to accomplish something especially tricky, or where he wanted a sense of privilege to outweigh another person's better judgement, a discreet invitation to his flat at the end of the day worked wonders. That was why he had asked Owen Cutler here tonight. Cutler was a backbencher in the Commons, the member for a seat on the Welsh borders in Shropshire and in general a staunch supporter of the government. Lockwood hadn't given him a job in his administration so far, because he needed three or four backwoodsmen like Cutler to accomplish the occasional unorthodox mission. Cutler, and others like him, were seen as independent of the government by both the opposition parties and the press, and that had, in the past, served its purpose. Now Lockwood was about to 'burn' Cutler.

It was what Lockwood thought of as the 'unhappy hour', the dead time before dinner. There were just the three of them in the sitting-room: Cutler, Lockwood and Eric Slocombe. The Prime Minister was waiting on the others – the absence of servants impressed people like Cutler. It emphasised how confidential, and therefore how important, the occasion was.

Having plied his guests with whisky, Lockwood then invariably blinded them with official gossip. 'See how small this room is?' He stood over Cutler as he said this. 'You should see the President's private quarters in the White House. Five times the size. *Five times!* Even the Australian Prime Minister has a better life than I do. Come through here a sec . . .'

Cutler got up and followed him through to the study.

'Have you ever seen one of these?' Lockwood took a dark-red leather-bound book from the desk. 'A Prime Minister's diary.' He kept the book a good way from Cutler but, when it was opened, the backbencher could easily make out how crowded with appointments it was.

Now it was time for Lockwood to turn on the charm. 'I hope you didn't mind coming up here at such an awkward time, Owen. You're probably going to the reception at the US Embassy – yes? Your wife won't complain, will she?' Lockwood smiled softly, as softly as he could, when he said this. Most people in politics would leave their wife hanging off an oil-rig for an invitation to the Number Ten sitting-room. 'How *is* Bridget, by the way?'

'I think she's rather missing the children, actually. The second one is at boarding-school now and she may have too much time on her hands.'

'Is Hugo already that old?' Lockwood couldn't really remember the names of Cutler's children. He had been briefed by Slocombe not twenty minutes ago, on the way back from a visit to the National Police College at Bramshill. Cutler would know all that, at some level. None the less, Lockwood could see that the man was still flattered.

'Yes, he's thirteen and nearly six feet. Taller than me already.'

'I've got three daughters, as you know,' the Prime Minister said, taking Cutler by the elbow. 'You're lucky having a son . . . But come back into the sitting-room, Owen. We're too far from the whisky in here. Eric and I have something we want to discuss with you. Let me freshen your drink and we can get down to business.' They stepped back into the blue chintzes of the sitting-room and sat down. Slocombe hadn't moved.

They all drank in silence and swallowed. Then Lockwood kicked off. 'How do you see us performing at the election, Owen?'

Cutler made a face. 'The polls aren't encouraging, Prime Minister. Not for an outright victory anyway.' He looked Lockwood directly in the eye. 'Your own standing in the polls is worrying, too. Unless you have something up your sleeve.'

Lockwood put down his glass. 'One or two ideas, Owen. One is for a brand new ministry. Do the media interest you? Eric here thinks we need a ministry for it. Run the BBC, promote British films, oversee the government's relations with all forms of broadcasting and the press. Run the government's adverts.'

Cutler's eyes gleamed. 'How are you planning to proceed, Prime Minister?'

'With maximum secrecy, Owen. We maintain radio silence about this until the campaign is announced. Then the opposition can't steal our clothes.'

'You think this is an election winner?' Cutler looked surprised.

'Not by itself, of course. But the press has been guilty of so many outrages in the last few years that I think a lot of people will be pleased that we are at last doing something to control it.' He paused for a moment. 'Whoever ran the thing would have a high-profile job, of course. Great public presence – but great risks, too. Eric thinks we need a few new faces in the government next time around and I agree with him.

'May I change the subject for a moment?' Lockwood smiled. He had managed that rather smoothly, he thought. 'I'm going to take you into my confidence, to show you how much I trust you, Owen, and how much I would value your advice and help. This is a matter of the utmost secrecy, as you will see.' And for the next twelve to fifteen minutes he described to Cutler the details of the blackmail threat to the Queen. He knew he could risk it because Slocombe's research had turned up the fact that Cutler was a devotee of the Palace. As Lockwood finished what he had to say, he got up and crossed the room to freshen Cutler's glass a second time. Cutler waved a finger, meaning not too much. But it was only a gesture and Lockwood was more than generous. 'Now we have a plan, Owen. But we need outside help. Someone like you. The government would be very grateful. In a practical way, I mean.'

There, the deal was on the table. As plain as it ever was in politics. The job offer had not actually been made, so that Lockwood, if he ever needed one, would always have a way out. But, that apart, the *quid pro quo* was as plain as a bank statement.

Cutler drank, and set down his glass. 'What would you have me do, Prime Minister?'

Lockwood didn't let it show but he breathed a silent prayer of relief. He paused briefly. 'We have to leak a story to the effect that the government is considering returning the Marbles to Greece. It has to be a strong leak, from a respectable source, so that the blackmailers accept it. But, as it is a form of bluff, it can't come from the government. As a senior backbencher, and someone who is a trustee of the National Portrait Gallery, you are perfectly placed to open up this issue. Eric?'

Slocombe nodded his head. Now the Prime Minister had hooked Cutler, the political adviser could come out of his shadow. 'I think this should surface as a *political* story, not an arts one. Do you know any of the political correspondents on any of the Sunday papers? The serious broadsheets, I mean. Not the comics.'

'I know all of them,' said Cutler. 'But I probably know Frank Metcalfe best. He's on the *Post*.'

'Good. What I'd suggest is this. Call him – either tonight or first thing tomorrow, Saturday. He won't have much time to check what you tell him, so he'll have to write it more or less as he gets it. Tell him that you've heard on the highest authority that the government is thinking of handing back the Marbles but that, so far, neither the Greeks themselves nor the British Museum Trustees know anything about it. Say that a secret Cabinet committee has been considering the issue and come up with a recommendation for their return. Tell Metcalfe it is all off the record, that you can't tell him *how* you know all this. But trade on your government contacts and your position as a trustee. Insist that he keeps your name out of it – that will make it seem more genuine. He'll check with Downing Street and we shall say that we cannot confirm or deny the existence of a secret committee and the same will therefore apply to the recommendations. That will sound so convoluted that he will think we *are* confirming it. And so the *Post* will run the story – right across the top of page one, I'm willing to wager.'

Cutler was silent again. He ignored his drink. Then he said, 'What happens afterwards? I mean, how will the story develop? Metcalfe will remember that I misled him.'

'But you may not be misleading him,' replied Lockwood loudly, full of bluster. 'It is certainly on the cards that we shall have to return the damned Marbles. But if we don't, if this all has a happy ending, we'll concoct some other story that will protect you. After all, Owen,' he added, just a little sanctimoniously, 'it is in my own interest to keep you clean.' Another reference, indirect but obvious, to a future for Cutler on the government benches. 'I've trusted you with everything, Owen,' the Prime Minister went on gently. 'You're now a trustee of the government as well as the NPG.'

Cutler beamed. That was a direct hit. 'I'll call Metcalfe straight away. As soon as I get home.'

Lockwood stood up and held out his hand. 'In that case, I'll send you home in a government car, Owen. Just to give you a taste.'

When Edward reached his flat, there were three messages on the machine. He sighed. He would never have thought it possible he could loathe a machine so much. He'd already had one whisky, at the club with Leith, and there'd be more to come at the midnight committee. So, for now, he squeezed himself a grapefruit. Then he sat at the desk and pressed the 'Answer/Play' button.

'This is Sammy. Great news about the concert: your effigy at school is still unmolested. In return we are taking you to the Hard Rock Café for dinner afterwards. Don't groan – you'll love it, and anyway it's all we can afford.' Edward didn't groan. In normal circumstances, he wouldn't have been seen dead in the Hard Rock Café – but then Sammy wasn't normal circumstances.

'Hello Edward, this is Lynne Irving. Harry says he met you at the I of A library today. We never see you now but Mason Inchcliffe from Harvard is coming to dinner next Wednesday . . . are you free? We'd love to see you. You know the number . . . Do try and make it. Bye!'

A pause. A warble. A click. Edward swallowed some juice. 'This is Nancy, with the laughing face. We can't go on, not meeting like this. At the tone, it will be . . . six forty-two precisely . . . We are getting to be like those couples in Swiss clocks – only one of them ever comes out at any one time. Never together. In case you have a map pinned up and a special operations room tracking my movements, today I was at Kirkleatham, near Middlesborough. Sculptures by Henry Cheere . . . Oh Woodie, there's not much cheer talking to your tape all the while.' She rang off.

Edward sat back in his chair. If she missed him so much, why hadn't she left a number where he could reach her? Why didn't she call late at night or early morning? And what was that crack about a map and an operations room? A coincidence or something more? And if she wasn't mixed up in this Apollo Brigade business why was she behaving so oddly? Edward felt sick.

He thought of his other message. He didn't think he could face dinner with Mason Inchcliffe. Inchcliffe was a distinguished scholar but a difficult man. He edited a journal, *The Fifteenth Century*, which combined history, art history, economic history, architectural history – and whatever else Inchcliffe thought worthy. He was a bit of a campaigner for causes – it made his journal very lively but it also made his company rather tiring.

Edward dialled the Irvings' number. He got Harry, not Lynne.

'Edward! Hey! Good to hear you. Can you come to dinner?'

'No, I don't think so, Harry. I'm very tied up just now – Hillier's in hospital, you know.'

'Yes, I heard. Too bad. Inchcliffe's here on one of his campaigns. He's hoping to do an entire issue of that journal of his on *one* subject.'

'God forbid!'

'You don't like the idea? He's asked me to . . .' And Irving was off, talking about Irving. It took Edward several minutes to disentangle himself and he only managed to do so by promising to try to look in for a drink on the following Wednesday, after the dinner party.

He put down the receiver but as he did so a thought struck

him and he lifted it again immediately. His movements slowed and he replaced the receiver a second time. He sat for a moment, his hand on the instrument, thinking. Finally, after a few moments, he picked it up yet again, and dialled.

'Lynne? It's Edward again. No, I haven't changed my mind about dinner – but may I speak to Harry again, please.' He waited while Harry was brought to the phone. 'Harry . . . hello again, sorry about this . . . Look . . . you don't happen to have a copy of the *Journal of Classical Greece* at home by any chance? Our conversation earlier reminded me that you might . . . Well, I'm interested in the style of the journal, the writing style I mean . . . Well, yes, I do have something I'm thinking of submitting . . . It's not sculpture, Harry, otherwise I *would* submit it to you . . . No, I'd rather not talk about it until I've got it all down on paper . . . Yes, I'll hold on.' He waited while Irving checked in his library. At length, Irving picked up the phone on his desk.

'You *have* got one!' breathed Edward. 'Wonderful. May I collect it now, please? . . . Well, I'm seeing Hillier tomorrow and I need to discuss it with him . . . Great . . . I'll be there in thirty minutes.'

Sixty minutes later, Edward was clambering down a gangplank just off Chelsea embankment. This time he had travelled not on his bicycle but in the very old but lovingly restored Aston Martin. Finding the row of houseboats had been no problem but he had found Victoria Tatton's number only with the aid of the headlights of passing cars. He hammered on what he hoped was Victoria's door.

'Yes? Who is it? It's ten o'clock, for pity's sake.'

'It's Edward. Invading your privacy.'

He heard the bolt being pulled back. Then she stood before him. She was wearing trousers and had a bright scarlet bandana around her neck. She looked spectacular and meticulous at the same time. She held a bowl in one hand. 'Couldn't resist the canelloni, right?'

'Wrong. Cancel the canelloni. I've got something else for you to cook. New names for the computer.'

Edward stepped over the outstretched legs of Bernard Midwinter and Bob Leith. 'I'm sorry we're late, sir,' he said to the Prime Minister. He lifted an upright chair from the doorway to the study and put it down where Victoria could sit on it. He himself perched on the arm of the sofa.

O'Day glared at him furiously but it was Lockwood who spoke first. 'We're not very formal here, Dr Andover, but we do believe in punctuality. All of us in this room are busy people. We all have jobs that we think are important. A midnight meeting starts at midnight, not at ten past, or twenty past. I hope I never have to say this again but – '

'We have a name, sir.'

Lockwood was annoyed at being interrupted. 'What do you mean?'

'What sort of name?' barked O'Day.

Everyone now stared at Edward.

Edward looked at Victoria and then back at the Prime Minister. 'Sir, as Commander O'Day has probably told you, he, Inspector Leith, Miss Tatton and I spent the day trying to find a name, a Greek name, of someone who travelled to Switzerland and is involved in one of the Greek groups that have views on the Marbles.'

'Yes,' said Lockwood. 'He's explained all that. Are you trying to tell me that you have more up-to-date – '

'Yes. Yes sir, I am.'

O'Day spoke sharply. 'What! How?'

The sofa arm was uncomfortable and Edward moved himself to prevent one leg from going to sleep. 'As the commander may have told you, sir, I found nine Greek names in the Institute of Archaeology library, nine names where the authors of articles in academic journals had expressed views that might mean they would support the aims of this Apollo Brigade.'

'And you drew a blank. Yes, we've heard all that.' Lockwood was listening but still looked stern.

'Well, when I got home, there was a message on my answering machine. It was an invitation to dine with an American academic, a very forceful character who edits a journal and uses it to campaign for causes he supports.'

'You will explain the connection, I hope.' Lockwood placed the whisky bottle he was holding on the mantelshelf.

'Yes . . . I had to refuse the dinner invitation but it set me thinking. Of the nine names I found today, four had published their articles in the same periodical, the *Journal of Classical Greece*. What I hadn't grasped this afternoon was that, even if none of the academics who wrote for the *Journal* would actually take action on their beliefs, one of the editors might. If this American academic I mentioned could use his journal for campaigning, so could one of the Greek editors.'

Lockwood's expression had softened.

'Around nine-thirty tonight I managed to get hold of a copy of the *Journal*. All the editors, four of them, are listed inside the front cover. Around ten o'clock, I picked up Miss Tatton and we went round to St James's Palace and spent a couple of hours with the computer, checking back through the passenger manifests of Olympic Airways and Swissair. That's what we've been doing. That's why we were late.'

'And?'

Edward looked at Victoria and motioned for her to take up the story.

'One editor of the *Journal of Classical Greece* has travelled between Athens and Zurich three times in the past fifteen months – '

'What! . . . What's his name?' Lockwood's fist clenched tightly.

'Dimitri Kolettis.'

'He's the senior editor,' added Edward. 'At least, his name comes top of the list, and the list is not alphabetical. It also says that he is a professor at the University of Thessaloniki.'

'Maybe he went skiing.' O'Day's voice was still sharp.

'Unlikely,' said Victoria. 'One meeting was in September and on each occasion he only stayed one or two nights. We've found his name on the return manifests.'

'He could have been using a Swiss bank.' O'Day wouldn't give up.

'And he could have been buying a cuckoo clock, or some fancy chocolate. Stop it, commander.' Lockwood nodded at Victoria and Edward. 'Well done. Of course there may be a perfectly innocent explanation for this man's trips to Switzerland but my gut tells me we are off and running.' He turned back to O'Day. 'Obviously, you will work all tomorrow checking this Kolettis character. Have Athens locate him and then, with luck, he will lead us to the others. I shall be at Chequers, not far away. You can reach me there if you need to.'

He addressed Victoria and Edward. 'As I explained to the others before you two came, I have arranged for a leak to appear in the *Sunday Post* this weekend. I therefore invite you all for lunch on Sunday to review progress. We can study reaction to the leak, Dr Andover will have talked to the blackmailers again and Commander O'Day will, with luck, have some information from Greece . . . So, thank you for coming. No midnight meeting tomorrow. We'll make it midday the day after, at Chequers.'

11

Saturday

Edward dabbed his knife into the mustard at the edge of his plate and spread it on to the bacon pinned under his fork. Every day of his life, when he was in Britain, Edward started his day with two rashers of bacon, two tomatoes – all grilled – and a slice of toast. Several women friends had hinted it was unhealthy, two had insisted it was lethal and only one had offered to cook it for him. Nancy liked cooking.

The morning's papers lay at his feet. He couldn't concentrate. What was he going to do about Nancy? Most of him still didn't believe she was mixed up in this affair in any way. Her odd behaviour – he had to admit it *was* odd behaviour – must be due to something else. Another man? But, if so, why did she bother to keep in contact? It was as if she was touching base with her phone calls, keeping a line open as some kind of failsafe in case . . . in case what? He bit into some toast. None of it made any sense. What if she *was* involved? Why, in that case, was she even calling him? To pretend everything was normal? Because she couldn't face him in person but needed to keep in touch so as not to make him suspicious, and in case she might need at some stage to understand the thinking at the Palace? He smeared more mustard on the rest of his bacon. He had to concede that Nancy's behaviour, weird as it was, fitted the second scenario better than the first.

If it was true, it was shattering. It meant that he had been used. It meant there had been no genuine warmth in Nancy at all. It probably meant she had lied to him about all sorts of things, not just her feelings about him or the fact that Rysbrack's sculpture was in the Pontefract church. It meant that Nancy had singled him out as a target a long time ago. He stared at the remains of a tomato on his plate. He and Victoria Tatton had been very excited last night when they had found Dimitri Kolettis's name on the passenger manifests. Edward had been too excited to take much notice of the dates he had flown to Zurich.

105

Now he saw their significance. The Greek's first trip had taken place several weeks before Nancy had introduced herself to Edward, after his lecture at the Courtauld Institute. She must have come to London – or been sent – with the express intention of meeting him. Of seducing him.

Now, suddenly, Edward realized why Nancy had kept in touch. He had told her everything that had happened in the early stages! He had been used again. He refused to believe it. Nancy had been too . . . too breezy to have made up her research in the north. He knew that to be real. Her lovemaking had been not only exciting, it had been genuine, he was convinced. She liked him, just as he . . . liked her.

He ate the last of his toast. His judgement was shot. He would have to talk to her – tackle her with his suspicions. He would know from her reaction. No sooner had he thought this than he realized he couldn't do it. If he did, and she *was* involved, the whole thing would explode. The Queen would be humiliated and eventually it would emerge that Edward, Edward who had had his suspicions about Nancy for days, and told no one, was responsible for the failure of – everything.

Edward found that, unconsciously, he had been holding his breath. He closed his eyes and sucked in some air. He was trapped.

As Edward approached the studio that morning, along the balcony overlooking the little courtyard, he heard a strange hum breaking into the Saturday silence of the palace. He inserted his key into the lock, turned it and pushed at the door. Frank got out of his chair but, seeing it was Edward, just nodded and sat down again. He was still reading the same paperback.

Edward stepped past the pictures to see Victoria hunched over a computer printer which was spewing out lines of writing. O'Day had a long sheet of paper in his hands and was scanning it.

'We've made an early start,' he said. 'Overnight I heard from Athens and I also had an idea. The news from Athens is a list of ten names. The good news is that six of the names were on our list of yesterday. The bad news is that none of the other four – all Greek MPs, by the way – features on the passenger manifests.'

'Why, then, the printouts?'

'Ah! That's the idea I had. What you and Tawsy here didn't think to check last night was if anyone came with Kolettis.'

'How could we? We didn't have any other names?'

'But we don't need one, do we?' O'Day grinned and tapped his temple, to suggest Edward and Victoria had not been using their brains. After his anger of the evening before, when he had clearly been a little jealous of the breakthrough Victoria and Edward had made in his absence, he obviously felt himself back in command. 'We're checking the other passengers on the flights which Kolettis made. If we find the same name on more than one flight . . . you see what I mean?'

Edward did. And it was true: Victoria and he had been too pleased with their discovery of Kolettis to think it through any further. He sat himself on a chair and said, 'Give me a printout.'

Victoria's fingers were doing a complicated jig on the keyboard. Even her fingers seemed tidy – composed, meticulous. Today she was wearing a bright scarlet suit, a welcome splash of colour in this room. The low collar of the suit made her neck seem even longer today. He was amazed that she could have such a long neck and yet be so tiny. Nancy had a long neck too . . .

The printer started to judder again and paper rolled forward. Edward could see the columns of names ranged against the left-hand margin. Victoria waited a moment, then got up from her seat. She ripped the paper from the printer, then tore off the separate sheets. She held two pieces out for Edward to take. 'This first one is the manifest for Kolettis's second flight to Zurich, in September last year, and his flight back two days later.' She smiled. 'And you owe me a pasta dinner. You should have seen that canelloni when I got home last night.'

Edward smiled and took the lists. Each of them contained between two and three hundred names, so comparing all of them was not easy. He tried hard to concentrate on the lists but his thoughts kept straying to Nancy. He even found himself looking for the name 'Tucker' on the passenger manifests. It didn't appear to be on the two he was holding. But the lists were not arranged alphabetically, so it wasn't easy to be sure.

Suddenly there was a knock on the studio door. O'Day looked up, alarmed. Frank had shot to his feet and was looking at O'Day. Edward moved round to the edge of the Canaletto and approached the door, O'Day motioning him to deal with whoever it was. Edward was just about to open the door when a voice rang out on the other side. 'It's Wilma! I've made a jug of coffee. Do you want it, or shall I drink it myself?'

Edward's sigh eased into a grin and he opened the door. As he took the tray, he gave Wilma a wink though he felt like kissing her. 'I didn't know you were coming in today. This is a real treat.'

'The son's gone mountaineering, the daughter's sailing, so she says, with friends. Besides, a crisis is a crisis. If you want anything, just holler.'

'Thanks Wilma, we will. Bless you.'

Edward carried the tray in and Frank closed the door behind him. They drank their coffee in silence and got back to work.

Suddenly Leith whispered, 'Yes! I've got one.'

Everyone looked at him.

'I have "A. Leondaris" travelling Athens–Zurich on Swissair on February the eleventh and Zurich–Athens, on Olympic, on the twelfth. Kolettis was on both flights. Anyone else got Leondaris on their lists?'

One of the phones rang out. It was the instrument Edward had used the first time he spoke to the blackmailers. He glanced at O'Day and Leith. They moved to their earpieces.

Edward picked up the receiver. 'Yes?'

Wilma's voice was heard. 'A gentleman. He says he called the other day. About the Second World War pictures.'

'Yes, Wilma. Thank you. Put him on please.'

There was a pause. Then, 'Good morning, Dr Andover.'

'Yes?'

'Yes, what?'

'Sorry?'

'You know the rules. The Victoria and Albert Museum, in South Kensington. There's a bank of phones near the restaurant at the Exhibition Road entrance. In half an hour, exactly.'

The line went dead.

O'Day turned first to Victoria. 'Little point in you coming, Tawsy. Stay here and keep on with the lists. We'll be back as soon as we can.'

When they reached the gallery, Edward led the way. He was familiar with the layout of the V & A. Inside the entrance he turned left and descended some stairs, past some early twentieth-century costumes. Ahead of them was the restaurant, newly refurbished in Scandinavian-style wood. To the left was the bank of phones. There were about six minutes to go and he used the opportunity to call Mordaunt, at Windsor, to keep him up to date.

Right on time, the phone near where Leith was standing gave a cracked ring. The inspector stepped back and Edward wedged himself into the cubicle. He picked up the receiver.

'Andover?'

'Yes.'

'You see. The arrangements work very well. Now . . . you have an answer for me?'

'I do. An announcement is being made tomorrow – '

'What do you mean? What sort of announcement?'

'A leak . . . to the newspapers, that the government is thinking of returning the Marbles – '

'I don't understand . . . What do you mean, that the government is *thinking* of returning the Marbles? Why can't they just announce it. That's our demand!'

'Don't panic! Or be naïve – '

'Watch your tongue, Andover. You're just the intermediary.'

'But I'm British. And Britain is a democracy. A genuine one. There are some things a government cannot do. Simply returning the Marbles, because you say so, is one of them.'

'Andover!'

'If the Prime Minister were simply to make an announcement that the Marbles were going back, all hell would break loose. There would be protests galore. The Greek Embassy might be . . . who knows? You want the sculptures returned. For that to happen, the way has to be prepared. The first move will be made tomorrow. The *Sunday Post* will carry a report to the effect that a secret government committee has concluded it would be diplomatically appropriate to return the Marbles to Greece – '

'Yes, but when?'

'Soon – '

'Soon! That's not soon enough.'

'Well, immediately then. I'm only the intermediary, remember.'

But the voice at the other end of the line now hardened. 'Look, Andover. Today is Saturday. You say this . . . report is to be released tomorrow. We shall have to study it. So the next call will be on Monday. At that time we want a much fuller explanation of your intentions, the British government's intentions. Chapter, verse, punctuation even. Otherwise . . . otherwise, remember that we can go public whenever we want. Is that absolutely clear? Chapter, verse – '

'Yes, yes. I've got it!' It sounded to Edward as though the voice was about to hang up and he didn't want that to happen on the current cool note. He struggled to find some form of words that would soothe and settle the voice. 'I'll do what I can, but I don't think – '

'It's not your place to think, Andover. Instead, just relay this to Lockwood. The British love their monarch; you Brits think the Crown can do no wrong. Well, then, why doesn't the Prime Minister issue a statement to the effect that the Queen has requested that the Marbles go back? That would settle it once and for all.' He chuckled and rang off.

Edward stepped out of the lift, and turned left. He knew his way around Windsor Castle better than most of the households. This was where the royal paintings not on show were stored; this was where the main library was; and this was where Sir James Hillier lived in a marvellous flat that went with the job. It was in the keep, above the library.

Edward followed the corridor around the curve of the building. Prints lined the walls: Rembrandt, Edward Lear, Hercules Brabazon Brabazon. And these were just staff quarters. He reached the door to Hillier's flat. Usually the two met in the director's office, two floors below, next to the library. Today that was impossible; Hillier had been out of hospital less than forty-eight hours.

Edward knocked and went in. The sitting-room was small but had a superb view of the Thames.

'Through here!' a voice shouted.

Edward followed the direction of the voice and turned in through a cream-painted doorway.

'Ah, there you are at last.' Hillier was flat on his back, though he could tilt his head so as to see Edward.

'Good afternoon, James. How are you feeling?'

'Well, the pain's not so bad, but I can't sit up of course and that makes it difficult to read. Sit over there, by the window. It's easier for me to see you there.'

110

'I bought you this,' Edward said sheepishly. He hadn't thought flowers or fruit quite suitable, given his relationship with the Director of the Queen's Collection. 'It's champagne, for when you can celebrate your complete recovery.'

'That's very thoughtful, Edward. Put it there, will you, next to the books.'

'How long before you can get up, do you think?' Edward sat where he had been directed.

'Another two to three weeks in bed. A month before I can come back to work properly. Think you can manage?'

'Well, I won't say you're not missed. There's a lot of paper-work, isn't there? But Wilma really comes into her own at a time like this.'

'So . . . what news is there? What problems have we got?'

Edward spent as long as he could discussing the leaky roof at Sandringham, then he switched to the request by Ottawa to borrow the Poussin. He explained that he had one of the palace's full-time restorers up at Balmoral making a condition report.

'Who's there?'

'Randall.'

'Hmm. Let him make the report. I'd like to see it when it comes in. I ought to be sitting up by then. But I don't think he's good enough to do the work. We must think of a specialist. Better prepare the studio – is the Canaletto ready to go back yet?'

Internally, Edward blushed. He wondered if it showed on his skin. The studio was not being used in quite the way that Hillier imagined. 'No. We had a problem when we were cleaning one of the figures. Some of it came away. I've ordered some of that pigment from Amsterdam – you know, the stuff which is produced in the eighteenth-century manner. But it will hold us up, of course.'

Hillier nodded. 'What else? Anything else been happening? Any new discoveries? Have I missed any new books? Any gossip?'

Edward thought. 'Mason Inchcliffe is in town. Oh yes – I hear that Foster Hale is tipped for the V & A job.'

'Is he now? Hmm. And your lecture at the Louvre, how did that go?'

Again, Edward felt as if he was blushing. 'I . . . I didn't go in the end.'

'Why on earth not?'

'Geneviève changed the day of my talk. And at the last minute. I just had too much on.'

'That's a pity, Edward. I like the Royal Collection to make a show now and then. It shows we aren't dead.'

Edward could see that Hillier was annoyed. But what else could he say? He couldn't tell him the truth and he didn't want to lie any more than was necessary. He changed the subject. 'Corning says he can start cleaning the de Vries in about three weeks. But he thinks it may take as long as six months to do properly.'

'Six months! How can it take that long? Leave that one to me. Margaret is coming in on Monday. I'll dictate a letter then.' Margaret was Hillier's secretary.

But at least the subject was safely changed.

'How is that friend of yours, by the way? The American woman. Nancy?'

Nancy and Hillier had met twice. Once at dinner here in Hillier's flat and once by chance at a private view at the National Gallery.

'She's well, thank you. Though I haven't seen her for a little while.'

'Marriage not discussed yet?'

Edward found this faintly embarrassing. 'No.'

'Ahh. She's a determined woman and I got the impression she was very keen on you.'

'But you only met her twice.'

'Three times, actually. I bumped into her in the London Library.'

'I didn't even know she was a member. And what has that got to do with marriage, anyway? It's a wonderful library but hardly romantic.'

'Not romantic, no. Not as such. But I very much got the impression she was interested in you, your job, etcetera. We met at the issue desk.' Hillier raised his head as much as he could. 'She had borrowed a couple of books on my predecessor. That old rogue, Anthony Blunt.'

'Dad – it's Edward. How are you both? The journey back was okay? . . . Good . . . Look, Dad, for once it's not you I want to talk to, but Barbra . . . Is she there? . . . Good . . . I'll hang on.'

112

As he waited, Edward stared up at the box of paperclips on his desk. They were upside-down. It was unlike him to –

'Barbra! . . . I'm fine, thank you – and you? . . . Good . . . Now, I have a favour to ask but it's an odd one. I want you to make some enquiries on my behalf but I don't want to explain why . . . not just yet. It's very sensitive – okay?'

Inwardly, Edward gave thanks for Barbra's incuriosity – and the fact that she appeared not to bear him a grudge for advising his father to buy the Ferrari rather than the Schnabel. 'I need some information on this girl I have been seeing: Nancy Tucker . . . Yes, it's an English-sounding name but in fact, as I understand it, the family were originally Italian and the name was Trucco before they anglicized it. I've never checked but my understanding is that the Tuckers or Truccos make icecream in the San Francisco region. I'd just like to know anything you can find out in a few days – who the family are, does she have any brothers and sisters, what sort of firm it is – big, small, profitable, and so on. Since you do have this head-hunting firm, I thought you might be used to finding things out about people.'

'How long have I got?'

'Two days . . . three. Is that too much to ask?'

'No. Not if you agree to do me a favour in return.'

'How could I refuse?'

'Great. I'll have an answer in three days.'

12
Sunday

'Good afternoon. You are listening to the BBC. It is one o'clock and this is the The World This Weekend. Here is the news, read by Douglas Davenport.' The gongs of Big Ben faded and the newsreader's voice filled the room. 'A spokesman at Downing Street has refused to confirm or deny a report in today's *Sunday Post*, which claims that Britain is considering returning the so-called Elgin Marbles to Greece. The report claimed that a special government committee, meeting in secret, has been examining the issue without reference to the Trustees of the British Museum, where the Marbles are on display, and has concluded that the Marbles should be returned "some time soon". More on this later in the programme.

'In South Africa, the controversial black leader, Mr – '

Lockwood leaned forward and turned off the radio. It amazed Edward that, so late in the twentieth century, when television invaded everything, including grief and shame, a mere radio programme should be so powerful. But *The World This Weekend* was still the pre-eminent slot.

Edward had never been to Chequers before. He had not realized it was so close to London and he had been surprised when the official car that brought him arrived at the house so unexpectedly; it really was tucked away. The architecture – red brick and stone mullion – did not impress him. The windows were large and he liked that, but the house had a suburban feel rather than that of the country. Inside it was comfortable, and human: it did not feel like an official residence, at least not in most of the rooms he saw. The furniture was the best feature, containing the most loved objects, those chosen with most care. The sofas were wide and comfortable. The chairs were walnut and eighteenth century, so far as he could see. The ceilings were elaborate but much restored, new even. The pictures were nineteenth-century portraits. There were huge jugs of fresh flowers everywhere.

There were twelve for lunch. Besides Lockwood and Edward, Mordaunt had graced the gathering with his elegant presence. Slocombe, Hatfield and Lessor, for the government, were all there. So were Midwinter, Evelyn Allen, O'Day and Leith. The Prime Minister's wife, Sally, and Victoria, were the only women.

Having switched off the radio, Lockwood set off on a second tour of his lunch guests. He had already made one circuit with the sherry decanter. He made sure everyone was looked after, then silenced the murmur of conversation by tapping his own glass against the decanter.

'I'm not one for talking with my mouth full – so the food isn't being served until a quarter to two. That gives us time to talk . . . so find seats and we can start.'

Everyone had been standing around talking, and they now searched out places to sit. Edward picked up an oak chair and placed it next to the sofa where Victoria sat.

'I'll begin with the usual moan about secrecy,' said the Prime Minister. 'Look at the number of people in this room – it's pretty large already. I really do not want this number to grow more than is absolutely necessary. This situation is going to get worse before it gets better – I want you all to appreciate that.' He placed his glass on a table and looped a thumb in the pocket of his waistcoat. 'However, we are over the first hurdle – at least, I hope we are. As all of you should know by now, the story in this morning's *Sunday Post* was a deliberate leak – from this end.' He looked at Midwinter, then at Edward. 'It ought to satisfy the blackmailers while at the same time not tying the government's hand. In that way, I'm hoping it will buy us time.

'You will not be surprised to learn that I've had a call this morning from Sir Martin Ogilvy, Director of the British Museum. I wasn't surprised and I told him I shall see him tomorrow morning. I'll have to tell him the truth. The next call from the blackmailers is also tomorrow. They have demanded from Dr Andover that they be put in the picture as to our detailed intentions. Tomorrow, therefore, Dr Andover will be able to tell them that we intend to close the Duveen Galleries later this week. It will take a few days to crate up the stones and then we shall send them by a slow Royal Naval ship – all ploys designed to buy us time. Each of these episodes will make the newspapers. There will of course be the most terrible uproar. The government will be deluged with protests. But a week or so from now, in good time for their damned Olympic Festival, Dr Andover will tell the blackmailers that we shall announce to the world that the British government is returning the Marbles – lock, stock and barrel – to Athens.'

Lockwood scratched the back of one hand. 'That, at any rate, is what we tell the blackmailers. It may be that, at the end of the day, we shall actually have to follow that course of action, but as of now we've got about two weeks to play with. Within two weeks we have got to convert what we have into a winning score. Now, what do we have? Well . . . thanks to Commander O'Day, Dr Andover and the rest of the team operating from St James's Palace, we now have two names for the members of this "brigade" – Dimitri Kolettis and A. Leondaris, who may be either a man or a woman. These two travelled to Switzerland several times. That is only to be expected if the paintings and documents surfaced in a Swiss bank but it does suggest also that they decided it was safer to leave the stuff in the bank while their little black-mail project got off the ground. Now, commander, I think you should add what you know.'

'Yes, sir.' O'Day glanced slyly at Edward. He had obviously kept something to himself. He was still smarting from Edward and Victoria's breakthrough on Friday night. 'My feeling is that Kolettis and Leondaris travelled to Switzerland initially to see the paintings and any documentation, check their authenticity and their likely impact. But the fact that they went back several times, over a period of months, also suggests that they decided to keep the pictures in Switzerland. In makes sense when you think about it. A numbered account in a Swiss bank is just about the safest place to hide anything. Also, it would avoid the danger of transporting bulky paintings and documents across borders and risk being found out. My second point is this. It also makes sense for the stuff to have been moved from the bank where they were found to a new one, which only the blackmailers know.

'My third point is that the Apollo Brigade, as it calls itself, probably keeps one of its members – one at least – in Switzerland. They need to have rapid access to the paintings in case they have to carry out their threat. Also, our experience has shown that, however ruthless people are, they feel nervous too. These black-mailers must be very nervous right now. They are trying to blackmail not just an individual, not just a queen, but a govern-ment, an entire country with enormous resources at its disposal.

116

I'll bet that someone, one of them at least, consults these paintings nearly every day – just to see that they are still there, still safe. That person, therefore, is very important to us, the most important of all. If we are to sort out this mess to everyone's satisfaction we must get back the pictures and any documents. The brigade member in Switzerland is the person who can lead us to them.'

Lockwood went to say something but O'Day beat him to it. 'Sir, I spent a lot of yesterday on the phone to Tony Riley, at the embassy in Berne. Kolettis and Leondaris always flew to Zurich. They always stayed one or two nights, no more, so Riley checked the hotels. Nothing. That stumped us, so next we tried a trick that I've often found useful in the past. If you are trying to find someone, there are always masses of hotels to check, scores of airlines, hundreds of taxis in any city. There are, however, only ever a handful of car rental firms. After a little bribery, Riley found that Kolettis had hired a car three times from the same firm, Alpine. We discovered two things: Kolettis's home address, or at least the one he uses on his driving licence. That saves us a little time, though our own people in Greece could probably have found it easily enough. More important, however, we found that on each occasion Kolettis had driven about a hundred and seventy kilometres – just over a hundred miles. That tells us he didn't stay in Zurich, and he probably went to the same place each time. So we can work out where he went.'

Lockwood looked up sharply. So did everyone else.

O'Day smiled. He was pleased with the effect his performance was having. 'If Kolettis did a hundred and seventy kilometres, that must mean that wherever he went was within a radius of eighty-five kilometres of Zurich. If you draw a circle around Zurich with that radius, you do of course find a whole raft of small towns and villages. However, you find only three places of any size – Liechtenstein, Lucerne and Basle. If you further assume that they were in Switzerland on business and not on pleasure, so they didn't spend any time touring around, then the mileage they did would tend to rule out Lucerne as a destination, since it's only about fifty kilometres – thirty miles – from Zurich. Which leaves Liechtenstein and Basle. Riley is checking Basle first, since after all Liechtenstein, strictly speaking, isn't in Switzerland. I spoke to him just before coming here but there's nothing more to report at the moment.'

He sat back, and there was silence in the room for a moment. A tractor or lawnmower could be heard outside.

'Say you locate the hotel Kolettis stayed in . . . so what? That doesn't lead us to any individual we can follow.' Slocombe hadn't touched his sherry.

'No, not straight away. But it narrows down the area we need to search. And there are other tricks we can try once we know for certain which town we have to deal with.'

'It must be Basle.'

All heads turned to Edward.

'How can you be so sure?' O'Day's glare was intense.

'Blunt was in Kornberg and Darmstadt, remember. If you study the file, as I have now done, you will find that he went missing for two days. Traffic was hopeless in the aftermath of war. He could only have travelled with bulky paintings in a jeep or truck. That would have taken some arranging. Think of the geography. He could never have made it to Liechtenstein.'

Lockwood sipped his sherry, looking over the rim of the glass at Edward. 'Any other thoughts, Dr Andover?'

Edward shrugged. 'Not at the moment, sir.'

Lockwood looked at Slocombe. 'We're getting to the point, I think, where we need to get out of London and start taking the fight to the other side.' Now he turned back to O'Day. 'Who do you have in Athens?'

'Haydon is the full-time man. Alex Haydon. He comes under Brooke, the military attaché.'

'Good?'

'Haydon's good enough, sir. Late thirties, Falklands veteran, ex our embassy in Colombia during the drugs war. He takes a bit of frightening.'

'Would he work well with Miss Tatton?'

All eyes turned on Victoria.

'I can't see why not.'

'Right. So that's our team in Athens. You, commander, had better join this man Riley in Switzerland.'

O'Day frowned. 'Don't you want me to stay here, sir? Someone has to do the day-to-day – '

'Who else is there? I've told you. I'm worried about security and don't want to involve anyone else. Dr Andover has to stay, to negotiate with the blackmailers, and we need Leith on hand to advise him. Anyway, Dr Andover has shown himself a very imaginative thinker so far, I think I'm happy to rely on him to run things at this end.'

For a moment O'Day appeared angry. But all he said was, 'Very well, sir.'

Lockwood looked at his watch. 'Lunch-time. Enjoy it. The Marbles were the lead item on *The World This Weekend*. I have a feeling that this may be the last square meal any of us is going to get for some time.'

The lights dimmed, there was a pause as blackness enveloped the room – and then the saxophones of the Sulphur City Saturday-Nighters barked out in unison. The lights came on again, the drums weighed in and the brass capped everything, a delicious wail that thrust itself against the eardrums and throbbed under the balls of the feet. Midnight, and the main set of the evening at the Albatross.

Edward let the sound and the vibration wash over him. He would have preferred it even louder, but that wasn't a complaint. He looked around the club. Considering the wildness, the flamboyance, the sheer energy of the music, the audience was a fairly sober bunch. On his visits here, Edward had often remarked to himself how straight, how tidy, how . . . worthy even the average jazz junkie was. How much the Albatross belied the world's ideas of what a jazz club was like. It would disappoint Sammy.

He lifted his whisky to his lips. The Albatross was familiar, comforting. He was well known here, though only as a regular. He had a vague idea that most of the regulars at the Albatross would be as thrown by his royal connections as Mordaunt or The General would be if they knew about his jazz habit. Nor had it escaped Edward that he too led a sort of double life, like Blunt. Edward's double life wasn't as deadly as Blunt's but . . . the Nancy connection was compromising. He had tried her home phone three times over the weekend. No reply – and no answering machine either. Wasn't that unusual, for an American? Or was he just being hypersensitive? He had tried the hotel where he had last spoken to her, where they were supposed to have spent the weekend, but Nancy had left no forwarding address. Just as he was about to ring off, Edward had had an idea.

'Excuse me,' he said to the receptionist at the other end of the line. 'I was supposed to spend last weekend with you but had to cancel at the last minute. A double room was booked, in the name of either Andover or Tucker. Is there anything to pay? Because of the late cancellation, I mean.'

'Just a moment, please. I'll check.' The receptionist wasn't long. 'No, sir. Nothing to pay. We have no record of a booking in either of those names.'

So Nancy hadn't booked the room when she said she would. Was that because she knew Edward wouldn't be able to go? Because she knew that the second picture would arrive and that, once Mordaunt was involved, everything would move up a gear?

Sitting in the Albatross, Edward was at his most clear-headed. At last he could admit certain things to himself. He had been set up – there was now no doubt about it. He was an integral part of the plan so that the blackmailers would know, in the early stages, how their demands were being received. Waves of anger engulfed him, like the saxophone sounds of the SaturdayNighters. He had liked Nancy Tucker more than any other woman he had known. Now she made him feel . . . a fool. Another wave of anger surged inside him and he gulped at his whisky.

As he lifted his glass, the movement caused Victoria to look across at him. It had been a sudden decision to come on here. After lunch Lockwood had taken a few of his guests for a walk of the Chequers grounds and then Edward and Victoria had shared a car back to London. She had invited him to the houseboat for tea and he had accepted. Tea had consisted mainly of Edward watching Victoria get ready for Greece: her flight left at ten the next morning. The houseboat fitted her character – what he knew of it. It was small – tiny. Almost clinically tidy. Small pictures, small jugs of flowers, a miniscule desk beautifully polished and preserved. Small items of silver or treen perfectly positioned. The houseboat was actually more cluttered than Edward's flat but it didn't feel like it. He had returned the compliment by inviting Victoria for dinner and she had accepted. That had been surprising, in view of the little time they had known each other and in view of the fact that she was travelling the next day. But he had been even more surprised when, after dinner, preparing to bid her goodnight, he had announced his intention of going to the Albatross and Victoria had said, 'Oh, I've heard such a lot about it but never been. May I come?'

As she looked across at him now and smiled, she seemed to be enjoying herself. So far as Edward was aware, Victoria was no jazz freak but at least the noise hadn't thrown her. They had heard nearly forty-five minutes of the Sulphur City Saturday-Nighters before she murmured, 'Take me home now, please.'

In the taxi he asked, 'You said you'd heard a lot about the Albatross – how come?'

'One of my neighbours is a musician. He's played there.'

'He has? What's he called?'

'Fraser Franklin – '

'The saxophonist!'

'The same.'

'And why have you never been before?'

'Fraser treats his wife badly. He's either playing around in London or he's on the road out of London and playing around. I like Fraser but any invitations to the Albatross with him would involve deceiving his wife.'

'You sound as though you get a lot of trouble from married men.'

'I don't think I'm hassled any more than any other woman.'

The taxi had reached the river. The embankment looked very pretty at this late hour, amber lights reflected in the water, the sparkling lace of the Albert Bridge, the explosion of light upstream at Chelsea Harbour.

'Why a houseboat?' said Edward as it came into view.

'I was left it by my communist aunt.' Victoria smiled. 'She was a character more than a communist, really. She'd been to all sorts of places which used to be exotic: Havana, Shanghai, Bucharest. She liked to say she'd been to Hanoi but not to Hackney. She was a snob but also an ardent feminist. No children of her own but four nephews and one niece – me. So when she died she made her point: I got everything. I liked her and I like her houseboat. It's a bit different. It faces west, you know. You get lovely sunsets over the river, the water seems to burn. Maybe, when this is over . . .'

Edward nodded. The taxi had come to a stop. 'Good luck in Greece.'

'Thank you for the jazz. Don't get squeezed between Lockwood and Mordaunt and O'Day.' She leaned across and, very lightly, kissed him on the cheek.

WEEK THREE

The Windsor Rubens

13

Monday

The clouds over Hyde Park were so low that the tops of the tallest buildings around its edge were lost in the mist. Rainy days sound different – not just the pellets of water on the window-panes but the traffic in the distance, slower than usual. Edward speared some bacon on his fork and brought his attention back to the newspaper in front of him. On the surface it appeared as though the rest of the press had not known exactly how to follow the *Sunday Post*'s exclusive. Owen Cutler hadn't spoken to anyone else, Downing Street was stalling, and of course no one else knew anything at all. In the event, most of the papers had hunted around for reactions and these had not been difficult to find. The Shadow Minister for the Arts had condemned the whole idea – but then he would, Edward supposed. More interesting were the views of one or two keepers at the British Museum, who said that the Trustees were the proper guardians of the museum and promised that there would be 'spirited resis-tance' from the curatorial staff if the government tried to impose its will without proper consultation. The director of the museum, Sir Martin Ogilvy, and the chairman of the Trustees, Lord Renfrew, both refused to comment. Edward was curious to see that, in the context of the stories as written, this made it seem that both men knew what was going on and were part of a campaign of secrecy, whereas Edward knew that the precise opposite was true.

One of the tabloids had had the cunning idea of telephoning the current Lord Elgin, at his home in Scotland. He had deplored the idea of returning the Marbles and complained that it would injure the good name of his distinguished ancestor.

The Greek reaction, understandably enough, was jubilant. The Greek Minister of Culture was fulsome in his praise for the British government, saying that it was a very 'civilized' move, that it would help enormously to boost the prestige of Greece's rival Olympic Festival. And he hinted that, if the Marbles were indeed returned as promised, the Greek nation would honour the British Prime Minister for his 'statesmanlike vision'.

The bacon and toast were finished. Edward looked out again at the rain. If anything it had worsened: he'd have to take the Aston today. With his finger he brushed some wisps of hair across his forehead. His hairdresser said he wouldn't recede any more but Edward didn't believe him. But for once he didn't dwell on it. He felt remarkably breezy this morning. He heard a plane in the distance but the clouds obscured it. It was too early for Victoria's flight to Athens anyway – it wasn't nine yet. He tried to imagine her as she was now, in all probability checking in at Heathrow. That kiss from Victoria . . . it was a slight thing maybe but he had liked it. Indeed, he liked Victoria. At the same time, there was Nancy. He tried to examine his feelings about Nancy. One minute he felt a longing, the next he felt sick. The sense of well-being he'd had a few moments before began to slip away. Where *was* Nancy? She had now not been in touch, even via the answering machine, for three days. Who was she, in any case? Was she really a casual west-coaster, able to pick up and discard relationships as if they were clothes or books – books which, once read, were no longer needed? Nancy's sudden disappearing act was entirely in character – but then perhaps she had deliberately created her 'character' so that when it came to her final disappearance he wouldn't be suspicious until it was too late.

After Nancy, after the doubts she had inflicted on him, Edward found Victoria's manner rather comforting, flattering even. She seemed honest, straightforward and, most important, happy with herself. Edward now realized, in comparing the two women, that Nancy had never been straightforward. She had seemed happy in her skin when they had met, but he couldn't be certain even about that.

The phone rang and he started. Was it Nancy at last? The chances were it was more mundane – the general maybe, or Mordaunt, God forbid. He picked up the receiver.

'It's me, at Terminal Two.'

'Victoria! Are you all right? Is the flight on time?'

'Everything's fine. Have you seen any of the papers?'

'All of them.'

'Nothing Lockwood can't handle, I would have thought.'

'I'm no expert. I actually rang to thank you for last night.'

'No need for thanks. Maybe . . . when this is all over . . . some canelloni?'

'Yes, canelloni, Ponte Alberto, the house speciality. Oh dear . . . the flight's being called. I was just going to . . .'

'Don't worry,' said Edward gently. 'Enjoy the flight, and don't do anything dangerous in Greece. Plenty of time when you get back.'

'No! Oh – all right. I was just going to say . . . I don't know what I was going to say. Dammit. All of a sudden, I find that English is a hard language!'

'Where next?' said O'Day. He and Riley were standing in the lobby of the Schlüssel Hotel in Basle.

'The Uster,' replied Riley. 'We can walk there from here. Along Eisengasse and then right, into Holbeinstrasse.' He led the way into the street.

As they walked, O'Day reflected that Riley had a cushy life here in Switzerland – and it showed. His most prominent feature was his stomach, which hung over his belt like an alpine roof loaded with snow. Hauling that thing around had given the man a wheeze. Yet he had a rather pleasant face, round, fleshy lips and blue eyes set wide apart. His main job for the department in Switzerland was to keep an eye out for financial shenanigans and to monitor the international organizations – Unesco, the Red Cross, the World Health Organization – in case they were being infiltrated. There was also a lot of drug money passing through Zurich these days. O'Day made a mental note that, after this was all over, he would have to find more for Riley to do. If nothing else, it would be good for his health.

They had reached the end of Eisengasse and turned into Holbeinstrasse. The Uster would be the eighth hotel they had tried so far. O'Day had flown in the night before, immediately after the Prime Minister's lunch, flights to Switzerland being rather more frequent than those to Greece.

They reached the Uster and went in. By now they had refined their technique. Although O'Day had yet to meet a Swiss who didn't speak English better than he did, he had none the less judged it prudent to conduct their enquiries in German. They needed co-operation and were more likely to get it, he thought, if they questioned people in their native tongue. It also fitted the plan they had concocted. O'Day therefore hovered near the entrance to the Uster while Riley approached the concierge: Riley was fluent in German and would take the lead for the moment.

For a short while, however, Riley hung back. It was a big hotel and there were three people behind the concierge's desk. Only one of them was suited for the story Riley planned to spin.

Eventually, his target – a grey-haired, tired-looking man in his early fifties – was free and Riley moved forward.

'Bitte?'

The man looked across and attempted a smile.

Riley proffered his embassy identification card. 'Anthony Riley, sir. British Embassy, Berne. I was hoping you could help us.'

The man looked more interested now, but he still hadn't managed a full smile.

Riley leaned over the counter, so that he could speak quietly. 'This is a confidential investigation, sir, because it is a delicate matter. We haven't involved the Swiss police yet because we don't think the Swiss taxpayers' money should be involved.'

Now the concierge was really hooked, though his near-smile had turned into a frown.

Riley nodded towards O'Day, still pacing the lobby near the main door to the street. 'That man, sir, is a British citizen. He's here because his daughter has been abducted.' The concierge's eyes flashed and Riley prayed that he had chosen his man correctly. He had waited for this particular concierge because he was more or less O'Day's age and therefore, in theory at least, might have children of his own who were the same age as the 'victim' Riley had invented.

'We have reason to believe, sir, that the girl was brought to Switzerland – at least to begin with. We are trying to trace her movements and to find out the names of the man – or men – she was travelling with. I can give you her name, the relevant dates – and this.' Riley handed across a hundred-franc note, about £30.

The concierge stared at it for a moment without moving.

Riley left the note on the counter. 'The British government would be very grateful for your help, sir.'

He was relieved when the man reached forward and took the note. Perhaps he did have a daughter who was a handful. 'Come through here, please.' The concierge led Riley around the counter and into a back room, where there was a computer screen. 'What were the dates and the girl's name?'

Riley gave him the three dates. 'Her name is Leondaris, first initial A.' Riley and O'Day were worried what to do about that initial. A father would certainly know his daughter's name. 'Her real name is Alexandra but she has several nicknames – Alex, Lex, Sandra.'

The concierge nodded and began to play the computer keyboard. The screen shone green, went blank, shone green again. There was a pause, then the screen went blank again, to be replaced almost immediately by columns of numbers and names.

'Yes,' said the concierge. 'Oh . . . I don't know. Look . . . Aristotle Leondaris stayed here on the first date you gave me. Is that a girl? Aristotle? Surely not?'

Riley did his best to control his wheeze, which always got worse when he was excited. 'She might have changed her name as part of the deception . . . You see, she was seduced away from Britain by her lover . . . Maybe the person she was with checked in on her behalf – and changed her name to be safe, to cover their tracks.' He paused, for effect. 'It has to be her. Of course it does! The times and the names fit too closely. Who was she travelling with – can you tell from your records?'

'Hold on.' More tapping on the keyboard. 'Yes, her bill was paid by a Mr Dimitri Kolettis. Just a sec . . .' He looked up at Riley. 'They had separate rooms.'

'Of course they did,' wheezed Riley. 'They would have done that so as not to attract attention to themselves . . . Tell me, who made the reservations? Was anyone else involved?'

The concierge turned back to the keyboard. After a moment, he pointed to a set of figures and letters on the screen. 'That code means that the reservation was made locally, by phone. No names, however, just Mr Kolettis's credit card number. Does that answer your question?'

Not really, thought Riley, but he nodded all the same. It confirmed there was someone here in Basle – but they already knew that. What they wanted was a name. 'Is there a list of the telephone calls they made?'

The concierge shook his head. 'Sorry. Our equipment isn't so fancy.'

Riley smiled in mid-wheeze. He thanked the man on behalf of

the British government and went back to tell O'Day. As soon as he had finished, O'Day approached the concierge himself.

'Excuse me, sir. Do you speak English?'

'But of course.'

'You have been most helpful – but I wonder if you could help me with one other thing?' Now O'Day held out a second hundred-franc note.

This time the concierge pocketed it straight away.

'My daughter's lover was Greek, but she may have been abducted with the help of people here in Basle – either Swiss or Greek. It is very important for us to trace this local person. The only other thing I can think of is this: my daughter was a great cook – she would have wanted to try the local restaurants. The reservation may have been made by the local man . . . in his name. Do you have a list of local restaurants? Good ones, I mean.'

The concierge dipped under the counter and produced a list. 'These are the best restaurants in the Basle area. Name, speciality, address, phone number. I can give you a photocopy.'

O'Day nodded and the concierge went along the counter and disappeared into another room. This was easily worth a hundred francs. He re-emerged after a short delay and handed across the photocopy. 'Good luck,' he said. 'Daughters are worse than sons, eh?'

O'Day tried to smile, sadly, playing his part. Then he and Riley crossed the lobby and stood near the door. 'We're no further forward just yet,' said O'Day. 'But if I had been Kolettis, and flown all the way here to see Blunt's Nazi pictures, and they had turned out to be blackmailers' gold, I would have felt like celebrating. A slap-up dinner would have been in order. But neither he nor this Leondaris person would have known the local scene. It stands to reason, therefore, that the reservation would have been made by the local man. We have confirmed that Kolettis and Leondaris came to Basle, so we can now switch from hotels to restaurants. We give them these dates and see if they have on their books any Greek names for the nights in question.'

No traffic had moved in Great Russell Street for ten minutes. Westwards it was backed up beyond Gower Street to Tottenham Court Road. Eastwards it extended to Southampton Row. All of these important north-south thoroughfares were choked. Solid. The cause was obvious enough: about fifty placards and posters held outside the main entrance to the British Museum. These were the brainchild of Madeleine Rolfe, wife of the leader of the Liberal Democrats and Chairman of the Friends of the British Museum. She had spent Sunday and this morning calling the rest of her committee. They had contacted others in their organization.

The 'call to arms' by Madeleine Rolfe had succeeded beyond even her wildest hopes. The placards ('Lockwood: don't lose your marbles'; 'BM = British Marbles') were surrounded by another two hundred chanting supporters ('S–O–S – Save our Stones – S–O–S – Save our Stones'). The crowd spilled from the gates of the museum on to the road but the police might have controlled it had not a number of customers at a nearby Greek restaurant in Museum Street been attracted by the noise and the placards.

To begin with, these customers, mainly Greeks, stood on the pavement opposite the museum, just watching. Then the Greeks among them had started shouting at the chanters. That soon grew into a sustained chorus. These two rival groups almost immediately attracted about the same number of onlookers, including people arriving or leaving the museum. Within an hour there were more than a thousand people milling around in Great Russell Street, and the traffic jam was forming.

Two police cars arrived, one after the other, blue lights flashing. Four officers tried to disperse the crowd. One of them, a chubby, sandy-haired man with a megaphone, started to shout. 'Please clear the road! This demonstration is illegal! The police were not informed in advance. Please clear the road! The traffic is blocked beyond Russell Square and as far as Euston Station. Ambulances cannot get to Great Ormond Street Hospital. The fire-engines at King's Cross are blocked. Please disperse – now!'

Nothing happened. At least, not to begin with. Then the sandy-haired policeman shouted again through his megaphone. Two policewomen on horseback had arrived but had been separated in the mêlée. One of them tried to force a passage through the milling crowds, which had become a congealed mass directly outside the museum gates. Behind her a black London taxi eased forward. Two of the Greeks from the restaurant tried to dodge in front of it but the driver accelerated a fraction to block their way. He overreached himself, however, and his front bumper just snicked the hind leg of the police horse. Surprised, and panicked, the horse jerked, and bucked. Not expecting it, the policewoman was dislodged from her saddle and slid to one side. Several people in the crowd screamed at once. Frightened even more now, the police horse bucked again and the policewoman was thrown to the ground. At this, the horse shied away – and stepped on a woman onlooker. The woman screamed, pushed at the horse, and all of a sudden the people around her moved together, as a wave. Several of the original demonstrators holding placards were unbalanced by this and fell. Seeing a whole bank of placards disappear, other demonstrators assumed they had been attacked by the Greeks from the restaurant. One of the remaining placards was thrown across the road, as a spear, towards them. A moment later four more followed in a concerted salvo. One grazed the police horse, which panicked yet again and ran forward a second time. Its hooves landed on several other onlookers. In no time, screaming and fighting had engulfed that area of Great Russell Street. The taxi was rocked violently.

The Greeks from the restaurant were heavily outnumbered and the few that remained to fight soon found themselves surrounded. No one paid any attention to the police megaphone. Four police could not control the hundreds of demonstrators and onlookers that now thronged the area. Angry drivers left their cars and joined in the screaming and shouting. The ten or so Greeks from the restaurant soon disappeared inside the mob. In the distance, police sirens could be heard as reinforcements converged on the scene. But their arrival was hampered by the traffic blockage that had attracted their colleagues in the first place.

Across the forecourt of the museum, Sir Martin Ogilvy, the director, had heard the commotion and now watched the fighting from his window. He could not make out the details but he had a very good idea of what was happening. He had never known anything like it but in some ways he sympathized with the demonstrators. He was still adjusting to the news which the Prime Minister had given him earlier in the day. On his appointment as Director of the British Museum, Ogilvy had signed the Official Secrets Act. The Prime Minister had reminded him of that fact and instructed him not to tell even his wife or secretary, and that was hard. Ogilvy was a reasonable man. By training he was an archaeologist, an authority on Roman Britain. He had been appointed to the museum by a previous government and therefore was not a particular fan of the present Prime Minister. Even so, he could see that Lockwood was in a dilemma. Clearly the Prime Minister couldn't leave the Crown in the lurch, and at the same time he had to appear to be taking action over the Elgin Marbles. But how long would the impasse last, Ogilvy wondered. This sort of controversy did the museum no good.

A fresh bout of shouting over in Great Russell Street suddenly rolled across the forecourt of the museum. Ogilvy was no expert on political matters, but it seemed to him as though Lockwood might have misjudged this one. He peered into the crowd, trying to make out what was happening. Unless he was mistaken, the bell he could hear ringing on the other side of the mêlée was not a police car: it was an ambulance.

Edward and Leith stood outside a row of booths in the South Bank Centre, the Hayward Gallery to be precise. It was mid-afternoon and they could see that, for some reason, the traffic on Waterloo Bridge was blocked.

The Apollo Brigade's call had come through to the studio about twenty-five minutes before, and Leith and he had scrambled down here, as commanded. So far, it had been rather a thin day for Edward. He hadn't heard from Victoria since her call from the airport, and as yet there had been no call from O'Day in Basle. And nothing from Nancy, of course. He had listened to *The World at One*, which had consisted mainly of Greek reaction to the *Sunday Post*'s story. The Greek Minister of Culture had called a press conference that morning at which he had announced he was sending a special emissary to London to ensure that the return of the Marbles really did go through this time. He had also disclosed that a special exhibition was to be mounted, in Athens and in London, featuring models which would depict how the Parthenon would look after the Marbles had been returned. Cheering demonstrators had appeared outside the British Embassy in Athens with placards showing Lockwood dressed in a classical Greek toga and wearing a laurel crown. In Paris, the Secretary-General of Unesco had welcomed the British decision to return the Marbles – he, at least, seemed to regard the 'final decision' as already having been taken. And in London the archbishop of the Aghia Sophia, the Greek Cathedral in Bayswater, had devoted a special service to give thanks for the British government's change of heart.

The forecourt to the Hayward was crowded. An exhibition of Georgia O'Keefe paintings had opened about a week before and was proving very popular. 'Do you think Lockwood was wise . . . with the leak, I mean?' Edward had been impressed and depressed by the reactions reported on *The World at One*.

'I'm no politician,' replied Leith. 'It wasn't ideal – but did he have any choice? The Apollo Brigade people want action. If we are going to string them along, we have to do something. Or appear to. He's under pressure – and there's also his grandson. A clot on the brain, apparently. They're going to have to operate.'

'Hmm. It's unlike Lockwood to misjudge events. But – '

'This O'Keefe woman.' Leith changed the subject. 'All those flower pictures with dark holes in the centre. Are they supposed to mean what I think they mean?'

A frown mixed with a smile on Edward's face. Leith was sharp and blunt at the same time. He was just about to reply when the phone rang.

He stepped forward. The booth smelled, the receiver needed cleaning, graffiti and cigarette ash formed patterns over the interior at eye level. He lifted the receiver from its cradle. 'Andover.'

'We've seen the papers. What does it mean?'

Edward's pulse raced. He stared at Leith as he spoke. 'The government has accepted your . . . terms. But . . . you must understand . . . We have to prepare the way. From now on, we shall do our best to comply with your timetable.'

'Do your best?'

'The Marbles are an emotive issue, for us as for you. There's likely to be opposition – but don't worry, you'll get your stones.'

'Does Ogilvy know?'

'He saw the Prime Minister this morning. The Duveen Galleries, which house the Marbles, will close on Thursday or Friday.'

'No. They must close forty-eight hours from now. In other words, on Wednesday.'

'That's hardly fair – '

'Andover! It's not your place to – '

'But it's madness!' Edward was suddenly very angry. Whether he was angry with this . . . voice, with himself, or with Nancy he didn't know. But all this deception and double talk . . . it overwhelmed him. He found he had raised his voice. 'You can't say one thing at one time, have us running around after you, and then say something quite different the next time. Where do you expect to . . .'

Edward faltered. He realized he was addressing thin air. The man at the other end had rung off. 'Damn!' he muttered to himself, replacing the receiver. He turned to face Leith. 'I mishandled that. He put the phone down on me.'

'Yes,' said Leith quietly. 'You stepped outside the script.' The inspector's face had hardened. His lips, thin at the best of times, had almost disappeared. 'Your job, Andover, is to be amenable, compliant, submissive even, if that's what is required. You accept what they say, however autocratic, inconsistent or misguided it appears to be. You play by their rules, not the Geneva Convention or the Marquess of Queensberry's idea of fair play.'

'It was just – '

'You lost your temper. For all they know, it was contrived on your part, designed to trick them into making a slip. You simply must never – '

'All right, all right. I'm sorry. I apologize. I didn't realize. It won't happen again.'

'There may not be another time,' Leith sighed. 'Come on, no use waiting here. The worst is: not only do we not know if they are going to call again, but, even if they do call, we don't know when. Lockwood's going to be livid.'

Edward bristled at this. 'I made a small slip. There's no need to get apocalyptic.'

Leith ushered Edward out into the fresh air before replying. They stood, overlooking the river, where they couldn't be overheard. The traffic still appeared to be blocked on Waterloo Bridge. 'You seem to forget, Andover, that the main risk is to you – to the Crown, I mean. If this thing blows up, the government may suffer – but another will be elected . . . But what will happen to your precious monarchy, eh? You'd better go back to the palace, stick by the phone and pray that our Greek friends call back. Otherwise you will have accomplished single-handed what Oliver Cromwell needed an entire army for.'

Victoria rolled down the window of the car and let in the warm evening air of Athens. All the cars she had ever owned had been built before the age of air-conditioning but Haydon's was a brand-new Toyota. Anonymous but air-conditioned.

'That's the flat,' Haydon said softly, getting back into the car and lighting a cigarette. 'The second floor, with the balcony. "Leondaris" is printed on one of the mailboxes.'

Victoria had taken an instant dislike to Alex Haydon. He was a good-looking bastard but cocky, supercilious, knowing. In view of the song and dance that the Greek press were making about the *Sunday Post*'s story, and the fact that the Greek Minister of Culture had held a press conference that morning, and because there were demonstrations outside the embassy, Haydon had booked Victoria into a hotel on the outskirts of Athens, away from the limelight. If she were to be seen, even in a television establishing shot of the embassy, it might alert the blackmailers. No one knew how much they knew.

Haydon had met Victoria at the airport and taken her straight to the hotel. After unpacking, he had insisted on hearing the full story from her. So, what with the journey and the two-hour time difference between London and Athens, it was after four before they had begun work proper.

Work proper involved, first, a call to Thessaloniki University. This established that Professor Kolettis was not at his desk. Big surprise. The professor, they were told, was away on an archaeological excavation and no one knew when he would be back. And the secretary would not say where the dig was, for security reasons. 'Who is calling?' she had asked.

'American Cable Television,' Victoria had lied. 'I am a researcher for a documentary on the classical world. I wanted to pick his brains. Will you tell the professor we were sorry to miss him.' That had seemed to satisfy the secretary.

A. Leondaris was easier. The number and address were in the book and there was only one. No one had answered the phone when they had called, and there was no answering machine. The address, Haydon had said, was in the university area of Athens, a pleasant, leafy district north of Sintagmatos, the city's main square. There were many boutiques, restaurants, art galleries and cafés. Victoria and Haydon had decided to go and see the flat for themselves and Haydon had just parked the Toyota, across the road and about fifty yards down a slight hill.

He looked at his watch. 'It's nearly five-fifteen. The question is: has he or she gone off "excavating" also . . . or not yet home from work?' He smiled at Victoria. He did a lot of smiling – his teeth were perfect and he knew it.

'We'll wait and see,' said Victoria.

They waited. Till six, seven, eight. At nine they decided that A. Leondaris could have gone straight out to dinner from work. Haydon left Victoria and went in search of some sandwiches. He came back with hamburgers, grapes and wine. They waited again: ten, eleven. At eleven Victoria, conscious that she ought to check with London, said: 'If Leondaris is out with a lover, they might spend the night together. How long are we going to stay?'

For reply, Haydon delved into his pockets. He took out a pen, his wallet, a couple of envelopes, a cheque book, a diary. He opened the glove compartment of the Toyota and put the things in there. He also took out from the compartment what looked like another cheque book, another diary, another wallet.

'What on earth are you doing?'

'Fieldcraft manual, chapter two. Didn't you do the course? You hard languages people must get sent into the field now and then. It's standard procedure. Any time we do anything that's remotely risky, or illegal, we have to change our identity, including our nationality.' He held up the wallet. 'That's what this is. Now I'm Gilles Broudin, from Montpellier. What's more, the address checks out if anyone follows it up. I have a wife there.'

Victoria said nothing. He was just as loathsome as Gilles or Alex.

'Wait here,' Haydon went on, opening the car door. He let himself out and strolled across the street. A minute or two passed. A taxi drove up behind the Toyota and stopped, its diesel engine clattering away in the night. Was this Leondaris coming home? No, a couple got out and disappeared into another flat.

Haydon seemed to have been gone a long time. Victoria kept one eye on the flat on the second floor, in case the lights came on. But the flat remained in darkness.

She looked at her watch, getting nervous. As she did so, Haydon emerged from the shadows. He was unhurried and walked slowly back to the car. He got in. He wouldn't say what he had done, or found, until they were in Victoria's room at the Holiday Inn and couldn't be overlooked. He took two whiskies from the mini-bar, reached into his pocket and threw half a dozen envelopes on the bed. 'The front door of the lobby was still open. I couldn't get past the inner door – well, I could but it was too risky. But all the mailboxes were in the lobby. I found these in our friend's box. I managed to force the lock – fieldcraft manual, chapter eight.' He grinned.

'It's Aristotle Leondaris,' Victoria breathed, holding one of the envelopes. She ripped into it, took out the sheet of paper inside and scanned its contents. 'It's from the Greek Bar Association. Looks like he's a lawyer.'

Haydon had opened another. 'This is an electricity bill.'

Victoria opened a third and threw it down. 'Phone bill. Pity Greece is so backward. No itemized billing – otherwise we could see what calls he has made to Britain, or Switzerland.'

'Look at the dates on the envelopes,' said Haydon. 'He seems to have been gone for about a week.'

'Sounds like our man.'

'And look at this!' Victoria whispered a moment later. 'It's got a letterhead from the Greek parliament. From a Stamatis Leondaris – '

'Father? Brother?'

'Cousin? Uncle?' asked Victoria. 'He sounds well connected, politically anyway. It's actually from Stamatis's secretary. It's a sort of circular: he's addressing a rally next week, on Greece and the Balkans since *glasnost* . . . Hmm,' she added after a pause, lifting the last two letters. 'This is an invoice for some plants he bought. And this, the last one, is an invitation to an art gallery opening.'

'Nothing definitively incriminating . . .'

'But you wouldn't expect that. He's our man, all right.'

'I'm inclined to agree,' said Haydon, as if his agreement was all that mattered in the world. 'But how do we get from here to there? If he has gone missing, or is with Kolettis, I don't see how we set about finding him.'

'There are two ways that I can think of,' replied Victoria. 'Either we continue to stake out the flat where we were tonight, and hope that he will return, so we can follow him. The drawback with that is he may not return until all this is over. Alternatively, we know a bit about Kolettis and we can find out more tomorrow at the British School in Athens. He's an archaeologist, don't forget. They may not be in hiding, not as such. They can't guess how quickly we have got on to them . . . otherwise, they wouldn't still be talking to London. So they may not be in hiding at all. The more we piece together Kolettis's career, the better an idea we will have about him. That may – *may* – tell us where to look.'

Haydon grunted approval as he knocked back another whisky. 'I hope the second approach works,' he said. 'We can't count on Ari.'

'Why not?'

'I'm afraid that when I broke into the mailbox, I rather messed up the lock. In fact, I mangled it badly. If he comes back, he'll see he's been broken into. It will probably tell him we're on to them. Then we'd lose all chance of catching them.'

'Good evening, everyone, and welcome to another edition of *The Eleventh Hour*. As you may have heard in the news, a seven-week-old baby died today when the ambulance taking it to hospital failed to get there in time due to a traffic blockage caused by a demonstration outside the British Museum. Traffic in London was stationary for more than two hours as far south as Waterloo Station and as far north as Camden Town. The approaches to Great Ormond Street Children's Hospital were among those streets choked with cars. Several people were injured during the demonstration, which was called to protest against a government plan to return the Elgin Marbles to Greece.'

Trevor Tennant turned in his seat as the studio shot switched from one camera to another. 'The injuries outside the museum seem to have been caused accidentally when a police horse panicked. Nevertheless, there was some fighting in the street outside the main entrance to the museum and a number of arrests were made. With me in the studio tonight, to discuss the issues raised by the Elgin Marbles, is Madeleine Rolfe, Chairman of the Friends of the British Museum and the organizer of today's demonstration, Chief Superintendent Colin Budgen of New Scotland Yard, Dr George Imittos, editor of the *Greek Times*, a weekly newspaper published here in London, and David Eady, Shadow Minister for the Arts. Before we begin our discussion, may I just add that we did invite both the Downing Street press office and the Director of the British Museum to be represented on tonight's programme – but both declined. Now, Chief Superintendent Budgen, I'd like to start with you. Are you blaming the demonstrators – people like Mrs Rolfe here – for the death of that poor baby?'

The policeman was in uniform and therefore very uncomfortable under the hot lights of the studio. It made him fidgety, and this came across as rather shifty. 'No. The demonstration was unfortunate; we had no prior warning and it soon got out of hand. But in fairness to the demonstrators no one could foresee the catastrophic effect it would have on the traffic. Traffic has been getting steadily worse in London for years. When something unexpected like this happens . . . it can trigger chaos. Also, I have spoken to the doctors at the hospital and we can't say for certain that the baby would have made it to Great Ormond Street even if the roads had been entirely free.'

Tennant turned to Madeleine Rolfe. 'Not everyone might be as charitable as the superintendent, Mrs Rolfe. I've heard it rumoured that the mother of the infant is thinking of suing. But let's leave that to one side. Your demonstration was called without notifying the police, it caused chaos, injury – people were arrested. What's your reaction to all that?'

'That I'd do it all again tomorrow, if need be.' Madeleine Rolfe had long dark hair and pebble glasses. She wore lots of make-up and a huge bow at her throat. 'There wasn't time to ask the police. This is a democracy, for pity's sake, and the government is plotting to act in a highly authoritarian way, going over the heads and against the wishes of the people. Strictly speaking, the government doesn't own the Elgin Marbles, the Trustees of the Museum do, although of course the government appoints the Trustees. Somebody has to stop the government doing what it is doing – me, if no one else wants the job. The fact that many more people turned up than we expected shows I was right to call the demonstration. People feel strongly.'

'Dr Imittos, may I bring you in here, please. Britain is a democracy, people have a right to demonstrate. How do you feel about that, given that some of your countrymen were injured and arrested today?'

'Democracy, of course, is a Greek word – and a Greek idea. As Greek as the Acropolis Marbles. I was outside the British Museum today. There were a few of us having lunch in a Greek restaurant nearby when we heard the commotion. We went to see what had been happening – '

'Had you been drinking?' Tennant never failed to spot an opportunity for mischief.

Imittos looked flustered. 'Well . . . wine, or course, with lunch. A few beers maybe.' He grew angry.

'What happened then?' Tennant moved him along, without conceding anything.

'A few of us stood opposite the main gates of the museum, watching. Just watching.'

'No jeers or shouts?'

'No, not to begin with. And you are not to assume that drink had anything to – '

'Madeleine Rolfe, did you see Dr Imittos across the street?'

'I certainly saw some people I took to be Greeks – '

'And who started shouting first?'

'That's not the point!' shouted Imittos. 'The point is: the Marbles are Greek and should be returned – '

'No!' shouted Madeleine Rolfe.

'But it *is* the point,' Tennant insisted, pleased that he had got some needle into the programme. 'The question, for the British at least, is that the Marbles are in Britain and belong to the nation. Is the government behaving properly in even attempting to dispose of them? David Eady?'

'Clearly, the government is not behaving properly. Indeed, it is behaving most improperly. Look at the strange, the awkward way this business has come to light – through an anonymous leak. The government did not want this story aired and it does not want it discussed even now. Look at its refusal to appear on this programme. We can give Madeleine Rolfe a mild slap on the wrist for not alerting the police to her demonstration but her mistake pales alongside that of the government. Is their refusal to appear here tonight the action of an innocent party? Is that an honourable action? No – it is disgraceful. Democracy may be a Greek word but the way the government is behaving is thoroughly barbaric.'

'But what I don't understand,' Tennant broke in smoothly, 'is this: what's in it for them? The Marbles are here, as you say. Why would the government give them away without asking for anything else in return?'

'You'll have to ask them.'

'But you are a senior politician, David Eady, Shadow Minister for the Arts. Can't you make a professional's guess?'

141

'I think we are on very murky ground here – '

'What you mean?'

'As you say, governments don't act like this for no reason. If the British government is to make the Greek government a gift, right out of the blue, we must be getting something in return. There's something wrong if we are not.'

'And what might that something be?'

'Your guess is as good as mine. But consider this: the oil in the North Sea runs out in four years' time. A fresh reserve of oil was discovered in the Aegean Sea last year – just off Thracos. Maybe the government has offered the Elgin Marbles as a sweetener to the Greek government, to allow British companies to drill there.'

'In which case, would that be such a bad thing?' The camera switched back to Tennant. 'Oil is more important than antiquities, surely?'

'Philistine!' cut in Madeleine Rolfe. 'There's oil all over the place, but only one set of Marbles. Besides, these stones were collected for the nation – and accepted. They can't just be given away by some temporary occupant of Downing Street.'

Tennant didn't like anyone else speaking out of turn on *The Eleventh Hour* – that was his job. So he ignored Madeleine Rolfe and returned to the shadow minister.

'But, assuming you are right about the oil, even a Prime Minister wouldn't conclude a deal like this one, surely, not without Cabinet authority?'

'Yes – in theory. But ask yourself why the story was leaked. Perhaps someone, some civil servant in the Foreign and Commonwealth Office, doesn't think the *quo* is worth the *quid*. And so they leaked part of the story, with the aim of scuppering the deal.'

'You have no knowledge that this might be so?'

'None at all. You asked me to speculate and that is all I've done. But I have absolutely no knowledge of what is going on. Indeed, that's my main complaint – that the House of Commons has been kept in the dark so much.'

'It is Tuesday tomorrow: Prime Minister's Question Time in the Commons. Are you going to tackle Mr Lockwood?'

'I would imagine that the entire House will be after Mr Lockwood tomorrow.'

Tennant turned away from Eady and said: 'We're running out

of time but I'd briefly like to ask Dr Imittos how he reads David Eady's speculation?'

The Greek shook his head. 'Idle speculation.'

'So why do you think that Mr Lockwood has taken this sudden turn on the Marbles?'

'Natural justice. It does happen, you know. There *are* good people in the world. Few, I know, and maybe that explains why he has kept this whole business so close to his chest. Few other people in this country are as civilized as he is.'

'Strong words, Dr Imittos. They make you sound anti-British.'

'Look what happened today,' cried Imittos. He was still smarting from Tennant's earlier jibe and his anger was not far beneath the surface. 'Madeleine Rolfe calls a demonstration without telling the police. As a result of that, more Greeks than British are injured and more are arrested. Earlier on in this programme, when I tried to put the Greek side, you insinuated that we were drunk. And you say I'm anti-British. It is you who are anti-Greek!'

Tension had risen again in the studio. Tennant tried to break in, to wind up the programme. 'Well, that's all – '

Imittos would not give way, however. 'Mrs Rolfe had her demonstration today – and because of that she's on television tonight. Well, we Greeks gave you democracy – so you should know that means it's our turn next.'

'You have let me down, Andover.' The Prime Minister was standing in front of the fireplace and shifted from one foot to the other. 'I let O'Day go to Switzerland because, in the past few days, you have shown yourself to be adaptable and imaginative. I thought it safe to leave you in charge. Now, as soon as O'Day is out of the way, you panic on me.'

'I think panic is a strong word, sir.' The news of Edward's mishandling of the discussion with the blackmailers had reached Lockwood and other members of the midnight committee long before it met – Leith had seen to that. As they had entered the Downing Street flat, each of the committee members had glanced over at Edward. He couldn't tell who was sympathetic and who was hostile.

'We're not going to quibble whether it was panic or not, Dr Andover. The result is the same. This whole affair may be over

– thanks to you. Two of the families mentioned in the Hesse documents have representatives in the government – and if that comes out it could do for us in a close-run election. So don't expect any bosom pals in this room, if it all hits the fan now. Me especially. If this goes wrong, Keld will be one of the lucky ones. It wouldn't take much to persuade him to stand against me – and this might just do the trick. You'll probably be out of a job, too – given what the royal family will come in for. Have you thought about that?' Lockwood passed the fingers of one hand through his hair. 'Still, we needn't dwell on that.' He looked around to the others in the room. 'For the moment, we have to proceed as if nothing has happened, as if our investigations can still make a difference, that we might still catch these buggers.' He turned to Edward again. 'What news from Athens? I hope that, when you spoke to them, you had the sense not to tell them about your mistake. They will only get somewhere if they believe that what they're doing matters. What did Victoria Tatton tell you – and what did you tell her?'

Edward was smarting from Lockwood's treatment. He well appreciated there was some justification for what the Prime Minister had said, but he also wondered if Lockwood wasn't taking it out on him for the fact that he, Lockwood, had misjudged the reaction there would be to the *Sunday Post* leak. There was also the question of the Prime Minister's grandson. Was that making him edgy, too? Edward could scarcely point out these things, however. Lockwood would fly at him. Instead, he said, 'Tatton and Haydon have been told that Kolettis is on a dig – but they don't know where. They found the Leondaris flat and watched it for a few hours but it appears unoccupied at the moment. They burgled the mailbox and from the letters established that he has a relative with the same surname who is a Greek MP.'

'And what did you tell them?'

'Nothing, sir.'

'How come?'

'Victoria Tatton didn't call until ten past eleven, London time, sir. We discussed what she and Haydon intend to do tomorrow – then I had to hurry to come on here.'

'Hmm. And what is the word from Basle?'

Edward relayed the substance of his conversation with O'Day in which he had felt it right to tell him about his conversation with the blackmailer. The commander had phoned at ten, eleven in Basle, by which time he and Riley were on their fifth restaurant but had so far had no luck. Edward didn't say much about the tone of the conversation. O'Day had made it plain that he thought legwork in the field was now beneath him, and that he should be where Edward was, having cosy chats with the Prime Minister. He had been scathing when Edward told him he had lost his temper with the blackmailer.

'So O'Day knows, eh?' the Prime Minister replied. 'Oh well, it's just as well in a way, I suppose. He might have some ideas as to what we can do.' He rocked on his feet in front of the fireplace, a distracted expression on his face. At length, he asked generally, 'Anything else?'

Midwinter coughed, then gave a synopsis of *The Eleventh Hour*.

'Eady's a fool,' Lockwood said when the press secretary had finished. 'Such waffle about oil.'

'But what about Question Time?' Slocombe leaned forward.

'Not a problem,' replied Lockwood. 'That's why we leaked the story in the first place in the way that we did. So that it is deniable. I shall simply acknowledge that the committee has met and produced a recommendation. No more, no less.' He turned back to Midwinter. 'Anything in tomorrow's papers?'

'The museum demo makes the front pages, and the death of the baby – though the heat has been taken out of that, after tonight's programme. One or two leader articles asking you to come clean. The Greek press conference – also on the front pages. Nothing startlingly new but it's all damaging in a drip-drip sort of way. The foreign press have been on in droves today – the *New York Times*, *Figaro*, *Die Welt*, *La Nazione*. So I expect we're going to get stick from all directions.'

Lockwood looked tired and fierce at the same time. 'How much was the other side leading by at the last poll?'

'Three points,' growled Midwinter.

'That must be five by now.' Lockwood fixed Edward with his stare. 'Maybe you've done me a favour, Andover. This business is already messy and could get messier still. If these Brigade people do go public, it does at least simplify things. The public's disapproval will all be directed at the Palace, not at Downing Street, and we'll be off the hook, ready to fight the election on straightforward issues. And the mistake will be down to a Palace employee.' The Prime Minister gave Edward a tight smile. 'On the other hand, if it does leak, thanks to you, Francis Mordaunt is going to be wilder than a bear in a beehive. And you will be out of a job.'

The green glow from Edward's answering machine seemed to fill the flat. It tinged the pale wood of the easel next to the desk, where a small pastel portrait by Hugh Douglas Hamilton was propped on the pegs. It was reflected in the glasses on the tray that he called a bar. It made the leaves of the plant on the window-sill unnaturally vivid. He approached the machine without putting on the light. He was feeling bruised and angry. This business had rushed into his life, picked him up and deposited him in some heavy company. Now it had turned on him: it threatened his job, his career, his self-esteem. He stared at the answering machine with dread. The figure four glowed up at him. One *must* be from Nancy. But if it was, would it contain more lies? At least her silence, much as he hated it, was cleaner. He pressed the button and the clicks and whirs began.

'Edward, this is Hillier. Please call after nine tomorrow. I've had some thoughts.'

Edward stared out of the window. A large black car was coming up the drive. The Waleses returning from some glittering affair? After today, he wasn't sure if he could ever feel the same way again about the royal family.

'Edward, it's Wilma. Just one important message among all the dross. Geneviève Chombert called from Paris. They want to publish your lecture in the proceedings of the conference as if you had given it anyway – can you send her a copy? I haven't done it yet but if you let me have a yea or a nay I'll send it off.' And would Geneviève Chombert still want it if he was no longer part of the royal household? God! His life was going to change if that happened.

'Edward, it's Mordaunt. I've been at Windsor all day with the Queen. We'd better confer very soon. Call me early tomorrow.' Cool, clipped tones, the equerry already distancing himself from impending disaster.

'Woodie, this is your Boston correspondent. Literally – I'm in Boston Spa, Lincolnshire. How do you like that?' She sounded perfectly normal. Normal for Nancy anyway. I'm changing my mind about your machine – I'm growing to hate it. I'm here for two nights, so, if you want, if you are missing me even a little bit, you can call me. So long.' She recited the number and rang off.

He scribbled down the digits. He was pleased and angry at the same time. Then it occurred to him that she was calling because the negotiations had foundered that afternoon. Did she want to find out how the Palace and the government were reacting? He was now far more angry than pleased.

14

Tuesday

'Good afternoon, gentlemen. For two? The reservation is in what name?'

O'Day said nothing. It was Riley's turn to do the honours. This was the seventh restaurant they'd tried and by far the most beautiful. It was called the Greifen and had a glassed-in terrace that overlooked the river. The sounds of a piano could be heard from the bar.

The woman at the reservations desk was very attractive in a stern sort of way: hair swept straight back, high cheekbones, and she was dressed in a navy suit, crisp and businesslike. Riley moved forward. 'We are not here to eat, miss,' he said, lowering his voice and adopting a confidential tone. 'I am British, but I live in Switzerland, in Berne – I'm attached to the embassy.' He showed his embassy card and then turned back to O'Day. 'This gentleman here is a British subject whose daughter has been abducted and has disappeared. We are trying to trace her last movements and we have established that she stayed in the Uster hotel. We believe she may have had a rendezvous with a man in one of Basle's restaurants. We don't know his name but he may well have made the reservation. I wonder if we could look at your reservations book for a particular date? . . . All we need is the name.' Riley paused and waited. From previous experience they sensed that, in the chic restaurants, the flashed fifty- or hundred-franc note did not work. People would help if they wanted to. Otherwise, no amount of bribery would do the trick.

The woman looked past them. Four other dinner guests had arrived. She checked their reservation, crossed out the name, and said: 'This way, please.' As she led them to their table, she called back to Riley, 'Wait in the bar. I'll find you there.'

The piano was in the bar. The pianist was quite clearly the other woman's twin sister. She wasn't wearing a business suit. Quite the contrary, she had on a low-cut dress. But her cheekbones and swept-back hair were identical. She was playing Chopin.

Riley decided to order a drink. They had earned it. Before the drinks arrived, however, the woman from the reservations desk came into the bar. She approached Riley and leaned over him. 'What date was it you were interested in?'

Riley turned to O'Day – they'd tried this gambit before – and asked a question with his gaze.

O'Day gave the last date when Kolettis and Leondaris were known to have been at the Uster.

'Hmm,' said the woman. 'That means the old book. It's in the bureau downstairs. I can't leave the restaurant – but don't worry, Inge will be able to fetch it when she finishes here in a few moments.' The waiter brought the drinks. 'Ah, good. Have your drink. I'll tell my sister what to do when she finishes. Just wait here.'

The drink made them hungry. They made do as best they could – and finished off a dish of olives and cocktail onions.

The Chopin finished, the sister got up, smiled at them and walked out. Across the bar, in the lobby, they could see the two sisters talking. They looked towards Riley and O'Day. Riley glanced at O'Day and winked. 'Twins, eh?'

O'Day frowned. This was hardly the behaviour of someone searching for a missing daughter.

They had now finished their drink and were contemplating another when O'Day noticed the pianist cross the hall a second time, towards her sister's desk. She was carrying something large and square. Moments later, the first sister, the one in the business suit, brought the book to them. She handed it to Riley. 'It's very simple. Each page is a different day. The dates are written at the top. The column on the left is lunch, on the right is dinner. I'll leave it with you, but please will you bring it back to me when you have finished. I need it to show the tax inspectors.' She smiled and went back to her chores.

Riley moved their dead glasses and the empty olive dish on to the next-door table. He pulled the book towards him. 'What was the most recent date – February?'

O'Day nodded. 'The seventeenth.'

Riley found the day easily enough. The handwriting was florid, very round and fulsome. It sloped, making it difficult to distinguish the 'a's and the 'e's, the 'k's and the 'h's. There were

149

some fifteen names for lunch and over twenty for dinner. He started to copy them all down, as they had been doing at the other restaurants. This was a bone of contention between them. Were they looking for a Greek name – or just *any* name? Certainly, if they found a name on two or more lists, coinciding with the dates Kolettis and Leondaris visited Basle, that would look very suspicious. O'Day, however, thought it was a waste of time. He was sure that, if they found it, the name they wanted would be Greek.

'Let's look at the other dates first,' he said. 'You know how distinctive Greek names are . . . it will be much quicker.'

Riley wasn't convinced but gave way. 'All right. There are no Greek names for February the seventeenth. What was the date before that?'

'November the nineteenth.'

Riley flipped back through the pages of the book. He found November; he found the nineteenth.

They were silent for a moment, reading. Or, rather, deciphering the florid handwriting.

'Look at that,' breathed Riley after a while. 'Doesn't that say "Evrotas" – or "Evrotes"?'

' "Evrotas",' repeated O'Day. 'Four for lunch.'

'Four! Another Greek? Or someone else in Switzerland?'

'Maybe neither. Look at the dinner list – Zakros, or Zekres . . . a table for three.' He was scribbling it down. 'That's our best bet yet. Pity they don't do as the posh restaurants in Britain or France do – take a phone number in case you leave something behind. Come on, let's check the first date.'

'Oh, shit!' hissed Riley when they had turned to the page. 'All the Greeks in Switzerland must eat here.'

'There's only *one* name. Keep it in proportion. "Stavroupolis . . . Stevroupolis." Another table for four.' He caught the eye of the first twin and she came over.

'Excuse me, I'm not sure of your writing. Is this Zakros, or Zekros?'

She looked. 'Zakros – but he can't be the man you are looking for.'

'Oh? Why not?'

'He comes here quite a lot. *Such* a nice man. Quiet, well-groomed, polite. Not at all the type of man you are looking for. He's not flashy . . . I really can't imagine him doing the sort of

150

thing you say has happened. He's respectable. I believe he's an art dealer.'

Sir Martin Ogilvy sat back in his chair and looked about him. He liked the Garrick. He liked the portraits on the walls of the lunch room, he liked the habit of serving spirits in small pitchers rather than measly glasses and he liked the members, those that he knew. He even liked his host, Marcus Proctor, sitting opposite him. This was – what? – the fourth time he'd had lunch with Proctor, since the latter had become Minister for the Arts over three years ago.

Proctor had instituted these regular get-togethers with the barons of the art world: directors of museums, of the opera, the ballet or the theatre, conductors of orchestras. One to one, no aides, no notes. Informal chat, gossip, nods and winks. Proctor enjoyed them and believed that others did too. The lunches were also useful. It was amazing what two men – two people, he corrected himself – could accomplish if each had the will. They were set up well in advance and usually were quiet, discreet affairs. In one sense, however, today's looked like being different. When the lunch had been arranged, more than a month ago, there had been no particular limelight attaching to the British Museum. As of the weekend, of course, all that had changed. This was going to be interesting. Proctor studied Ogilvy from across the table. The museum man had his eyes trained on the menu just now but, as Proctor watched, he snapped it shut.

'I'll have the whitebait to start with, then the mixed grill. And I think I'll have beer rather than wine.'

Proctor wrote the order on a small pad at the side, where he had already recorded his own choice. A waiter approached and took the pad away. 'Has Madeleine been up to any more tricks today?' Proctor decided there was no point in avoiding the issue.

'Did you see her on the box last night?' Ogilvy broke his bread roll. 'She was a bit scared by what happened, I think. Underneath it all. The Trustees are meeting later this week.'

'What can they do?'

'It's an interesting point, Marcus. It's true that things in the museum, which are not on loan, belong to the nation, and in that sense to the government. But in law the objects are ceded to the Trustees, and the government of the day does not – theoretically – have the right to dispose of them against the wishes of the Trustees without an Act of Parliament. Of course, the Prime Minister could dismiss the Trustees and replace them with lapdogs . . . Anyway, so long as this all remains a bluff, it shouldn't arise.'

Ogilvy's whitebait arrived, with some soup for Proctor. The minister sipped his consommé and tried to work out whether he had heard right. Bluff? What bluff? He knew nothing about any bluff. Not that he knew much about anything in this matter. In fact, unless he had misheard, Ogilvy knew something Proctor did not. More, Ogilvy assumed that Proctor knew what he knew. Because he was a minister, he supposed. Proctor racked his brains as to how to respond.

'But you see why it has to be kept secret?' The minister tried to look knowing.

Ogilvy stared at him sharply.

Proctor lifted his soup spoon to his mouth but didn't take his eyes off the other man.

Ogilvy glanced around the club room, to make sure he couldn't be overheard. 'Lockwood wouldn't tell me what kind of threat was being made against the Queen, just what the demands were, and that the Elgin Marbles may have to go in the end.' He paused to fork some of the whitebait into his mouth. 'What's the threat, Marcus?'

At that precise moment, Proctor was bloated with a general rage against the Prime Minister. Something was going on, something that sounded like the biggest art scandal there'd been in a long time, and although Ogilvy knew about it, or a great deal about it, he – Marcus Proctor, Minister for the goddam Arts – was out in the cold.

Proctor hadn't wanted the arts job in the first place. He'd hoped for a position in Treasury, that's where the power was. But Lockwood had insisted. Although Proctor had quite enjoyed his three years, the arts were not the mainstream, not the fast track. Treasury, Foreign Office – even Defence, where his wife's brother was – they were the powerful ministries. Yet if this really was the biggest art scandal it was his chance to get back centre stage. Ogilvy seemed to be saying there was some sort of threat against the Queen and that it was related to the Elgin Marbles. That sounded a big enough story for anyone. He wiped the soup from his lips with his napkin.

'Martin, I can't tell you. You should be flattered you know so much. Lockwood has played this one very close to his chest.'

'Do you know how many pieces of stone make up the Elgin Marbles, Marcus? I'll tell you: ninety-three. It's an enormous job to take them down, pack them up and ship them to Greece. I hope you know what you are doing in the government, Marcus. It must be one hell of a royal scandal if this is the result.'

Proctor tried to look sanctimonious. 'It is, Martin, it is. Very big. That's why I can't tell you anything.' His mind was already elsewhere. This was more like it. A genuine, juicy, old-fashioned political scandal. Proctor hadn't the faintest idea what the scandal was but he wasn't worried. He had no feelings, one way or the other, for the royal family. All he knew was that he didn't much care for the Prime Minister. He had been left out of this business but now he knew the important bits. He had contacts, in the security services, in the Home Office, in the police. In the Cabinet Office, come to that. He'd have no trouble fleshing out the details. The real question was: could he use it against Lockwood? If Lockwood were to be ousted as Prime Minister, as leader of the Party, would Proctor get a better job from his replacement? Nothing was certain in politics, of course. But if Proctor were to hand that replacement, on a plate, the means to unthrone Lockwood, he could surely count on a big ministry in return. Especially if that candidate was his brother-in-law.

'Archimedes Iridakis, the man appointed by the Greek government to liaise with Britain over the return of the Elgin Marbles, arrived at Heathrow airport this morning.' The television screen switched from the newscaster to film of Iridakis walking up a jetway surrounded by reporters. He was a tall man, swarthy, with a fine head of grey hair. The skin on his heavy eyelids was a shade darker than the rest of his face.

Edward could not remember ever watching television in the middle of the day but all his old habits were, for the time being, in abeyance.

'Mr Iridakis,' asked one of the television reporters, 'What do you hope to achieve by your visit? The British government has made no official statement on this matter and the reports published so far indicate only that a committee has been considering the question. Isn't your visit just a little bit premature?'

'Not at all!' beamed the Greek. 'My job is to do anything which facilitates the return of these glorious works of art to Greece. My government attaches the highest priority to this matter, and no expense is to be spared, no stone left unturned, as you might say, in order to realize the ambition of every Greek – to have those Marbles back on the Acropolis, where they belong. And in time for the Olympic Festival.'

'Has anyone in the British government agreed to meet you?'

'No . . . but then I haven't asked to meet anyone yet. I shall be conferring with our ambassador here in London and the cultural attaché later today. We shall decide together how to proceed.'

'How long are you planning to be here?'

'As long as it takes.'

The shot changed again and the newscaster was back. 'Downing Street is still offering "No comment" on this issue but the Prime Minister is expected to come under strong pressure at Question Time in the Commons this afternoon. Abroad now. In Poland, the – '

Edward switched off. He was eating a chicken sandwich which Wilma had brought in. He, Leith and Frank, the security guard, were the only ones in the studio. So far, today had been a little better than yesterday but that wasn't saying much. He had not yet spoken to Nancy, despite having her phone number. When he had called that morning, she had already gone from the hotel but had left a message for him to call that evening at 6.30. It thus looked as though he would finally get to talk with her.

The blackmailers had not yet gone public – but then they hadn't been in touch again either. Edward had spoken to Hillier, who had telephoned Ottawa over the weekend and got them to improve the sum of money they would make available for the restoration of the Poussin, thus demonstrating that he might be flat on his back at the moment but he wasn't out for the count. O'Day had called with the news that they now had a third name – and an address they had found with the help of the telephone company. He and Riley were en route to keep the address under surveillance. So Edward would at least have something to tell Lockwood at tonight's meeting.

The phone in front of Edward flashed and he reached for the receiver. It was Mordaunt.

'I called this morning,' said Edward defensively.

'Yes, I was in with Lockwood and Her Majesty. The Tuesday audience.'

And this time, Edward thought, I wasn't invited.

'I have to tell you, Edward, that Her Majesty is not at all pleased by this turn of events.'

'I –'

'It would be unseemly for someone of your standing to be dismissed but of course if this . . . catastrophe comes about . . . you could not – you would have to resign. You do appreciate that.'

There. It had been said. That last sentence was not a question. Mordaunt certainly did not waste any time.

'It was a slip, a momentary thing. I didn't ask for this job.'

'It could be a calamitous slip, Edward. An historic slip. Unfortunate for you – but there it is.' He put down the phone.

Edward too replaced the receiver in its cradle.

Leith said, 'You realize what will happen, don't you, if all this hits the fan?'

Edward didn't speak. He wasn't sure what, exactly, the policeman was getting at.

'I don't know how they will do it, or what the details will be. But I can see it coming.' He shook his head slowly from side to side. 'They will make you the scapegoat.'

Victoria felt Haydon's eyes on her. There were some men who could look at a woman admiringly without leering. Not Alexander Haydon. He was handsome, but almost too perfect. He'd obviously had it easy in life and had never felt the need for any old-fashioned charm. Victoria shuddered inwardly. He was not going to find her easy; he was going to find her impossible. She picked up another journal, the last of a pile in front of her.

The British School in Athens, where they had been since ten o'clock this morning, was situated not far from Aristotle Leondaris's flat in much the same sort of leafy street. Its library – devoted to classical archaeology – was on the ground floor. Haydon, to do him justice, had got them in here without raising any suspicions. He had produced his embassy card and explained that Victoria was from the National Audit Office, a government outfit whose job it was to assess whether the taxpayer was getting his money's worth from various governmental agencies. This was a clever ruse because it was in the nature of things that people from the audit office should turn up unannounced and meant that Victoria was given total access and left completely alone. Together, she and Haydon were going through piles of academic journals, looking for references to Kolettis, anything that might lead them to him. It was already close to four o'clock. The library closed at five, although Victoria reckoned that if she insisted upon it they would stay open for her, given what she was supposed to be. But it wasn't necessary; they were at the end of the journals. They had delved systematically through all the recent archaeological journals – but to no purpose. Kolettis appeared to have published nothing in the past two years. She closed the final journal. There was nothing in that, either.

Victoria sat back. Now what? She was looking for an archaeologist but was supposed to be from the audit office. What else could she ask to see?

Several things occurred to her. She got up and approached the librarian. 'You have people on digs – right? Do you publish reports? . . . May I see them, please? Do you publish a newsletter? May I see the subscription list as well? What other records do you have?'

'We hold conferences from time to time – there are lists of lecturers and the people who attend. And we have press cuttings.'

'Yes, I'll see all of those,' replied Victoria.

The folders were brought. Victoria took the conference brochures and gave Haydon the cuttings. However, there were far more cuttings than brochures and Victoria had gone through her bundle long before Haydon had finished his. She reached forward and took a fistful from the pile he had not yet examined. It was immediately clear that the cuttings had not been put into any order of date or subject. But, whether from Greek newspapers or British ones, they all related in some way to the classical world. There were reports of excavations, reports of conferences, reports of classical antiquities sold at auction. There were book reviews, travel features relating to 'cultural holidays' in Greece, and there were concert reviews of performances played in ancient Greek amphitheatres. Victoria did not at first realize that Professor X. D. Kolettis was the name she was looking for and she went on to the next cutting. But then, a slight sweat breaking out above her upper lip, she turned back. It was a cutting taken from a Greek newspaper and it appeared to be a leader article entitled 'Bleak future for a glorious past'. Victoria scanned the contents. It was a polemical piece chiding the Greek government in colourful language for its lacklustre support for archaeology. It held nothing of material interest for Victoria save the fact that its tone and subject matter confirmed that Kolettis was politically aware and prepared to be involved.

Her pulse began to slacken again. She shoved the cutting over towards the pile made up of things she had read. As she did so, however, she noticed two lines at the foot of the article which had been set in italic type: 'The author is currently at work researching a new biography of Praxiteles.' She turned it around and passed it to Haydon.

He scrutinized it, then said: 'So? Praxiteles was a famous sculptor. There's a restaurant named after him in the Kallithea district. We could have dinner there tonight.' He grinned.

Victoria shook her head. 'See the date. The cutting is only six months old. If he's on a dig it has to be something to do with the sculptor. I don't know anything about Praxiteles – but I know someone who does.'

'David Eady!'

The Shadow Arts Minister stood his ground as the six or seven other MPs who had been trying to attract the Speaker's attention all sat down. Briefly, he acknowledged the cheers from his own party's backbenchers. They knew what was coming and were looking forward to the government's embarrassment. The hubbub in the chamber fell as low as it ever did and he took advantage of that. 'Mr Speaker, will the Prime Minister please confirm or deny a report in last Sunday's press that his government is considering returning the Elgin Marbles from the British Museum, where they are currently on display, to Greece?'

As he sat down the hubbub rose again. Members not already in the chamber crowded behind the Speaker's chair to hear Lockwood's reply.

Lockwood rose and stepped forward. Three-twenty. In ten minutes the operation on his grandson would begin. Lockwood's hands clasped the dispatch box. His face was shiny, as if he had just stepped out of the shower. Or was sweating. 'Mr Speaker,

I can confirm that the government is *considering* returning these sculptures to Greece . . . but no decision has yet been – '

The rest of his words were drowned in the din created by the opposition. A deep roar filled the chamber, an angry noise spattered with old-fashioned cries of 'Shame!'

'Order! *Order!*' shouted the Speaker. 'Order!' He let the noise ride for a while. There was no way Lockwood could be heard above the row. The Prime Minister took a step back and sat down. He stared at the dispatch box in front of him.

The Speaker stood up. House of Commons protocol dictated that now every other member must be seated. 'Order, order,' he said and this time he was heard and obeyed. 'The Prime Minister!' he shouted, and sat down again.

'Thank you, Mr Speaker,' said Lockwood and then sped right on before anyone could interrupt him again. 'No decision has been taken yet on this difficult matter. There are arguments on either – '

David Eady was on his feet again and Lockwood gave way, sitting on the edge of his bench. 'If no decision has been taken, why did the chairman of the Friends of the Museum see fit to organize a demonstration outside the building yesterday – a demonstration that resulted in injury and arrest? Why were the Trustees not informed of the government's thinking on this matter? Why have Trustees at all if they are to be treated in this way?'

A second roar now broke out behind and above Eady as the backbenchers of his own party voiced their approval of his line of attack. The Prime Minister stood up and waited for this second commotion to die down. 'This is a delicate matter – '

Another roar from opposite. 'Only if you are up to no good,' shouted someone.

'Order!'

'This is a delicate matter, Mr Speaker. The House will appreciate, I hope, that there are diplomatic and political matters which I cannot go into at this moment but which have an important bearing on the conduct of policy. That is all I feel I can say just now.'

Eady was on his feet again. 'The Prime Minister is clearly speaking in code, Mr Speaker, or classical Greek for all I know. Could he please decipher that gobbledegook for the benefit of the House.'

'It wasn't Greek,' said the Speaker with a twinkle. Everyone knew he had been a professor of classics before he took to politics. But as he said this he looked at Lockwood.

The Prime Minister put one hand on the dispatch box and said, 'That is all I feel able to say at the moment, Mr Speaker.'

'Will the Prime Minister – '

'Roger Dempsey!'

A government backbencher rose to his feet. He was the Member for Wirral. 'Will the Prime Minister confirm that the agricultural subsidy cannot – '

His words were drowned in a groan from the opposition benches. They had been looking forward to seeing the PM baited some more, but now the House had moved on and the moment was lost.

Lockwood leaned along the front bench so that his head was close to Hatfield's. 'Off the hook for a few hours,' he whispered. 'Is Dempsey one of your tame lions?'

The Chief Whip said nothing. But he winked.

'I'm sorry but I didn't recognize your voice.'

'You're the one who's elusive. A different town or church or sculpture every day. You're like a gypsy.'

'But without a crystal ball. Or a caravan or violin, come to that.'

'You're obviously itinerant, though. Restless or nervous?'

There was a pause. Had Edward gone too far?

'I'm not nervous. Woodie. Why would I be nervous? That's an odd thing to say. Restless, yes. I miss you.'

'Well . . . here I am.'

'So, let's start again. Hello, Woodie. How lovely to hear you at last. You can't get any gossip out of a machine. What's the gossip in London town?'

Careful, thought Edward. Was that a leading question? He played safe. 'Oh, Hillier is recovering, so I'll be able to get back to research soon. I've had an invitation to go to Romania – to give a lecture on the Royal Collection. Some Belgian thinks that one of our Rubenses is a fake. Paxton & Whitfield ran out of Parmesan cheese – that's the worst news so far.'

Nancy chuckled. 'What about the demo at the British Museum? What do you think will happen?'

'Can't say,' breathed Edward, trying to sound as relaxed and offhand as possible. Nancy's question was natural – but it could have been a probe.

'Do the British like art that much, Woodie? Do you really care whether the Elgin Marbles go or stay?'

'You tell me, Nancy. You've been here a while now. What do you think?'

'I'm biased, Woodie.'

What did *that* mean? 'Oh yes?'

'Sculpture's my subject. I'm bound to think the Marbles belong on the Acropolis.'

She was leading the conversation neatly, Edward recognized. And trying to pick his brain. At the same time, she had just given him a motive for why she might have joined this bunch of . . .

But all he said was, 'I'm glad I'm not Lockwood.'

'I'm glad you're not Lockwood too. He's so *small*. I like tall blonds. What about the weekend, Woodie?'

'Where will you be?'

'I'm not exactly sure. Here in Yorkshire, or further north. Durham, Northumberland.'

'Book a room somewhere, just to be on the safe side. A double room.'

Did she hesitate? Had she caught the tone in his voice? Maybe that crack had been a mistake. God! How Edward hated this fencing.

'Okay,' she said, and if there was a delay in her reply it was very brief. 'I'll tell you when I've done it. Get into another clinch with the machine, no doubt.'

'Fine. Till tomorrow, then.'

'Goodbye, Woodie.'

Edward put down the receiver. Something Nancy had said itched at the back of his brain. What was it? Something . . . something out of the ordinary . . . something Nancy had said that she normally didn't say. He swallowed hard. Normally, when she wound up a conversation she used that Americanism, 'So long'. Not this time. This time it had been 'Goodbye'.

O'Day shifted in the passenger seat of the Toyota, trying to get comfortable. Given his height and the cramped dimensions of

Riley's car, that was virtually impossible. 'If this goes on much longer,' he groaned, 'we're going to have to get a bigger car.'

They had been waiting for more than six hours. Once they had found Zakros's name in that restaurant, the Greifen, they had prepared to stomp around all the hotels once more, to find out where he was staying. Riley, however, had first called the phone company on the offchance that he had rented a house with a phone. *Bingo!*

'Why a house?' O'Day had wondered out loud.

'I can think of two reasons,' said Riley. 'One, it's cheaper, much cheaper, if you are staying around for more than a few days. Two, it's better security. When they first got these pictures, they may have needed to examine their condition, to check that they were not damaged in any way and that they were genuine. It would have been a risk traipsing them in and out of hotels.'

O'Day nodded, agreeing.

There was no car outside the house, no one had come or gone since they had been there, so they were waiting for dark, in an hour's time at around nine o'clock, to see whether any lights came on. That would tell them if he was home or not.

'Not your usual line, is it?' asked Riley, with a sideways glance at O'Day.

'Fieldwork, you mean? Legwork? Not any more, no. But security on this is as tight as a moneylender's fist. O'Day sucked his teeth and squinted through the windscreen. 'If this Zakros isn't at home . . . we might indulge ourselves later.'

'Well, we've survived another twenty-four hours.' Lockwood surveyed the room from his regular vantage point, leaning on the mantelshelf. 'Thanks to Joss here, Question Time was nowhere near as messy as it might have been. What are tomorrow's papers saying, Bernie?'

'That you were let off the hook, that the opposition weren't allowed to nail you, that the Chief Whip displayed some sharp practice with Dempsey. The Greek emissary was in the House, by the way. He said he thought the Commons was a game and he is still pressing for an appointment.'

'Let him press. The blackmailers have held off. They haven't been in touch either but at least we are all still in jobs for the time being, Andover included. In fact, Dr Andover has been quite busy today. He rang me just before lunch to say that O'Day and Riley, in Basle, have got a name – Nicos Zakros – for the Swiss end of the team. So we are half a pace forward and no further back.' Lockwood glanced at Edward. 'And what have you got to say for yourself this time?'

Edward felt himself blushing. 'I've heard from Athens, too. Victoria Tatton came across a newspaper cutting in the library of the British School which was only six months old and said that Kolettis is researching a new biography of Praxiteles.'

Lockwood stared at him. 'Forgive me, Dr Andover, but what good does that do us? Unless I'm very much mistaken, Praxiteles has been dead for . . . two-thousand-odd years.'

'Yes, sir. But . . . you're forgetting that when Victoria called Thessaloniki University she was told that Kolettis was away on a dig. That may have been moonshine, of course – but say it wasn't. Whatever you think of Kolettis, he *is* a scholar. There have been lots of biographies of Praxiteles . . . therefore Kolettis would only produce another one under a particular set of circumstances: *he has discovered something new!*'

Lockwood looked puzzled. 'And this is relevant because . . . ?'

'*Because* Praxiteles only worked at a small number of sites. I haven't had a chance to check them all out, but as soon as the libraries open tomorrow morning it shouldn't take more than an hour to narrow down the places where Kolettis should be.'

Lockwood stared at Edward, who couldn't immediately read the Prime Minister's expression. At length he shook his head. 'That's about the most fanciful piece of reasoning I've heard in a long time. Thank God I've got O'Day in Basle to rely on.'

Haydon stood in the shadow and watched as the policeman strolled down the street. The Greek police were not so different from their British counterparts. These days even a backbench MP got some special treatment, even if it was only the fact that the local patrolman kept a closer eye on the politician's home than those of ordinary, non-political souls.

Haydon's eyes had adjusted to the gloom and he watched the policeman disappear into the night. There wasn't quite enough light to read his watch but he reckoned it must be after two. The houses were quite large in the part of Athens where Stamatis

Leondaris lived. There were small gardens at the front, rimmed by a wall as high as a man.

Haydon gripped the skeleton keys in his pocket and moved from one set of shadows to another. Apart from the sound of a train in the distance, all was still. He approached the small wrought-iron gate that gave entrance to the garden. He undid the latch and pushed it back. The gate whined on its hinges and for a moment Haydon stepped back again, into the deeper shadow. He waited.

He let fifteen minutes go by. The noise of the gate did not appear to have set off any dog that might have been hiding in the shadows of the house. As more time went by, there was no sound of movement from within the house; Leondaris and his wife were deep asleep. Haydon hadn't told Victoria what he had in mind; he would rather surprise her in the morning – if he found out anything.

After fifteen minutes he moved forward. His movements were tidy, rapid and economical. He hurried down the path, then to the side of the house where there was an entrance beneath an architrave. Haydon inspected the door. It was mainly glass. He found the keyhole, inserted one of his skeleton keys into the lock, and manoeuvred it until he felt the lock give way. He turned the handle.

The door wouldn't budge. He didn't curse or sweat. He moved on round to the back of the house. The side door was obviously bolted as well as locked. If the other doors were like that, he was lost.

The back door was on a kind of porch, or 'deck' as his American friends would have said. He approached the door and without any delay inserted the skeleton key into the lock. As before he manipulated the rod until he felt movement inside the lock. He tried the door handle: the door wouldn't give. It was only as he turned away that a thought struck him. He tried the skeleton key in the lock again, felt movement a second time and immediately pressed on the door. It swung open. It had been *open* all along.

He didn't dwell on it but moved rapidly into the house. The door gave on to an eating-room with the kitchen opening off that. Haydon passed quickly through both. He reached a hall or corridor. Along the passage he could see the front door and the staircase. Opposite was another door, open. Haydon saw immediately that this was what he was looking for: the study.

He stepped inside. This was a well-organized room – a large desk with stacks of papers, bookshelves crammed with books, pamphlets, large-format art books. He knew by now, from the embassy's reference library, that Leondaris's wife was a jeweller, and he could see that some of these books were on precious stones. He had seen her workshop across the garden at the back, but clearly she kept some of her books here.

On the desk there was a small stack of opened letters, with an airline ticket on top and a passport. Next to the passport was an expensive pen and a watch, both of which Haydon immediately pocketed. He wasn't a thief, but in case he was disturbed a few valuables would help cast him in the role of a thief and deflect attention from what he was really interested in.

As he was pocketing the pen, he also noticed, in the wall between two of the shelves, a small safe. Now *this* was interesting. He smiled. The safe was British and he knew the model well. He put his ear to the dial and listened carefully, concentrating hard. The difference in sound when he moved the dial to the right position would be miniscule and the feel in his fingertips would be the lightest of touches.

It took him more than fifteen minutes to feel the first one. That was always the most difficult, however. Now he knew how the dial *felt*. How many numbers would there be? Five? Six? Eight? He couldn't remember from his training but this wasn't a new model. Six, he guessed.

Within half an hour he had three done: two, three, zero. Then he had a thought. He went back to the desk and picked up Leondaris's passport. He opened it and found what he was looking for. Leondaris was born on 23 May 1950 – 23.05.50. It was embarrassingly simple.

He went back to the safe, turned it to five, five again, then zero. He pulled on the door – and it swung open.

Haydon grunted in pleasure at his own cleverness and reached inside. He came first to some small velvet bags. He opened one and a large gem fell into the palm of his hand. More of Leondaris's wife's handiwork. He put the stone into his pocket and then emptied another little pouch. This time there were three small stones but they still caught what light was going in the darkened study: diamonds. They too went into his jacket pocket.

But now he turned back to the safe. His fingers searched the space at the back and touched some smooth cardboard folders.

Ah! Was this what he was looking for? He moved more little pouches out of the way and gripped the documents.

At that moment, a red flash seemed to erupt inside his head and a hot pain zipped across his skull. He went to cry out but had barely begun when his breath was cut short. The dark-red world went black.

Edward nodded to the policeman at the gate of Kensington Palace. He was becoming familiar with the night staff. The midnight committee was giving him very late nights and keeping him away from the Albatross. Not that he was tired – far from it. Lockwood's tone in Downing Street had been upsetting and demeaning.

Edward walked around the side of the palace, parallel to a wall with some rosebeds adjoining it. He unlocked a door which led to his staircase, climbed the steps and let himself into his flat. It was more untidy than ever. Dictionaries and other reference books stood in their own pile next to his desk.

The glow of the answering machine greeted him. He walked over to it: a figure 1 stared up at him. Not Nancy again? He pressed the button.

'Edward, it's Barbra. Call me – I've got a surprise for you.'

He looked at his watch. One-thirty a.m. in London meant it was five-thirty, early evening, in California. Barbra would probably still be in her office.

She was. 'Look,' she said, after the briefest of greetings, 'I've turned over all my contacts – everything and everyone from the phone book to the local CIA resident. So I can categorically tell you that there is no Tucker Icecream Company, no Trucco Icecream Company or any variant, anywhere in California between Stanford in the south and Mendocino, which is some 160 miles north of the Golden Gate. There are several Tuckers in the book, of course and there's a Tucker's Timber, a Tucker's Grain Company and a Tucker & Peabody Law Firm. But I can't find a Nancy Tucker anywhere, not in the places I've tried, anyway.'

Edward closed his eyes. 'And Trucco? What about Trucco?'

'Only one – and that's a man. Aldo Trucco, MD.'

Edward massaged an eye with the ball of his hand. Barbra's news appeared to settle things. 'Thank you,' he said softly. 'And I won't forget I owe you a favour.'

'Now, on that, you may be able to help, sooner rather than later. We've been gazumped on the Ferrari. Some Italian offered a hundred thousand dollars more than your father. He's livid but won't compete. Which means,' she added, a note of triumph creeping into her voice, 'which means that a picture is back on the agenda. I want you and me to choose something together. Think of something suitable I might like and can eventually persuade your father to like – yes?'

'I'll do my best, Barbra. Can you give me a couple of weeks to come up with something?'

'Great. Well, it must be late in London. You'd better get some sleep.'

After he had rung off, sleep still seemed a long way away. Nancy *had* to be involved. Barbra's evidence confirmed everything that had gone before. But how could Edward tell anyone now? If he did, what with his delay and his mistake over the negotiations, Lockwood would go wild. Edward himself might even become a suspect.

As he stood by the window of his flat, looking down on the policeman he had greeted moments before, another conviction took root inside him. Nancy had deceived everyone, but Edward most of all. *She* had singled *him* out. If he told Leith or Lockwood, he would certainly be made a scapegoat, should anything go wrong, and then they would deal with Nancy. He didn't want that. He would deal with Nancy himself.

'Will there be an alarm?' O'Day inspected his watch. It was just coming up to two-thirty.

'This is Switzerland,' whispered Riley. 'They have alarms on their wallets.'

Both men were dressed in their darkest clothes. That afternoon they had bought dark caps, leather gloves, long silk scarves to wind around their heads to obscure their faces below their eyes. They had watched Zakros's house from two in the afternoon until dark. No lights had come on, so he wasn't at home. They had waited until now to be certain he wasn't coming back and to give everyone in the street time to slip into their deepest slumber.

'Let's finish the soup and get started,' grumbled O'Day. 'It could take a while to unscramble the alarm.'

Riley passed him the thermos flask which contained the remains of the soup. He himself took a nip of whisky from a flask and held it out to O'Day.

The other man shook his head as he swigged down the soup. He took a breath. 'Afterwards.'

He put the cap back on the thermos, set it down on the back seat of the car and slipped on his gloves. He wound the scarf around his head and put on the cap, pulling it well down. Riley did much the same. They got out of the car, eased the doors shut, but did not lock them. They walked quickly across the road and were soon in among the shadows of the trees surrounding the house. They split up, O'Day going to the right, Riley to the left, as they had agreed in advance. A few minutes later they came across each other at the back of the building.

'I have what looks like a window into a small loo on the ground floor, steps down to a basement and these french windows just here, which open into a dining-room.'

O'Day thought for a moment. 'I think I may have something better. Look.' He retreated the way he had come, with Riley following. He stopped outside a big sash window made up of small panes of glass. 'I think this is the study. Anyway, there are curtains on the inside, with a pelmet. The pelmet covers the top layer of panes.'

Riley nodded. He knew what O'Day meant. O'Day took a large sheet of plastic wrapping which they had bought on their way to Zakros's house, along with a glazier's knife. He laid the plastic sheeting under the window.

O'Day took the glazier's knife from his pocket and climbed on to the window-sill. With one hand he held on to the window as he started to cut away at the putty round one of the panes in the top row. It was difficult work and having to do it one-handed didn't help. Flakes of dried putty fell on his hair and into his eyes, causing them to itch. He worked steadily, unhurriedly, telling himself he had hours if need be. Riley stood below, watching that the putty fell on to the sheet, breaking off every now and then to scurry to the trees at the front of the house and check that there was no one else about.

After perhaps forty minutes, O'Day handed down the knife and said, simply, 'Tape.' Riley handed up a role of heavy-duty masking tape they had bought that afternoon in the same shop as the other things. O'Day unrolled a length of tape, then tore it off with his teeth. He flattened the strip against the window-pane but left about six inches free, twisting it to give it added strength. He repeated this five or six times, spreading the tape out over the pane of glass in a rosette. Each strip was left with a loose, twisted piece near the centre. When the circle was complete, he passed the roll of tape back down to Riley.

'Ready,' he whispered. He gathered up all the loose strips into his one hand. With the other he gripped the window for balance. Then he began to pull. The window budged and he thought it was going to come. But no, it held.

He saw a place where putty jutted out from the window-frame. 'Knife!' he called down. He cleared the putty and returned the knife to Riley, who laid it carefully on the plastic sheeting. They would replace it later, if they had the chance. He gathered the strands of tape and pulled again. This time, after a moment's pause, the pane came away. One or two of the strips dislodged from the glass but enough of them held to prevent the pane falling to the ground. He lowered it to Riley. Now O'Day got down from the window-sill and took off his shoes. He climbed back on the sill and, using the frame where the glass was missing as his holding-point, he put his weight on one of the lower frames and lifted himself up. The open pane was too small for him to crawl through but instead he reached inside and undid the clip that fastened the top half of the sash window to the bottom half. He got down again and put on his shoes. 'Now, the alarm,' he whispered. 'That's your department.'

'It will be an infra-red alarm,' replied Riley. 'One that detects movement or sudden changes in temperature. Leave the window an inch open for half an hour. With the air that gets in through the pane you removed, and through the gap between the two halves of the frame, the temperature will go down, but too slowly to trigger the alarm.'

'You mean we've got to wait for another – '

'Yes.'

And so they waited. They were good at that.

At half past three, Riley got up from where he had been sitting against the wall of the house. 'Now, here's the plan. Ninety-nine people out of a hundred have their alarms set to cover only the main rooms and the stairs. Burglars have to move around via the stairs, after all. Also, nine hundred and ninety-nine people out of a thousand have the control panel of their alarms somewhere in the hall – usually you've got to be able to reach it within thirty or forty seconds. To judge from the layout of the house, our man's control panel is either in this room here or somewhere in the main hall next to it.'

'And if it isn't?'

'It isn't. We're sunk.'

Riley eased the window up a little more and waited. No wail from the alarm. Gingerly he rolled himself through the gap and dropped gently on to the floor inside. He stayed there for a while, letting his eyes adjust and surveying the room. It *was* a study. A desk, easy chairs, a computer. Bookshelves and a filing cabinet. He scanned the room but he already knew there was no sensor unit in here; otherwise it would have detected him the minute he dropped through the window. But the control panel might be in a desk drawer or a filing cabinet. He walked across. There was no control panel in any of the desk drawers. There was no control panel in the filing cabinet. There was nowhere else it could be in the study.

Riley grunted. Now it got tricky. The panel must be in the hall and there would certainly be a sensor there. Fortunately, the door between the study and the hall was open. That might have been awkward, if he had had to pull back the door; that alone could trigger the alarm. He dropped to the floor and started to crawl forward. This wasn't foolproof but it did minimize the risk that he would be detected by a sensor. He inched towards the door, a wider vista of the hall opening up before him as he did so. There were some stairs, there was a table with some flowers on it – a light from the street shone in through the glass in the front door. Beyond the stairs was a desk, untidy with papers. This was more like it. There was a phone on the desk, more bookshelves lining the wall by the desk. But Riley's eye fixed upon a small door beneath the bookshelves. A small cupboard – perfect for a control panel. He inched forward further – *there it was*! He jerked back, his breath producing a reedy sound in his throat. A tiny red eye was affixed to the cornice, above a door that led out to the garden at the back of the house. The sensor, exactly where he would have put it himself. Although he had been momentarily disconcerted by the red bead, now – as he got to his feet – he reflected that it was, in its way, reassuring. The owner of the house had employed an alarm company which appeared to be very conventional in its habits. That could mean

– he prayed it *would* mean – that they also sited the control panels in conventional places too. Like that cupboard near the desk.

Riley now took from his pocket a small tube, barely three inches long. From that he extracted a very fine metal rod, thinner than a refill for a ballpoint pen. He slid the end of it back and forth, to check that it was working. At the far end a small metal circle opened out, like a tiny umbrella. He repeated the process several times. Satisfied that it was working smoothly, he set it down on the desk in the study. Now he took from another pocket a small metal container, shaped not unlike a Coca-Cola bottle, except that this had a thin spout on the end and what looked like a trigger. He depressed the trigger for the briefest moment and a fierce whoosh of compressed air shot out of the nozzle. Satisfied that his tools were working, he went back to the window.

'O'Day!'

O'Day emerged from the shadow he had been hiding in. 'Here.'

'In a very short while this alarm will start to pulse, before it screams, unless it's rigged to the police station only. I want you to go and start the car. If I'm not galloping across the road in thirty seconds, which is all I've got, stop the car and come back. It will mean I've fixed the alarm. Clear?'

'Yes.'

'I won't make a move until I hear you start the car.'

O'Day walked back across the road, got into the car and switched on the engine.

Riley stood near the door to the hall, just out of range of the red eye, and juggled his tools in his hands, getting the feel of them. As soon as he stepped into the hall a pulse would beat throughout the house. Within thirty seconds, forty at the most, that pulse would burst into a screeching wail and, most likely, set off a bell at the local police station. All alarms gave their owners a period of grace, so they could deactivate them with a simple key. Even if he was right and the control panel, with the all-important lock, was in the cupboard next to the desk, he wouldn't have time to pick the lock. That was where the 'umbrella' and metal bottle came in. He gripped them more tightly, counted to three and rushed into the hall.

He was four steps down the corridor before the pulses started, like someone insistently banging the wrong key on a computer.

Four more steps and he had reached the cupboard. He yanked back the door – *yes!* the control panel was there. He put the bottle on the carpet as he knelt down. Quickly, he reached towards the lock and inserted the metal rod. He missed the first time! The pulses were still insistently throbbing down the hall – ten seconds must have elapsed already. His fingers found the lock and hurriedly he inserted the rod. If it jammed almost immediately, it meant the lock had a blind end and he wouldn't need the rod. No, the rod slid through until it must have come out the other side. He slid the slot at the end so that the 'umbrella' would have opened. Now he pulled the rod *towards* him until it would come no further. The 'umbrella' now covered the other end of the lock, converting the chamber into a closed cul-de-sac. Fifteen seconds. Holding the metal rod with his left hand and pulling it towards him as hard as he could, he picked up the bottle. He manoeuvred the nozzle into the keyhole of the lock below the other metal rod. Seventeen seconds. Now, as he pulled hard again with his left hand, he pressed the trigger of the bottle with his right thumb. A hissing sound filled the hallway as the jet of high-pressure air zoomed into the lock. The theory was simple: the pressurized air would force itself against the entire surface of the lock interior, making any movable parts yield. The only problem was whether the 'umbrella' was wedged tightly enough against the back of the lock, and whether the parts of the lock itself fitted snugly together, preventing too much air escaping and making the pressure drop. Riley counted to four to give the jet a chance to work.

The pulse raced on, ricocheting around the hall. Twenty-one seconds.

He stopped the air, slackened his grip on the metal rod and twisted the 'umbrella' into a different position. Then he pulled hard on the rod again. Twenty-three seconds. He jabbed the nozzle against the mouth of the lock for the second time. He pressed his thumb against the trigger and held it there. The hissing all but drowned out the pulsing sound, but not quite. And then it did. The pulse had stopped and now only the hissing, the awful hissing was to be heard. The lock parts had moved. Riley eased back his thumb.

Not a sound, save his own breathing, disturbed the night there in the hall. Calmly, he pocketed his tools. With his handkerchief he wiped the front of the lock so as to obscure and minimize any scratches he might have inflicted on the metal barrel. He closed the door. Then he went back to the study.

O'Day was outside the window. He rolled through. 'Brilliant.'

Riley bowed slightly. He looked at his watch. 'Quarter to four. Let's work together – it's easier to communicate if we're disturbed. We'll start at the top.'

Upstairs there were four bedrooms and as many bathrooms. Two bedrooms were empty, save for carpets and curtains. Zakros obviously hardly ever did any entertaining. There was one guest bedroom but that was scarcely any different from the other rooms – just an empty room with a bed.

The next room was the master bedroom. O'Day went to the cupboards. Rows of suits, lines of shoes, maybe twenty ties. Shirts, underpants, socks, black in one drawer, red in another, yellow in a third. 'Bit of a ponce, our Zak.'

Riley was in the bathroom by now. 'Enough cologne to sweeten an elephant,' he said. But there was nothing to help them. He went back to the bedroom, looked under the bed and then delved into the cupboards either side of the headboard. Magazines, a soft-porn movie, tapes and videotapes, a pair of black Porsche sunglasses. A pair of ski gloves and a pocket calculator. Discarded toys of a grown-up. 'Okay, downstairs. We can split up there. I'll take the kitchen and dining-room, you do the living-room. We'll rendezvous in the study and make our exit from there.'

'No, let's turn the study over straight away. Zakros is only a lodger here. The study is the only room he spends any time in. Come on, you know I'm right.'

O'Day led the way. When they reached the study he said, 'You look through the books. I'll do the desk.'

For twenty minutes they worked in silence. O'Day went through each of the drawers in the pedestal desk, carefully taking out any papers or documents and then replacing them in exactly the same arrangement as he had found them. After half an hour he had finished. 'Nothing here.'

'Same here.'

'It's a quarter to five. Be light soon. Better think about leaving. Can you reset the alarm?'

'Oh yes.' He held up his skeleton keys. 'I've got all the time in the world now to play with these.'

'Right, let's move, then. We should have known, I suppose, that he would be too canny to leave anything incriminating lying around. I'll just close these drawers and make sure the desk is tidy and free of scratches.'

The blotter had been dislodged in all the activity and a lamp had been moved. O'Day rearranged both objects. 'Ready?'

There was no reply from across the room.

'Riley! What is it?'

'A book on Blunt.'

'A coincidence, I agree. But hardly incriminating – '

'There's a paper inside the front cover.'

O'Day said nothing. Riley came towards him with his hand held out. 'It's an envelope, addressed to him . . . Look.'

'Yes. But I don't – '

'Look at the postmark. It's one of those special franking devices. Look where the letter was posted from.'

O'Day was already looking up at Riley. 'Zakros has a penfriend in the British Museum.'

15

Wednesday

'Haydon has disappeared!'

Edward's hand, holding the phone, went clammy. 'You're sure? What happened?'

Victoria's voice was trembling. 'I don't know what happened. We had an early dinner together last night, and then he dropped me at the hotel. He was coming over for breakfast this morning and we were going to head out of Athens, after I had talked to you, to wherever the Praxiteles sites are. He didn't show, so I called his flat. No reply, so I called the embassy. He's not been there today.'

'That doesn't mean he's disappeared.'

'Edward! I went to his flat. He's not there – his bed hadn't been slept in and his car is not in its parking slot. He went somewhere last night and hasn't come back.'

'Maybe he's with a woman.'

'And maybe I'm a trombone! Haydon's a professional, Edward. Even if he was with a woman last night, he'd still have been here this morning.'

Edward said nothing and, after a pause, Victoria went on. 'What frightens me is this: if they knew about Haydon, *how* did they know? And do they know about me?'

'Don't worry,' said Edward as soothingly as he knew how, though he was growing anxious himself. 'There may be another explanation.' He thought fast. 'I'd better talk to Lockwood, as soon as I can. You stay in the hotel – you must be safe there. I'll get back to you. Soonest.'

He rang off and instructed Wilma to call Number Ten. While she was doing this – as naturally as if she had been doing it all her life – he stared out of the studio, across the slate roofs of the palace. If anything had happened to Haydon . . . his mind turned to Nancy. What if she did know? What was her role in all this? How . . . how tough was she?

Edward's phone flashed and he snatched at it.

Wilma said, 'It's Midwinter.'

Edward had already called the press officer once this morning and relayed O'Day's worrying news about another Apollo Brigade member inside the British Museum. Now he had more bad news.

Midwinter, however, got in first. 'They've gone public.'

Edward winced. 'Oh, no!'

'Yes – but in an odd way. A Vienna newspaper received a key yesterday; it was dropped off at their editorial offices, with a note to say that it fitted a left-luggage locker at the main railway station and that inside the locker they would find a front-page story.'

'And – ?'

'They did. It's all over the *Wiener Zeitung* this morning. Our embassy there faxed it over to us a short while ago. The locker contained two things. There was a painting, by Rubens, of the Annunciation. It was apparently looted by the Nazis during the war from the Kunsthistorisches Museum in Vienna. You can imagine the fuss they are making in Austria. It's like the return of a kidnapped son or daughter.'

'And what was the second thing? You said the locker contained two things.'

'Yes, and very ominous it was too. With the Rubens, there was a photograph – showing the Duke of Windsor with Hitler.'

'Jesus! What does the *Wiener Zeitung* make of that?'

'Nothing. Not for the moment, anyway. They know nothing, so they are puzzled. But they have reported it, on page one. Which means that any number of people may read it.'

'It's a sort of warning – yes? It suggests they are not going public with everything . . . that they will be in touch again.' Edward felt a weight lift. Till he remembered Haydon.

'Let's hope so. The story will probably be reported on British television tonight and in the rest of the world's press tomorrow. Other people may begin to put two and two together. But, by and large – yes, I suppose this is good news.'

'Hmm,' Edward grunted. 'And I'm afraid I've got some bad news. Lockwood should be informed immediately.' And he told Midwinter about Haydon's disappearance.

Midwinter groaned. 'How did they know? How could they know?'

'We can't be certain they did know. But I suppose we must assume so.'

'It's too much of a coincidence – and you realize that this cancels out the Vienna business, don't you?'

Midwinter groaned again. 'I'd better get on to Lockwood. It looks all over to me.' He rang off.

Victoria opened the door of her room and peered around the frame. The corridor was empty. She stepped out and locked the door behind her. She hurried to the lift and pressed the button. Waiting for it to arrive, she kept glancing nervously along the corridor to be sure that she was alone. Victoria had still not heard from Haydon and it was now coming up to seven o'clock. Neither had the embassy heard and it was now closed. There was still no reply from Haydon's flat. Edward was probably right to say she was safer in the hotel – but that rather depended on how much the other side knew, and whether they had established links between Haydon and herself.

She had felt fairly safe in her room while it was daylight, but now that it was getting dark she didn't feel quite so happy. She had decided to transfer downstairs, to the sitting area near the lobby where there were lots of people. She had left word with reception so that they knew where to find her if London called.

At last the lift arrived and the doors slid back.

Victoria was startled to see two women inside. They looked like tourists but . . . she had no choice other than to get in. One smiled at her and she began to relax. But then she felt the lift move *up!* She tensed all over again: they simply couldn't have known she was about to enter the lift – could they? Two floors up, the lift stopped and the women got out. Victoria pressed the button for the ground floor and the doors slid shut. The lift began to descend – only to stop at the floor where Victoria's room was located. The doors opened – to reveal two men, obviously Greeks, waiting. Victoria wanted to scream. The men entered without speaking and stood on either side of her. She held her breath. Should she dash out of the lift at the last moment? But the doors slid shut and it was too late.

The three of them sank down through the floors. The men didn't move or speak. Were they waiting until they reached the lobby, when they would forcibly 'escort' her outside? How did they know what she looked like?

They reached the lobby and the doors opened. The men didn't

176

move. What were they waiting for? Then one said to her, in Greek, 'After you.'

She stepped forward and turned right, towards the hotel shop. Were the men following? She half turned and looked back. No – thank God. They joined two women who had been waiting and were making for the hotel's main door. As Victoria relaxed, she felt her cheeks glow as her fear dissolved throughout her body.

At last she was surrounded by people. She had a book and looked for somewhere to sit, somewhere in the middle of a crowd but where she could hear easily enough if they paged her. She walked forward, past the shop. As she did so, the evening paper caught her eye. She bent and picked up a copy. It was folded in two and she turned it over. Suddenly she was frightened all over again. A face stared up at her at the foot of the front page, a face that she knew despite the fact that it was distorted. She read the headline. It said: 'Body of Frenchman found in sea.'

Edward contemplated the stone bust on the other side of the corridor. White marble, depicting Pitt the Younger, according to the caption. Parliament had quite a few works of art – hardly spectacular, but some good sculpture, quite a lot of rare books and a few decent pictures. Nothing quite as remarkable as the building itself. He looked along the corridor to the entrance to the chamber of the House of Commons. It was early evening and there was no shortage of MPs toing and froing.

Edward sat with Midwinter, Leith and Mordaunt. It had been a tense day, waiting to see the Prime Minister, made even worse when Victoria had rung an hour earlier with the news about Haydon. Lockwood was spending the evening at the House, since there was a crucial debate on the loans to Russia. Lockwood's parliamentary office, outside which the others were now gathered, was at the corner of the building, so that Edward could look along two corridors running at right angles to one another.

The door to Lockwood's office opened and Hatfield beckoned them in. The Prime Minister's inner office was square, with a low ceiling fashioned in elaborate stone patterns. Two leaded windows looked out over the river and the row of amber lights stretching across Westminster Bridge. What was the PM's mood?

Edward wondered. The grandson, he had been told, was in intensive care and not yet out of danger.

Lockwood waved them to seats but didn't speak until they were all settled. He turned to Slocombe. 'Eric?'

'I'm stumped, Bill. The news from Vienna this morning was encouraging in its way. The other side's response to Andover's mistake seemed to suggest that they had stepped up their threat – but weren't going fully public. In other words, we were still in business, still had a trade. But for Haydon, we could have expected another call tomorrow. The Haydon business, however, is a real joker in the pack.'

'What happened exactly?'

Slocombe looked at Edward.

'According to Victoria Tatton's account of the newspaper report, Haydon's body was found floating in Piraeus harbour. He was bound hand and foot and, although he died by drowning, he had been hit over the head before being thrown into the water.' Edward paused as they all took in the terrible details. 'Victoria Tatton told me that it was routine for Haydon to change his identification documents whenever he was doing something illegal or risky. That's why the Greek newspaper – and presumably the police – identified him as a Frenchman, Gilles Broudin. Victoria Tatton doesn't know what he was up to last night – he never told her. So I'm afraid we don't know who killed him or why, and what connection, if any, it has to the Elgin business.'

'That's why I say it's a joker, Bill.' Slocombe spoke again. 'Put yourself in the other side's shoes . . . This is speculation but that's all we've got to go on . . . You're nervous, tense. In the middle of a delicate and dangerous negotiation. Someone breaks into your house or your office, some sort of property belonging to one of your team. If that person was British you could be pretty certain you had been found out. But in this case the invader, the burglar maybe, is French. Or you think he is. Were you burgled for some other reason? Or was the Frenchman on contract to the British? Was he not a Frenchman at all? Or . . . final scenario . . . is Haydon's death nothing to do with the other business? Did he make enemies in Colombia who have finally caught up with him? Did he have hidden habits that were always likely to land him in trouble?' Slocombe sat back and patted his toupee gently.

No one else spoke.

'In a sense, of course, it's academic,' Slocombe eventually continued. 'There's nothing we can do except wait. We'll either get a call or we won't. This thing will either blow or it won't.'

Lockwood bit his lip. 'Eric, I agree that we are forced to wait for them to call. But that's not all we can do. I've had some ideas, so let's not be too negative.' He cocked his head at Midwinter. 'Tomorrow's papers.'

'Go further than the television did on tonight's news. All the serious papers have the Vienna Rubens story but the *Telegraph* and *The Times* each put it on the front page. The headline in the *Telegraph* is: "Mystery link between Duke and Nazi loot?" *The Times* doesn't go so far, but inside there's a piece about Windsor's war – which concludes that there is no known link between the Duke and any stolen masterpieces.'

Lockwood fiddled with a pen on his desk. 'Bloody close. Too close. Now,' he said, turning to the others, 'what about this Brigade member actually inside the museum itself? Do we have any ideas?'

Lockwood looked at Midwinter again. The press officer shook his head. 'There are seven hundred people at the BM and it could be anybody – '

'No, it bloody well couldn't. It has to be someone with access all over the place, it has to be somebody senior enough to use the museum franking machine. These people are not going to trust anyone. From what I've been told, all the others in this Brigade are middle class and politically involved. You can bet that whoever they've got at the BM will be the same. And maybe Greek, too.'

'Sir?' Edward sat up.

'Yes?' barked Lockwood.

'O'Day has already faxed us a copy of the envelope he took from Zakros's study, and he's sending us the original by courier. So we have a sample of the handwriting of the Brigade member who works at the British Museum. We can check that against the various people who fit our profile of suspects – '

Lockwood nodded his head. 'But how will you do that without alerting the suspect?'

'I know a bit about the BM – I helped organize an exhibition there a few months ago. There is a central archive for the museum, in the director's wing. A handwriting expert could go through each person's file, comparing scripts. We could send the expert into the museum during the day, along with masses of other visitors. The director could tell us in advance where the expert can hide while the museum is closing. We arrange for this expert to have a key to the archive. So long as he stays there all night and leaves next day when the museum is again thronged with people, there is no way anyone will even know he is there, apart from the director, that is.'

Lockwood again played with his fountain pen. 'Leith – you've got a handwriting expert, I take it?'

Leith nodded.

The Prime Minister sighed. 'The London end, and Basle, seem under control. As much under control as these things ever are. But what are we going to do about Athens? Victoria Tatton isn't enough.' He glanced at Edward. 'You really think Kolettis is on a dig, researching this . . . sculptor?'

'Praxiteles.' Edward shrugged. 'I can't think of a better plan.'

'Are you thinking we should send Andover?' Slocombe looked at Lockwood.

'O'Day would be best, but he's locked into Basle. Leith has to stay here, to advise on the negotiations – '

'If there are any,' whispered Midwinter.

'If there are any,' repeated Lockwood. 'Security is a first consideration. I'm terrified Keld will hear of this. He *mustn't*. We could send someone from O'Day's outfit but . . . if Andover is right and Kolettis *is* on a dig then some specialist knowledge might come in handy . . .'

'But what about the Brigade – how do we explain Andover's absence, and who will take over?' It was Midwinter again.

Lockwood looked from Edward to Mordaunt. 'We tell them what in fact nearly happened – that Andover has been fired. We say that, after his display of temper last time, when he lost control of himself, we have decided not to risk him again. That will show them how seriously we take their Vienna manoeuvre. We'll need an official alibi, too.' He looked at Mordaunt. 'Any ideas?'

Mordaunt sniffed. 'The Queen is scheduled to go to Berlin later this year. An exchange of paintings has been discussed. We could pretend Andover's gone to Germany to sort it out. I'll tell Hillier it had to be done now.'

Lockwood nodded. 'And I think it's about time the Palace took a more prominent role in the affair. Sir Francis, I think you should take over from Andover.'

Mordaunt's hand gripped his chin. 'I must of course ask Her Maj – '

'No! This issue is already taking up a great deal of government time. I want you on board, Mordaunt. Fully. We're in this together and that means you will take over from Andover. I'm sure Her Majesty would agree. If Andover is going to Greece, he's going first thing in the morning and you are going to cancel everything to be on hand, in case the Brigade do call. I hope I make myself very clear.'

Mordaunt returned Lockwood's stare and for a moment there was an icy silence in the room. But Mordaunt knew when he was beaten. He uncrossed his legs and smiled. 'Of course, Prime Minister . . . I shall be glad to help in any way I can.'

Lockwood grunted. 'So, we all hold our breath overnight to see what Haydon's death brings with it. Now, before we disperse, anything else?'

'Yes, there is.' All eyes turned to Hatfield. 'Owen Cutler bearded me in the House today. He's a trustee of the National Portrait Gallery, as you know, and therefore linked in to the art-world mafia. It seems there is an extraordinary meeting of the British Museum Trustees tomorrow. There's nothing we can do about it, of course, but I'm told there's a distinct possibility that some of them – maybe more than half – will resign.'

'I could get to like this street.'

'Aren't you the comedian. At least we've got better soup tonight.' Riley handed O'Day a mug. Earlier in the evening they had cruised past Zakros's house. It appeared as if it were still unoccupied. There was no police car outside, nothing looked as though it had been disturbed in any way. Accordingly, they had eaten a late dinner and returned to the road near the house at eleven. They had now been waiting for just over an hour, parked a little further away this time.

'Do you think he'll come now?' Riley continued. 'Why would he return home in the middle of the night? Surely he would stay somewhere warm and comfortable and then come on in the morning.'

'You're probably right,' answered O'Day. 'On the other hand, speed still matters above everything else. He must come back here at some stage and we can't afford to miss him. So we stay. More soup?'

Riley shook his head. 'These stake-outs don't get any easier, do they? Makes me wish I was in – oh, maybe the Riesbachli in Zurich. Fricassee of lobster, simmered in champagne – '

'Shut up!'

Riley chuckled. 'The longest I've ever been on a stake-out was eight whole days . . . Our tip-off got the day right but the week wrong. That was in Southampton waiting for a drugs rendez-vous. I've hated Southampton ever since.' He lit a cigarette. 'In the old days of the Cold War I was in Vienna. Waiting for people to come over from the east was no joke either. A four-day wait was routine. And often, of course, no one ever came. People forget how far north Vienna is. God, it was cold – '

'Car!'

As O'Day hissed out the word, headlights lit up the inside of their own car and they settled lower in their seats – O'Day was in the back so he was able to lie flat. The silver glow of the lights gradually filled the car as if it were a searchlight beam directed right at them, except that all the time the shadow moved, sliding over their shapes like mercury. As the car passed them, it slowed. Now the interior of the car filled with an amber light, on and off, on and off. O'Day raised his head a fraction so he could peer over the ledge of the car window. He smiled . . . in fact, he almost burst out laughing. Although it was approaching one o'clock in the morning, although there was not another waking soul, so far as he knew, for miles around, this was Switzerland and so the driver of the car was signalling that he was turning in. O'Day poked Riley in front of him in the shoulder. 'He's here!'

Both of them, like a couple of cats in a bin, stuck the top half of their heads above the window-ledge of the car. The winking amber light had been killed. Now the sidelights were switched off. The driver's door opened and a figure emerged. He was tall and slim but that was all they could make out. He took a suitcase from the boot of the car and walked to the front door.

'Fingers crossed and let's hope he doesn't notice the window.'

Riley looked at O'Day in the gloom. 'How will we know?'

'If he's at all suspicious he'll clear off straight away.'

'Fine. Then we follow him.'

'Then we follow him. First, though, I'd like a peek in that car. Might make our job easier.'

A light had gone on in the hall of the house. Then another came on in the study, at the side. Things remained that way for several minutes.

'He could be reading his mail, or telephoning. Either way, he doesn't appear to have noticed the window.'

Riley murmured agreement.

Moments later the study light went out. Then nothing.

'He's in the kitchen, pouring himself some water or juice. We can't see that light from here.'

A few minutes later a light came on upstairs and immediately the hall light went out. 'He's going to bed,' said Riley.

'Huh-uh. And, since he's arrived back from out of town, at one o'clock in the morning, it follows that he must be exhausted. He should be comatose inside half an hour. More soup, I think.'

They kept their eyes on the light as O'Day sipped the hot liquid and Riley finished his cigarette. After seven or eight minutes, the light was turned off. Riley inspected his watch and then took from his pocket the skeleton keys he had used the night before. 'Did you get training with these?' He looked at O'Day.

'Yes – but a long time ago. You can do the honours.'

'I've never had to break into a hotel room with those new-fangled electronic keys. They must be tricky.' Riley held up the rods. 'These are wonderful, though. Never fail.' He wiped the rods with his handkerchief. 'Right. I think it makes sense for you to wait outside the front door. He's got to come down the stairs if he hears anything and you'll be able to sound the alert. Agreed?'

O'Day nodded.

Silently, they opened the car doors and stepped out into the road. It was cooler than last night. O'Day made for the front of the house and Riley moved swiftly across to Zakros's Peugeot. He had the car door open in little more than a minute. The lock's design was predictable and he got in behind the wheel. The interior of the car was empty. There was nothing on the leather seats. He felt the pockets behind the seat backs. They too had nothing in them. He felt under the seats. Still nothing. He pressed the button on the glove compartment. It was locked. Now that was interesting. It was almost unheard of, in Riley's experience, for anyone to bother locking a glove compartment. He reached again for his skeleton keys.

It was a simpler lock than the one in the driver's door and he had it open in no time. Inside there was a tin of boiled sweets, the car handbook, the insurance document and another piece of paper. He opened it out and looked at it. There was a list of numbers. Each line was six digits long, grouped in pairs, so it looked as though they were telephone numbers. Some of the numbers began with the same order of digits, as if they were from the same exchange. But what did the numbers mean? Did they mean anything? Were they numbers Zakros had to call? Riley thought hard. The numbers were intriguing but they were also a little disappointing. He couldn't take the piece of paper, in case Zakros noticed that it had gone. So should he copy out the entire list? He thought that, first, he would try the boot: there might be something more obviously useful to them there. He slipped out of the car, taking the skeleton keys with him. The boot lock opened as quickly as the others – he hadn't lost his touch. Inside, there was a spare wheel, a blanket, a number of maps scattered loosely over the floor and, to his surprise, a punctured football. But that was all. Quietly, he closed the lid and then waved at O'Day for him to stay where he was. He ran back to their own car and reached for the paperback he had brought with him to help pass the time. It had some blank pages at the back. Inside a minute he was back in the Greek's car and writing down the numbers. There must have been twenty or thirty sets of them – why so many? It didn't take him long to get it done, then he replaced the list back in the glove compartment and pushed its lid closed. Gently, he relocked the Peugeot's door, looked across to O'Day, then both of them hurried to their own car. Leaving the doors slightly ajar, they held on to them as Riley accelerated gently away. Only after they were clear of the Greek's house did they slam them closed.

Back in Riley's hotel, whiskies in hand, they pored over the list of numbers. 'They're definitely Basle phone numbers,' said Riley. 'I recognize some of the exchanges.' He pointed to several sets of digits.

'But they may have nothing to do with this whole affair. Let's see.' O'Day picked up the phone and took the list from Riley. 'I'll try the top one first.'

'Is that wise?'

'We're in a hurry.' O'Day punched the numbers, then held the receiver to his ear. 'It's ringing,' he said after a few moments.

Then: 'No reply . . . I'll try the next . . . No reply there, either. Let's see if the last number produces anything . . . No,' he said after a further delay. 'No one's home anywhere.'

'We're wasting our time. We should get some sleep.'

'He won't be up before seven.' O'Day looked at his watch. 'Quarter past two . . . we can give ourselves a four-hour break.' As Riley made to move, O'Day added: 'I'm not so sure I agree with you about these numbers. They must be linked in some way. You don't just keep a list like that for no reason. Not in a rented car.'

'But there are twenty or thirty of them. Do you think there are twenty or thirty members of this Apollo Brigade?'

'Nnno. No, I don't. But maybe they have an elaborate communication system and these are the numbers he calls at a pre-arranged time.' O'Day shrugged. 'Sleep, Riley! We don't want to miss him in the morning. Our masters in London would not be pleased if we did that.'

16

Thursday

'If that waiter knew what he was talking about, the site should be along here, on the right.' Victoria had a map, opened on her lap as Edward drove. It was high afternoon near Eleusis, the sun bleaching the landscape all around as far as the eye could see. White hills hurt the eyes and the warm, sweet smell of figs filled the air.

Victoria had received a call in the early hours that morning, from Edward. He was arriving on the first flight from London. Victoria, now less frightened than before but still in shock after Haydon's death, had checked out of the Holiday Inn and met Edward at the airport, where they had rented a car. They had left Athens by the Corinth road, coming off to the left before the junction which led to Thebes.

As they drove, Edward had brought Victoria up to date on the thinking in London. He also explained why they were heading for Eleusis. 'Yesterday, I phoned the Classical Association, for a list of current digs in Greece. Most of these digs use volunteer labour so they're perfectly happy to give out information over the phone to "amateurs", which is what I said I was.'

'And?'

'There are only three current digs in the area associated in any way with Praxiteles: Eleusis, Olympia and Knidos. Eleusis is closest to Athens, so we start there.'

Eleusis may have been closest but it had still involved driving back through Athens. That had been a hot, sticky experience so they had stopped for a coffee in Eleusis itself, which had also provided an opportunity for Victoria to ask the way to the site. They were now leaving the town on its north side and Edward felt better than he had done in days. The Apollo Brigade still hadn't gone public and the warmth of Greece had a mellowing effect on him, as if it loosened the joints of his limbs. Victoria's presence wasn't a hardship, either.

Hills sloped gently away from the road, white stone blazing in the sunshine. 'What's this?' Victoria murmured, leaning forward in her seat. 'Look.' She pointed. A narrow track ran off to the right, like a line of chalk drawn in the landscape. 'There's a sign . . . see.' It was a makeshift affair, a stretch of board nailed to a post. The writing was in Greek. 'It says "Temple".'

'That must be it.'

'We're a bit exposed, aren't we?' said Victoria as Edward slowed the car and turned off the metalled road. 'They'll see us long before we see them.'

'We'll pretend we're tourists – so don't let on that you can speak fluent Greek.'

The track went straight over the hill, without any allowance for the gradient, and they soon lost sight of the road. Ahead of them now, low slopes stretched away, each one whiter than the last until they were lost in the haze of the day. There were hardly any trees – just low bushes. After about five minutes they came to an area that had been levelled. It was about the size of a football field and the far end had been cut into the hill. It was deserted.

'No one could dig in this heat. They must have been mad to build here in the first place.' Victoria turned in her seat, looking this way and that, to make sure there was no one observing them.

'Or very devout in their belief that the gods inhabited these lands. This is the wrong place. The Classical Association misled me. The digging has been finished for some time. The ground has already been smoothed over.'

It was getting hot in the car. 'Where next?' asked Victoria, turning up the air-conditioning.

'Olympia,' said Edward, putting the car into gear, ready to turn round. 'I pray to God it's the site we want.'

'Why? What's wrong with the other place – Knidos?'

'There's nothing wrong with it. It's just that it's on a narrow spit of land north of Rhodes and actually in Turkey. It's very isolated. If Kolettis is hiding there, he will almost certainly see us coming.'

Sir Francis Mordaunt stared in horror at the lines of people queuing for the Tate Gallery cafeteria. In his life he rarely had to deal with the mass of humanity and he didn't relish being so close to it now. He looked down at the little Welsh policeman, standing nearby. Leith was more like the people in the cafeteria queue. He wore the same kind of clothes, probably lived in much the same area and held his knife and fork in much the same way. Mordaunt was a snob and accepted the fact. Secretly he felt it was beneath him to be here but of course he had no choice. Since the meeting with the Prime Minister, he'd had to rearrange his schedule, hand over various duties to the Lord Chamberlain, and hold himself in readiness for the call that had finally come just a little while ago.

His eye fixed on a swarthy – Greek-looking – youth in the cafeteria queue. They had all received a shock first thing this morning. The breakfast news had carried a story to the effect that, during the night, a group of buildings across Britain had been attacked and daubed with graffiti. Each of the buildings – the National Gallery in Trafalgar Square, Downing College in Cambridge, Birmingham Town Hall, the Royal Scottish Society in Edinburgh – had one thing in common: each was modelled on the Parthenon, or had some prominent classical Greek features. In each case the graffiti had been daubed on the columns of the façade of the building, one letter per column, each several feet high and spelling 'KLEPHTES'. This, it had turned out, was Greek for 'Thieves'.

That had been worrying enough but, during the morning, the BBC had received a phone call from an organization claiming responsibility for the attacks. The organization called itself 'The Enemies of Elgin' and had demanded the return of the Elgin Marbles immediately. Otherwise, the spokesman had threatened, its action would be stepped up. That was bound to inflame the situation, Mordaunt reflected, introducing yet another 'joker', as the Prime Minister's political aide had put it, into the equation. Mordaunt also knew that the Trustees of the British Museum were meeting about now . . . they could make trouble, too.

The call from the Apollo Brigade had come at about eleven-thirty and they had been given the usual half an hour to scramble down here to the Tate. Leith, to Mordaunt's left, occupied the time by sucking a mint. Mordaunt found it difficult to stand still. He stared as a thin, shabby West Indian went along the bank of telephones inserting his finger into the slot in each machine where returned coins were deposited. He was just cruising, on the offchance someone would have left money there. What a way to –

One of the phones rang.

Mordaunt was startled, but then stepped forward into the booth. The West Indian moved away.

'Andover?'

'No . . . it's Mordaunt.'

'Where's Andover? What's going on? I thought the voice was different when I called before.'

'Andover lost his temper last time. He was too . . . excitable. The Prime Minister decided to replace him. I am his superior at Buckingham Palace. I . . . I am closer to Her Majesty.'

The voice hesitated, the man behind it calculating. 'And where is Andover? Physically, I mean?'

'Scotland.' This story had been agreed with Midwinter only moments before. 'He's been given a holiday. Out of the way. Don't worry . . . nothing else has changed. You can speak with me just as you would have done with Andover.'

'I'm not worried.' But the voice hesitated again, as if the man was wondering whether to go on. Then, 'You know about the Rubens in Vienna?'

'Yes.'

'That was a warning. There will be no other.'

'Yes, I know. Don't worry, we are complying with your wishes. I, as Andover's superior, have been appointed to show how seriously we take your . . . warning. It is now Thursday. The Duveen Galleries will close at the weekend, so the sculptures will be ready to leave about a week after that.'

'Good – but not good enough.'

'What! . . .' Mordaunt lowered his tone. 'Go on.'

'Listen. You pay a price for what you did. What Andover did. We are bringing our deadline forward. The Marbles have to be at sea, on their way to Greece, a week from today –'

Mordaunt groaned.

'I'll say this one more time. You are an intermediary. I am not interested in your views and reactions. Just do as you are told. We don't care when you close your precious Duveen Galleries, or whether you leave them open. Just get the Marbles on their way within a week.'

'Yes.'

'That's better. Now, listen again. I shall call next on Saturday

– but next time not even you, Sir Francis, not even you with your special relationship to Her Majesty, will be enough.'

Mordaunt stopped breathing for a moment. Now what? 'Go on.'

'The next . . . exchange will be the most important of all. We shall need certain assurances. And so, Sir Francis, I – we, the Apollo Brigade – need that assurance from where it really matters. The next time I call, it will be to Buckingham Palace, and I shall expect to speak with the Queen herself.'

'He's going back to his car. We're going to have to split up.' Riley swallowed what was left of his coffee and put some change on the table. They both rose and hurried out of the station. 'Okay, I'll stay with him,' said Riley. 'You check out the phone and then catch a taxi back to near the Greek's house. He's bound to return home at some stage.'

After only four hours' sleep in the hotel, O'Day and Riley had returned to the Zakros house that morning and resumed their vigil. He had not stirred until mid-morning. When he had finally appeared, Zakros had driven from his house to a café in Basle where he had bought a paper and taken a late breakfast. He had then gone for a walk by the river. At least, they had thought he was going for a walk but in fact he had made a telephone call from a payphone at a jetty. It was a relatively short call, however, and they had decided to stick with him and return to the phone later to check out its number. They had then followed the Greek to the main railway station. There they had been able to enjoy a coffee themselves, at the station café, for Zakros had waited in front of a bank of payphones, occasionally glancing at his watch. By then it was nearly one o'clock.

Suddenly, O'Day had whistled softly. 'Yes! Riley, we've been as thick as elephant shit.' He had stared at the other man, his eyes aglow. 'That call from the phone at the jetty. It could have been the early call to the Palace, to Mordaunt. He's given him the location to go to and now he's waiting to phone him again, from here. Zakros is the man at the sharp end. He guards the pictures *and* he does the talking.' O'Day was really excited now, pleased he had been given Basle after all and not left at home. 'You keep an eye on him. I'll try to call Lockwood from one of the other phones.'

And so Riley had watched both O'Day and Zakros, only three booths apart. O'Day too kept a weather eye open for Zakros, in case he made a hurried exit. But in fact O'Day finished first and rejoined Riley. 'Looks like it,' he whispered. 'I couldn't get Lockwood but I spoke to Midwinter. He confirmed that Mordaunt had just spoken to the Greek and was on his way to receive the next phone call – at the Tate Gallery.'

That was when Zakros had broken off his conversation on the telephone. Riley followed him at a distance.

O'Day waited for both of them to get well clear of the station. In fact, he watched both cars leave before returning to the bank of phones. It was not impossible that the Greek was being shadowed by a colleague when he made these crucial calls. There was a newsagent next to the phones and O'Day browsed through the magazines until the booth the Greek had used was free. He strolled towards it, picked up the receiver and dialled a number at random. In case he was being observed, and feeling rather foolish, he pretended to speak into the receiver. As he did so he inspected the number near the dial. He memorized it and put down the receiver. Then, repeating the phone number to himself so that he wouldn't forget it, he crossed the station forecourt to the lavatories. Inside a cubicle, where he couldn't be observed, he took the list of numbers from his pocket, wrote down the number he had just memorized and checked it against the others. It didn't take him long to establish that the number was not on the list.

'Oh Christ, look at the coaches! There must be two thousand people here.' Victoria focused her binoculars on the site. 'It couldn't be more different from Eleusis. It's teeming with people.'

The ruins of ancient Olympia stretched out before them, a mass of white stonework in a saucer-shaped hollow rimmed with cypress and olive trees, a few oaks. They had overnighted in Corinth and arrived here in time for a late lunch, after finding a couple of hotel rooms. It was already past two o'clock.

'Where do we start looking? And how?' Edward held his hand up, to shield the sun from his eyes.

'Easy enough to pose as tourists in among all the others.'

Edward and Victoria followed the road leading to the site. The heat was still intense but thankfully the road was lined with trees and there was no shortage of shade. They crossed a bridge and came to the site; there was a small queue at the entrance but once they were inside there was plenty of space. They found the path which led to the Heraion, and then walked up to a ridge where there was a map showing the whole layout of the ruins.

'Look,' Victoria said, pointing to the map. 'There's a section here in red, meaning that it's closed to the public. Is that where they're digging, do you think?'

Edward looked over Victoria's shoulder. He could smell her hair. Then he grabbed her wrist and led her into the sunshine. 'Let's see for ourselves.'

They tried to follow the patches of shade as they wound their way through the site. The white stones and columns of the different temples and the Heraion were laid out like the bleached bones of a strange, enormous dead animal. Eventually, they came to an area which had been chained off. A sign, white on red metal, said 'Private'. Beyond the chain there was a short path leading to two wooden huts and a low area where the excavations were presumably taking place. However, as these were actually below the level of the ground, it was impossible for Victoria or Edward to see anything.

'Let's not be seen to stare,' said Victoria quietly. She looked over her shoulder. 'Follow me.' She led the way up a short incline to where more white columns reached further than most into the sky and offered shade. They stood behind the columns. 'We can keep watch from here.'

'Keep watch for whom?' said Edward. 'We don't know what Kolettis looks like.'

'We watch for anyone coming or going, anyone on the dig. Then we follow them, contrive to meet them . . . and then we ask after Professor Kolettis.'

'Just like that? What do we say . . . . and why do we say it?'

'We'll think about that tonight, over dinner. There's no point in hanging on now. They won't dig in the afternoon, not in this heat. We'll have to come back at opening time tomorrow.' She led the way down the slope towards the exit.

Back in the town, Victoria went for a walk by herself while Edward returned to the hotel to take a cool shower. He was wearing just a towel when she returned – their rooms opened on to the same balcony. As she joined him there, she held up a newspaper, a Greek one.

'Anything in it? Anything interesting?'

'You could say so. The government has announced that the Duveen Galleries will close at the weekend.'

'Imagine a newspaper ad for this job,' said Riley gloomily. 'No meals, no sleep, virtually no pay. We could be at the Cocotte now, in Copenhagen, scrambled eggs with quails and caviare, duck with–'

'You're spoiled,' growled O'Day. 'And you wouldn't change it. You love it really.' O'Day had rejoined Riley on the vigil, taking a taxi to near Zakros's house. He had walked the rest of the way.

'I'd love a piece of that turbot they do in sweet peppers at the Buerehiesel in Strasburg, or a plate of courgettes with truffles that you can get at the Chantecler in Nice, or –'

'There he is!'

They both sat up. It had been dark for a while and their eyes were attuned to the gloom. The light in the hall of Zakros's house had flashed on, then off again almost immediately. Now the front door opened and they saw him getting into his car.

'Nine-thirty,' whispered Riley, inspecting his watch in the light attached to his key-ring. 'Bit late for dinner in Switzerland.'

'Give him a good start,' said O'Day. 'We don't want him cottoning on now.'

Riley let the Greek get out of sight before he started the car. The road where Zakros lived was just two blocks from a main thoroughfare; they knew they could catch up with him there and the road would be so busy he would never notice them. Zakros drove through the centre of the town and for a moment O'Day thought he was heading for the phone booth by the river. The Irishman had checked it out after inspecting the booth in the station; but it was not on the list of numbers they had either. Now Zakros was driving out the other side of Basle. He pulled up in a square with a cinema complex at one corner.

'Don't say he's going to the movies,' said O'Day. 'That would be a real treat.'

Stopping their car on the opposite side of the square, they watched Zakros cross the tramlines and walk back towards the cinemas. He did not go in, however, but hovered at the edge of the arc of light given off from the complex.

'Maybe he's meeting someone who's already watching the show?' Riley tried to keep the Greek in view in the driving mirror.

'That's worrying,' said O'Day. 'If they have another person in Basle, they might have spotted us.'

'No. If that were true, they wouldn't meet. They would just shake us off, or let London know, and the whole thing would blow. He's moving again!' Riley had lost the Greek in the mirror.

'Not far!' whispered O'Day. 'Hell, we should have noticed. He's got a phone call.'

Riley sat up in his seat and turned his head. In the centre of the square was a short row of three or four phones. Zakros was already talking, indicating that he had been called, rather than that he was doing the calling. 'This must be how they keep contact. They must figure it's too dangerous to phone his house, or to have him phone them from home.' They watched as best they could as Zakros alternately spoke animatedly into the receiver, then stood still as he listened to the other end. As he listened, people started to leave the cinema; the performance was ending.

'Maybe he's meeting someone too,' whispered Riley. 'Keep looking.'

But almost as Riley said this, Zakros hung up and hurried back across the tramlines to his car, alone. 'Right,' said Riley. 'Same as before? I'll trail him, back home probably. You can look at the phone. Then take a taxi back to the Greek's, as you did earlier.'

'Fine,' said O'Day. 'But drop me a couple of blocks from here and I'll walk back, just in case the phone is being watched.'

Riley nodded and started the car. At a distance, he followed the Greek out of the square. He had to wait while a tram went by but Zakros's car was still in view. He caught up with him and then, after a couple of streets, stopped to let O'Day get out.

O'Day strolled back to the square, pausing to look in shop windows every now and then. He didn't want to arrive back near the cinemas too quickly. Even when he got there he spent a little while examining the posters advertising the movies. While doing this he fished from his pocket a piece of paper with some writing on it. Then, just in case he was being observed, he scrutinized the paper as if he was searching for a phone number. In this way he approached the booth that Zakros had used a few minutes before. As he reached the open doorway, it struck him that Zakros had taken the call at precisely ten o'clock. Interesting. Could it be that the Greek had an arrangement, that whoever called him did so, on a different public phone, each time but always at the same hour? Clever. But it now gave O'Day and Riley a tactical advantage. He put coins in the aperture and dialled Riley's number. As it rang out he memorized the number of the phone he was using. He let the phone ring for a while, then put back the receiver and strolled casually away. A little while later, he picked up a taxi. Inside the cab he wrote down the number in the paperback book where Riley had copied out all the other numbers they had found in the Greek's car. This time he saw immediately that the number of the phone near the cinema complex *was* on the list.

'I take it that Her Majesty will have no objection to talking with . . . the Greek?' The midnight committee was in session and Lockwood was in his usual position, in front of the fireplace at the top of Number Ten. 'Now that the negotiations are on again, we can't risk losing them a second time.'

'She is not happy about it.' Mordaunt felt uncomfortable at these meetings. He was outnumbered and he looked tired. 'But of course she will play her part.'

The Prime Minister nodded. He prided himself that his edginess was controlled. His grandson was still in intensive care, but conscious now. 'It sounds to me, from the wording the Greek used, that they are about to make some fresh demand. Is that fair?'

Mordaunt nodded. 'Zakros said that the next exchange – and I quote – "is the most important of all".'

'Anyone have any bright guesses as to what that might mean?'

No one spoke.

Lockwood stared at the equerry. 'We'll just have to sit tight and wait. Meanwhile, in case anyone hasn't heard, the entire Board of Trustees at the British Museum resigned this morning, in protest.'

Mordaunt nodded.

'Coming on top of these "Enemies of Elgin" . . . it takes some of the shine off the fact that the blackmailers have been back in touch. We're getting in deeper. On the other hand, the fact that all the Trustees resigned gives me a free hand. That was a tactical mistake of theirs – but then most of them aren't politicians.' He looked at Leith. 'What other news today? Anything good?'

'Nothing from Greece, sir. Tatton and Andover made a tour

of Olympia but don't expect any progress before tomorrow. O'Day and Riley observed Zakros receive a phone call at a public booth in Basle. The number of the phone in the booth turned out to be on the list they found in the Greek's car, so it could be that he is contacted regularly on a different phone. That's good security from their point of view, and if we could find out where these booths are located we could bug one in advance and listen in to the conversation. Unfortunately, we have no idea at the moment where the other phone booths are located.

'I'm told by the Foreign and Commonwealth Office that there are still demonstrators outside our embassy in Athens. The emissary sent by the Greek government has given up trying to see you, I understand, and is now petitioning the Foreign Secretary.'

'I'm surprised the Greeks haven't tried harder.' Midwinter held his glass for Lockwood to fill it.

'Why should they?' asked Slocombe. 'We're in enough trouble as it is. If they did anything else they might rock the boat.'

'We might be in more trouble than we know.' Hatfield spoke quietly and the others looked at him. 'It might be a tricky Cabinet tomorrow.' Hatfield clenched his fingers. 'George Keld is planning to raise the whole business of the Marbles.'

Lockwood grunted. 'How do you know?'

'One of the deputy chief whips saw him in the main lobby with Henry Misco, one of the BM Trustees who resigned this morning.'

'That doesn't mean he's going to raise it in Cabinet.' Cabinet meetings were traditionally held on Thursdays. This week's had been held over for a day because that morning Lockwood had rushed to the hospital to see his grandson the minute he knew he had regained consciousness.

'Not by itself. But he's given notice to Evelyn Allen that he wants to raise a "delicate matter" under AOB. What else could it be?'

'Yes, you're right. Damn. How much does he know, I wonder. And how the hell did he find out?' The Prime Minister turned to Slocombe. 'Hear that, Eric? He's got to be stopped.'

'Do we have anything on Keld?' Slocombe looked from Lockwood to Hatfield to Midwinter. 'Anything we could trade off against this?'

Lockwood said nothing. Midwinter shook his head. Hatfield

looked uncomfortable. 'There's one thing . . . I don't know how useful it is.'

They all looked at him.

'He has an illegitimate daughter.'

'What!' said Midwinter.

'Perfect,' whispered Slocombe.

Lockwood remained silent.

'It happened a long time ago,' said Hatfield. 'Keld is fifty-seven now and the girl – woman – is already twenty. He's paid the mother all these years, enough for maintenance, education and a little bit more – enough to keep her quiet. But the important thing, from our point of view, is that he was already married when she was born.'

'How do you know all this?' Lockwood had at last found his voice. He hated what he was hearing but he had been in politics a long time and, distasteful as it was, he was not the type to look a gift horse in the mouth.

'My election agent's son was once the lover of Keld's illegitimate daughter. The daughter told her lover, lover told his father, my agent told me. Years ago, I might say. I'd forgotten it until a few moments ago. It had never mattered until now.'

'And now it might matter very much,' muttered Slocombe.

'But illegitimacy is no longer the stigma it was,' said Midwinter. 'Half the country's illegitimate, from what I read.'

'Half the country isn't trying to be Prime Minister,' growled Slocombe. 'Keld won't risk it being made public. He'll settle out of court, as it were. Out of Cabinet.'

'I hope you're right.' Lockwood spoke quietly.

'I'd bet money on it. My own money,' said Slocombe with a sly grin. 'Come on, Bill, cheer up. Don't look so pious. We've been in deeper than this before. Are you losing your appetite for the game?'

Lockwood shrugged. 'Maybe I am. If he stands against me for leader . . . even if he doesn't win, it will show the strength of the opposition. That could be damaging.' He moved across the room and put the whisky bottle in the cupboard where it was stored. Speaking with his back to them, he said: 'You're probably right, Eric. Keld will be warned off once he finds we know about his illegitimate child. On the other hand, he may just explode and blow us all out of the water.'

*

Giles Wittington briefly shone his pencil torchlight on to the filing cabinet. The card on the door read: 'Jaffe–Newman'. He pulled open the drawer as silently as he could. He was a careful, tidy, quiet man by nature, and because his job demanded it. And he was not nervous either, which was just as well tonight.

Sir Martin Ogilvy had arranged things as best he could. Wittington had strolled into the museum like any tourist at around four-thirty this afternoon. He had been briefed as to how to find the records department which, the director had assured him, would be empty of people from five o'clock onwards. The records office had two windows which looked down on to an inner courtyard of the museum. It also had a boxroom, with no windows, where the stationery was kept. Wittington had hidden in there until it was dark because the director had said that, although the security guards did not routinely open up the records department at night, they would do so if anyone saw a figure moving about in the office after five o'clock.

Bob Leith had given him about thirty names of people who worked at the museum and whose profile seemed relevant in the current context: like most political terrorists, they were all aged between twenty-five and forty. They had all joined the museum in the last five years. Also, everyone in the Department of Greek and Roman Studies was included.

Moving into the records room proper, Wittington found the files, three or four at a time, and then took them back to the boxroom where, with the door closed, he could inspect the documents at his leisure and with the lights on. He'd had no luck with the first and second batches. Now it was nearly one o'clock and he was on the third batch. In front of him was the employment file of one Helen Maynard, a Keeper of Ceramics at the museum. Wittington saw immediately that her handwriting was nothing like that on the envelope Riley had found in Basle which had been couriered to Downing Street that very day. The next file was marked 'Errol Merton', a metalworker in the conservation department. He had a beautiful hand, a calligrapher's hand; but it wasn't the one Wittington was looking for. The next two were also in the clear and it was not quite two o'clock. That made twelve names gone already. He gathered the files together, put out the light and went back into the outer office. An amber light from the courtyard outside shone into the room, casting deep shadows. As best he could, Wittington moved from one area of shadow to another. He replaced the files in their correct places and then moved on to the next drawer: 'Opie–Sonnabend'. This drawer was in the amber light so that he didn't need even to use his torch. Consulting the list he had been given by Leith, he saw that there were just three files in this drawer that he needed to remove: Vivian Russell-Roberts, Bernard Sackler and Eugenie Shelby. Ahh! Eugenie . . . wasn't that a Greek name?

Back in the inner room, he turned to that file first. The signature on Dr Shelby's application form stared out at him. It was sometimes more difficult with handwriting than non-experts realized, especially if there were few letters that appeared in both specimens of handwriting, or if different inks or pens had been used. He set what he had side by side:

Eugenie Shelby   Mr Nicos Zakros
         Gstaadstrasse 57,
         00662 Basle
         SWITZERLAND

There was surprisingly little overlap. In fact, there were only the letters 'e', 'i', 'S' and 'l'. The 'e's looked similar, though in two cases they were poorly formed. The 'l's looked closer still but the 'i' . . . Wittington had his doubts. The capital 'S's weren't much help, as one was joined to the 'h' of Shelby and the other, in SWITZERLAND, had been printed. This was possibly the same hand, Wittington concluded, but he couldn't be absolutely certain, and was that good enough? Bob Leith had emphasized how important this was and that the Prime Minister was taking a special interest. Perhaps he should go through the remainder of the names to be on the safe side. He was just about to close the Shelby file and turn to Vivian Russell-Roberts, when something caught his eye. It was a typed entry high up the page, a good way from Eugenie Shelby's signature. It was simply headed: 'Maiden name'. That was an old-fashioned term, Wittington reflected, hardly used these days. The forms were very old. Not that it really mattered. What mattered was that, inside this box, the word that had been typed was 'Chrysostomou'. By birth, Eugenie Shelby was Greek.

17

Friday

'I thought the site would be empty, this early in the morning.' Victoria looked at her watch. It had just gone nine-thirty.

'Germans and Dutch all get up early. And it's cooler at this time of day. But it's good for us. If there weren't many people around, we would be more noticeable.'

The site had opened at nine. Edward had thought it not clever to be first in the queue but they hadn't been far behind. Now they were watching the entrance to the dig as best they could. Several people had gone in and no doubt others were already inside when they had arrived. But so far no one had left.

It promised to be another baking day. The evening before, Victoria and Edward had eaten dinner at a restaurant in the main square of Olympia, and had returned to the hotel fairly early. At Corinth, Edward had been exhausted following his journey to Athens and their long drive immediately afterwards. So he had gone to sleep immediately. At Olympia they had talked for a while, about Haydon mainly. Victoria had suddenly been affected by delayed shock. They had kept moving the day before, and Edward had arrived from London, and these events had put off for a while the full power of what had happened to Haydon. Victoria wasn't frightened now, as she had been in the hotel in Athens; instead she was prone to bouts of depression which engulfed her unpredictably. They had adjoining rooms in the hotel, and shared a balcony. Edward had sat on the balcony, reading, until Victoria had finally dropped off to sleep. He noticed that she travelled with a few tiny objects from home – silver things, a treen animal. They were laid out tidily on the table by the bed. She had seemed better this morning.

'How many people would be on a dig like this one?'

Edward shielded the sun from his face with his hand. 'Difficult to say. Fifteen, twenty . . . maybe more. In Britain there are always lots of volunteers. People love it with a passion. It's one activity where labour is not a problem. In some ways there is too much. Throughout southern Italy, parts of Greece and Turkey, there are lots of illegal digs. There's big money nowadays for people who find decent antiquities. Is that someone leaving?'

Victoria looked up. She had been bitten by mosquitoes during the night and was scratching one of her bites. 'Yes. Shall we both follow him?'

'Why shouldn't we?'

'One of us could stay and follow someone else. Double our chances.'

'I don't see how. Kolettis is either here or he isn't. If there are only fifteen to twenty people on the dig, or even if there are forty, they will all know about him. Also, it will be less suspicious if we approach people as a couple. We can pretend to be married. Come on, before we lose him.'

The person who had left the dig was a tall, thin, dark-haired man who was walking slowly back towards the town. Victoria and Edward followed him, at a distance. 'We can't just accost him in the street,' she said. 'Let's wait until he goes into a shop or a café. Then we can think of something.' But the man didn't go to a shop or a café. He went to the post office. They watched him queue for nearly fifteen minutes and saw him come away with a bundle of letters. 'Looks like he's got letters for several people,' said Victoria. 'Perhaps the archaeologists from out of town all have their mail delivered here.'

'What's he going to do now? We should have approached him in the post office.'

But now the man did go to a café. They watched him order a coffee and water and then open one of the letters. 'At least that tells us he's from out of town himself,' whispered Edward. 'He must know who Kolettis is.'

They sat down not too far from the man and ordered coffee of their own. 'Leave this one to me,' said Victoria. 'Let's hope he likes women.' She got up, walked across to the man and stood over him. For a moment he didn't see her but then he looked up. 'Excuse me,' she gushed. 'Do you speak English?'

He nodded.

'I may be wrong, I know, but my husband and I' – and she waved vaguely in Edward's direction – 'believe we saw you at the excavation this morning. That is true, isn't it?'

Again, the man nodded.

'Oh, good! Then perhaps you can help us. We are old friends

of Dimitri Kolettis and we heard he was on a dig somewhere near here. We were told he is working on a new book on . . .' She faltered and looked across at Edward.

'On Praxiteles,' said the dark-haired man.

'Then he is here!' Victoria's eyes shone.

'No, he's not. You were misled, I'm afraid. He has never been here, so far as I'm aware, and I've been in Olympia for the last four months.'

'Somewhere nearby, then?'

Edward registered with amazement Victoria's ability to gush when she needed to.

'No, there are no other digs near here. Not for miles. I'm sorry but Kolettis isn't here and I don't have the faintest notion where he is.'

Ten-forty-five in Olympia meant it was eight-forty-five in Downing Street. Lockwood faced George Keld across the breakfast table. A cold summer's rain rattled the windows at the top of the house. Keld was not much taller than Lockwood. His iron-grey hair seemed to hold the pearly light of the day and framed his head, like a silver halo. His eyes also caught the light, making them appear wet. Lockwood offered Keld tea and toast. The other man had already turned down anything more elaborate. 'Is Susan well?' the Prime Minister asked.

'Thank you, yes. And the boys, both doing well at school. Sally?'

Lockwood inclined his head. 'Still hates this flat and is very on edge about our grandson in hospital . . . but otherwise . . . we're fine.' He paused. The invitation to Keld had been sudden – peremptory – and both of them were uneasy with small talk. 'Hatfield says you wish to raise a certain matter in Cabinet.'

Keld's cup, half-way to his lips, suddenly stopped.

Good, thought Lockwood. First round to me. He didn't know that we know. 'I don't know how you found out about all this but I'd prefer it if you didn't raise the matter in Cabinet, George. I can't risk this thing leaking.'

Keld had flushed red but was beginning to recover. 'I think you're wrong, Prime Minister. Very wrong. From what I know of this matter, you are placing this government in jeopardy and all over something that is fifty years old.'

'The popularity – or otherwise – of the royal family is hardly a dead issue, George. And two members of the Cabinet are involved. Are you suggesting I should have just stood to one side and let Her Majesty cope with these people . . . this Brigade . . . all alone?'

'Quite frankly . . . yes, that's exactly what I would have expected had I . . . I would have given you that advice, had you asked me.'

'And if the whole thing leaked . . . you would have been prepared to sit and watch the Queen go through hell, in public?'

'It's not the government's fight, Bill. Why should we suffer for the foibles of a man who has been dead for years?'

'I'm not aware that we have suffered yet. And it *is* our fight. As I say, two members of the Cabinet are involved – their families, at least. That's a risk best avoided.'

'But look at the mess you're getting into . . . demonstrations, the Trustees resigning at the British Museum, all those buildings daubed with paint. This could be your nemesis, Bill.'

'Not unless you insist on raising this matter in Cabinet, George. We do have a team working on this whole thing, and we're making progress all the time. We'll be ready to move against them soon.'

'Soon may be too late.'

'As I say, George, not unless you insist on raising the issue this morning. If you bring this matter to Cabinet, we can kiss goodbye to secrecy and therefore any chance of catching the Apollo Brigade and disposing of them quietly. The royal family would be exposed to terrible publicity . . . I don't know where it will lead but, if I can avoid it, avoid it I will. The government would be seen as divided and as having co-operated in a cover-up – and what effect that would have on our chances at the election I simply don't know.'

'I don't see it your way, Bill. I'm sorry. I think you have shown a grave error of judgement here. Not just in the fact that you chose to help the Palace in the first place, but also in the fact that you kept the secret to yourself and chose not to tell the rest of your government. If ever there was a question which required a Cabinet decision, this is it.'

Keld was obdurate. Lockwood saw that he would have no choice but to use Hatfield's piece of slime. 'But there are uses for secrecy, don't you think, George? Even you can be secretive at times.'

'What do you mean?' Keld frowned.

'I'm thinking of an episode . . . a long time ago . . . a very long time. When you were much younger and, well . . . not so much irresponsible as . . . unlucky.'

Keld said nothing. He was certainly tough, Lockwood reflected. He must know what the Prime Minister was alluding to but he was going to make him say it. 'As I'm told the story, George, you were married at the time of this . . . accident. A child, a daughter. Linda, I believe she's called – yes? In her early twenties, by now, I should think. Possibly with children of her own. A whole secret side to you, George. Don't think I'm disapproving, by the way –'

'Stop!' Keld glared at Lockwood. 'Let me get this straight. You are proposing a trade? If I raise this royal business in Cabinet, you are going to leak the existence of Linda . . . One blackmail leads to another.'

'I prefer your first choice of words. A trade.'

'And if I don't agree –?'

'If you don't agree, you will probably bring us both down.'

'How do I know that, even if we agree this time, you won't use the fact of Linda's existence at some other point in the future?'

'You don't, George. You'll have to take my word for it. But that's why I say I prefer the word "trade". I mean to imply that this is a clean swap. One favour for a favour in return. Non-reusable. One day you hope to take over from me. Since we're being so frank, let me say that I believe you hoped to take over from me sooner rather than later. That you thought you might stand against me in this year's leadership contest, in October. That is part – even the main part – of your desire to raise this blackmail business in Cabinet today. You'd like to see me replaced as leader of the party and preferably before the next election. What I'm saying is that you can take your chances later. When I decide to bow out, I shan't stand in your way and I won't use Linda. But I'm not giving up this address – much as Sally hates the flat – in a coup organized by my own party. I promoted almost all the present Cabinet, you included, George, so don't think you can leap-frog me. If you try, you'll get bitten in the balls!' Lockwood looked at his watch. 'Now, we've been talking long enough . . . You've got work to do and so have I. Do we have a trade – or not?' The Prime Minister sat back in his chair but his eyes held Keld's.

Keld wasn't shifty, Lockwood allowed him that. The Defence Secretary looked the Prime Minister full in the face for a full minute, without flinching. He was no doubt turning everything over in his mind for the last time. At long last, he spoke. No emotion registered on his face as he said: 'We have a trade.'

From the front page of the *Evening Standard* newspaper:

ARSONISTS ATTACK GREEK CATHEDRAL
Aghia Sophia torched
in reprisal raid.
Valuable Holy Screen destroyed.

The Greek Orthodox Cathedral in Moscow Road, Bayswater, was broken into last night and set fire to by arsonists. A painted screen showing several saints and worth millions of pounds was destroyed in the fire which also consumed many pews, the altar and choir.

Police and fire service officials say that graffiti daubed inside the church suggest that the raid was a reprisal for the recent attacks on 'Greek-style' buildings such as the National Gallery in Trafalgar Square, or Downing College, Cambridge.

According to Ronald Old, of Notting Hill Fire Station, one daubing inside the Cathedral said: 'Goodbye to the Kebab Cathedral.' Another said: 'Greeks go home – but the Marbles stay.'

A spokesman for the office of Archbishop Gregor Lysiptos, religious head of the Greek community in Britain, deplored the arson. 'The Greek community in Britain has long enjoyed very friendly relations on all sides and this attack on the holiest site of our religion here is shocking and an outrage. If the attack was in response to the recent daubings on classical-style buildings in Britain, the archbishop can only deplore both sets of actions, and urges the British government to seek a speedy solution to this problem.'

The spokesman added that the screen, or iconostasis, which in a Greek Orthodox church separates the main body of the congregation from the altar area, consisted of several pictures of saints which are especially revered in the Greek Orthodox church. 'They were painted by unknown masters in the fifteenth and sixteenth centuries and were brought to Britain in the 1920s, some from mainland Greece and some from Cyprus. In the current art market, they would be worth millions of pounds and their loss is a grievous and dreadful blow to many Greeks who live and worship in London.'

A spokesman for the Association of Greeks in Britain, Mr Costas Kyriacou, blamed the government for the outrage. 'The British government should explain to its own people, and to those of Greece, just what is happening in the matter of the Parthenon Marbles. Are they going back to Greece or are they not? Having announced that it is "considering" the matter, the government has now chosen to sit on the matter. As a result, the situation risks getting out of hand. No one wants to see the sort of happenings we have been witnessing lately. Mr Lockwood should act – and he should act now.'

The Press Officer at New Scotland Yard said that, so far as the Greek Cathedral fire is concerned, police are following up a number of leads and that a fuller statement would be issued shortly.

Giles Wittington had never seen so many famous faces close up. Tom Lessor's was the first he recognized. He had been on television only last week and now he came out of the Cabinet Room into the hall at Number Ten along with James Hammond, Environment Secretary. Frank Massie, Chancellor, was next, talking to Ian Dunlop, Secretary of State for Scotland, and John Waymouth, Education Secretary.

Wittington was waiting with Mordaunt, Leith and Eric Slocombe. They were to see the Prime Minister as soon as Cabinet was over.

As the ministers began to leave, the front door opened, letting a weak sunshine flicker into the corridor. Jocelyn Hatfield, Chief Whip, came out of the Cabinet Room next, with Mary Fraser, Social Services Secretary. Then came George Keld, Defence, by himself and looking rather stern. Robert Standish followed – he was Trade and Industry.

Wittington felt a tap on his shoulder and turned, to see Leith holding a piece of paper in his direction. 'This is Eugenie Shelby's address. She's separated, apparently. We're trying to trace the ex-husband at the moment.' Wittington looked at his watch – a quarter to one. He was beginning to feel a little jaded after being up for most of the night. He had remained in the archive until just before dawn, when he had transferred, as Ogilvy had instructed him, to the staff lavatory nearby, and locked himself in. He had been told the security guards would not use it and they hadn't. He had left the lavatory a minute or two after ten. Some unknown early member of staff had tried to get in but no doubt assumed that a fellow keeper had beaten them to it. Then, posing as an early visitor to the gallery, Wittington had strolled around for half an hour, and then left. He'd gone straight to Leith, who had debriefed him, sent him off for breakfast and then brought him on here. It had been quite a night.

'I think we can go in now,' said Slocombe. 'All the ministers have left.' He led the way into the Cabinet Room where Evelyn Allen was talking in subdued tones to the Prime Minister. Slocombe and the others all stood on the opposite side of the table and waited for the Prime Minister and Cabinet Secretary to finish. Eventually, Allen looked across at Slocombe, nodded, and left the room. Slocombe took the lead and sat at the table. The others did likewise.

'How did Cabinet go?' Slocombe asked.

Lockwood shrugged. 'Our secret is safe . . . for the time being.' He looked at Leith. 'This cathedral burning is a bit of a setback.'

Leith nodded. 'But there is progress to report on other fronts, sir. This is Wittington, by the way.'

Lockwood and the handwriting expert exchanged nods.

Leith continued, 'The woman we want at the BM is called Eugenie Shelby. Wittington is fairly certain the handwriting matches, but equally relevant is the fact that Shelby is her married name. By birth she is Greek. The Shelbys are separated now and we're trying to trace the husband, in case he can be a help. As for Eugenie, she works in the conservation department of the museum – I've spoken to Ogilvy this morning and he knows her . . . She specializes in sculpture conservation.'

Lockwood nodded but spoke to Wittington. 'You're certain this Shelby woman is the person we want?'

'Sir, I found her file at about two o'clock this morning. But I had to spend the rest of the night in the museum, so I didn't just go to sleep. I looked at all the other files on the list which

Inspector Leith gave me. With only signatures to compare, it's never easy or foolproof with handwriting. But hers is definitely the closest match of all those I looked at. I'm sure you've been told that there are seven hundred people employed by the museum. Obviously I only looked at a couple of dozen files.'

Lockwood nodded again. 'Anything else?'

'Not much, I'm afraid.' Leith leaned forward, his hands spread out on the Cabinet table. 'At the moment, Riley is tailing Zakros in Basle, while O'Day is legging it around the city, making a survey of all the public phones. We might get lucky.'

'And in Greece?'

Leith made a face. 'Zilch. Tatton and Andover were at the second site earlier today. No sign of our friends. In fact, they were told Kolettis definitely wasn't there. They are now on their way to the third site, at Knidos –'

'Remind me,' said Lockwood. 'They are still sticking to the sculpture trail – yes? Where is the next stop, exactly?'

'Knidos. The excavation site is about twenty miles from Datça – that's on a narrow spit of land leading out from Marmaris.'

'Turkey? Would a Greek be able to dig in Turkey? They are hardly the best of friends.'

'Scholars are a funny bunch, Bill. If Kolettis *is* the authority on Praxiteles which Andover says he is, he'll be very welcome. Also, in a way it's good cover for them – no one would think of looking for a Greek operation run from Turkey, for the very reason you have just voiced.'

Lockwood shrugged. 'At least Tatton speaks Turkish – yes?'

Leith nodded.

'And how do they get to . . . Datça?'

'They could go to Izmir but that would probably take too long. I expect they'll take a plane to Rhodes. Then the ferry to Marmaris. And by road from there. They won't be in Datça until after dark tonight, if that's what you want to know.'

Lockwood looked at Slocombe. 'Don't bother with Shelby's husband. If we question him, he might alert her. They were married – he might still feel his main loyalty is to her.' The Prime Minister bit his lip. 'What would be the psychological impact if we simply moved in now, and arrested two of them – Shelby and Zakros?'

Slocombe steepled his fingers. 'They'd be shocked, but the others would go to ground. The fact remains that, so long as they have the remaining Nazi pictures, they have the upper hand. We can't put Zakros on trial, even if we could get him extradited, and that would be difficult enough – we've been through all that before. And I doubt whether we could make anything stick against this Shelby woman. All we have, when it comes down to it, is an envelope that is probably in her handwriting, which was found in the Greek's house and, remember, was obtained illegally and therefore not allowed as evidence in a court of law, even if we wanted to bring it into a court of law. So we don't really have a great deal. The chief value of the Shelby woman is that we now know who she is, but she doesn't know that we know. She may be worth following. It might also be worth tapping her phone, although, since the Greek in Basle is so careful with his, she probably is too.' Slocombe pushed his fingers through his hair. 'I'm afraid it all comes down to Tatton and Andover in Greece. If they can locate Kolettis, then we stand a chance of winning. The odds are that Aristotle and Stamatis Leondaris are with him but, even if they aren't, Zakros and Kolettis seem to be running the show . . . Unless there is someone else in this Brigade, whom we know nothing about, we could apprehend the three of them simultaneously and barter their freedom in exchange for the paintings.'

'What do we know about the second Leondaris, the MP?'

'I asked the political attaché at the embassy. Stamatis is rather right-wing, or makes a lot of noise in that direction anyway. Interestingly, he's the member for a Thessaloniki constituency – where Kolettis is professor. His wife is a jeweller, highly thought of. And he's Ari's brother, by the way. There's still no reply to Ari's phone in Athens and, according to the political attaché, Stamatis didn't show the other day for a rally in Thessaloniki. No excuse was given, but it does seem that he's out of the way somewhere.'

'And so we carry on as before?' Lockwood sucked the tip of his pen.

'For the time being, Bill. But I feel a bit calmer now, don't you? We're making progress.'

Lockwood nodded. 'I suppose. But I don't know how much longer we can hold off in Greece. This burning of the cathedral . . . it's a bad business. Where is it going to stop?'

*

O'Day was growing to loathe Basle. He had quite liked it to begin with. The wide river, bisecting the city, gave it space and provided some pleasing, and surprising, vistas. But if this had been an American city, laid out in a grid pattern, his job would have been easier. Easy. He could have covered the entire town systematically. As it was, he'd been forced to buy a large-scale map and mark off the streets he'd walked along, otherwise he would never have remembered and could have wasted precious time doubling back on himself. He'd started near the Mittlere Bridge and the old fishmarket fountain, and worked south towards the large synagogue, then across to the museum area, completing an arc and coming back to the river at the Wettstein Bridge. That had taken no fewer than five hours to cover properly and so far he had discovered only one phone on his list, at the edge of a small park across from the History Museum. That was gratifying but hardly sensational and, since the number was higher up the list than the one on which Zakros had received his call the previous evening, it had almost certainly been 'used'. He decided now to cross the river, to try somewhere completely different. He walked across the Wettstein Bridge and turned left, back towards the centre. He had no luck. Now he went away from the river, towards the freight-marshalling yards and the more industrial parts of Basle. Nothing. He started to get angry. How many telephones were there in this goddam city, for Christ's sake?

Near the freight-marshalling yards, there was a smoky brasserie and he dipped in there to get himself a late lunch and a beer. The place was crowded, thick with people and cigarette fug. He ate his lunch quickly – sausage, onions and red cabbage – and then opened out the map on his table. Was Basle laid out in any systematic way or with any features that would determine where the Greek might have chosen the phones? The more he looked, the more irregular and unplanned Basle seemed. That sort of thinking was no help at all. As he drained his beer, he thought back to the two sites where he knew the telephones were located. One was in a small square with a cinema; the other was on the edge of a small park, across from the History Museum. No . . . that sort of reasoning was silly. After all, the Greek may well have chosen the sites at random – that would be the most secure system.

It had started to drizzle outside and he ordered a coffee. He looked at the map yet again and tried to put himself in the blackmailers' place. One thing had struck him about the list of phone numbers when Riley first showed it to him. The list was very long and yet there were no addresses. Surely that could only mean one thing: there *was* a rhyme or reason to their arrangement around Basle, something that the Greek could remember in his head. There had to be a pattern – it was there, if only he could discover it. He stared out at the drizzle. A yellow tram went clanking by. His coffee arrived. He looked at the map again. The main roads were in red, the smaller ones in black. The parks were marked with stippling which made them appear grey, as was true of the river. The major public buildings – the museums, the fishmarket fountain and the large churches – were blocked out in black. Tram routes were marked as straight black lines along the streets they ran on, with round blobs every so often.

Trams. The square with the cinema complex was on a tram route. Deliberately, O'Day located the site of the other telephone, the one in the park near the History Museum. So far as he could tell, it was on the same tram route as last night's phone. O'Day drew the map closer to him. His fingers closed around his coffee-cup as he examined the symbols more carefully. No, he couldn't see what he was looking for. He looked up, caught the waitress's eye and signalled that he wanted the bill. He folded the map and finished his coffee. The waitress put a tiny slip of paper on the table. He examined the amount and left enough cash to cover it.

Outside in the drizzle he looked up and down the street. There was a tram stop some hundred yards to his right. Even better, there was a tram coming, headed back into the centre of town. O'Day sprinted for the stop, arriving more or less abreast of the tram. He climbed the steps, paid his fare as if he was going the whole way on the tram but did not immediately search out a seat. He was looking for the feature which he knew existed on most public transport systems – a map. He could see one at the back of the tram where, fortunately, there were very few passengers. He stood in front of the map and found the route he wanted. As he had hoped, it was highly stylized and simpli-fied, but each tram stop was marked. As he examined the map he made two discoveries. First, there were two numbers between the two sets of digits for which he knew the locations – and there were two tram stops between those locations. Second, the first number he had located was seventh in the list – and it was near the seventh tram stop from the beginning of the line at Spalentor. Therefore, it did not require a first-class degree in mathematics to reach the conclusion that the Greek's telephone numbers were laid out along one particular tram route and that each successive call came to a phone that was the next stop out, along that line. This was presumably how Zakros could remember where the phones were without having to write down their addresses.

O'Day was excited now but he'd have to check. From the map in front of him, it appeared as if the route he was now travelling on came closest to the one he was interested in at the Steinenberg Strasse. That was in about five stops' time. He found a seat and waited. The tram clanked back across the Wettstein Bridge, turned right past the Kunstmuseum. O'Day got down where the route passed Steinenberg Strasse. It was now approaching three-thirty. Riley would be wondering what had happened to him but that couldn't be helped. Another half-hour and he might just have an answer . . . According to the map on the tram, most of the routes started either from Spalentor or the square where the Falkenstrasse met the Kohlenberg. He walked west, crossed Steinenvorstadt and reached Leonhardsgraben, which took him to Spalentor. There he found a stationary tram waiting to begin its journey. He got on.

As it moved off a few minutes later, he began counting the stops. The first phone he had located should come into view after seven stops, the second after ten stops and, if all that went according to plan, he would get off at the next, the eleventh, stop.

The tram swung into Gerbergasse, rolled passed the fishmarket fountain and, close to the river now, turned left into Blumenrain. The seventh stop was reached just before the Johanniterbrücke – O'Day knew it well, for it was indeed near the phone he had found earlier in the day. The tenth stop was just on the St Johannes Ring, near the square with the cinema where they had watched the Greek receiving his call the evening before. Now very excited and pleased with himself, O'Day prepared to descend from the tram. The St Johannes Vorstadt had now changed its name to the Elsassestrasse and the tram's next stop was where this street crossed Mulhauserstrasse.

O'Day was slightly apprehensive when he saw this intersection; it was one of the busiest, and one of the biggest, in the city. He could see phones in several directions. Still, it was a lot more

212

manageable than surveying the whole of Basle and he set about systematically examining all the booths he could see. There was a bank of three outside a department store. No. There were two across the street, near a kiosk selling newspapers and magazines. No. Beginning to sweat a little he looked around for more. There was a cinema on the far corner and, on the other side of the entrance, he could make out three more phones. He waited for the lights to change so that he could cross the road. As he did so, however, he noticed a little alleyway between a shop selling fishing tackle and a post office. There was a line of six phones there. He decided to try them first. He knew the number he was looking for by heart now: 47 78 11. The first booth was empty – and the number was wrong. The second booth was occupied . . . he would come back to that. The third booth was occupied . . . he would have to come back to that also. But the fourth booth was free. He lifted the receiver so that he could read the number. He groaned in pleasure. The number was 47 78 11.

Edward reached across, took the bottle from the bucket and held its neck over Victoria's glass. 'More wine?'

She shook her head. 'I don't feel thirsty, I don't feel hungry and I certainly don't feel happy.'

Edward nodded but helped himself to wine all the same. Their journey to Datça had been uneventful and they had arrived at around seven in the evening. They had found a hotel but then had immediately gone to enquire about the excavation at Knidos. All the taxi drivers knew where the dig was, but Knidos was about twenty miles away, and at that hour, of course, the site was closed. They had returned to the hotel looking forward to their dinner – after travelling all day they were both famished. But then Victoria had called London, to be told that O'Day and Riley were making real progress and hoping to tap the blackmailers' phone very soon, and that Wittington had unearthed the name of an Apollo Brigade member in the British Museum. 'In other words,' as she had pointed out to Edward once her conversation with Leith in London was at an end, 'we are the only people with no progress to report. I'll bet Lockwood is getting itchy.' She also told Edward about the Aghia Sophia in Moscow Road. That had deepened their gloom still further. And ruined their appetite.

'We ought to discuss our plan for tomorrow.' Edward put the bottle back in the bucket. 'The same as last time? Watch out for one of the diggers, follow him or her, ask about Kolettis?'

She seemed not to hear him. 'What worries me . . . is that we took that man's word too easily. The man in the café at Olympia, I mean. If I were Kolettis and were involved in what they are involved in, I would have some sort of security system. At the least, if someone came looking for me, I would leave standing instructions, to the effect that I wasn't there.'

'Not necessarily. Even allowing for Haydon's murder, he can have no idea we're on to him. He's here as an archaeologist. He's not in hiding as such and is not acting as a terrorist – or indeed as a blackmailer – normally does, keeping himself to himself in a closed cell. There is nothing suspicious about him.'

'Hmm. Maybe. One of the main points of security is that it secures you against the unexpected. He may not expect us to have tracked him down so quickly, but if he is professional he will still have taken precautions against what might happen rather than what he expects to happen.'

'What makes you think Kolettis was at the last site?'

'Nothing. Nothing concrete anyway.' She smiled a rather sour smile. 'Two things, really. I thought it through as we were travelling today – it took a while before I could admit my doubts to myself . . . I will have some wine now, please.' She spoke as he poured. 'It seems to me that, given what he's doing, or trying to do, a site on mainland Greece would be preferable. This peninsula is really out of the way, impractical if you are a budding blackmailer, wouldn't you say? Leith said on the phone that it might be a clever ploy to run a Greek terrorist attempt from inside Turkey, but that may be too elaborate. There's another thing. So far, this Apollo Brigade consists of a negotiator in Basle, a restorer at the British Museum, a Greek archaeologist, a Greek lawyer and, according to Leith, his brother, a backbench politician. We don't know how many more there are – and there are probably not many, I agree. But there must be at least one other person with some political weight. More weight than Stamatis, I mean. The motive behind this blackmail is political – if the Marbles do return, the impact will definitely be political. I'm growing convinced that there must be at least one other person in this Brigade who is a heavyweight politician. Kolettis appears to be the motivating force intellectually but Stamatis Leondaris, if he *is* involved, and we're not certain of that yet, is just a backbench MP. Useful, yes, but hardly a figurehead. There must be someone else. And if that's true, this heavyweight and Kolettis must meet from time to time. A Greek political figure would stand out in a Turkish town, but if Kolettis was somewhere in Greece he could easily travel to Athens whenever it was required. In Athens they could meet – secretly or openly – without it seeming remarkable in any way.'

She drank her wine. A silence stretched between them, across the table.

'I understand why you're worried,' said Edward at length. 'But perhaps you're worrying too much, especially as we've only just heard how well the others are doing. It seems to me that you could turn your reasoning on its head. An isolated place like this is a good place to hide. If there's a genuine dig, it provides perfect cover – and the phones are very good these days.' He let the matter of the Brigade's size and strength slide. He couldn't tell Victoria about Nancy. Not yet.

'What about the political angle?'

'You may have a point, I agree. But I'm not sure, once the actual blackmail had started, that Kolettis and the political figure, if there is one, would have to talk so much. The blackmail is an 'operation', so to speak. Only its effect is political . . .'

Another silence descended between them. Neither was wholly convinced by the other's arguments nor, indeed, by their own.

Edward lifted the wine bottle out of the bucket, but there was nothing left. 'Coffee?'

'How about having coffee somewhere else? The harbour looked as though it had one or two decent places.'

He nodded, smiled and got up. As they went out, he signed for the dinner: it would go on to the hotel bill. They strolled to the harbour. Here the sweet and sour smells of the sea mingled with those of cooking – kebabs, hot olive oil, coffee. There were children, dogs and restaurants everywhere, old women in black, the crews of a few big yachts, in brilliant white.

'Let's walk first, look at the boats. See how the rich live.' Victoria led the way. 'Afterwards, I might just have a brandy with my coffee. I need something to give me a lift.'

It was a very warm night and, as they strolled around the harbour, they passed yet more children who were still up and wearing only bathing costumes. One or two wizened fishermen

215

sat smoking in the gloom, young girls on scooters wove in and out of everywhere. Datça was not comparable to one of the fashionable French or Italian Mediterranean ports – Portofino or Saint-Tropez – but it had its share of smart boats. One, however, towered above all the others. It was not a sailing boat but rather resembled a miniature hotel. It was white, with lights everywhere and a wide deck area at the stern, which now overlooked the jetty. As Edward and Victoria strolled past, they could see several people on board playing cards. The men were in shirtsleeves, the women in flimsy dresses. Servants in white moved about them, removing plates, holding trays with glasses on them. Wine or whisky winked in the lights of the boat. Victoria and Edward walked on to the end of the harbour wall and sat for a moment looking out to sea. The sky was like ink, studded with stars. Then they retraced their steps and took coffee and brandy in one of the two harbour cafés.

'I can't believe that I'm here, feeling like this,' said Victoria. 'This has to be one of the most beautiful spots on earth – and yet it's all lost on me.'

'I'd feel better if there was something else we could do. Not just eating and drinking.'

'Maybe that's where your talents lie.'

'Thank you.'

They sat for a while, not speaking, watching the life of the harbour. They were both worried. At length, Victoria drained her brandy glass and said, 'I feel a talent for sleep, right now. Back to the hotel?'

'Yes – but give me a moment. The wine and coffee seem to have zoomed right through me.'

When he came back, he sat down and reached across the table. He covered Victoria's hand with his own. She looked at him: it was their first physical contact. But she left his hand where it was.

He said, 'There were two men in the loo. They were talking – in English – about a dig.'

Victoria's eyes glowed. 'Was Kolettis mentioned?'

'No. But they weren't archaeologists. They were both dressed all in white. They were crew members from that gin palace over there.'

18

Saturday

'Now, sir . . . sir! Could you come here for a moment? . . . Yes, you, sir. You're Indian, aren't you?'

The man looked straight into the camera. 'That is correct.'

'May I then ask why you are here today, on this demonstration?' The reporter, a red-headed twenty-nine-year-old with a Yorkshire accent, thrust the microphone to and fro enthusiastically between himself and his interviewee. 'As I understand it, this march was called by the United Greek Fellowship to protest against the torching of the Greek Orthodox Cathedral in Moscow Road and to press the Prime Minister to speed the return of the Elgin Marbles back to Athens. And yet half the march seems to be made up of Indians, Pakistanis and even a few Irish.'

'Yes, that's true – '

'But why?'

'I'm coming to that, if you'll let me answer. In the first place, it is a question of sympathy. I am chairman of the Indian Workers' Association and we are only too aware of the hostility of some British – not all by any means, but some – the hostility of some British to different religions. We have had our places of worship desecrated in the north, several times. So, in the first place, our presence here is a gesture of solidarity with the Greeks. What happened in Moscow Road was a disgrace and a tragedy. But there is also the question of the Elgin Marbles themselves. These pieces of stone arouse great passions but they are not the only cultural objects which are in Britain illegally – '

'You mean there are also Indian and Pakistani objects which you would like back?'

'That is exactly what I mean. There is a Hindu throne in the Victoria and Albert Museum, which is very beautiful and of great importance historically. It was taken out of the country at the end of the eighteenth century. That definitely ought to be returned. There are a number of Benin bronzes here in the British Museum that the Nigerian government would like back – and in the Museum of Mankind, an offshoot of the British Museum, there are valuable masks and a canoe that were produced by the Indians of Canada. They are unique and should be back in their native land.'

'If I may ask you just one more question, sir, then you can rejoin the demonstration . . . What do you hope to achieve by this march?'

'Publicity, first. Interviews like this one so that we can make known our views to a wider group of people, to the nation at large, in the hope that they will join us. But today we are marching from the museum here in Bloomsbury, to Downing Street, where we are going to present a petition to the Prime Minister, urging him to return the Marbles without any delay, and then to turn his mind to other cases where grave injustice has been done.'

The camera followed the interviewee as he ran a few steps to regain his place in the march and then refocused on the reporter. 'And so the saga of the Elgin Marbles takes a new twist today. I remind you also that this demonstration is only one of two taking place here at the British Museum. Inside the building, about a hundred keepers are staging a sit-in, with placards and speeches, in the larger galleries. Their object is the exact opposite of the Greeks and Pakistanis and Indians you see before you on the screen. The keepers want to stop the return of the Elgin Marbles and they have been joined by Lord Renfrew and some of the other Trustees who have resigned over the government's action. We return to the studio for now, but I hope to report later from inside the museum. This is Brian Welch, for BBC TV.'

'If someone else comes and looks over my shoulder, I'm going to die of embarrassment.'

'Don't be so touchy. You're not that bad.'

'Alongside you, I'm terrible. And you're not Mary Cassatt.'

Victoria turned and speared Edward's shoulder with her pencil. 'You're getting freckles on your forehead. All this sun brings them out.'

'And I've got such a lot of forehead – yes?'

'Don't be so touchy. A high forehead can be very distinguished.'

They were both sitting against the harbour wall in Datça with sketchpads on their knees, pretending to be artists. They were in the shade as the white day blazed around them. They faced into the harbour where they could see all the boats, especially the gin palace. That morning they had staked out the dig, as they had intended. They had watched plenty of people come and go. Overnight, however, they had had second thoughts about adopting the same tactics as they had employed at Olympia. If Datça was the headquarters of the Apollo Brigade, Victoria had argued, then their planned approach – to ask after Kolettis – was too blatant and too dangerous. They needed something subtler. She hadn't been sure what fresh approach would work but had suggested they keep watch on the boat, which was called the *Strabo*, in the hope that such observation might help. The sketchpads – bought in the village at lunchtime – were simply an excuse to be able to sit in one place for a long time, without appearing suspicious. They had now been leaning against the harbour wall for more than an hour. Since it was high afternoon there wasn't much activity anywhere, just a few tourists foolish enough to brave the sun. It was some of these who kept looking over Edward's shoulder at his handiwork.

'Hello,' said Victoria, lifting her head from her sketching. 'Competition for *Strabo*.'

Edward followed her gaze. Another enormous yacht was nosing into the harbour. This one was also white – at least the main bodywork was. But it was very modern, sleek and swept back, and all its windows were smoked glass, almost black against the rest of the boat. Edward and Victoria watched as the boat slowed, moved into reverse and then gently approached a vacant slot at the jetty.

'It's British!' said Victoria. 'Look, it says "Ginfizz: Brighton" on the stern.'

Edward nodded. 'How many would that sleep, do you think?'

'I haven't a clue. Count the portholes, that might help.'

He watched as *Ginfizz* tied up. A man dressed in a white short-sleeved shirt and white shorts descended from a staircase which the *Ginfizz* had lowered. He carried a briefcase; this was presumably the captain going to find the harbour master, to pay his dues and declare his passengers. There was little sign of life on board apart from that. No doubt they were all sleeping off lunch.

'Which bits do you find easiest to draw?' said Victoria softly. 'People, things or the landscape?'

'It's all equally hard to me. And I'm hopeless at everything. Do you think we're doing any good here. I'm thirsty.'

'You're too impatient. We've only been here an hour, at a quiet time of the day.'

'Well, let's have a drink and come back in an hour, when everyone starts waking up. There'll be more happening then.'

'Oh, all right. Beer comes first, as usual.'

They collected their things together and stood up. Then they strolled back to the bar. It too was nearly empty at that time of day and they chose to sit inside, in the shade. Edward ordered the beers while Victoria went off to find a newspaper. By the time she came back, he was half-way through his drink. 'Any luck?'

'No British newspapers, just yesterday's *Rhodes Daily*. The Trustees of the British Museum have resigned. The British Embassy in Athens is still surrounded by demonstrators, peaceful but noisy if you see what I mean. A lot of shouting but no trouble yet. That could change after the Aghia Sophia business.'

As they talked they saw the captain of the *Ginfizz* enter the bar. He had presumably finished with the harbour master and was beginning to relax. They heard him order a coffee and water.

'He looks about twelve,' whispered Victoria.

'Your type? You do live on a houseboat, after all.'

'He's good-looking but his skin's too smooth. He must be gay.'

'Is this someone else from the same boat?'

Another man had entered the bar and was making for the captain. He addressed him in English. 'You forgot the passenger manifest.' He held a sheet of paper in his hand.

'I know. I'll have to go back to the harbour master after my coffee. Thanks for bringing it. Saved me a walk. Want a coffee?'

'I'd rather have a beer. I can't do my shopping yet anyway. Nowhere's open.' His beer was poured and the two men chatted away. They were obviously regular cruisers of the Mediterranean, the second man being the ship's chef. Victoria browsed through the paper and Edward just sat, as the Englishmen talked around him. After about ten minutes they left, the chef going off in search of shops in which to buy food, and the captain back to the harbour master with the passenger manifest.

Edward watched the figure of the captain as he crossed the harbour. How on earth did Victoria know he was gay?

She lifted her head from the paper. 'Passenger manifest!'

'What?'

'That captain has to deliver a passenger manifest to the harbour master's office.'

'Yes.'

'Other captains must do the same.'

Edward sat up. 'Including the captain of the *Strabo*.'

'Exactly.'

'But . . . how do we get to see the manifest? . . . We'd have to break into the harbour master's office.'

'Exactly.'

Edward was silent, digesting what Victoria had said.

After a while, she added: 'We'll have to go in tonight. It won't take long, not once we're inside, anyway. Are you any better at breaking and entering than you are at drawing?'

'Mordaunt! I thought we had agreed – ' Zakros's voice grew petulant.

'Don't hang up!' the equerry half whispered, half screamed into the phone. 'Don't hang up. Her Majesty is here. I just want to say that . . . the Duveen Galleries, which contain the Elgin Marbles, are closed and . . . it hasn't been announced yet but the Prime Minister has recalled a Royal Navy frigate – HMS *Anglesey* – from a tour of duty off Norway. The Marbles are being crated over the weekend and the *Anglesey* will collect them from the Port of London on Monday or Tuesday, depending on the weather in the North Sea. Anyway, she will meet your deadline. She will then deliver them to Piraeus. It will take her – oh, four or five days . . .' He tailed off.

'Hmm.' Zakros was non-committal. Then he said, 'I will speak with Her Majesty now.'

The Queen took the phone. 'Yes?' Earpieces were affixed to the instrument so that Leith and Mordaunt could listen in.

'There is one other thing we require of you, Your Majesty.'

The Queen was taken aback. 'Is . . . is that fair?'

'Don't worry, we are not changing the rules, like common blackmailers. You will understand when I tell you. I'm sure Mr Lockwood has been expecting it – or something very like it.'

'What is it?'

'First, you need to buy a certain make and model of typewriter.'

'What on earth for –?'

'You'll see. Just listen. Then do it. Have it done for you. Buy an Olivetti 509E. I'm told they can be bought almost anywhere. Harrod's certainly. It must be Olivetti and it must be a model 509E. Is that quite clear, ma'am?'

'Yes, yes . . . I'm writing it down.'

'Good. Now, I'm going to dictate a letter to you. You are to have this typed out, using the Olivetti, on your own personal Buckingham Palace stationery and it is to be signed by you, in ink in the normal way. But – and this is an important instruction, which must be observed exactly – when you put the paper into the typewriter, you must press the "Return" key eight times. Do you understand?'

'Eight times. Yes. Why?'

'I'll ignore that. Now, the letter. I'll dictate slowly . . . Are you ready? . . . It should read as follows: "I am writing . . . to express . . . my appreciation for all the help and guidance . . . you have given concerning the return of the so-called Elgin Marbles to Greece. When we met, in London, all those months ago, it was your inspiration and discreet energy which helped me to encourage the British government that its decision to return the Marbles was the right one. I thank you too for all the help you gave in little ways, finding solutions to obstacles, overcoming difficulties, smoothing the path imaginatively and seeing through the whole project with enthusiasm and tenacity. Greece can be proud she has such a son and I hope that your role in all this will not go unrecognized or unrewarded. Yours sincerely and in friendship . . . Elizabeth R." '

The Queen made a sound half-way between a groan and a sigh. 'I can't write this. It is not the sort of thing the monarch can write.'

'Yes, you can, ma'am. You'll have to.'

'But . . . it will involve the Crown . . . in a political matter – '

'But nowhere near as controversial as the other . . . matter, hmm? Look upon it as good news, as a piece of insurance. When this is all over, when the Marbles are safely back in Athens, it must have crossed your mind that we – the Apollo Brigade, that is – would still be free to give our story to the newspapers. This letter shows you we don't intend to do anything of the sort. We shall only go public if you do not keep your side of the bargain. Otherwise, the letter I have just dictated will be made public – and only that. We have an Olivetti 509E . . . and shall simply insert the name of the . . . addressee at the top of the letter. It will be a significant social and political boost for that . . . person . . . acknowledgement from the Queen of England for the role . . . that person has played in this affair, this affair which all Greece will know about.' Zakros chuckled. 'The Apollo Brigade must have some sort of credit for all our hard work. You must have been wondering how we would go about that – I'm sure Mr Lockwood has. Now you know.'

The Queen went to speak but then changed her mind.

Zakros grew more businesslike. 'On a Saturday it shouldn't take more than an hour or two to track down an Olivetti 509E. Say a few minutes to tap out the letter. Half a day's work at most. I shall telephone again at this time on Monday. Then I'll tell you where to post it.'

'Coming to you . . . nine, eight, seven, six . . .'

Brian Welch counted silently to five and saw the light over the camera lens flash red. 'I'm standing now in the King's Library of the British Museum, surrounded by priceless items of Britain's heritage, mainly books in this gallery but of course the British Museum is famed throughout the world for its treasures of every kind – cuneiform tablets, Etruscan vases, the Rosetta Stone, the Portland Vase, Egyptian mummies . . . and of course the Elgin Marbles.'

At this point the camera turned away from Welch to take in a group of keepers and curators of the museum seated on the floor of the library, holding placards. Then the camera slowly turned back to Welch, who by now had a man and a woman standing next to him.

'With me is Brenda Peachey, who works in the museum as a curator in the Department of Greek and Roman Antiquities, and Sir Henry Misco, the architect who is – or was, until very recently when he resigned – a trustee of the museum. Brenda, if I can come to you first . . . It has now been six days since this story first broke. Why are you demonstrating today when you have had all week? And what do you hope to achieve?'

'Well, I would have thought that it's obvious why we're demonstrating today. Quite frankly, we never imagined for a moment that the government actually intended to carry out the policy that this secret Cabinet committee recommended. Not until the

223

Duveen Galleries actually closed was it clear that the Prime Minister really is set on this course. Add to that the fact that the Trustees have now resigned and we had no choice but to make our views known. This museum is in crisis.'

'Earlier today, several hundred Greeks, Indians and other sympathizers marched on Downing Street to petition the Prime Minister. Why haven't you done that?'

'William Lockwood seems to us to be beyond reason. Our aim therefore is to enlist the support of the public. My colleagues are giving lectures today in a variety of galleries, explaining the issues and asking members of the public to approach their MPs with a view to getting an emergency debate in parliament.'

'Are the security staff and warders on your side?'

'Some are, yes. I understand that one or two warders refused to close off the Duveen Galleries last night. But it has been done now. The doors are locked and we can hear the packers.'

'The director of the museum, Sir Martin Ogilvy, has refused to see us. Have you seen him?'

Brenda Peachey shook her head. 'No, he's in the museum today, supervising the packing of the Marbles. But he won't talk to anyone.'

'What do you expect to happen now?'

'Two things that we know about. The Reading Room will be closed on Monday, in protest, so the public will not be able to use it. Second, the Print Room will also be closed. We are talking to the warders and they may mount a protest. If they did, then the whole museum would have to be closed.'

Welch moved the microphone across to Misco. 'Sir Henry, mass resignation has a fine ring to it. But aren't you now a spent force? Might it not have been more cunning for the Trustees to have fought the Prime Minister from inside?'

Misco tossed back his head, throwing his silver hair in a way that made him look much younger than his seventy-three years. He had obviously done it before. 'The Prime Minister is using brutal tactics – we must do the same. But don't imagine that our opposition to him stops with our resignations. Brenda here, and her colleagues, will try to force a debate in the Commons. We shall certainly get a debate in the Lords. Lord Renfrew, our chairman – or ex-chairman, I should say – will certainly raise it next week. We shall be asking other national museums to join us in protest.'

Welch pulled the microphone back to his own lips. 'Does either of you know when the Marbles are due to leave?'

Peachey and Misco shook their heads.

Now Welch addressed the camera directly. 'So . . . a chaotic week ahead in London's museums. Protests, closures, debates in Parliament . . . The Prime Minister appears to be easily out-numbered on this issue – but he has the power. Will he use that power to push through this controversial repatriation? Here at the British Museum the mood is ugly but as yet not violent. Will the coming week change all that? This is Brian Welch for BBC TV.'

Riley had rented a new car, a green Mazda. A different make and a different colour. Now that they knew where Zakros was going to be at ten o'clock in the evening, they didn't have to tail him at all times. Not that they would have been able to, since they had had to spend some time earlier today fixing the phone he was going to use. It was rather easier to fix public phones than any other kind – for the very simple reason that you could get at the instrument. Riley had done the honours in this particular case, unscrewing the plastic casing of the receiver while O'Day kept watch. There had been plenty of time to make a good job of it and to affix a tiny radio transmitter so that they could listen in to the conversation a few yards away. That is why Riley had hired the Mazda. Now there was no reason for Zakros to be suspicious about the car – he had never seen it before. For the past two hours they had been sitting in the Mazda, watching people go into the booth and make calls. O'Day and Riley had heard every single one of them perfectly.

'Ten to ten,' said Riley.

'I can tell the time,' said O'Day.

'Just trying to be helpful.'

'It would be a help if you passed the whisky flask.'

'At the Bruegel in Bruges, they simmer tiny snipe in whisky. It has to be males apparently – '

'Shut . . . up!'

They sat in silence as O'Day took a gulp of alcohol. They had experimented earlier in the evening, and found that it was impossible to see into their car from the booth. Zakros wouldn't spot them. Each of them had long since passed the point at which they felt the need to keep talking. The minutes passed as they kept their eyes peeled for the first sign of the Greek.

'There! By the travel agent. Wearing a raincoat.'

'Got him. You're right. Chic, eh? Bit of a playboy, our Zakros.'

'Don't knock it . . . it could be our saving. If he was a provincial Greek, he'd only speak Greek. As it is, he must speak German or French, to have been sent here to Basle. And English when he calls the Palace.'

They watched in silence as Zakros inspected one shop window after another, gradually moving closer to the phone booth. They saw him look at his watch twice and then, exactly on ten o'clock, he stood in front of the booth and lit a cigarette.

'Christ! What's that?' hissed Riley as a raucous noise filled the car.

'Moron! It's the phone ringing. We haven't heard it before . . . No one else has taken a call here.'

Almost immediately the noise was cut off. Zakros had lifted the receiver.

'Yes?' Zakros spoke in English.

'What happened today?' It was a woman's voice. She spoke English too.

'I talked to Queen Elizabeth. I really did. It was amazing. They do everything we ask – '

'Of course. We hold all the cards.' There was a chuckle. 'The court cards.'

'I dictated the letter. Me . . . I dictated to the Queen. Literally.'

'What else happened?'

'Oh yes. Mordaunt spoke first. He said Lockwood has arranged for a British Navy ship – a frigate – to load the Marbles – '

'When?'

'He said the ship was being recalled from Norway, would pick up the Marbles in two days, from London, and then proceed to Piraeus, which would take another four days.'

'Do you trust him?'

'I think so.'

'You're not sure?'

'. . . Yes . . . I'm sure.'

'Good. When do you speak to the Palace again?'

'The day after tomorrow – '

'When either the stones are on their way, or they aren't. You'll have to be firm.'

'Don't worry, we're too close to success now.'

'You're being very brave. Kofas is most impressed. If the plan works, there'll be big jobs for all of us. To think that a group like ours, just seven people, could accomplish what generations have failed to do.'

'There are many demonstrations, I hear.'

'Oh yes. Here in London and in Athens. That's all to our advantage . . . We always knew there would be a lot of support for the cause. You will be the biggest hero of all. You deserve it.'

'I am blushing. I never imagined, that time when Blunt came to Athens, that . . . that it would end like this. He was so unfriendly, so snobbish.'

'We've discussed all this before, Nicos. He hated losing his knighthood, silly man. You know how the British love a title.'

'He was certainly a lot friendlier afterwards, I agree. Lucky us.'

'*Not* luck, Nicos. You played him well. He loved the idea of one end of the royals being used to blackmail the other end. You were brilliant. Now it's paying off.'

'I'm blushing again.'

'Go and have a drink. I miss you.'

'And I miss you. Give my regards to Kofas.'

'So long. Tomorrow, as usual.'

'Yes.'

The phone went dead, and O'Day and Riley watched the Greek walk away from the booth. His cigarette must have gone out during his conversation for he stopped to light it again and then resumed his walk. They watched him in silence until he had disappeared. Later on they would dismantle the phone and remove the tapping device. But they would let him get well clear first.

'Who, then, is Kofas? And what was all that about Blunt?' said Riley.

'Search me. At least we found out one important thing tonight, besides Kofas, I mean.'

'Oh yes?'

'Christ! Weren't you listening? This character referred to a group of seven. That's the first time we've had it confirmed that there are seven of them. The question is: who are the others? We now know about Kofas, we know about Aristotle and Stamatis Leonardis and about Kolettis. That makes four. We know about

Zakros in Basle and Eugenie Shelby in London – that makes six. The voice on the phone was in London – '

'Shelby?'

'No. Shelby's Greek. That woman's voice just now was American.'

'I don't believe it,' Victoria whispered, pulling on Edward's sleeve.

'What don't you believe?'

'What a break . . . Look, there's a window open.'

For two-thirty in the morning, the light was surprisingly good, thanks to an entire galaxy of stars overhead. Victoria pulled on Edward's sleeve again and they crept behind the harbour master's office. They had used the old lovers' routine to reach this end of the harbour. Victoria had leaned against Edward, her head on his shoulder and her arm around his waist as they strolled past the boats, now all wrapped in silence. He hadn't objected. At the end of the jetty they had leaned against the office, apparently kissing, should anyone have been watching at that late hour. 'My aunt would have disapproved of this,' whispered Victoria. But, after a moment, their kissing had become real.

They had observed earlier in the day that the harbour master's office was a simple affair, two offices in an L-shape with a reception area in between and what looked like a small kitchen and a lavatory behind that. It was not exactly a fortress, and Victoria had said she would easily be able to break in. Now, checking behind the building to be absolutely sure there were no hippies or tramps or drunks sleeping there, who might be awakened by what they planned, she had found the open window.

'They're just asking to be burgled,' whispered Edward.

'There can't be much worth stealing in here,' she replied. 'Just records – they probably take the harbour dues, those that are paid in cash, home every night and pay them into the bank next morning. It's very hot here during the day, as we know. Maybe they leave the window open at night to keep the building aired. Anyway, lucky us.' She led the way towards the window. 'You're taller than I am,' she whispered when they had reached it. 'Can you lift me up?'

Edward bent and grabbed Victoria around the thighs. He lifted her bodily so she could reach the catch on the window and pull it further open. Still holding her, he moved back so she could keep out of the way of the window as it swung round. Then he shoved her still higher as she bent over the window-sill. She tipped the upper part of her body forward and disappeared inside. Edward, who was wearing rubber-soled pumps, now jumped as high as he could and caught hold of the window frame. He got some purchase on the wall from his pumps, enough to stick his elbows over the sill and haul himself up some more. Inside the room, Victoria was just getting to her feet. She was rubbing her head.

'I landed on the wash basin. If you can, sit on the sill and then step on to the basin.'

Edward managed that with difficulty – he was bigger than she was – but eventually he dropped down safely into the room. Victoria led the way through to the kitchen – a refrigerator, sink and electricity point, really – and on towards the main rooms.

'You try that one,' she hissed, indicating the door on the left. 'I'll do the other.'

Edward tried the door. It wasn't locked. Inside, he found a desk and three or four filing cabinets. None was marked, so he opened them at random. The files were in Turkish but in one there were some drawings; he couldn't be sure but they looked like designs for a new jetty. He tried another drawer – more plans, this time for shops lining the harbour. He tried a different cabinet. The first two files were filled with printed documents – official communications from Istanbul, by the look of them. In another drawer he found large-scale maps of the peninsula, all the inlets, coves and beaches. Emergency maps, maybe, in case of shipwrecks. He turned to the last cabinet. As he opened it, he smiled. It was empty, save for some flippers, goggles and snorkels. The desk-top was empty so he tried the drawers. Notepaper, envelopes, a date-franking machine, an old telephone, some phone books and what looked like a harbour master's hat were all he found. He tiptoed through into the other room.

'A complete blank – '

'What was that?'

'What was what?'

'Listen!' They both stood very still, not even breathing.

There was a noise in the distance.

'Sounds like a boat,' whispered Edward.

'Coming in here!' hissed Victoria. 'Shit!'

'The harbour master will never come out at this hour, surely? They'll do the paperwork in the morning.'

'You want to take that risk?'

'Are you getting anywhere? The other room's useless.'

'Yes and no. It's very tidy in here. I've found the records of boats coming and going. I just haven't hit on the most recent ones yet.' She peered through the window, back to the bar and café. 'Can't see anyone yet . . . but let's not risk it. If we get caught now the whole thing's up in smoke.'

She led the way swiftly out through the kitchen and into the lavatory. Without even looking back, she stepped on to the lid of the lavatory seat, then on to the wash basin, then turned and sat on the window-sill. Bending her legs and swivelling her body, she dropped outside. Edward followed suit. As he landed, the noise of the boat suddenly swelled as it came abreast of the natural promontory that formed the basis of the modern harbour.

'It's bigger even than *Ginfizz*,' said Victoria. 'Push the window shut. If anyone does come to the office, let's hope they don't notice it's a burglar's paradise.'

They decided to stay where they were. They couldn't walk back into town, because if the harbour master did come out to his office they would have to pass him. That might look suspicious in itself and if, on top of that, he happened to notice that certain things in his office had been moved he might recall their faces.

The sound of the new boat faded as its engines were cut. They rumbled as reverse was engaged and there was a swirl of water. One or two voices could be heard giving instructions. Victoria and Edward watched in silence as the bulk eased backwards to berth a few spaces from *Ginfizz*. Unfortunately, the stern of the new boat was obscured by the *Strabo* so they couldn't see if anyone had disembarked. They had no choice but to wait.

They waited half an hour, an hour, ninety minutes.

'It's four-thirty,' said Edward at last. 'It'll be getting light soon. No one is coming, Victoria. Come on.'

'Okay. Let's both work the room I was in.'

They climbed back into the harbour master's offices, using the same technique as before. When they reached the main office, Victoria worked through the filing cabinets while Edward searched the desk. 'The *Ginfizz* papers are still here,' he said after a moment and began to go through the documents on the desk with more care. They worked in silence for perhaps ten minutes before Victoria said, 'Ahhh. Look at this.' She held out two sheets of paper. On the top one there were some words in Turkish, but immediately underneath, the international form was in two languages, Greek and English, and it read: 'PASSENGER MANIFEST FOR' and then, written in ink, were two words: Strabo: Piraeus'.

'And look.'

Two-thirds of the way down the list of names was the entry: Dimitri Kolettis.

19

Sunday

Archbishop Gregor Lysiptos stood in front of the scaffolding and waited for a moment before speaking. Ahead of him the Aghia Sophia was crowded; he had never seen it so full. He was moved but also angry: the size of the congregation only demonstrated that the power of publicity was greater than the power of God. He paused, not only to allow the crowd to settle down, but also to allow himself to settle down.

'Friends,' he said at length. He had a fine voice, as rich and as dark as his beard. 'Friends, I have never seen this fine cathedral so full. So many newcomers. So many television cameras, microphones, reporters with their notebooks. Perhaps it is a reflection on our times that the Lord could never fill the Aghia Sophia as well as the devil can. With your forgiveness, therefore, I will say a few words in English. Greek, the Greek of Sophocles and Aristotle, of Herodotus and Homer, is the usual language of our service. But for today, and in these circumstances, I will speak in English. I want our newcomers to hear what I have to say.' He shifted on his feet. His white and gold robes glowed beneath the television lights. 'Behind me you see scaffolding. It supports what remains of our beautiful iconostasis, a holy screen showing some of the Greek Orthodox religion's most venerated saints. Not that there is much that remains – a few square feet only. A beautiful gold-leaf screen, the work of hundreds of years, is no more. Many of you are sitting on flimsy chairs, lent to us by the Red Cross. You should, of course, be sitting on hardy pews, pews that no one would call beautiful perhaps but all of which were given by members of this church, pews which were dedicated to the memory of our ancestors, Greeks who came to London over the years and, in one way or another, enriched the city. Now, like the screen, many of these pews are no more and the memories have disappeared with them, literally gone up in smoke, just as the wooden pews themselves did.' His gaze raked the room.

232

'This, as you know, is the first service to be held in this cathedral since that black night last week. I look around you and I see policemen, policemen who are no doubt trying hard to find the culprits of this horrendous crime. I see politicians, distinguished men and women from our community, actors, professors, lawyers, bankers. This first service is emotional for all of us who know this church and love it. The people who started the fire took away not just the screen and our pews, not only the memories of our forebears . . . they took away our belief in our fellow men.

'Look at the progress man has made in two thousand years!' Lysiptos was shouting now, bellowing his words so that they rang around the cathedral. 'Two thousand years ago, men spent their lifetimes carving beautiful shapes out of stone. They did so to create one of the most beautiful things the world has ever seen – maybe the most beautiful thing the world *has* ever seen.' He paused. 'I refer of course to the Parthenon in Athens. Now, after more than two thousand years of progress, after more than two hundred decades of better education, where are we? I will tell you where we are: we are in a world where a quarrel between governments – a quarrel moreover about beautiful objects, the same beautiful objects which, all those years ago, made up the most wonderful place of worship the world has ever seen – can cause hatred, can cause intolerance, can cause destruction. That is where we are today, friends.

'The whole history of mankind has been a fragile undertaking. Every leap ahead has, as often as not, been accompanied by a slide backwards. Never was this illustrated more clearly than in the treatment meted out in this cathedral.' The archbishop was bellowing again. 'What happened here on that black night was evil, unholy, barbaric. The perpetrators were heathens, ignorant criminals. But worse, worse than all that is this fact . . . These black deeds, these terrible actions, were preventable. I don't mean by the police. I mean that these cruel people, whoever they are, were stimulated to act, were prepared, primed, goaded into what they did. I refer here to the Prime Minister! To William Lockwood! The Prime Minister, by his shilly-shallying, by his inability to make up his mind, by his spreading of confusion, by his high-handed incompetence has created a climate in which this sort of grave act can occur. I do not mean to excuse the people who broke into this church, who spread petrol over the screen and the pews, who scrawled obscenities on the walls. They will be caught, I trust, and dealt with according to law. No! I speak out now, in this place, in this sad place, against the man who is the real cause of the ravages you see before you. And, as an archbishop, as a man of God, I cannot recognize the difference between peoples, between nations.

'I now call upon the Prime Minister, I beg him, to bring this matter to a swift conclusion. Already this church has been desecrated, already several magnificent buildings throughout this fine land have been attacked, already demonstrators have been injured. The Prime Minister, by his statesmanlike vision over the Parthenon Marbles, has nevertheless unleashed emotions that were buried. By delaying the return of the Marbles, he has allowed reactionary forces to fester. They will not go back beneath the surface, not now, not after what has happened. Friends, I believe there is only one way, one way for this situation to be resolved. I say this as a man of God but also as a Greek man of God. I say to the Prime Minister, I implore him: return the Marbles now! This was a wrong committed more than a century ago. Nearly two centuries ago. Now is the time to put right that wrong. If the Prime Minister does that, now, it will also, in its way, put right the wrong that was done in this cathedral a few nights ago. I call upon the Prime Minister to act, and to act now!'

At the front of the congregation, the local mayor sat next to the Commissioner of Police and Bayswater's local MP. The mayor leaned forward and whispered across to the MP. 'Are you going to make anything of this in the Commons, Arthur? It's explosive stuff.'

'Yes,' said Arthur Page, Leader of the Opposition. 'Yes. It's about time I did.'

'This is the first time in days that I feel decently hungry.' Victoria smiled as she spoke to Edward.

He leaned forward and helped her to some red wine. They were dining outside the harbour restaurant. 'Tell me what you see.' He stroked the back of her hand.

After their success in locating Kolettis's name in the *Strabo's* passenger manifest, they had studied the other names. Among them were A. and S. Leonardis. So this was obviously where the

Apollo Brigade was hiding out. There was also a G. Kofas on board.

They had returned to their hotel in good spirits, Victoria especially. At last they were getting somewhere, she felt. At five in the morning, however, even Turkey was chilly, so Victoria had invited Edward to share her bed. He had not refused.

'I see three men. The older one, the big one who is nearly bald, is doing all the talking. The other two are listening. There's a resemblance, you know. Maybe they are the brothers. One of them keeps looking over his shoulder, as though he is expecting someone else to join them. There's a spare place at the table so maybe they *are* expecting someone else.'

Victoria and Edward had spent the day discreetly watching the *Strabo*. Now they knew Kolettis and the others were on board, their next priority was to identify them physically. Victoria had called Leith in London with the news of their discovery. He had promised to have the British Embassy in Athens check out the *Strabo*. He had informed them that the embassy had finally located Haydon's car. It had been left in an Athens street and had finally been reported to the Athens police, who had notified the embassy. 'And here's the interesting bit,' Leith had said. 'It was five streets – three minutes' walk – away from Stamatis Leondaris's house.'

Edward and Victoria had debated what that meant. 'Haydon must have burgled Leondaris – and been caught. They couldn't have known he was a British Embassy man but they wouldn't have wanted to take risks,' said Victoria. 'A burglary, with Leondaris involved, would not have been welcome just before their big coup.'

'But they must have been very suspicious,' said Edward. 'It was a hell of a coincidence.'

Victoria nodded. 'On the other hand, if they thought Haydon, or Broudin as his papers said, was anything to do with our side, a bit of brutality wouldn't have gone amiss, would it? It would show they are serious in their threat. Anyway, they decided to go ahead. Leondaris's wife is a jeweller – maybe they thought Haydon was a jewel thief.'

Edward said nothing. Suddenly the danger was so close he could touch it.

During the day, he and Victoria had watched the *Strabo* from various locations around the harbour, posing once again as artists. It had been embarrassing for Edward but he'd had no choice. Around seven-thirty they had watched a party of three leave the boat and head for the restaurant. They had allowed them fifteen minutes' grace, then found a table for themselves at the same restaurant where they could observe, and even overhear something of what the *Strabo* party were saying.

'Describe the others.' Edward was itchy that he couldn't see what Victoria could.

'One man has silver hair, a thin neck, rather effeminate hands. Quite swarthy. The other is fatter, rounder, whiter. He's going bald too.'

'Like me.'

'Bah! Don't be so vain. I like a high forehead – I told you.' Victoria smiled. 'Everything looks so normal here, so jolly.' She nodded towards the other table. They look as though they're celebrating even before their victory.'

The waiter brought Victoria and Edward their starters. As he leaned across to serve them, there was a movement at the table they were watching. Victoria had to crane forward to see.

Another figure had arrived, a fourth man.

'What kept you?' The big man spoke in rapid Greek, so that Victoria had to strain to understand.

The fourth figure remained standing. He was a squat, pugnacious-looking man with dark crinkly hair that hugged his skull. 'I was reading, George,' he said. 'Working.'

'Relax!' said the big man. 'Sit down. Have some wine.'

Victoria hardly heard. The man who had been reading was still carrying a book. Except that it was too big and too flimsy to be a proper book. It was, instead, an academic journal. From where she sat, Victoria could even read the title: *Journal of the Classical Greece*.

'That's it, Zak, right on cue. The phone's to your left. Keep going.'

O'Day and Riley were in high spirits. After days of trailing the Greek, they were now, as they saw it, more or less in charge. Earlier in the day, they had found the next phone, near the next tram stop, easily enough. They had affixed the same bugging device as on the previous day. And now Zakros, or Zak as they half affectionately thought of him, had turned up at the appointed place, at the appointed time. Their world was behaving a little more predictably again.

'I wonder what's on the agenda for tonight.'

'Not anything, necessarily,' replied O'Day. 'They most likely use these rendezvous just to keep in touch, in case anything should go wrong, or something unexpected crops up.'

Riley drummed the steering wheel with his fingers. 'Unless Zak actually goes to the bank where the pictures are kept we'll never find them.'

'You're right there . . . At some point we're going to have to worry him, panic him, so that he thinks the documents are in danger and goes to check them – and leads us to where they are hidden.'

The car – a red Ford tonight – suddenly filled with sound as the phone in the booth across the street started to ring. 'Here we go,' said Riley.

They watched the Greek walk quickly to the booth and lift the receiver.

'Yes?'

'Two things only to report.' It was the same woman's voice.

'Go on.'

'The English church in Athens has been attacked. As a reprisal for the Aghia Sophia.'

'Was there much damage?'

'Windows smashed. Graffiti, the altar overturned.'

'That suits our purpose.'

'Yes.'

'And the other thing?'

'It's more complicated. I've been trying to contact Andover, just in case he might let slip something that would help. I know he's not at home but he always checks in with his answering machine. I left a message for him to ring me. He always does – or he always has until now. He's supposed to be on holiday, in Scotland – '

'Yes – that's what Mordaunt told me.'

'I know . . . but I'm beginning to have my doubts. I wonder . . . I wonder if he's suspicious of me . . . and that's why he's avoiding me? Maybe the other side know more than we think they do.'

WEEK FOUR

The Stones of Treason

20

Monday

Given what had been happening, it was natural enough to assume that the throng of people outside the British Museum was a demonstration. But it wasn't, not in the strict sense. Among the faces milling around, there were a number of well-known academics and art historians from across the world. The Reading Room of the British Museum, what was left of it after the British Library had decamped to St Pancras, had failed to open on time.

Not everyone had seen the television news the previous Saturday, when Brenda Peachey had forecast that the protests at the museum would spread, and some of those who had seen the programme did not believe what she had said. In fact, she had understated the case. On their way into work that morning, the British Museum staff had seen seven dark-blue lorries drawn up in Russell Square and another three already backed up inside the museum's deliveries entrance. It was obvious why they were there. As a result, while some of the world's most distinguished scholars gathered at the front of the museum, almost the entire professional staff who worked there milled around at the back. There was no shouting or overt demonstrating: they were librarians, archaeologists, classicists, not the demonstrating types. There were one or two newspaper photographers and some protesters but the mood at the back of the museum was sullen and resentful rather than rowdy. Nevertheless, the sheer number of people on the pavement caused some of them to spill over into the road and, despite the presence of the police, this caused the traffic in Malet Street and Russell Square to back up. It was Monday morning and that area of London was very busy at the best of times. Traffic was inching along.

One of the cars in line was driven by Sir Martin Ogilvy, arriving at the museum after a meeting of the Review Committee on the Export of Works of Art. He saw his staff before they saw him. But he was trapped by the traffic and for the last fifty or sixty yards, before he reached the gates of the museum, Ogilvy's car was surrounded by members of his staff. No one shouted at him, no one screamed. In fact, no one spoke. Everyone was spontaneously mute as Ogilvy ran – or rather crawled – this silent gauntlet. He was unnerved by the silence, the control shown by the people standing there. He was distressed by the looks he received from people he regarded as colleagues. He had shielded himself so far; now, for the first time, he saw their collective reaction. As he turned into the gate, he looked in his rear-view mirror, to see those colleagues staring after him as if he was some hateful object. Until now Ogilvy had played the part the Prime Minister had asked of him. He had kept the secret – his wife and secretary were still in the dark, though he'd had that one conversation with the Arts Minister. He had realized that what he was doing would be unpopular but he had regarded it as his duty to help out and, more important perhaps, he had regarded the whole business as temporary, or theoretical. He had assumed that Lockwood would win, that the Marbles would never have to leave. Seeing the blue lorries in the deliveries yard, and the staring faces behind him, he suddenly realized that the situation was now very different.

The Elgin Marbles were about to leave. They might never return – and he would be known in history as the director, the only director, of the British Museum to connive in the disposal of major art objects. Years from now he would be vilified, reviled, laughed at, dismissed out of hand. The sullen hatred he had seen in the eyes of his colleagues would eventually turn into contempt. His name would be recalled only with disdain.

He parked his car in the space reserved for him. He entered the building by the side entrance, opposite the wooden hut where the cuneiform tablets were conserved. He nodded at the guard. There was only one, he noticed – some of the others were watching the lorries and standing outside. Even they disapproved of what was happening. As he went deeper into the building, he realized how quiet it was today. And dark. Not all the lights had been turned on, half the doors were locked – or closed at any rate. They should have been open. He decided to see what was happening in the main lobby. As he approached it, through the King's Library, he heard a hubbub of voices. He turned the corner and stopped. Ahead of him the lobby was choked with people. But they weren't tourists or visitors. They were scholars – yet more colleagues – come to use the Reading

Room, which had obviously not opened this morning. The threat had been carried out.

As he realized this, he was spotted – by David Seebag, an historian he knew from Manchester, an authority on Italian medieval pottery. Seebag pulled the sleeve of another man, whom Ogilvy also recognized. He was one of the top three authorities on St Patrick, and was talking to an Australian Chaldean scholar. They all looked in his direction – and then moved towards him. Seebag was about to speak when Ogilvy, surrounded and alone in his own museum, turned and ran.

'What was all that about?' Victoria held her treen animal – it was a horse's head – cupped in her hand.

Edward lay in bed. He had just put down the phone. He looked tired. 'There's something I didn't tell you.'

She looked at him sharply.

'I didn't tell anyone. But now Leith knows – they all know.' He explained about Nancy and the phone conversation Riley and O'Day had overheard.

When he had finished, Victoria got off the bed, put down her treen animal and went into the bathroom. When she came out, she was wearing her dressing-gown. She picked up her coffee and sat, not on the bed, but on a chair by the dressing-table. 'I think you owe me more than the few details that you gave Leith.'

Edward nodded. 'I was in love with Nancy – at least, I think I was. She certainly had an effect on me that no one else did. But I didn't realize she had used me until . . . until this whole business was well under way. By that time I had . . . mishandled that telephone conversation with Basle and if I'd told Lockwood I'd have been out on my ear and very likely locked up.'

'But you were taking one hell of a risk.'

'See it my way and you'll see I had no choice. And I thought Nancy's main role was to observe – through me – how the negotiations were developing.'

'Even so, she could have been followed – she might have led our side to one of the main characters.'

'Yes . . . yes. But I didn't know – I couldn't be sure – she was involved. All I had was circumstantial – '

'Edward!'

243

He took a breath. 'All the evidence I had was circumstantial and – well, I did . . . we *were* close once. Or I thought we were.'

'Oh dear.'

'All right! All right! What I did was wrong. Foolish.' He took another breath. 'No! That's not fair. I was foolish, maybe. But you don't turn on your friends, not immediately, not at the first suspicious circumstance. Not at the second, even. If they're friends they get the benefit of the doubt. It may not be the way politicians behave, or the security services. But I'm not one of them.'

'What did Lockwood say?'

Edward shrugged. 'Leith was cool, but not spitting. Maybe he understands. Maybe the Prime Minister understands – more than you seem to.'

Victoria was silent for a while. She put down the treen horse and sipped her coffee. When she next spoke, her voice was different. 'If you were in love with her, what was . . . what were you doing last night and the night before? With me, I mean.'

Edward pulled the bedclothes up to his chin. 'I can't give you a definitive answer. People talk about love at first sight: everyone accepts that can happen in a flash. But what about the opposite – being turned *off* people just as quickly? Nancy used me, she lied, she deceived, she pretended. When I think about it, I get hot waves of anger and embarrassment. I think of her way of laughing, her habit of cocking her head to one side when she was being sarcastic – a hundred little intimacies that I assumed *were* intimacies. And I feel betrayed. I feel I've lost a race badly, a race I didn't know I was in. And of course I *have* lost.' Edward turned on his side to face Victoria. 'What do you think happened to my feelings as a result of all that? Do you think love could survive that?'

'Feelings are unpredictable.'

'Well, not mine. Anger is one thing. I suppose you can be angry with someone you love. But you can't embarrass someone and expect them to love you back. Embarrassment and love, shame and love, can't coexist.'

'But you're talking about Nancy and you. Not about us.'

'You asked, Victoria,' he said gently. Then, 'Neither you nor I could govern the time when we met. Whenever you meet some-one you have a past, an immediate past, as often as not with someone in it. So does the other person. That can't be helped –

it's normal. Nothing I've done with you, Victoria, nothing I've said, has been anything other than natural or honest. Yes, I think about Nancy a lot. But when I think about her it's with embarrassment, anger and shame, not with tenderness. Not any more. A week – ten days – ago, I was in love with her. Now I could kill her – and I mean that. She has destroyed something inside me.' He smiled at Victoria. 'It so happens that you seem to be the perfect antidote to Nancy. You are so fresh, intellectually, emotionally, sexually. When I'm with you I hardly think of Nancy.'

'Hardly! Jesus, my aunt was right! Men *are* a pain.'

'Victoria! We are in Turkey for a reason.' He added softly. 'Nancy is part of that reason.'

For a while, neither of them spoke. Then Edward said, 'Come and sit next to me on the bed. Please. There's a lot more technical stuff which Leith told me.'

Victoria stared back but didn't move.

'Please . . . come over here. I'm sorry if I've made you angry.'

Edward threw back the sheet and stood up. He walked around the foot of the bed to where Victoria was sitting and led her back to where she had been lying.

She said nothing but allowed herself to be manoeuvred by Edward. He got back into bed and put his arm around her.

'Leith thinks I should call Nancy – '

Victoria tried to roll away from him but he held her tight. 'Listen! From what Riley and O'Day overheard, it seems that she is suspicious about my really being kicked off the case, so to speak. Leith thinks I should phone her today.'

'Won't that look suspicious? One day she says she hasn't heard from you – and you call her the next day?'

'Not necessarily. Don't forget, she didn't know the conversation was being overheard.'

Again, neither of them spoke. Edward still had his arm around Victoria but she sat upright, stiff, unyielding.

After a while, she said, 'You could be sailing.'

He looked at her.

'It would explain why you haven't been in touch. I used to do quite a bit of sailing at one stage.' She eyed him. 'Part of my past you didn't know about. You could have been sailing around the Western Isles and put ashore after several days at sea. Then you called her straight away.'

Edward grinned, leaned across and gently kissed her cheek. 'Brilliant. But the only problem is: what if she wants to call back? As I say, she's cunning. If I just get her answering machine it's one thing. But if she's at home, and we have a conversation, she'll think up some reason to call me back, to check out that I really am in Scotland.'

Victoria sat thinking. Edward couldn't be sure but the stiffness in her body seemed to have lessened. Outside in the street a mule suddenly screamed.

Edward went to move, to start shaving, then stopped. 'How about this? Say we make it the Orkneys, not the Western Isles. That would help explain why I sounded so far away on the telephone. I say that I've just arrived at Overbister – that's on Sanday. I say that I've been sailing with some Scottish friends who know people on the island and we're having one night ashore. I leave a number – '

'How can you do that? Do you know anyone up there?'

'I know there's an RAF base at Sanday, about twenty miles from Overbister. My father stayed there the other week, with friends. I'm sure Leith, or someone at Downing Street, can get them to co-operate. They must have some sort of line that, for a short amount of time, can be used as a decoy: whoever answers the phone pretends to be one of my friends.'

Now Victoria tapped her temple with her finger. 'And that person, when Nancy calls, says you're not in – you're at the pub or a restaurant or shopping. But then they call here quickly and you call Nancy back straight away. She will have telephoned Scotland and reached you almost immediately. It ought to satisfy her.'

Edward tightened his grip around Victoria's frame. 'That ought to beat Nancy.' Again he lightly kissed her cheek. But this time his lips sought hers. She resisted to begin with but he would not be put off. With his other hand he loosened the belt of her dressing-gown. He slid his hand inside and stroked the tips of his fingers down the inside of her thigh. He looked at her.

For a moment, she returned his stare. Then she closed her eyes and opened her lips.

Captain Kenneth Lynn stared down from the bridge of HMS *Anglesey*. He did not like what he saw. He had been enjoying his voyage off Norway, paying courtesy calls on some of the fishing villages along the coast. Compared with the fiords, the Port of London, despite all its recent development, was a wreck.

Not that it was the architecture that he objected to as he stared down from the bridge. He was suited to the sea because he liked privacy, he liked the detail and the clarity of purpose of a naval captain's job. All that had gone by the board with this latest assignment. His ship had berthed about an hour ago and he had been told to expect the first items of cargo – ninety-three crates holding the famous, the notorious, Elgin Marbles – before the morning was out. The Marbles hadn't arrived yet but the protesters and the demonstrators had. How they had found out which dock was being used, he didn't know. Still, it was hard to hide a frigate. The demonstrators were kept away from the quay but from the height of the bridge Lynn could see them and their banners lining the road that led to the entrance to the dock. To Lynn it appeared as if there were two sets of demonstrators – Greeks on one side, who were in favour of the Marbles being returned, and everybody else on the other side, who were against the return. The police were in between, receiving abuse from both sides.

Lynn disapproved of the Royal Navy being used for this sort of business. It was demeaning. The navy's good name should be saved for cleaner causes. Still, orders were orders and HMS *Anglesey* was now ready to receive its cargo. He prayed that the crates would arrive soon. It would take all day and most of the next day to load them. He had orders to leave as soon as possible and that suited him: while the cargo was on board and the ship was in dock, it was a perfect target for demonstrators. The sooner he put to sea the better. As he watched, he heard a shout go up from the demonstrators. He saw a policeman on horseback suddenly do a sort of jig as his horse took a few paces to one side. Then he saw what the commotion was about: the first of the blue lorries with the Marbles was coming into view. Two white police Rovers led the way. Behind them, he counted five lorries, then two more white Rovers. It wasn't all of the Marbles, just the first batch. He saw banners being slapped against the sides of the lorries as they went slowly past the demonstrators. A line of police, three deep, prevented the demonstrators from getting close to the gates.

Like all his naval colleagues, Kenneth Lynn regarded himself as a firm and loyal supporter of law and order. His sympathies were instinctively with the police, whatever the issue. In this case, however, he was trying not to devote too much thought to the issue and had forbidden discussion of the Marbles at mess times: it could be unsettling in a community as small as the *Anglesey*'s. He wasn't sure where he stood on the issue himself. He watched now as the dock gates were pushed closed as the fifth of the lorries came inside. There was more shouting from the demonstrators but maybe they would disperse now that there was nothing to see. Lynn watched the lorries disappear into the customs shed and found himself thinking back nearly two hundred years to the time when the Marbles had left Greece. What sort of customs shed would they have had then? Were they brought to Britain by naval ship – and did they all fit into one vessel? How did they pack the Marbles and how long did the journey take? He stepped inside and picked up the ship's phone. He rang down to his bosun.

'Yessir!' cried the bosun on the second ring.

'Prepare to receive cargo,' said Lynn. 'The Marbles have arrived.'

From the front page of the lunchtime edition of the London *Evening Standard*:

MURDER AT THE MET!
Copycat demo leads to killing of guard

REUTERS/AP: NEW YORK: A security guard was killed earlier today when three men broke into the Metropolitan Museum in Manhattan and made off with eight valuable Hindu religious objects. The guard, Mr Spiridon Panottis, interrupted the three burglars and was hit over the head, possibly with a gun. Mr Panottis suffered a brain haemorrhage and was dead on arrival at Lennox Hill Hospital.

A second guard, Mr Chessy Mlodzanski, was also attacked. He was admitted to Lennox Hill suffering a fracture of the skull but regained consciousness and was able to tell police that his three assailants were all Indians. They were armed, he said, and forced him at gunpoint to hand over his keys to the museum display cases on the second floor.

A note left by the burglars in the empty display cases links the theft in a bizarre way to the issue of the Elgin Marbles in Britain. Police released the text of the note, which reads: 'The religious objects we have liberated today belong in India. They were stolen from our country just as the Parthenon Marbles were stolen from Greece by Lord Elgin. Now the Marbles are going back where they belong – and so are our beautiful Indian sculptures.' The note was signed: 'Hindu Heritage'.

A spokesperson for the mayor's office in New York described the crime as an outrage. 'This is an unusual motive for theft. I hope it is not going to be a new trend. It just shows that the fate of the so-called Elgin Marbles is a matter of great interest right across the world.'

Mordaunt stared out at the gardens of Buckingham Palace, but he didn't really see the summer rain bouncing off the surface of the pond. He was oblivious to the photographs of his friends and relations all around him. He was even oblivious, for the moment, to Leith, who since Saturday had been sharing his office. With O'Day, Victoria Tatton and Edward Andover all abroad, it had made sense to move the operational headquarters into the equerry's office.

Mordaunt was preoccupied with the news, which was all bad. What with the demonstrations at the British Museum and the docks, the morning newspaper reports of Archbishop Lysiptos's fiery sermon, and now the dreadful news of the murder in New York, the situation appeared to be deteriorating badly. Getting out of hand. Lockwood appeared to have lost his touch drastically. Now that there had been this killing . . . with that note linking it to the Marbles . . . if the royal role in all this ever got out . . . Mordaunt found himself sweating despite the wintry summer.

His own loyalties were not to the Prime Minister of course but to Her Majesty. So far both she and Mordaunt had been prepared to let Lockwood make the running, give the lead. Now, with Lockwood's plan in tatters, Mordaunt found that he had begun to think how the Prime Minister could be . . . not overruled exactly but . . . well, perhaps he, Mordaunt, should take a more active role . . . think up a fall-back which would protect Her Majesty. He didn't know what to do – not yet. Indeed, it had only just become clear in his own mind that this was a role he could – he should – take on. But . . . now that he had made the adjustment, now that he had made that advance, the answers oughtn't to be long in coming.

'Phone!' hissed Leith.

But the equerry had seen it and he snatched at the receiver. He spoke firmly. 'Mordaunt.'

'Write this down.'

'What? . . . No –'

'Write this down!'

Mordaunt was amazed. There was to be no public payphone ritual today. 'Yes,' he breathed. 'I'm ready.'

'Gilbert Tignet, Thierry et Tignet SA, 56 Rue Grenoble, Lausanne. Mail the Queen's letter today. Don't have it delivered by hand; post it properly. If you make any attempt to trace it, or attach any bugging device, you won't hear from me again.' The line went dead.

Mordaunt looked at Leith. He too was scribbling down the address. 'Well?'

Leith finished writing before replying. 'We'll check the address, of course. 'But Monsieur Tignet will be a fiduciary. In case you are not aware of these creatures, Sir Francis, a fiduciary is a peculiarly Swiss institution: a lawyer who guarantees his clients' anonymity –'

'But surely, in the circumstances, he would help –'

'Almost certainly he doesn't know where or who his instructions come from. He'll have been paid cash for his services, which are simply to take receipt of the letter. He'll be called at some point – they'll use a code, no doubt – and asked if the letter has arrived. Then, much later, he'll be told to mail it on. I've dealt with these fiduciaries before and they take their role very seriously. No amount of coercion or persuasion on our part will have any effect.'

Mordaunt was unimpressed. 'That seems a bit –'

'Phone!'

This time the equerry had missed the flashing. He turned in his seat. 'Yes?'

'It's Ogilvy. At the British Museum. I'm looking for Andover.'

'Andover's away. May I help? Has something happened?'

'Hmm. In a way. I must see Lockwood. I was hoping Andover could swing it.'

Mordaunt frowned. 'I'm not sure I could arrange that. You know how busy the Prime Minister is. Is it anything I can help you with?'

'Not really. This thing is getting out of hand. I seem to be the only academic involved in all this besides Andover. That's why I wanted to speak to him – he might understand. Unlike him, my role is public – and I can't take all the stick. There's a row of placards outside my office right now, saying things like "Lockwood's stooge", "What are you giving away next?" and "Free offer: 93 marbles".'

'And . . . what? You want the police to get rid of them? Inspector Leith is here – '

'No. No! That's not it, not at all. I've had enough, Mordaunt. I want to see the Prime Minister so I can resign.'

'Nancy, it's Edward. I'm sorry I haven't been in touch but . . . well, things got rather complicated regarding that matter . . . that matter I wasn't supposed to talk about. The long and the short of it is that I'm in Scotland. Part holiday, part exile, part punishment. I've been sailing, trying to blow all the nastiness away. I'm with Neil and Ian Cashel and we've just put into Overbister on Sanday. Sorry to miss you but if you still want a chat you can try me on . . . the number here is Brae . . .' Edward gave the code and number.

Leith had jumped at the idea Edward had worked out with Victoria and set it up within two hours.

Edward finished his message. 'We're in and out all today, restocking the boat, but do try me – I'd love to talk to you. We leave tomorrow for the Western Isles – that's, oh . . . two to four days at sea, depending on winds and weather. So, it's now or never. Bye.'

He rang off. The plan now was for Victoria to keep an eye on the *Strabo* while he manned the phone in the room.

Victoria was preparing to leave, getting ready her paintbox and watercolour pad.

'Be careful,' said Edward softly. 'In some ways, a single woman is more noticeable than a couple.'

'You too,' replied Victoria. 'Nancy's beaten you once already, Edward. We can't afford to let it happen again.'

*

251

'Coming to you in one minute,' said a voice over Brian Welch's earpiece. 'Stand by camera, stand by sound.' The crew on the pavement in front of Welch suddenly snapped into action. People all around stared at this tiny piece of theatre. 'Fifteen seconds,' said the voice inside Welch's ear. 'Ten, nine, eight, seven, six . . .'

Welch watched for the red light on the camera to wink on. He held the microphone closer to his mouth. 'Here, in Downing Street, the pavement opposite Number Ten is more crowded than usual. The reason is that police have allowed two hundred demonstrators inside the gate from Whitehall, though many more have been left outside.' As Welch said this, the camera panned across to the line of Indians with placards crowding the pavement opposite the PM's residence. It settled on Welch.

'With me I have Ayod Janata, leader of today's demonstration, and the convener of Indian Nationalists Abroad, British sector.' Welch turned to Janata and the camera pulled back its focus to take in both men. 'Mr Janata, a security guard was murdered earlier today at the Metropolitan Museum in New York, when three Indians broke into the gallery and stole eight objects. Yet your demonstration has gone ahead this afternoon. Why have you done that? It could look like exceptional bad taste to hold a rally in these circumstances.' He held out the microphone to Janata.

'First, you say it was murder in New York. I am sad for what happened – but it was really an accident – '

'But in the course of a burglary – '

'The people who carried out that raid were merely taking objects that had been stolen from India in the first place, many years ago. You ask me why we are demonstrating here and I would have thought it was obvious. Like the Metropolitan Museum, like many of the museums in Europe and North America, British museums contain heritage objects that were stolen from India. In particular, there is a valuable and important throne that was taken from the country in the eighteenth century. That is in the Victoria and Albert Museum. Now, it appears to us that the British government is having a change of heart over the Elgin Marbles – and returning them to Greece. We Indians feel the same way as the Greeks do . . . we want our beautiful objects back. Now is the time for us to act, to mount this demonstration. We are naturally very sorry that a security guard, and a Greek security guard at that, was accidentally killed at the Metropolitan Museum. And in fact the Indian community in Britain is making a collection to send to the guard's widow. But I want to make it clear that we agree with the aims of our countrymen in New York, we agree with Hindu Heritage, to the extent that we want to see many cultural objects returned to India. The West has – '

Welch pulled the microphone back towards his own mouth. 'Are there any circumstances in which you would go beyond demonstrations? Would you, for instance, ever contemplate breaking into a museum and stealing objects, as happened this morning in New York, with such tragic consequences?'

For a moment, Janata hesitated.

Very quickly Welch again pulled the microphone back to himself. Looking into the camera and raising his eyebrows, he simply said: 'From Downing Street, this is Brian Welch for BBC TV.'

'Nancy? Can you hear me? This is a lousy line. It's Edward.'

'Woodie! At last. You sound like you're on the moon.' Nancy had responded to his call and Leith had relayed the fact not three minutes before. Fortunately, Edward had got through to her flat in London the first time he had tried. Barely seven minutes had elapsed since Nancy had phoned Scotland.

'Close, but I'm an earthling all right. I still feel I'm going up and down after days at sea.'

'But why the sea, Woodie? What happened?'

'I'm not supposed to tell you. The operation is still going on.'

'Is this all to do with those paintings you told me about?'

'Did I say that? I wasn't supposed to. Yes.'

'And why were you –?'

'Nancy! I can't talk about it.' Edward had discussed with Leith whether he should give Nancy a false line, something that would give the other side a false sense of security. In the end, however, they had decided that Edward should give nothing away, should behave very properly. In that way, she might not want to talk to him again. Now he changed the subject. 'How's the sculpture research?'

'Finished. That's why I'm back in London. Now I have to write it all up. Do you like sailing? You never mentioned it.'

'I did it quite a lot as a boy. This trip with the Cashels came up just at the right time. It's a good way to get away.'

'You're not getting away from me, are you?'

Edward felt his breathing grow shorter. An image of Nancy, naked, her flesh half in shadow, danced before him. He was angry, shamed and embarrassed all at the same time. But he was also aroused. 'Nancy . . . it's difficult for me. The phone here is . . . a bit public. But . . . I made a mistake, a bad mistake . . . Don't forget my flat – my home – is in the royal household, not just my office. I had to get away. But not from you.'

'When will I see you?'

The bitch! thought Edward. 'I don't know. I shall stay away until . . . until I can come back. Sailing is quite demanding. You have to concentrate – that's good for me, given what's happened.'

'What do you think about New York?'

'What do you mean?'

'Haven't you heard? Maybe Scotland *is* on the moon.' Suddenly she sounded suspicious.

'I've heard nothing. You don't get the papers at sea and at these latitudes we keep our radio permanently tuned to the weather forecast.'

Mollified, somewhat, she told him about the murder at the Metropolitan Museum.

'Oh, no!'

'You may have made a mistake, Woodie, but Lockwood's hardly a shining example to follow.'

Edward closed his eyes. Nancy was certainly pushy, turning the conversation to her own purposes at every opportunity. 'I must go, Nancy. Other people are waiting to use the phone.'

'All right, all right. Just call me from the Western Isles.'

'I will. I promise.'

'Who knows? I may just fly up to meet you.'

'You may have whatever you wish, so long as it's Dewar's.' Lockwood smiled at Sir Francis Mordaunt. He was playing host again, in the flat above Number Ten. It was midnight.

'Then I'll have Dewar's, please.'

Lockwood stood over the equerry and poured his drink. The flat was full tonight. Besides Slocombe, Midwinter and Leith, Tom Lessor had been invited, and Hatfield, the Chief Whip, was expected. Lockwood made sure everyone had a drink, then stood with his back to the fireplace, looking down at them all. 'Tomorrow is going to be the worst day yet. I can say that with authority because today was the worst day and tomorrow it will be in all the papers. None of you will know everything, so here goes . . .' And he gave them a tour of all that had taken place in the previous twenty-four hours, from the break-in and death at the Metropolitan Museum, to the arrival of the *Anglesey*, the demonstration in Downing Street and Mordaunt's conversation with the blackmailer.

'How does this change things, Prime Minister?' asked Mordaunt when Lockwood had finished.

The Prime Minister made a face. 'Good question. This business with the Indians in New York was a surprise, of course, a shock, and no one could have predicted the break-in, or that someone would have been killed. The demands on the Queen, over the letter, I see as encouraging in a way. We now know the motives of this Apollo Brigade and they seem rational, in a sense, even if we don't agree with them. We know where each member of the Brigade is so we can move in on them as we wish. The only thing we don't know is the same as before – the whereabouts of the Blunt paintings. O'Day and Riley tapped Zakros's conversation again tonight but we are none the wiser, except that they are going to step up the pressure in some way. I've come to the conclusion that we cannot expect to find out much more from the phone taps in Basle. We have five days, give or take, before the *Anglesey* reaches Piraeus. Between now and then we must persuade the Greek in Basle to lead us to the documents.'

'How do you know the documents are kept in Basle?' Mordaunt swallowed a large gulp of scotch. He reflected how Blunt himself had been a heavy drinker.

Lockwood nodded. 'This Zakros character is still there. There must be a reason why he is. They have to assume that at some point they might have to deliver their threat – otherwise this whole thing is a charade. And the simplest thing, after this Brigade got hold of the paintings, would have been to move them from one Swiss bank to another. I accept Inspector Leith's reasoning on that. No frontiers to cross, and Switzerland is in any case one of the most secretive countries there are. That's why Blunt chose a Swiss bank in the first place. No, it all points to Switzerland, and to Basle.' There was a short silence in the room. Lockwood looked from face to face. 'One thing you might be able to explain, Sir Francis, is the link between Blunt and

Zakros. You were told about the exchange that Riley and O'Day overheard in Basle?'

Mordaunt nodded, placing his whisky glass on the table. 'Yes, and afterwards I went back through the Blunt file at the Palace. As you may know, Blunt retired in 1971 but of course he kept up his relationship with us. He updated his book on Poussin, wrote about other aspects of the collection and acted as a general adviser. I noticed in the file that he had arranged three loans from the Royal Collection to Greece – in 1968, and then again in 1973 and 1978. Presumably we used him because he knew the country, all the classical bits anyway, from his earlier work and contacts. He could have met – and befriended – any number of Greeks on those occasions. He always accompanied the pictures: that's our standard arrangement, from a security standpoint.'

'And,' the Prime Minister interjected, 'if, as you suggested some days ago, the Greek end of the royal family knew about his wartime mission, he might have been approached?'

'It's a possibility. But, you know . . .' Mordaunt sat up. 'Blunt was a terrible snob, a very good hater and someone who really knew how to harbour a grudge. And he was really embittered by the removal of his knighthood. It would not surprise me in any way if he isn't behind all this. He had more than three years, between his public exposure and his death, to put everything into place. This is exactly the kind of cunning plot Blunt would have relished. I can't prove it of course but, deep down, I believe *he* thought up this plot, *he* gave the Greeks the idea, for use after he died. *He* told them where to find the paintings and what their significance was. He may have recruited Zakros as an art dealer with the "correct" political attitude, primed him, and then sent him the crucial bit of information, about the paintings, but to reach him only after his own death. He might even have told Zakros to try to get the Elgin Marbles returned. I come back always to the fact that Blunt never forgave the British establishment for what he thought it had done to him at the end of his life, for the humiliation heaped on him. So he conceived this plan, as revenge, to be realized after his death, when he couldn't be touched.'

Lockwood gazed at Mordaunt without blinking. For a while neither man spoke, then the Prime Minister murmured, 'We'll never know, but what you say is plausible, Sir Francis. Only too plausible. And Blunt isn't beaten yet.' Lockwood seemed to shake himself, as if to change his mood. 'Anything else we should know?'

'Yes, there is.' Mordaunt picked up his glass and swallowed some Dewar's. 'Ogilvy wants to resign.'

'What?' Lockwood wasn't the only person in the room to say it.

'I've just come from Soho, where I had dinner with him at a discreet restaurant I know. He says the didn't count on so much protest and he says he never imagined the Marbles would actually leave Britain. He's obviously feeling very exposed – he's the only academic or scholar who is in on all this and so he's the only one who is not protesting. He clearly feels isolated and, since the truth can never be told, he thinks he will never be able to explain his position and rehabilitate himself. Hence he feels his only course is to resign.'

'Has he actually done it? He's supposed to resign to me.' Lockwood punched one fist into the palm of his other hand. 'That would be a real blow. A coup for the professors.'

'Never mind that,' said Slocombe. 'He could be a security leak.'

'As I say,' Mordaunt continued, 'I had dinner with him. He really wanted to see you, Prime Minister, to tender his resignation immediately.'

'So? Has he done it yet?'

'No . . . I managed to hold him off for a while.'

'How did you do that, may I ask?' Lockwood looked hard at the equerry.

'He had originally asked to see Andover. A bond between academics – but that, of course, was impossible. However, before seeing him, and because of what he had originally said, I called Andover in Turkey and I picked his brains. He was quite creative, I must say.' Mordaunt's face suddenly looked very cunning. 'I'm afraid . . . I told him a lie. When he first phoned us, during the day, I asked him to delay at least until dinner. I said I would do my best to talk to you in the interim. I know you've been very busy today, with those Brussels commissioners who are here – so I didn't in fact even bother to trouble you. I talked to Andover instead.'

They were all engrossed in Mordaunt's narrative, Lockwood especially.

'When we had dinner, I lied and told him that I had spoken to you. I said that you didn't want him to resign, that you would be very disappointed and angry if he did, and that if he didn't resign he could expect a seat in the Lords. But I added that precautions had been taken during the day, that in view of all that is currently happening at the museum at the moment a new director would have to be appointed straight away. I said that preliminary soundings had been taken and that your preferred candidate, Prime Minister, was Richard Salford. That was Andover's suggestion.'

'Why did you say that, Sir Francis? And who the hell is Richard Salford?'

'According to Andover, he's Martin Ogilvy's fiercest rival, sir. Like Ogilvy, he is an archaeologist, but when you've said that you've listed all that they have in common. They hate each other with a loathing that not even Cain had for Abel. They disagree totally on every professional issue there is and are not on speaking terms. Ogilvy dropped his fork when I told him and wouldn't touch his fish after that. The lure of the Lords and the spectre of Salford seems to have done it for the time being. He agreed to stay on.'

Lockwood was looking at Mordaunt rather oddly. Then he looked at Slocombe. 'What do you think, Eric?'

'I think I could be out of a job soon. It's brilliant, Andover's bloody brilliant. Ogilvy won't resign after this – he'll be in too deep. Today was the time to resign, if he was going to. Well done, Andover.'

Lockwood was smiling, too. 'A narrow squeak,' he said, 'but the political jungle is full of such noises. On to the next.' He looked around the room again. 'What I need now is some brainstorming, from the minds assembled here, as to how we might persuade this Zakros character to panic and rush off to the place where the Blunt paintings are hidden.'

For a minute or so no one said anything. A late-night plane droned overhead. 'I have an idea, Bill, but may I have another drink first?' Slocombe held out his glass. There was a faint smile on his lips.

Lockwood reached for the bottle, filled Slocombe's glass and did the same for some of the others who had also finished. He went back to the fireplace and waited.

'You said it yourself, in fact. The one way we can be certain he will dash to the documents is if he thinks we're going back on the deal. Remember when Andover argued with him over the phone? He went AWOL for a couple of days and then that picture turned up in Vienna. Now we're on his tail, if we could do the same again, he would lead us to the hiding place.'

'Bit risky, isn't it?' Lockwood looked at Slocombe and frowned.

'This whole thing is risky.'

'Say we accept your reasoning, Eric . . . if we provoke the Greek, how do we know he won't go public with the whole thing?'

'We don't know. But for once I think events may be on our side. Tomorrow or Wednesday the *Anglesey* leaves for Piraeus, and the Apollo Brigade will be much closer to success – or so it will seem to them. If, at that point, we throw a spanner in the works, they are not going to throw over a victory so easily – it's not in human nature. They will redouble their threat – yes, I see that. But I'm willing to bet that they won't junk the whole enterprise.'

Another long silence ensued before the Prime Minister said: 'Thank you, Eric. A clear statement, leaving the decisions to me. Every time you say something, I get another grey hair.' He smiled grimly. He was about to say something else when the door to the flat was opened by the security guard and the Chief Whip rushed in.

'Jocelyn, I'd given you up for lost. We're almost finished, I'm afraid.'

'No you're not, Prime Minister.' Hatfield looked flustered. Slocombe rose, poured a fresh whisky and held it out to him.

Hatfield took the glass and gulped down some of the contents. 'I've just come from a long meeting with Ted Adams, the opposition's Chief Whip. They've got some Commons time coming up very soon. Arthur Page has indicated he wants a full-dress debate on the Marbles affair. The Speaker has agreed and there's nothing I can do about it. Bill, I don't like it. This could turn into a vote of censure against you.'

21

Tuesday

From *The Times*:

US AMBASSADOR WARNS INDIAN GOVERNMENT
UN seen as first step in America
response to Museum murder

UN Plaza, New York: Mr Mason Farmer, the American ambassador to the United Nations, last night delivered a strongly worded protest to the Indian government regarding the recent killing at the Metropolitan Museum, when a group of burglars, calling themselves 'Hindu Heritage', killed a security guard in the course of the theft of religious artefacts.

Mr Farmer, who is known to be close to the President and to Mr Dixon Thayer, US Secretary of State, said that the American government expects the Indian government 'to do all in its power to apprehend these murderers, these thieves'. Speaking from the rostrum of the main UN chamber, he added: 'We expect the government of India to return to us both the objects and the criminals themselves to this country to stand trial. Should the Indian government fail to do this, the US government reserves the right to take whatever action it deems necessary to protect its interests and to prevent the recurrence of this dangerous precedent.'

'Good morning, everyone, you are watching the breakfast-time news on the BBC and it is just after 8.20. An opinion poll in this morning's *Daily Telegraph* shows that 73 per cent of those asked say that the Elgin Marbles should not be returned to Greece. More than 65 per cent say that the government has handled the affair badly, and a similar proportion say that even now, at this late hour when the Marbles are due to be shipped abroad any moment, they should be brought back. The Prime Minister's personal popularity has also slumped. Only 32 per cent of those asked thought he was doing a good job, compared with 66 per cent who think that Arthur Page is doing a good job and 61 per cent who think that Anthony Rolfe, leader of the Liberal Democrats, is doing a good job. The most popular member of the government is George Keld, Secretary of State for Defence, who has the backing of 65 per cent. This may have something to do with the fact that Mr Keld has not been involved in the Elgin Marbles affair. It also emerged overnight that the opposition leader, Arthur Page, has decided to use one of his party's emergency days in the Commons to debate the issue. Mr Page is with me this morning in the studio.'

The camera pulled back to take in both figures, the presenter and the politician. 'Mr Page, there is an election not too far away. Aren't you just making political capital out of this issue?'

'That's a damn-fool question, if I may say so. I'm leader of the opposition and I don't like what's happening. So yes, I am forcing the issue. The opinion poll you quoted proves my point – that what the government is doing is unpopular. But it is not only unpopular, it is wrong.'

'You say it's wrong, but many experts say that the Marbles were illegally exported from Greece. The present Lord Elgin has said – '

'The present Lord Elgin doesn't come into this. But the feelings of the British people do. And the majority of them – the great majority – do not want these objects given away.'

'But, Mr Page, I come back to the legality of their original export. Does that count for nothing?'

'Look around the world – there are pictures in Lyons that were stolen by Napoleon from Milan, pictures in New York that were stolen by the Swedes in Prague, there is a whole library in the Vatican, for pity's sake, that was stolen in Germany.'

'All those wrongs don't make a right.'

'In this case I think they do. These objects were moved around the world hundreds of years ago, when law and order was a very different matter from what it is now. Things were accepted then that would not be tolerated now.'

'What issues will you be raising in the debate?'

'Well, we object as much to the style of Mr Lockwood's government as to the substance. It is not simply the fact that he has chosen, unilaterally and almost single-handedly it would seem, to return the Marbles, but he has mismanaged the affair so that it has become embarrassing for this country. Around the world we are either vilified or ridiculed. From the very first moment when it leaked out that a government committee was considering returning the Marbles, right down to the murder yesterday of the security guard in New York, Bill Lockwood has mishandled this matter. It is a disgrace. The Americans, as we have seen from this morning's papers, are much firmer where their interests are concerned.'

'Now let me get this straight: are you saying that the Prime Minister is to blame for the murder of Spiridon Panottis, the security guard at the Metropolitan Museum, yesterday?'

'Not directly, of course. The Indians who coshed the man over the head with a gun were the ones who actually killed him. But where did they get the idea to take back the Hindu treasures? Who has made the return of cultural property such a hot issue politically? Our very own Prime Minister.'

'But these are grave charges, Mr Page. You are saying, in effect, that Mr Lockwood has blood on his hands.'

Page looked hard at the presenter. 'That is why we have called this debate. That is exactly what I am saying.'

'Do you see what I see?' Edward motioned with his head towards the *Strabo*. He and Victoria were on the other side of the harbour today, in a little square which overlooked the jetties. From there they could still keep an eye on the yacht. And it was the kind of move real artists would have made.

'I see what looks like Kolettis carrying a jug of something good – is that what you mean?'

'No, very much no. Look at the funnel – '

'What do you –? Got it ! Smoke. Jesus!'

Edward was packing up his things. 'They're moving out! We should have thought of that. Why have a boat if you can't move every so often?'

'What are you doing? Where are you going?'

'I'm going down to the harbour to see about renting a boat. You are going to the harbour master's office. The *Strabo*'s captain will have had to inform them where they are bound. I will leave it to your charm to find out our destination.'

'What about the hotel?'

'Boats don't move that fast – we'll have time to check out and get back down to the harbour before the *Strabo* is out of sight. Now come on.' He led the way at a fast walk down to the jetty. As he slowed to look at the various notices on the boats that were for hire, Victoria went on along the jetty to the harbour master's office. The heat was beginning to rise as the sun reached its full height. Harbour life was dying for the moment. However, the front door of the harbour master's office was still open and Victoria wondered if she dare go in. What would she say? She decided to play the ignorant tourist. Would an ignorant tourist have her command of Turkish? Almost certainly not, but it couldn't be helped.

She knocked on the door and stepped in.

'Yes?' said a voice in Turkish. 'May I help you?'

'Hello,' she replied brightly. 'I hope you can help me, yes. My husband and I have been holidaying here and we now feel like going to Greece. Are we allowed to do that – can we go direct from here, I mean?'

He smiled and waved her to a seat. 'Have you got your own boat?'

'No, we'd have to hire one.'

'You could take a hire boat from here to Rhodes or Kos. There's a ferry to Rhodes from Marmaris.'

Victoria nodded and flashed the man a smile. 'We've been to Rhodes . . . we'd prefer somewhere else. Where would you suggest?'

He considered for a moment. 'If you wanted to go to mainland Greece, Rhodes is best. Rhodes or Samos – there are ferries or flights to Athens from both places.'

She looked around the harbour master's office. 'Does everyone have to tell you where they are going?'

He nodded. 'We have to keep track of the shipping – otherwise smuggling and other crimes could get out of hand.'

'Don't you ever wish you were on some of the big yachts that come in here, sailing to exotic places?'

'Sometimes.' He shrugged. 'I was born here. I've been to America, to Paris, to Rome, to Australia, to Africa. I like it here.'

'But wouldn't it be romantic to leave here one evening and arrive in . . . oh, Alexandria or Haifa the next day?' She looked around and pointed at the *Strabo*. 'That big yacht, for instance, that would be a lovely way to travel. They're leaving now – I saw the smoke coming from the funnel. Are they going anywhere exotic?'

He made a face. 'It depends whether you think Kithira is exotic. I've never been.'

'No, nor have I.' She had what she had come for but had to keep up pretences a moment longer. 'No, I'd rather go to Samos, I think. It sounds good – and we can go on to Athens from there, you say?'

'Yes, that's no problem.'

She thanked him and went back out to the harbour. She found Edward talking with a tall, thin man sitting on an upturned rowing boat.

'I'm not sure I understand,' said Edward, 'but I think he's saying that he has a boat for hire – but that it's not back yet – '

'Forget it,' Victoria interjected and waved him over to her.

Edward disentangled himself from the boatman, who was reluctant to see him go, sensing a killing. Victoria had turned and was watching the *Strabo* slowly ease away from the quay and turn its prow towards the harbour opening. 'What did you find out?' he asked her. 'Where are they going?'

'Kithira.'

'That's miles away.'

'About three hundred, to be exact. I looked it up on the map outside the harbour master's office. We'll never get a boat to take us that far, or keep up with the *Strabo*.'

'Lockwood's going to love us if we lose contact now.'

Victoria didn't answer straight away. Then she said, 'A yacht like that cruises at about . . . oh, twelve to thirteen knots, call it fifteen miles an hour. That makes it roughly twenty hours to Kithira.' She looked at her watch. 'It's nearly noon now, so they should arrive around eight tomorrow morning. The question is: can we get from here to Kithira by then? If we can get a boat to Rhodes tonight we should be able to fly to Athens or Crete first thing. Whether we can get to Kithira from there, and in time . . . I just don't know. Is there an airport on Kithira? How do we find out?' She punched Edward's arm. 'We've got to try. You go back to the hotel, call London and tell them what we're doing and I'll use my female charm on your boatman, to see if he'll take us to Rhodes.'

In the end, though, the boat plan didn't work out and they decided to take a taxi back to Marmaris and the regular ferry to

Rhodes from there. The boat left Marmaris at six-fifteen and took four and a half hours, which gave them plenty of time to buy bread, wine, grapes and some salami so that they could have dinner on the ferry. Only when Turkey was slipping away behind them and had become nothing more than a jumble of lights in the distance did Edward voice the fear he had felt ever since he saw the *Strabo* steam out of the harbour at Datça. As he poured Victoria some wine into her plastic mug, he said: 'Let's hope the captain of the *Strabo* was telling the truth when he said they were going to Kithira. Kolettis might have bribed him to lie. If he was lying, then we've lost them.'

'Bit of a flirt, our friend, eh? Did you see the way he looked at that woman?'

Riley shrugged. They were sitting in their car, a blue Opel, parked on the St-Alban-Rheinweg, overlooking the river. This morning they had tailed Zakros ever since he left his house at nine-thirty. He had gone first to a cigar shop, where he had remained for twenty minutes, then he had taken coffee in the Three Kings Hotel, where he had bought a paper and made a telephone call. Now, at midday, he was strolling by the river. It was threatening rain but the wind was probably too high. There were small waves on the Rhine. O'Day was surprised at how yellow the water was today.

'He's looking at his watch,' said Riley. 'He's moving back into town.' They watched as Zakros left the Rheinweg, climbing the steep incline towards the St-Alban-Vorstadt. 'You follow,' said Riley. 'I'll do my best to keep in touch with the car. But don't bother about me. Stick to him and call London the minute anything happens. I'll tell Leith where I am and you can find me through him. Do you think we need reinforcements?'

O'Day frowned. 'Lockwood's still paranoid about security. We'll have to manage. We're okay so long as our Greek friend doesn't spot us.'

O'Day got out of the car and walked after Zakros. He turned left into St-Alban-Graben, right into Steinenberg, along Steinenberg and right again into Gerbergasse. It was now just coming up to twelve-thirty. A hundred yards along the street, Zakros stopped and looked into a shop window. From where O'Day was, it looked as if it sold model railways. O'Day had seen such behaviour in the Greek before, but in the second that he realized Zakros was waiting for someone or something the Greek crossed the road, reaching a doorway at precisely the same time as a woman who had been walking towards him, on the opposite side of the street. In a flash, O'Day understood Zakros's odd behaviour and why he had been killing time all morning. It also probably explained the phone call at the Three Kings. He had been calling the airport! This woman he had met in Gerbergasse had flown in from somewhere! From Greece? Was it Eugenie Shelby or the American who had duped Andover? It was impossible to check.

O'Day watched Zakros and the woman. They embraced, kissed and then disappeared through the doorway. He gave them a couple of minutes, then crossed the street and strolled down Gerbergasse. As he came to the door, he could see to one side a small brass plate which read: 'Drachen und Stoller'. It certainly looked like a bank. At last!

What should he do now? Find a phone and call Leith? Look for Riley? Stay here in Gerbergasse? After a moment's thought, he opted for the last. He must stay in touch. The wind had dropped and the rain was beginning. There was a tiny alley leading from Gerbergasse to Falknerstrasse and he hid there, though it gave him no protection from the wet. Ten minutes passed. He wondered where Riley was and kept an eye open for the blue Opel. Smells from a nearby restaurant wafted along the alley, tweaking his salivary glands.

One o'clock came and went. The rain intensified and he began to get some odd looks from more sensible souls in their raincoats. His hair had by now trapped a fair amount of rain and periodically he was forced to shake his head to dislodge it. His neck was freezing from the water. At about a quarter past one a blue Opel swished down Gerbergasse but it was driven by a blonde woman. O'Day lapsed back into his wet hideout. What time did banks close in Basle he wondered. How long was he going to have to wait? Was the woman flying straight back to Britain or wherever she had come from? Another, panicky, thought struck him. If they came out with the Blunt pictures and documents, and then split up, whom should he follow? There'd been more than enough time to call Leith since they had been in the bank. Was there still time to try a call? No sooner had he thought this, however, than he saw two figures, a man and a woman, emerge from the bank. It was them. The woman paused to open her umbrella and then they walked away from him, towards the market place. O'Day stared before following them. They were carrying nothing. Did that mean they had small documents in their pockets, or in the woman's handbag? Or perhaps a tiny Nazi picture, rolled up?

They talked as they went and, when they reached the market place, walked on until they came to the Three Kings Hotel. O'Day followed them through the lobby and watched as they turned left, into the restaurant. Now was his chance: they were taking a late lunch. Quickly, he found the men's room, towelled his hair and his face dry. The hotel phones were in the lobby so at the least he could see Zakros and the woman if they left.

He reached Leith immediately and relayed the morning's events. Riley had already checked in and was waiting by a phone for Leith to call back with O'Day's location. Leith confirmed that his men had established that it was Nancy Tucker, the American, who had gone to the airport. Eugenie Shelby was still in the British Museum. Then he added: 'You're sure they have nothing with them?'

'Nothing bulky. I would have seen. Unless they're going back after lunch, to pick up things.'

'So we can't be certain Drachen und Stoller is the bank we want?'

'Oh yes . . . I think so. Why else would the woman come all the way out here? They rendezvoused outside the place.'

Leith listened. 'I'll call Riley now. I'll tell him to stay outside the hotel, in the car. He should be there in a few minutes.'

Leith rang off and O'Day moved back into the lobby. If he stood near the terrace overlooking the river, he could see into the restaurant. Yes, they were still there. He bought a paper and sat down to read. After a few minutes, Riley came in. He didn't acknowledge O'Day but he too bought a paper and took it back outside to the car. The waiting resumed. O'Day rarely read more than the political news on most days but now he found himself reading the sports pages, the business pages, the horoscopes, the women's pages. He found himself reading about events in Sarawak, Timor and Antarctica.

After an hour and a quarter, Zakros and Nancy Tucker emerged from the restaurant. They stood in the lobby talking for a moment although O'Day couldn't hear what was said. He was forced to admit that Andover had taste. He could see why the Queen's Surveyor of Pictures had fallen for the American. She was not only beautiful; her skin and her hair glowed. O'Day found he had read the same paragraph about Helsinki four times. They moved out of the lobby, to the steps which led to the street. He let them get on to the pavement and followed. As he came out of the hotel, however, he almost bumped into them. They hadn't gone anywhere – on the contrary, the American woman was getting into a taxi. O'Day couldn't stop without looking very suspicious, so he folded his paper under his arm and strolled off. As he went, however, he heard Zakros call out: 'Have a good flight, darling.'

So she was going back to the airport. Back to London or on to Greece? Riley, presumably, would find out.

O'Day crossed the street so that he could use the shop window to observe Zakros unobtrusively. As he did so, the blue Opel moved off, following the taxi.

The rain had eased but hadn't stopped entirely. In the shop window, O'Day saw Zakros looking hard after the taxi – or was it the Opel? Had Riley been too enthusiastic, and too obvious, in his pursuit? Had they blown the whole thing? Despite the rain and the wind, O'Day found himself sweating as he watched the Greek turn back into the hotel and disappear. He hurried back himself and mounted the steps to the lobby. There was no sign of Zakros.

Yes, there was. He was in a phone booth. O'Day's heart sank. Had Riley given them away?

Rain drummed against the windows of Francis Mordaunt's office. He stared down at the green and white marquees on the lawns outside, bulging with people. He felt sorry for the hundreds of souls who had never been to a Buckingham Palace garden party before and today would see only the inside of a massive tent. He was feeling a bit sorry for himself too. The opinion poll in today's paper had been a shock for Mordaunt – and indeed for them all. No one had known quite how unpopular Lockwood's actions had been. Now they did know. If it ever became public that the Marbles were being returned to Greece to save the royal family's skin . . .

The Commons debate didn't help, either. Now that Page had

come out so firmly against Lockwood, that would identify him, in the public's mind at least, as anti-royal, should the story ever leak. The Crown was thus likely to become a political issue between the two main parties. Mordaunt shuddered. Outside, the rain was worsening. He watched as a policeman in a black cape examined someone's pass. The woman was wearing a large, floppy, pastel-blue hat. She had not expected such God-awful weather and was already looking bedraggled. The rain still gusted in sheets across the marquees. Looking down again, Mordaunt saw the opposition front-bench spokesman on education, scurrying from one marquee to another. That made him think of Arthur Page and his damned debate.

Page. Once more, it occurred to Mordaunt that his own loyalty, as equerry, was not to the government. It was to the Queen. It was true that Lockwood had behaved very loyally over this matter but, at the same time, he had also mishandled it badly – to the point where this potentially very damaging debate was to take place. Where the royal family could lose more, in the long term, than by having the Windsor/Blunt business made public. Mordaunt stared at the wet marquees. Maybe there was a way in which the debate, at least, could be avoided. He'd have to choose his moment . . . but in principle there was nothing to prevent him briefing Page on the secret.

The conductor had just taken the rostrum, and the welcoming applause was dying down, as Mordaunt and Leith were shown into the private dining-room behind the royal box at Covent Garden. Tonight the table was laid for ten. Eric Slocombe, who was seated at one chair, had pushed the table setting to one side. He gripped a tumbler of mineral water. Midwinter sat at another chair, muttering into a mobile phone. Evelyn Allen stood near a window. A waiter offered Leith a glass of champagne. Behind him, in the auditorium, the first strains of Puccini's *Turandot* could be heard. Suddenly, the noise level jumped as the door to the dining-room banged open. Mordaunt turned, to see Lockwood and Hatfield enter, both dressed in black tie. The Chief Whip stared at the waiter. Holding the door, he barked one word. 'Out!'

The waiter put the bottle on the table and left the room. Hatfield closed the door behind him. They all found seats.

'We can't meet at midnight tonight,' said Lockwood matter-of-factly. 'As you can see, I am entertaining the German Chancellor and it will probably go on for ever. If I fall down on my public duties, there'll be no shortage of comment and criticism. At least, now that the lights are down, no one can see I'm away. Herr Schenker is a polite man with problems of his own. He won't draw attention to my absence . . . Now, the first interval is in thirty-six minutes – I've checked. So we've got to get a move on. A lot has happened today – who's first?'

Evelyn Allen made his customary cough. 'I am afraid, Prime Minister, that there is absolutely no way you can prevent the Greek issue coming up at the Cabinet on Thursday. Almost every senior minister has contacted me, announcing his or her intention of raising it.'

'And I'm besieged by backbenchers, Bill. They're all worried by what's happening – and they're worried by Page's debate.'

Lockwood looked at the Chief Whip. 'Have we got a date for that yet?'

'Nothing definite but it's probably Monday. Page is using opposition time so I can't interfere.'

Lockwood nodded. He looked tired tonight. Sally was still at the hospital with his daughter and son-in-law. His grandson was not improving. The Prime Minister turned back to the Cabinet Secretary. 'Evelyn, make the Greek business the top item in Cabinet. Circulate a new agenda first thing tomorrow. We'll see off all the fainthearts. Now . . . the backbenchers, Joss. I'm not going to see them. The more people I see, the more I'll have to lie to – they'll resent that when it's all over. I'm relying on you to protect me from extraneous things . . . We're getting to the critical stage now and must keep our minds on the important details. Now, Eric, you've got one of your theories for us, I believe.'

'It's a bit more than a theory, Bill.'

'Well, shoot.'

Slocombe sat up. 'I've been putting together all that we know and trying to draw some conclusions. You never know when that will come in handy. It would seem from our observations that Kolettis and this Kofas character actually call the shots. For some reason, possibly security, they only contact Zakros indirectly, using the Tucker woman in London as go-between. She certainly seems to be a number, incidentally. She strung

Andover along for months but the Greek in Basle, Zakros, is her real lover, if O'Day's observations are anything to go by. Kofas incidentally is very well known to our political attaché in Athens. He has a very high profile, unlike the others. He owns ferries, hotels, petrol stations, travel companies, a publishing house, which includes the *Journal of Classical Greece* among its titles. I've had the embassy in Athens do some digging on him. He is about sixty, too old and too authoritarian to try for parliament but does have political ambitions. The most interesting thing about him, from our point of view, is that he is a staunch monarchist.

'Now, see what you make of this . . . When the Basle Greek dictated the letter which the Queen had to sign, we assumed that the addressee was to have been . . . well, someone like Kofas. But how about this for a different scenario: say the addressee was not Kofas but King Constantine, in exile in England! There's no shortage of Greeks who would like to see the monarchy in Greece return – but how can they create favourable circumstances? What better than to have the ex-King instrumental in the return of the Marbles? With a letter from our Queen congratulating their ex-King, who knows how much a popular movement might not develop, demanding his return? The Marbles are a fantastically emotive issue in Greece – all Greeks would applaud their return and support anyone who had a hand in it.'

Lockwood's eyes were fixed on the menu card in the middle of the table. He digested what Slocombe had said. 'Do you think the ex-King knows anything about this?'

Slocombe brushed his moustache with a finger. 'No. He knows there's a lot of support for him in Greece, he'd like to go back in the right circumstances . . . but no, I don't believe he'd put the reputation of the British royal family, and the monarch who allows him to live here in exile, at risk for a plan like this. All that the Apollo Brigade can do is make the note public during the euphoria that is bound to accompany the return of the Marbles, and hope that the rest follows on.'

'I agree with Mr Slocombe, Prime Minister.'

'Yes?' Lockwood turned and eyed the equerry. Mordaunt hadn't touched his champagne but he fingered the stem of his glass. 'As you know, we weren't supposed to hear from Zakros again until he received the Queen's letter – probably Thursday or Friday. Well, today, Nancy Tucker turned up in Basle and both she and Zakros went to a bank. This afternoon, Zakros called me.'

'To say what?' Lockwood spread his hands across the table-cloth, his fingers splayed like two starfish.

'The exact wording was: "If the *Anglesey* doesn't leave within twenty-four hours, we go public with Titian's *Ariosto*." '

'Go on.'

'I've checked, and Titian's *Portrait of Ludovico Ariosto* was looted from the Oriani Collection.'

'And,' Leith took up the story, 'if they link *that* to the Duke of Windsor, people *will* start asking awkward questions. Coming on top of the Vienna Rubens.'

Lockwood stared at Leith. 'What about this bank in Basle?'

'Well, sir, the name is Drachen und Stoller. Zakros must have got the Tucker woman over to Basle this morning, to help him out. They obviously wanted a really important picture that would scare the daylights out of us and force us to act quickly. According to Andover, she's an art historian, which would help explain her involvement. The good news of course is that we now know where all the stuff is hidden. How we get into Drachen und Stoller is a different matter. But at least we know its location.'

'We still can't act against anyone yet, though, can we?' Lockwood saw the difficulties immediately. 'When we go in we have to go in against all of them, simultaneously. We can't do that until this yacht turns up again, tomorrow. What do you think the chances are that it really is going to . . . where did you say, Kiritha?'

'Kithira, sir. Pretty good. I'd say.'

'Oh yes, why?'

Leith looked from the Prime Minister to Slocombe, and back again. 'Kithira is slap in the middle of the stretch of water that separates mainland Greece from Crete. That's right on the route the *Anglesey* will take on its way to Piraeus. They're not taking any chances, sir. They'll pick up the *Anglesey* when she rounds Cape Malea and then follow her. The minute you call her off her direct course for Piraeus, Kofas and Kolettis and the others will know.'

22

Wednesday

Four thousand feet below, the waters of the Mediterranean looked green and inviting. The tiny plane was cramped and, in the sunshine, very hot. Both Victoria and Edward were deeply uncomfortable and it wasn't surprising, considering the last eighteen hours. The crossing to Rhodes hadn't been so bad, but owing to strong winds, which had made the sea choppy, the ferry had been late getting in – nearly midnight. They had found a hotel only with difficulty; by then it was after one. They had been too tired to make love, and Victoria had had to telephone London, where she was told by the duty officer that a small plane had been chartered for them at Heraklion in Crete and that two seats were booked for them on the first commercial flight out of Rhodes the next day, at ten-thirty. That plane had been half an hour late, so they hadn't arrived in Crete until after midday. It was now nearly half past one and they were beginning their descent into Kithira. Ahead of them they could see the single mountain that dominated the island.

'Where is the airport?' shouted Edward, above the rattle of the small Cessna.

'To the west of Kithira town,' said the pilot, who spoke excellent English. 'We fly out over the sea and then come in from the west. The prevailing winds today are from the north-east.'

'Is that where the port is?'

'What? I can't hear.'

'I said: is that where the port is – Kithira town?'

'No. Kithira town is part-way up the mountain – look, you can see the white roofs straight ahead.'

They all stared to where he was pointing. A line of white buildings could be seen some nine hundred feet above the sea.

'But there *is* a port here?' Edward tried not to sound too pathetic.

'Oh yes, Kapsali, near Kithira, and Aghios Pelagias, near Potamos, in the north-eastern corner of the island. Kapsali is very small.'

'How big is Kithira?'

The pilot shrugged. 'Fifteen . . . twenty miles, north to south.'

'Can you fly over Potamos for us?' said Victoria.

The pilot frowned. 'I've already told flight control I'm coming straight in. It will look very odd to change now.' He looked at his watch. 'And I have to get back to Heraklion as soon as I can.' He turned his head to look over his shoulder at Victoria. 'I'd rather not.'

Victoria didn't press it. She could see Kapsali from the plane: there were no large boats of any description. They'd have to travel to Potamos/Aghios Pelagias by taxi.

The pilot dipped the plane and curved it to their left. They dropped to two thousand feet. For about a minute and a half he held the plane's nose down, flying north-west and losing height to fifteen hundred feet. Then he curved the plane right, looking over his shoulder to where they could now see a tiny white and brown strip sticking out into the sea. He straightened up at about a thousand feet and prepared to land.

The landing was uneventful and they taxied to the small pastel-blue building which stood next to a massive red-ringed wind-sock. There was nothing to pay – that had all been arranged during the night by London and the embassy in Athens. But they did have to arrange a taxi. The man in the blue hut, who doubled as flight control, customs and porter, agreed to phone for a car in Kithira town and, exhausted, they both sat on the ground in the shade of the building and watched as their pilot took off again, heading back to Heraklion. By now it was twenty to two.

The car arrived after about twenty minutes. It was actually a small pick-up truck so Edward let Victoria take the passenger seat and got into the back with their luggage. The road wound right over the main mountain and they were soon back at a thousand feet, though this time anchored firmly to the ground. There was no shade for Edward but fortunately there was so little traffic on the road that the pick-up could maintain a good speed, making a breeze that kept him cool. There was sea in all directions, with the mainland of Greece just visible in the north. Everything else, including the horizons, was lost in a heat haze. After about twenty-five minutes they started coming down again on the other side of the mountain. Edward twisted to look ahead. Aghios Pelagias was now in view, the usual Greek huddle of white and pale-blue walls and flat roofs. At about a quarter to three they reached the outskirts of the town, then a square with a few old olive trees, providing shade, and a church. Here the driver stopped. Victoria got out. 'The driver says cars can't get to the port; we have to go down these steps here.'

Edward handed down their bags and rolled over the edge of the pick-up. A group of small boys gathered round, their hands held out as Victoria started to count money for the taxi. Edward lifted the bags and led the way down the steps.

Victoria caught up with him and took her bag.

'Nervous?'

'I ought to be too tired to be nervous . . . but I'm not. Too tired, I mean.' He nodded ahead to where they could see a stretch of water between the walls that lined the steps. 'As soon as we get down there we're going to know whether this has all been a terrible waste or not.'

They hurried forward, feeling anticipation with one step, dread with the next. What were they going to do if the *Strabo* wasn't here? What were they going to do anyway? At the foot of the steps they were met by the usual harbour smells of fish and diesel. The usual harbour water, slicked with oil, cardboard cartons, half-submerged bottles, used cigarettes. Edward looked right: a line of cafés, a ship's chandler's, a gas station for boats, a police station. He looked left: a lighthouse, a small grey derrick, a very old, wooden-hulled fishing boat with a high prow and masses of orange netting. And, on the far side, the *Strabo*.

'Half ahead.' In these modern ships, Kenneth Lynn didn't need to bellow as his predecessors would have done. He gave the order quietly.

'Half ahead it is,' replied the bosun.

The *Anglesey* had just reached the middle of the river. The loading of the Marbles had gone smoothly enough, though there now wasn't enough room for the crew to play volley ball. The ship's departure had been curiously quiet. If the radio was to be believed, the docks were pulsing with protest. At one point the police had been unable to keep the rival demonstrators apart, and fighting had broken out. But that, of course, was outside the docks. At the water's edge there had been only a few stevedores and a representative from the Admiralty to see them off.

Lynn sat down. The route down the Thames and into the Channel, indeed as far as Gibraltar, was fairly straightforward. He had asked for the charts of the eastern Mediterranean to be brought up, so that he could study his approach to Piraeus. He spread the largest-scale chart in front of him and scanned the area. Greece, of course, was a mass of islands, and his first officer had pencilled in what he thought was the best route. Lynn told himself he would make a more careful inspection later but, at a first glance, the most direct route took him between the western tip of Crete and an island called Kithira, then –

'Sir – look!'

Lynn raised his head. 'What is it?'

'Boats, sir. A chain of them . . . blocking our way.'

Lynn saw what the first officer meant. 'Oh Lord, I thought our departure was too good to be true.' He focused his binoculars. Ahead of them, abreast of Greenwich Pier and the Royal Naval College, were five small boats, each manned by six or seven people and all roped together in one line. They were drawn up across the main channel of the river and each one had a huge board nailed to its gunwale. A single capital letter was painted on each board so that the whole chain read: 'E-L-G-I-N'.

The boats were about a quarter of a mile ahead. There was plenty of time for the *Anglesey* to stop, but, Lynn calculated, there was not enough depth in the river for him to go around them. What was he to do? He used his binoculars again and examined the banks of the river either side of the boats. Hmm. Ferry Street and Factory Place, on the port bank, were deserted, but the starboard bank – Thames Street, the pier itself – was packed, scores of people milling around and – he should have guessed as much – several brightly coloured vans from the TV companies. Whatever Lynn did it would be on television tonight.

He thought quickly. One option was to radio the Admiralty for advice. He dismissed that. He was a captain and expected to use his initiative. If he slowed, or stopped, the image of five small boats holding up the might of the Royal Navy would flash around the world as surely as that picture of the individual Chinese who had stopped the tanks in Tianenmen Square. Lynn turned to the bosun. 'Get out the launch.' Then he called down to the engine room. 'Randall! Stand by with the S3 canisters.'

There was a pause. Then: 'Aye-aye, sir.'

While the launch was being made ready, Lynn gave the bosun his instructions.

Two hundred yards short of the line of boats, he throttled back to 'Slow ahead'. He raised his binoculars again. The launch, with seven men aboard, shot forwards. At its prow was the bosun and his mate. The launch approached the boats between the 'L' and the 'G'. As the launch closed with the line of other boats, the bosun extended his boathook and lifted the rope from the water. He brought a length of it aboard. His mate had an axe which he now brought into view. He lifted it – and slammed it down on the rope, snapping it at once. The 'L' and the 'G' boats jerked apart. Through his binoculars on the bridge of the *Anglesey*, Lynn observed all this. 'Half ahead,' he ordered quickly.

The *Anglesey* picked up speed. It was a hundred yards from the line of boats. The tide was taking the 'E' and 'L' boats to the left, to the port bank, whereas the 'G', 'I' and 'N' boats were still more or less where they had been. The launch kept its position between the two.

The *Anglesey* closed . . . fifty yards, twenty, ten. At that point, Lynn stepped out from the bridge and raised his arm. The bosun threw the throttle on the launch, its bow rose in the water, and it screamed downstream. At the same moment, Lynn shouted into his intercom: 'Full ahead! Set S3 . . . fire!'

The frigate rumbled forward, into the gap between the small boats. At the same time, smoke began to pour from the rear of the *Anglesey*. In a matter of seconds, the line of boats, the entire river – including its banks where the television crews were located – was choked with dense, grey-black cloud.

Ahead of the line of smoke, completely obscured and thus unobserved by the TV cameras, the *Anglesey* made her escape.

Riley poured some soup into the mug. He passed it to O'Day. 'There's this place in Vienna, the Winkler . . . does a soup made from beer and – '

'Shut up. I've had enough soup to last me a lifetime. And enough "compact" cars.' Tonight's was a green Taunus. It was ten to ten and they knew from experience that the phone would ring exactly on time. They sat in silence as Riley sipped his soup, watching Zakros, who had already arrived and had seated himself on a bench near the phone. By now they were in the suburbs of Basle but still near the same tram route.

Five to ten. Zakros stood up, took something from his pocket and began to fiddle with it. He put something into his mouth. 'Chocolate,' breathed Riley between sips. 'There's a place in Montreux, does Italian icecream with home-made orange-flavoured chocolate.' The Greek walked forward a few paces and threw something, probably paper, into a waste bin. Then he returned to the bench and sat down again. At two minutes to ten he went to the booth and closed the door behind him. With the light on him, O'Day and Riley watched as he read the various posters inside the booth.

The phone rang. They watched as the Greek picked up the receiver. 'Yes?'

'Nicos – '

'Shut up!'

'Nicos!'

'Remember that Frenchman Stamatis had to . . . get rid of? And the disappearance of Andover?'

'Ye-es.'

'I . . . I think I may have been burgled.'

'What? Why do you say that?'

'Well, this will sound odd – but there's *dust* all over the hall. I don't know what kind of dust it is, and I don't know how it got there. But it's there all right and it isn't normally. It's as if it was blown there, when a door opened maybe.'

'Is anything missing?'

'No . . . I don't think so.'

'Well, then – '

'Nancy, they could be bugging us, following . . .'

'Did you find a bug in the house?'

'No.'

'All our calls are to public booths. How could they bug you there? It's a different one every day. We've been through this.' She paused. 'On the other hand . . . I wonder . . . Let me think . . . Look, go to the next phone. I'll talk to Dimi and come back to you. Don't panic – but hang up now – and watch, to see if you are followed.'

'Ssshhit!' hissed Riley. 'There's no time to tap the next phone, and we daren't follow.' He looked at O'Day. 'I don't like this one bit.'

*

Lockwood stared at the television screen. It was hardly ever switched on in the Number Ten flat but tonight was different. All of them – the Prime Minister, Hatfield, Slocombe, Midwinter and Leith – were staring at it grimly and in silence, listening to the presenter.

'. . . The two ships which collided in the Thames today, blinded by the smoke released from HMS *Anglesey*, were the Venezuelan refrigerator ship, *La Gran Sabana*, and the Greek oil tanker, the *Astakidhon*. The *Astakidhon*, as these pictures show, was holed amidships, and three crew members were injured, including the captain, Samos Elasson. The tangled ships blocked the Thames for nearly three hours before they were both towed clear, to safety. We understand from the London Hospital that the condition of two of the crew is satisfactory but that Captain Elasson is in intensive care, having suffered a fractured spine. A spokesman for the Greek Embassy in London said . . .'

'Enough!' growled Lockwood, 'Turn it off.' He gulped some whisky as Midwinter pressed the remote-control button.

'Damn!' the Prime Minister breathed. 'You take one pace forward, you're shoved a giant leap back. Whatever possessed that frigate captain?'

'Might've seemed like a good idea at the time, Bill.' Slocombe was less fazed by this latest catastrophe than was anyone else.

Lockwood shook his head. 'We've had enough bad luck. You'd think something good would come our way soon. The news isn't any better from Basle. If Riley and O'Day can't tap the phones, we lose contact with the way the other side is thinking.'

'On the other hand, Bill,' said Slocombe slowly, 'Zakros does have to return to the bank at some stage, if their side is ever to deliver its threat.'

'That's all very well, Eric, but how are we going to force him to go to the bank? We never did decide that.' Lockwood looked at Leith. 'I understand that, if Lynn doesn't mess things up again, the *Anglesey* will be off Kithira some time on Sunday?'

'Yes,' replied the inspector. 'The captain has told us he intends to send one of the ship's launches on ahead, to the western side of the island where it can't be seen by the *Strabo*. They will take off Tatton and Andover some time during the hours of darkness.'

'How on earth will they find them?'

'Apparently the runway of the local airport juts out into the sea. Tatton and Andover will be waiting there. It's hard to miss it, I'm told. They should be on board the *Anglesey* by dawn on Sunday. The frigate will then sail quite close to the east side of Kithira so there's no chance of the *Strabo* missing her. We'd rather know where they are. Once she sets off in pursuit she will probably zigzag about, so that the crew of the *Anglesey* don't notice she is following.'

'That's convenient in one way,' said Lockwood. 'It means we have four of this Brigade all together on the one boat. That means we have to take care of just the three others, separately.' He looked at Slocombe. 'I can see that the Shelby woman will be quite easy. And Tucker. But what about the Greek in Basle?'

'Easy enough to pick him up, Bill, but the problem is still the stuff in the blasted bank. You know what the Swiss are like. If we just lift him, there's no telling if they will play ball and let us get into the account. In an ideal world we would trap him into taking everything out and then, the minute he steps on to the Gerbergasse, bingo! We land the lot, him and everything else.'

'Any ideas?'

Hatfield started to shake his head but Slocombe said, 'Hold on a mo'. How about this . . . If the *Strabo* does follow the *Anglesey*, then, knowing what we know, all you have to do, Bill, is to order the frigate to change course away from Piraeus. Better still, she could change course and bear down on the *Strabo*. They would realize, at the last, that we had got on to them, they would also realize pretty quickly that we had been stringing them along, that we have been biding our time – and with luck they will panic and instruct Zakros to go public as they have threatened all along.'

'But will they?' Hatfield leaned forward in his seat. 'Won't they realize that, if we are on to them, we are on to the man in Basle as well? If they do, they'll realize the best thing he can do is to go to ground. We might not catch him then but, even if we did, we wouldn't get the paintings or documents.'

'Aren't we making too much of all that artwork?' said Midwinter. 'Why wouldn't the Swiss government play ball, once they knew what was in that bank in Gerbergasse?'

'Then you don't know Swiss banks, Bernard.' Lockwood smiled grimly. 'Ask the Chancellor what he thinks.' He looked at Slocombe. 'We need a better plan.'

Everyone lapsed into silence.

'What about this?' Leith shifted on the sofa. 'Why not have

Ogilvy, at the British Museum, call in Eugenie Shelby and tell her that the *Anglesey* is not going to deliver the Marbles after all, that it is just a fake run, that the government never had any intention of handing over the Marbles but that it was just playing for time. He says the government is involved in some murky political game with the Greeks that he has no knowledge of but that it is all coming to a head and they are to prepare for the return of the Marbles. Her job as a conservator, a sculpture conservator, will be to check their condition after the voyage. I would imagine that the first thing Eugenie Shelby will do is alert Tucker, who would in turn alert the *Strabo*. They won't know what to think but, the minute the *Anglesey* changes course they will believe that what she tells them is true. Then they will alert their man in Basle and he will hot-foot it to the bank.' He drained his glass. 'Then comes the tricky bit: to have it all working smoothly, we need to arrest Zakros at the same time as the *Anglesey* turns on the *Strabo*. At the same time, of course, we pick up Eugenie Shelby.'

There was another silence in the room, broken only by the Prime Minister walking across to Leith and refilling his glass. He turned back and faced Slocombe. 'Seems good to me, Eric. Can you see anything wrong with it?'

'Just this: they are already suspicious, because of the dust from Riley's blow-machine. So . . . will they fall for this new thing?'

Leith shrugged. 'Maybe that's the luck the Prime Minister is looking for. Riley and O'Day aren't following the Greek at the moment. It's now Wednesday, four days to Sunday. Enough time, maybe, for them to lose whatever suspicions they have. And think how excited they will be, the closer the *Anglesey* gets to Greek waters.'

Lockwood nodded. 'It's worth a try, I think. What should be our timing on all this? When will the *Strabo* sight the *Anglesey*?'

Leith sipped his whisky. 'According to the Admiralty, who are keeping in touch with the ship on our behalf, if she maintains her present speed, she should be abreast of Potamos around six to six-thirty their time, on Sunday morning. A bit early, I would have thought. Easy enough to slow her down, of course. No one will notice, especially under cover of night.'

'Let's work backwards,' said the Prime Minister. 'Kithira is about a hundred and forty miles from Piraeus, am I right?'

281

Leith nodded. 'Give or take. At twelve to fifteen knots, that's around ten hours' steaming.'

'Ssso . . . if she keeps up her present pace, she'll be in Piraeus by . . . half past three on Monday afternoon, Greek time.'

'Correct,' said Leith. 'Half past one in London.'

'Now let's switch back to Eugenie Shelby. For it to look natural, we must have Ogilvy call her not too urgently. After all, the Marbles will take several days to return to Britain. Say he contacts her later in the week, or over the weekend even, and suggests a meeting on Sunday. If that meeting were to take place after lunch, here in London, it would be four or five o'clock in Greece. It would take her an hour to get through to the *Strabo*'s phone.' Lockwood smiled at Leith. 'The more I think about your idea, Bob, the better I like it. But here's another gloss . . . The *Anglesey* must change course while the banks are open in Basle and with enough time for Kolettis and Kofas and Nancy Tucker to alert their man in Basle and give him time to get to the Gerbergasse.' He helped himself to more whisky. 'That means . . . that the *Anglesey* mustn't change course until the next day, Monday morning – '

'In which case, Prime Minister,' said Hatfield, 'may I suggest this: let's assume the *Anglesey* picks up the *Strabo* some time on Sunday morning – when it follows her at a distance. The *Anglesey* could steam north for five hours at, say, ten knots, a respectable speed, and then hove to. That would make sense because, were she to carry on, she would arrive in Piraeus at around midnight, hardly a good time to berth, given her mission. The captain could let some men relax – water-skiing, swimming, exercises on deck, for instance – while others dressed the ship for arrival: flags, lights, that sort of thing. I was in the navy – years ago – and they do dress ships for arrival in foreign ports. That would all be happening around the time the people on the *Strabo* were getting their message from Eugenie Shelby – '

'Excellent, Joss,' said Lockwood, taking up the story. 'For a while they would be getting conflicting signals. Either they would tell Zakros in Basle to act first thing the next morning, and remove the pictures and documents from the bank as soon as it opened – '

'Or,' said Slocombe, 'they would wait all night, to see if the story from Mrs Shelby was really true. After all, with the crew relaxing, and with the ship being dressed, it would seem as if the ship was still preparing to enter Piraeus.'

'Exactly. Only at dawn the following day will the Shelby story be confirmed, when they see the frigate turn for home. Then they will contact Basle, Zakros will have all day to visit the bank and, as he sets foot on the Gerbergasse with the pictures, the Marbles and the Queen, not to mention the government, are safe.' Lockwood looked from one face to another. 'Can anyone see any problems? Let's have them now, while there's still time to think them through . . .'

But no one could add to what Hatfield, Leith and the Prime Minister himself had conceived. On the contrary, an air of subdued excitement had entered the room. At last it looked as though events were coming their way after days, weeks, of seeing them beyond control.

'Thank you all for coming,' said Lockwood, putting the whisky bottle back on the trolley and thus ending the meeting. 'Please use the back staircase . . . we need tight security more than ever now.'

23

Thursday

From the *Daily Telegraph*:

STOLEN STATUES GO ON SHOW IN INDIA
MUSEUM OBJECTS SURFACE IN HINDUPUR
From our own correspondent

The eight religious statues stolen last weekend from the Metropolitan Museum in New York have gone on show at the sacred Hindu shrine in Hindupur in the southern half of the country. The shrine is heavily guarded by Hindu zealots and only selected members of the press are being allowed access.

Hindu Heritage, the organization which claimed responsibility for the theft, issued a statement yesterday, saying: 'The eight religious statues reclaimed from America are now back where they belong, at the holy centre of the religion which inspired them. This action was not done for personal gain, as may be seen from the fact that Hindu Heritage has handed over these sacred objects to the officials at the shrine.

'Hindu Heritage apologizes again for the accident at the Metropolitan Museum, in which a security guard suffered a fatal injury. We are exploring ways of making amends to the security guard's widow. We are also exploring ways of returning other items of Hindu Heritage which have been stolen from our homeland.'

A spokesman for the Indian government declined to comment on this latest development. But he said that Indian officials were studying remarks made by Mr Mason Farmer, US Ambassador to the UN, following the theft and that a reply would be issued shortly.

Our New York correspondent adds: The funeral of Mr Spiridon Panottis, the security guard at the Metropolitan Museum, who was killed last Sunday in the attack by Hindu Heritage, took place yesterday in Astoria, the predominantly Greek suburb of the city. More than a thousand people turned out to hear Mr

Panottis's brother, Mr Sophocles Panottis, denounce the Indians who made the raid but also Mr William Lockwood, the British Prime Minister.

Mr Panottis said: 'Deep down, the British government and its Prime Minister, Mr Lockwood, bear a responsibility for my brother's death . . . let the British government mark their responsibility for their action not just by returning these Marbles but in addition by paying Greece compensation for the loss she has suffered over many years. The British government should pay for the Marbles to be mounted back on the Parthenon – that would mark the Olympic Festival but also, I say, it would be a fitting memorial for my brother.'

'One of the crew is sunbathing – topless. Nice figure. Bit like yours.' Edward held the binoculars to his eyes though Victoria couldn't see him. He was like a duck shooter in a hide. He had rigged up a number of towels on the balcony of their room, using a clothesline and the branch of a tree that was conveniently close. They could observe the *Strabo* without being seen. It was very hot already. There had been just the one room available in the hotel, and the bed could have been bigger. Victoria was still not entirely sure about Edward's feelings regarding Nancy and hadn't been able to relax as much as she might. But she was coming round.

'You know, it's a pity I can't lip-read. I can see clearly enough to see them talking.'

'Them? Who's she talking to?'

'Kolettis. He's brought her a drink.'

'Hard life, being a blackmailer.'

'Now he's kneeling over her. He's put his head on her stomach. Now he's – '

'Are you making this up?'

'See for yourself.'

Victoria took the binoculars and crouched in the 'hide'. 'Oh . . . goodness! He's got freckles, Edward, like you but all over . . . Dear, dear . . . you're missing the best bit.'

Sir Evelyn Allen nodded his silver mane and the security guard gently pulled shut the shiny mahogany doors to the Cabinet

Room. Twenty-one ministers were inside, plus Sir Evelyn. It was three minutes past eleven. There was the usual chatter, jokes, gossip. But there were more silences too, glances at Lockwood and Keld. The noise was muted, people were filling the void, waiting for the Prime Minister to start proper proceedings.

He looked to his left where the Secretary of State for Scotland was still standing. 'Douglas, please! We are late already.' Douglas Rothes blushed a bright vermilion and plonked on to his seat.

'We will follow the new agenda as circulated. I'm told by the Chief Whip that some of you object to the way I have been conducting this Elgin Marbles business. I am willing to listen . . . to my colleagues in this room. Who will begin?' Lockwood's breezy manner so soon in the meeting unsettled some of the Cabinet and, to begin with, there was silence. The Prime Minister was feeling better this morning – his wife had just called from Great Ormond Street to say that little Tommy, his grandson, was out of immediate danger. Lockwood was about to speak again, about to challenge men he had promoted into high office, when George Keld got there first.

'Prime Minister, I will begin. And let me say to start with that I believe I speak for most of the Cabinet – more than half . . . We have, quite frankly, been puzzled – amazed – by this Elgin Marbles business all along. We cannot understand where the issue came from, we cannot understand why this special committee had to consider the matter at all, let alone in secret. We don't know who was on this committee. And since it did become public we cannot understand why you have arranged things in the way that you have. You seem to have been in a hurry to dispose of these works of art, so much so that you have provoked unnecessary protest, chaos, confusion and damage. There has simply not been due process of consultation. This, in the view of many people here – and not only here, I might add – has encouraged the wilder elements to make trouble, in the hope that other objects might be dislodged. We have all seen where that has led . . .' He paused and looked around the table. 'We have all seen the papers this morning and I am bound to say, Prime Minister, that there is some truth in what is being said across the Atlantic. The way the affair has been handled here has, in some curious and indeterminable way, sparked what has happened there. But the way the American government has handled the matter is in marked contrast to the way the British government has handled things. They have handled it firmly and as a government – the UN ambassador spoke out straight away, unambiguously and with the full approval of the President himself. In Britain, however – and everyone is remarking upon it – the matter has been handled only by you. Most people in this room are as much in the dark as everyone else. The collision of those two ships on the Thames, in the wake of the *Anglesey*'s smoke trick, was the most miserable and embarrassing episode of all. The fact that one of the ships damaged was Greek, and that the British taxpayer now risks paying out millions of pounds in damages, is just too galling. The Greeks are the very beneficiaries of this sudden rush of generosity on your part, which is quite out of keeping with what is called for.

'The worst thing, however, is that . . . all this comes in the run-up to an election – an election which it is by no means certain we shall win. Indeed, it is the opinion of many of us that the way this Elgin Marbles business has been conducted may well have been losing us votes. It may lose us yet more support in the country. This is undignified, Prime Minister, undignified and unfair. It seems especially unfair to the Cabinet Ministers around this table, who do not know what is happening and yet, under the tradition of collective responsibility, must shoulder the blame for anything that goes wrong, who must answer to their colleagues in Parliament and their constituents in the country, for any loss of support – and ultimately for any defeat in the election. We therefore feel that an explanation is owed the Cabinet, a full explanation not only for the way the matter is being conducted now, but why this issue reared its head – its increasingly ugly head – in the first place.'

Keld sat back and sipped some water. Ministers did not actually cry out 'Hear, hear' in Cabinet but there was a chorus of grunts from around the table, murmurs of approval, quiet slapping of the table which left no doubt as to how much support Keld had.

'Thank you, George.' Lockwood knew he had to move swiftly. Any delay now would look like deviousness, or uncertainty, which was worse. But Keld had been very clever. He had been in no way disloyal, had not even hinted to Cabinet that he knew what lay behind all the 'shilly-shallying'. In so doing he had kept to the bargain he had struck with the Prime Minister. At the same time he had put himself at the head of Lockwood's critics, at the head of those ministers who claimed to have the rest of the party – both inside and outside Parliament – in mind: the custodians of the party's majority and its right and will to govern. Lockwood could see that Keld had a lot of support. It was probably support born of disaffection, for the seemingly high-handed way in which he, as Prime Minister, had been handling this affair. It was support that would be easy to dislodge if he could bring something dramatic out of the hat – but for the time being, for another few days, he couldn't.

'It is natural that, with the opposition debate coming up in the House, which has now been confirmed for next Monday, some of us should get worried. I acknowledge that the opinion polls are not encouraging. I regret the resignation of the Trustees of the British Museum. But that is all I regret. Most of you around this table have known me for years. You know my wife, you know my children – and I know yours. You therefore know – or should know – that I am not high-handed, I do not keep my colleagues in the dark unnecessarily, I am not a shilly-shallyer.' He smiled. 'If there is such a word.'

'But, Prime Minister . . . is that an acknowledgement that you are keeping us in the dark over something?' It was Geoffrey Scylde, the Secretary of State for Employment.

Lockwood fixed him with his stare. 'Geoffrey, there are twenty-two people in this room, some of whom are better at keeping secrets than others.' He looked quickly up and down the table. 'I think we can agree on that. Each ministry around this table has its own secrets – some more than others. Very few of you know what George Keld, at Defence, knows. Very few of you know what Tom Lessor, at the Home Office, knows. Very few of you know what Geoff Scylde, at Employment, knows. There are financial secrets that only the Chancellor of the Exchequer knows. No one questions any of that – it is a necessary part of the modern state. But – '

'But, Prime Minister, few of those secrets – perhaps none – are Cabinet matters, few of them have an effect on our standing in the polls, few if any of them are the subject of an opposition debate in the House.' Alan Pritchett, Secretary of State for Wales, joined the attack.

'It therefore follows', Lockwood stormed on, 'that when such matters do arise it is the Prime Minister who deals with them. I cannot . . . I will not say any more about this matter here, around this table. I realize that, for many of you, this will not be a

288

satisfactory answer and it will offer small comfort ahead of Monday's debate. It cannot be helped. I do not ask you to like my decision but I do ask you to trust me, to accept that I have good reason for doing what I do. The debate will carry a three-line whip and it goes without saying that everyone in this room will abide by that. And I now ask that we move on to the next item on the agenda, the proposal for a second Channel Tunnel – '

'No, Bill.' It was Keld. His body had gone very still and his eyes looked straight into Lockwood's. 'No. We all appreciate what you've just said, and we agree with most of it. It's just that the part we disagree with is the most important part. Monday's debate is crucial. I've made no soundings so I don't know how close the vote will be. I doubt if anybody on our side will break with the whips and actually vote with the opposition, but who knows who might abstain? The point is: we shouldn't be having this sort of damaging debate so close to the election; the leadership of the party should not land us with this difficult – this very difficult – dilemma. I appreciate, we all appreciate, that this . . . this secret you are keeping so close to your chest may be vital for this country. But that very fact means we cannot see why you do not share it with us. If you do not trust the rest of your Cabinet, well . . . you have no right to expect a reciprocal trust from us. Everyone in this Cabinet admires you and admires what you have done for the country. For the party. Quite frankly, Bill, that makes it all the harder for us to comprehend, and to sympathize with . . . whatever it is that you are up to.'

Keld unbuttoned his jacket and put the palms of both hands on the table. 'This is hard to say – I was going to add "Prime Minister", but "Bill" is just as natural. You see before you, around you at this table, twenty politicians, twenty ministers, all of whom want your job. There's nothing unusual in that. What you don't understand, Bill, or appear not to, is how damaging this whole business has been, and still is. We could lose the debate next week – I happen to think that we will. And it is your leadership that has brought us to this point.' Keld stuck out his chin a fraction. 'Even now, next Monday's difficult situation might be averted, if you would let us all help. But you won't, will you? Your mind is made up.'

Keld stared at Lockwood.

Lockwood stared back. And nodded.

For several seconds – what seemed like much longer – there was complete silence in the room.

Keld stood up. The sharp sound of his chair being scraped back across the tiled floor shot around the room. 'I thank you for the opportunity to serve as Secretary of State for Defence, Bill. I have found every minute rewarding and I venture to think that I have been of some use. But I cannot sit by and allow the actions of one man, albeit the leader of our party, to imperil future achievements of that party. What you are doing is wrong, terribly wrong. I shall feel free to say so in the debate – and I shall feel free because, from this moment, I resign as a member of your government.' Keld picked up his papers and his pen, and, with a last look at Lockwood, marched out of the room.

O'Day had been confused when Riley had bought an electric drill. He had been even more perplexed when, instead of renting a car, Riley had gone to a different agency and hired a large Ford van. But when Riley had drilled two small holes – one in the back door of the van and the other in a side panel – O'Day saw the light.

'We can park in the Gerbergasse and watch in safety from here,' Riley said.

They had done so. In the circumstances, they had made no attempt to follow Zakros or to tap the next phone on the list. Now it was nearly three o'clock and the bank would be closing soon. There had been no sign of the Greek. They watched as the heavy doors of Drachen und Stoller were banged shut. They let themselves out of the back of the van and climbed into the driving cab. Riley pulled away – and then braked suddenly as a tram rang its bell angrily. 'Menace!' O'Day hissed.

'We can have a proper dinner tonight,' Riley said as he turned the van into the market place. 'And a proper eight hours' sleep.'

O'Day wiped a large hand across his face. 'And if Zakros manages to get into the bank outside normal hours? We're going to look like a couple of Swiss gnomes.'

Slocombe, Midwinter, Hatfield and Leith trooped up the stairs of Number Ten. Above them the Prime Minister held the door open. 'Tell me the worst,' he said to Hatfield as they filed past him.

'It's as bad as can be,' said the Chief Whip. 'Keld's resignation pushed Page over the edge and now Monday's debate is full-dress: a censure motion on your handling of the Elgin Marbles affair.'

Lockwood closed the door and followed the others into his sitting-room. As he made for the bar, they all threw themselves into the easy chairs. It had been a wearing day. Lockwood poured the whiskies. 'What's your arithmetic, Joss?'

Hatfield took the glass that was offered, helped himself to water from a jug and took a healthy guzzle. 'The opposition, plus the Liberal-Democrats, plus the Scot Nats, will all vote against us. No one on our side is going to break a three-line whip wholeheartedly and vote against you, Bill. The question is: how many will abstain? That could lower our total and let the other side in. Some of our own backbenchers might do that: they might feel they'd get better treatment from Keld, and that our chances at the election would be better with the Elgin affair forgotten. That would be easier with you out of the way. That poll in the *Telegraph* didn't help.'

'And? The *arithmetic*!' Lockwood gave the others their glasses.

'Keld's immediate entourage is twelve strong. They will all stay away from the voting lobby. His brother-in-law will do so, too. Then there are the people theoretically on our side who you have made enemies of, while you have been Prime Minister. Seven ministers, of one sort or another, who were sacked; three very ambitious backbenchers who consider themselves to have been snubbed in being left out of the government; those three Welsh members who still resent your allowing the nuclear power station to be built near Haverfordwest; two others who still believe the second Channel Tunnel could ruin their constituencies, with heavy traffic. That's twenty-eight out of nearly three hundred . . . but, with a majority of thirty-four . . . well, you don't need me to work it out for you.'

'If it's that close,' said Midwinter, 'isn't it time to go public with that damaging stuff about Keld? The illegitimate child, and all that.'

Tonight Lockwood wasn't standing in front of the fireplace. He too was slumped in a chair. 'Too late for that, Bernard. In the first place, if we were to release it between now and the debate, it would look very sleazy, as indeed it would be. But, worse, the gloves would be off then and Keld would regard himself as free to release what he knows in the debate. After the debate, it goes without saying, would be too late to have any effect on the result.'

'But can't we threaten him with it? He must know it will ruin his chances of ever being Prime Minister.'

'Wrong again, Bernard. If we threaten him he may just go public in the debate, which we don't want. But in any case he's chosen his moment very well from his point of view. Say we do lose the vote on Monday. I shall have to announce that I intend to resign as leader and fight a leadership contest. If, after that, the sleaze about Keld is leaked, the only thing it will achieve will be to make the party more unpopular before the election. People in our own party will blame me for that – and quite rightly. That will kill any chance I have of being re-elected leader. It may or may not help Keld, but it is no help to me. Am I right, Eric?'

'I couldn't have put it better myself. The bastard child business is a dead duck, so to speak. Events have played into Keld's hand and he has played that hand perfectly from his point of view. All we can do is pray that nothing else goes wrong between now and Monday – like someone breaking into the V & A and stealing something – and we should devote our energies to trying to keep a few of those wayward backbenchers on the team.'

'Any ideas?' Lockwood swallowed more whisky.

'It will have to be imaginative,' said Hatfield. 'Any promises we make about a role in the next government are going to look desperate – we are hardly in a position to guarantee that our side *will* form the next administration. I might be able to do something with the Channel Tunnel waverers, but don't forget Keld sits for a Scottish constituency . . . the Welsh MPs might like that Celtic link. They may think they would be listened to more by Keld.'

There was a long silence, as usual broken only by the ticking of the Thomas Tompion clock in the corner.

Presently, Hatfield continued. 'How is the other matter progressing?'

Lockwood rubbed his hand across his face. 'Everything is in place. But we have to wait for the *Anglesey* to arrive in Greek waters – on Sunday. Just keep your fingers crossed that, between now and then, the Louvre isn't invaded by Algerians, or the

Uffizi by Sienese brigands, or that British tourists don't go barmy on Mykonos.'

'On the other hand,' said Hatfield slowly, 'this whole thing could be solved on Monday before the debate even gets under way.'

'But we can't use the information, Joss.'

'We can't tell the whole truth, I agree. Jesus! Even if we can't announce the real reason why the Marbles left, only to come back again, can't we make up a story that fits some of the facts? If you could announce, right at the opening of the debate, that the Marbles were returning to Britain and that they had only been sent away in the first place because . . . oh, I don't know . . . because a certain problem, of terrorism or kidnapping or another kind of blackmail, had been successfully resolved . . . I'll bet the debate would collapse.' Hatfield's eyes were glowing now and he sat up. 'What do you say, Bill? I'm right, aren't I? You would come bouncing back.'

Lockwood had got to his feet and was refilling Hatfield's glass. 'What do you think, Eric?' he said over his shoulder, as he poured. 'He's got a point.'

'I agree in theory. In theory, it's beautiful. But would someone like to tell me just what story we should concoct? It would have to be the most convincing lie in history.'

24

Friday

Victoria's gaze spanned the square of Aghios Pelagias and her features widened into a grin. 'Look, Edward. A market. Figs, shoes, olives, hats, grapes, socks – '

'And customers, my dear.' He pointed. 'Including the chef from the *Strabo*.'

It was true. A thin, blond man with a white sweatshirt and a blue gingham kerchief around his neck was standing at the stall which sold tomatoes. The word 'Strabo' was printed in blue across the back of his shirt.

'Let's sit here,' said Edward, indicating a small café with a dim, but cool, interior. 'It's out of the sun and it's out of the way.'

They went in, found seats and ordered two Cokes. They watched the *Strabo* chef. He had a huge straw bag with him, which he filled with grapes. He stepped to one side and Victoria saw Kolettis next to him. Instinctively, she stiffened. She nudged Edward and pointed, but he too had seen the archaeologist. They both got up and moved to another table, where they couldn't be seen from the market. At the back of the café a radio was playing and a number of men were standing by the bar. They stared at Victoria and at Edward, but then went back to their gossip. Edward got up and went to stand in the arch that formed the front of the café. The chef and Kolettis had disappeared; presumably they had gone back to the *Strabo*. Edward returned to the table inside the café. Victoria was leaning back in her chair, her head cocked to one side, her eyes gazing blindly at the vaulted ceiling.

'Is that supposed to be sexy?'

She held up a hand. 'Ssshh!'

Then he realized she was listening to the radio behind the bar. The other men had stopped talking and were also listening. As Edward sat down, the men suddenly burst into chatter and Victoria rocked forward on her seat. 'That was the news, from Athens.'

'Saying what?'

'The British School was attacked during the night. As a reprisal for the Greek tanker that was holed in the Thames. The school burned down.'

Riley balanced a tin of beer on the bulge of his stomach. 'Terrine Toyota,' he sighed, passing O'Day some pâté he had hurriedly bought earlier that evening, while the Irishman kept watch alone on the Zakros house. 'The man said it was made from the same recipe they use at the Stucki – that's one of the best restaurants in Basle.'

They both swallowed in silence. Then Riley, in between sips of beer, added: 'Say Zakros doesn't behave as he is supposed to. Are we ready?'

O'Day nodded. 'I was thinking about that, too. I raised it with Leith but . . . now there's to be that debate on Monday, in the Commons, security's tighter than ever.' He swallowed some more beer. 'No reinforcements.'

'Let's think it through, then – '

'What is there to think about? Either he goes to the bank or he doesn't. Whatever he does we follow him. If anyone else in the Brigade comes here to join him, then either Athens or London will alert us.'

'Are we certain we aren't expecting any more of the Brigade who we don't know about? People who've been sleepers so far.'

'No, of course we're not certain. But my guess is that there aren't any more. The Tucker woman said there were seven of them. No one else has ever been referred to in their phone conversations, and they wouldn't need anyone. Security's important for them too, don't forget.' He drained his beer can. 'One thing, though: we *do* need another vehicle, just in case anyone joins Zakros. That would bring Tatton and Andover, or Leith, as back-up for us, but, in a chase, the other side could still split up. Better get another car first thing tomorrow.'

Riley nodded. 'And the more I think about it, the more likely it is that Zak will have support. Paintings are bulky objects: he couldn't carry more than a few by himself.' He paused. 'Say he does make a bolt for it. Where's he going to head for?'

'Do I look like a gypsy?' O'Day held up his beer can. 'This isn't a crystal ball.'

'Just trying to be prepared.'

'All we can do is keep mobile.'

Riley rubbed his hand over his chin. 'I wouldn't mind a shave, though.'

'You think you look any prettier without the stubble?'

'Nnnno.' Riley eyed himself in the car mirror. 'But would you rent even a Toyota to someone who looks like me?'

William Lockwood looked down at his grandson, Tommy. The boy seemed so small in the hospital bed. 'May I kiss him?' the Prime Minister asked.

'Next time,' whispered the nurse. 'He's been asleep less than an hour. He should have been asleep hours ago. We don't want to risk waking him now.'

Lockwood nodded and hugged his daughter instead. 'Shouldn't you get some sleep?' he asked her. 'You look shattered.'

She nodded. 'I will now. Thank you for coming, Daddy. You're in the wars, too, like Tommy.'

Lockwood looked down at the boy again. 'Not like Tommy,' he whispered. 'Not like Tommy at all. We act as though it's life or death in politics, but it rarely is. When you see . . . when you see such a little head, almost lost in the pillow . . . and you realize how close it was . . . what it would have done to you if . . . Politics is just – *tawdry*.'

His daughter hugged him back. 'I'll tell Tommy you came, when he wakes up in the morning. And I'll give him the chess set.' Lockwood had brought his grandson a gift. 'He'll be thrilled.'

The Prime Minister kissed his daughter's cheek. As he did so, he saw the door to the room open and, in the corridor outside, the figure of Bernard Midwinter. 'Looks like I'm wanted,' he whispered. 'No peace for the wicked.'

His daughter squeezed him a last time. 'Tommy doesn't think you're wicked. And neither do I.' She let him go.

Outside in the corridor, Midwinter led the way to a quiet spot away from the nurses and doctors and where they couldn't be overheard. 'How's the boy, Bill?'

'Better, they say. Not completely out of harm's way yet, though. Thanks for asking. But that's not why you're here.'

'No, in fact, I've just come from another hospital. From the London Hospital. The Greek tanker captain died an hour ago.'

25

Saturday

'I like Greek wine, I like Greek grapes and I like Greek sunshine. But what I wouldn't give for a good British breakfast!'

Edward smiled at Victoria. They had taken to eating breakfast – bread, jam, fruit and coffee – on their balcony. It was sunny but not yet hot and they could keep an eye on the *Strabo*. 'You didn't get that figure on bacon and sausage,' he said.

'Wrong. I eat like a horse in the mornings. Like a horsefly in the evenings.'

'You had two kebabs last night, one more than I did.'

'Yes, well . . . all this tension, plus your constant attention, gives me a larger appetite than usual.'

'Jam?' He passed it to her. 'What happens after we get taken off tomorrow morning?'

'Leith didn't say. He said that the captain of the *Anglesey* would fill us in but that it rather depends on how the *Strabo* reacts to the frigate's change of course.'

Edward stood up, still holding his coffee-cup. He stood at the edge of the balcony, amid the towels, and looked down on the *Strabo*.

Victoria continued. 'Apparently the Shelby woman, the conservator, is not being called in to see Ogilvy until tomorrow. Our side doesn't want them to have too much time to think – so from then on it's all going to be very closely timed. The idea is that at some stage after we have gone on board, the *Anglesey* will change course. That's designed to provoke the *Strabo* so that they alert Basle to withdraw the Blunt pictures and documents from the bank. That should happen some time on Monday – '

'In time to head off the censure motion.'

'You can't blame Lockwood for that. After the risks he's taken for the Queen.'

'I don't blame him. But I hope he's not counting on the Greeks to do exactly as he hopes.'

'Why do you say that?'

Edward finished his coffee. 'Because, my dear, unless I'm very much mistaken, the *Strabo* is getting up steam. There's smoke coming from her funnel and that can only mean one thing: she's preparing to leave again.'

'We now have a back-up vehicle: a purple – would you believe? – Ford. Hardly discreet, I know, but that's all they had. It's just out of sight, round that corner over there. Oh, and I got this.' Riley handed O'Day a cardboard box.

The Irishman opened it. Inside there was a pastry. He bit into it lustily. Between mouthfuls, he asked: 'You called London?'

'I did.'

'And?'

'The captain of the Greek tanker – the one that collided on the Thames when the *Anglesey* loosed off all that smoke – has died. The Greeks are incensed. Some British tourists were attacked in Athens late last night. Three of them are in hospital.'

Sir Francis Mordaunt put down his propelling pencil and rubbed his eyes. It was late and he had been working all day. Sir Francis was a very definite type of Englishman (though his ancestors, generations ago, had been Huguenots). Though he was in theory surrounded by relatives, nieces, godchildren, he was in practice a fairly solitary soul. The only two people he saw frequently were the Queen and his manservant, and he was more of a valet really. A long time ago, Mordaunt had been married. But Mordaunt had found he preferred his job to his marriage and when Angela had phoned from Italy to say that she was staying on indefinitely with Toby and Georgia Mitchell they had both known that it was the end. Mordaunt hadn't minded, not really. It had taken them years to get round to a divorce, by which time he was quite friendly with Angela's new lover. Mordaunt was aware that some people thought he was homosexual. His solitary lifestyle, his rather sharp features, the care he took with his clothes . . . in fact, it wasn't true. Not strictly true anyway. Mordaunt's job was still his life, his mistress, his ruling passion. Sex, any form of sex, played no part in his existence. He wasn't ashamed of that, nor was he particularly proud. He was just relieved. It made life a lot easier.

He got up and went to the fridge. He took out a piece of cold chicken and a bottle of Chablis. He felt tired and slumped on the sofa. After a moment he leaned forward and, with a long, bony finger, switched on the television.

'. . . Here, then, are the headlines again. Another earthquake in China is believed to have killed seven hundred and fifty people . . . The Italian Prime Minister has resigned over a bribery scandal . . . Twenty people were evacuated from a North Sea oil-rig after it appeared to shift on its supports . . . The US Secretary of State has stopped all American aid to India as a result of the murder at the Metropolitan Museum and because the stolen statues have gone on show at Hindupur . . . and at the Crystal Palace two world-class Nigerian athletes mounted a protest, demanding the return of the Benin bronzes in the British Museum. That's it . . . Goodnight from everyone in the news-room.'

As the music played, Mordaunt tried to digest that last item. Did that mean the Nigerians were taking a lead from the Greeks and the Indians? He groaned. No doubt the story would be all over the Sunday papers tomorrow and he would find out all he wanted to know. Another hurdle for Lockwood. And what about the other item, the American response to the theft of the objects at the Metropolitan Museum? He bit into his chicken. These were deep waters.

Another programme was starting. It was called *No Strings* and featured puppets, marionettes, carved or modelled to look like well-known figures. It was incredibly childish and vulgar and very, very funny. It had a cult following and Mordaunt loved it. The Queen herself often came in for quite a bit of stick. He gnawed at his chicken leg and settled back, trying to ignore the Crystal Palace episode.

Immediately, he saw a face that he recognized and he sat up again. It was Lockwood's, more or less. The creases in his cheeks were very deep, he was miniscule in comparison to everyone else around him and his iron-grey hair appeared to be fashioned from real wire. The Prime Minister was dressed, however, not in his habitual dark-blue suit, but in a white toga. He wore a crown of laurel leaves. Mordaunt also realized that the puppet Prime Minister was standing in front of a model of the Parthenon. Behind him was the head of Hatfield, also in a toga but carrying a lyre and a jug of wine. Arthur Page was next to Hatfield. He also wore a toga and carried Cupid's bow and arrow.

'I say, Bacchus,' said the Page puppet. 'Zeus is being a bit authoritarian these days, even for him!'

Bacchus hiccupped. 'He *is* god of gods, you know, so he can do as he likes. The Greeks may have given us democracy but that was for mere mortals – Aristotle, Sophocles, buncha humans. We gods just carry on, as we always did. More wine, Cupid?'

Cupid swallowed from the jug, wiped his mouth, and then went on, 'But why does he want the Parthenon restored?'

Bacchus nodded his head. 'It's all Greek to me, old boy. The Greeks are Christian now, whatever that means.' He hiccupped again. 'In their new services, they set fire to the churches. Very quaint.'

At this, Zeus turned and pointed to Bacchus. A flash was seen and then the puppet with the jug went up in smoke. Next, Zeus pointed at Cupid, with the same result. The camera closed in on Zeus's face. 'There's nothing a good thunderbolt can't cure,' Lockwood was made to say. He put his finger to his lips and sighed. 'I hope I've got one left for the debate on Monday.'

The show moved on to another skit. But Mordaunt didn't notice. He replaced his chicken leg on the plate on his lap. Lockwood was becoming an object of ridicule. This whole business threatened débâcle and it had to be stopped. It really was time to call in Arthur Page.

26

Sunday

The bridge of the *Anglesey* was, so far as Edward could judge, some thirty to forty feet above the water-line, and fairly breezy. That was why Kenneth Lynn had chosen it for their conference. It was impossible for anyone to disturb them unawares and they could not be overheard. Indeed, they could hardly hear each other. Victoria and Edward had been taken off Kithira at about two-thirty that morning. Getting back to the airstrip had proved no problem. They had taken a taxi to Kithira town and then, since the strip was so exposed, they'd walked the few miles to the coast after dark. It was only then, during the walk to the shore, that Edward suddenly thought of Samantha. In the rush of things he had quite forgotten! Tonight was the night of the concert and the dinner at the Hard Rock Café. He'd let Sammy down – his effigy would be all but destroyed by now. It was the first time he'd ever let her down and he was upset. He'd make it up to her – but it would take some doing.

Once on board the *Anglesey*, he and Victoria had gone straight to bed – they'd had very little sleep in the last forty-eight hours and both went out like bad boxers. They had been roused at ten, given a good, old-fashioned English breakfast and then brought to the bridge. It was now eleven-fifteen – nine-fifteen in London. 'Here are copies of the messages I have received from Inspector Leith, via the Admiralty,' Lynn said, giving them slips of paper. 'I must emphasize that, apart from me and the radio operator, you two are the only people on this ship who have the faintest idea what is to happen. And even I don't know everything, or why we've been told to slow down. It's my ship, but I have been told to do as you suggest.'

Victoria and Edward studied the slips of paper in turn. The shock they'd had, the morning before, when the *Strabo* had put out to sea, had proved to be short-lived. She had moved about a mile away from the harbour and then dropped anchor again. Edward was the first to realize why. 'Her radar wouldn't work in port – she was in the shadow of the island. Now she'll be able to pick up the *Anglesey* much sooner.' Certainly the *Strabo* had held her position all day, until they'd had to leave for their rendezvous.

'Where are we exactly?' said Victoria, handing the slips of paper back to Lynn.

'During the night, while you were asleep, we changed course slightly and slowed down. We are currently about forty miles south of Kithira and some twenty miles west. From here on we steam steadily north, at ten knots, reaching Kithira this afternoon, around four-thirty or five. Assuming all goes to plan and the *Strabo* picks us up, we shall continue north – well, you know the rest. We stop around five or five-thirty, relax, dress the ship and so on. What I don't understand is what happens after we change course that final time and head back to Britain. Can you fill me in?'

Victoria nodded. 'First off, you don't head back to Britain, not straight away.' She held her face to the sun but kept her lips close to Lynn's ear. 'The next part is going to be very tricky – and I can see why they didn't try to explain it to you either over the phone or by telex. You need some background.'

As she outlined the whole blackmail business, Lynn stared at her. At times he seemed to sway, though whether that was the waves or the impact of the story was difficult to tell. She brought the narrative right up to date and then added: 'First, as you say, you change course. You do that in such a way as to claim the attention of the *Strabo* – you make a large change of course but you do it slowly. We don't want to lose the *Strabo*. By tomorrow morning, the people on board the other ship will be expecting you to change course but they will want to see it for themselves before they take any action. You will change course at approximately eight o'clock . . . you don't need to know why but the timing is important. I say "approximately" because it will help us greatly if you can make the change when there is no one else around to see it. Much safer. When you change course, that will set in train a chain of events – again, you don't need to know what they are. That chain of events will take . . . oh, somewhere between two hours and three and a half hours to unfold. During that time, the *Anglesey* needs to maintain her change of course but she also needs to remain in visual or radar contact with the

Strabo. This period, when you are on your new course and yet keeping in contact with the *Strabo*, is the second phase.

'At some point we shall hear that the chain of events which you have set off has, or has not, unfolded successfully. If the chain of events is not successful, then I shall have to do some sharp negotiating and you will have to put on speed – and resume your old course, for Piraeus. If, on the other hand, the chain of events is successful, the *Anglesey* will change course again, put on speed – and close with the *Strabo*. We have to catch her and arrest her.'

'In Greek waters and in broad daylight?'

'Yes.'

'I'm not sure that isn't an act of war.'

From the *Observer*:

AMERICAN AID WITHDRAWAL PROVOKES BITTER REACTION
From our own correspondent, New Delhi

Senior political figures here have responded bitterly to the announcement made in Washington on Friday night by Mr Dixon Thayer, US Secretary of State, to the effect that the US is suspending all aid to the sub-continent as a consequence of the raid on the Metropolitan Museum last week. During the raid, by an organization calling itself Hindu Heritage, eight statues were stolen and a security guard was killed.

Mr Thayer, who was addressing the Foreign Press Club's annual dinner in Washington, said that both the President and he himself had been outraged by the fact that the stolen treasures had gone on show at a Hindu shrine in Hindupur. He said that all US aid to India, currently running at $886 million a year, would be held up. A consignment of trucks, due to leave Baltimore yesterday, has already been cancelled.

Mr Vishwanna Chota, government spokesman for foreign affairs, described the move as a 'gross over-reaction'. 'We recognize that one death is one death too many,' he said. 'But it is still only one death. America's aid to India saves hundreds – maybe thousands – of lives. They are now at risk.'

Mr Seba Herma Chandra, deputy leader of the opposition

coalition, went further. 'This is a disaster for India,' he said. 'But it also shows how muscle-bound and simplistic American foreign policy is. Not everyone in India is Hindu – so why should the rest of the country be forced to suffer for the crimes of others? Where is the democracy in that? America is currently trying to persuade India not to develop a greater nuclear capability. Why should we listen any more?'

Our Washington correspondent adds: Secretary of State Thayer's remarks were endorsed yesterday by two leading North American politicians. The Governor of New York, addressing a rally in the state capital, Albany, praised the secretary of state for his 'firm grasp on the important essentials of foreign policy'. And Mr Robert McReady, Prime Minister of Canada, speaking in Calgary, said that Dixon Thayer's 'prompt action had hopefully done enough to nip in the bud this new notion of cultural terrorism.' In a clear reference to the British Prime Minister, he added: 'The museums of the West are open to all. Their contents belong to us all – and should not be allowed to become the playthings of the powerful.'

'Now, your traditional Sunday lunch is the best, of course. Roast beef, nice and red. Gravy. Peas, though personally I can't abide Yorkshire pudding. But . . . well, I had thirty-six oysters in Galway one September Sunday, years ago. Then there was a seal in Oslo . . . bit tough but delicious in its way. Giant crabs – *sushi* style – in the Seychelles, that I shan't forget. And this one, of course. Alcohol-free lager and chocolate. *Warm* alcohol-free lager at that.'

'Tell me, Riley,' O'Day shifted in his seat. 'These fabulous meals . . . did you really eat them? Or are you making it all up?'

'Of course they were real. Look at that.' He patted his stomach. 'That's real.'

O'Day fixed him with a stare. 'And I suppose they all went on expenses, didn't they?'

'Two weeks ago, on this programme, we reported the first news of the government's plans to return to Greece the so-called Elgin Marbles. No one imagined at that time that this would be such a critical issue for William Lockwood. In fact, tomorrow in the House of Commons he faces a censure motion on this matter. In a moment, we shall be talking to a brace of politicians and asking them how they think the debate will go. First, though, we are going over to our correspondent in Athens, Ellis Kirby . . . Ellis, what is the mood in Athens this weekend?'

'Well, Douglas, although all eyes in Britain are on the Commons debate, with perhaps a thought for the injured Britons in hospital in Athens, here in Greece we are all awaiting the arrival of HMS *Anglesey*, carrying the Marbles. About a hundred small boats are gathering in Piraeus harbour. They will go out to greet the *Anglesey*, as soon as she is sighted, and escort her into the port. Tonight there is to be a vigil on the Acropolis. Anyone who wants to is taking a candle or torch – and thousands are already streaming up the hill. The entire Acropolis will be lit tonight by flamelight and it should be visible from the sea, the hope being that the lights of the vigil will be the first thing the crew of the *Anglesey* sees.'

'No one knows, do they, when exactly the *Anglesey* will arrive?'

'No. The embassy here says that the secrecy is due to security reasons. The embassy itself is ringed by police though there aren't many demonstrators outside at the moment. Most people have been taken with the idea of a vigil – and it should be a pretty spectacular sight.'

'Thank you, Ellis Kirby. Now, with me in the studio I have Frank Whiteman, deputy leader of the opposition, and Jocelyn Hatfield, government Chief Whip. Joss Hatfield, if I may come to you first . . . All of the Sunday papers this morning carry the picture on the front page of the two Nigerian athletes demonstrating at Crystal Palace yesterday and reports on the injured British tourists in Greece. In sharp contrast, there is the firm action of the US Secretary of State, which has been widely welcomed. Isn't all that going to damage the Prime Minister's position still further? According to your calculations, how close is it going to be tomorrow?'

'I don't think the Nigerian protest changes things at all. In fact, if you look closely at the situation, it is a non sequitur. There is some doubt about the legality of the Marbles' export from Greece at the beginning of the nineteenth century. But there is no doubt that the Benin bronzes were legally exported from Nigeria. Therefore the comparison does not arise. I am of course very sorry that our fellow countrymen were attacked by Greek thugs late on Friday night and I hope the culprits will be caught and punished.'

'And the debate tomorrow? How close will it be?'

'The government has a majority of thirty-four. Tomorrow's debate is a three-line whip. A few people on our side may abstain but we'll have no problem surviving.'

'Can you put a figure on what your majority will be?'

'I can but I won't. I'm too long in the tooth to give hostages to fortune.'

'Frank Whiteman, Joss Hatfield won't give a figure. Will you?'

'Yes. I think the government will lose. At our last count – on Friday, before this Crystal Palace business, before the holiday-makers were attacked, and before we knew about the vigil in Athens tonight – we calculated that exactly thirty of the government's backbenchers would abstain tomorrow. In one of the papers this morning, there's an article reporting that a couple of other backbenchers, from dockyard constituencies, who were not in our calculations, rather resent the fact that the Royal Navy has been used to return the Marbles. I also didn't know that Glen MacTaggart, the member for Fife, is married to one of Elgin's descendants. He may find it difficult to vote for the government.'

'But isn't that a rag-bag of reasons for abstaining? It's not as if your side was arguing a noble cause and persuading people by eloquence and passion, is it?'

'That's modern politics for you. Tomorrow's debate is a three-line whip because the government is fighting for its life. It has a rag-bag of reasons too. It is not persuading by reason or passion but by force. There will be eloquence tomorrow, and passion. But there are always other reasons – personal reasons – why some people vote as they do. That is perfectly proper in a democracy.'

'In one of this morning's other papers,' said the presenter, 'it is suggested that the Queen should intervene to prevent the Marbles being landed in Greece. How would you feel about having the royal family on your side, Frank Whiteman?'

'I would welcome support from wherever it came,' Whiteman replied. 'But this is a party political matter now, so of course the royals ought not to be involved.'

'And you, Jocelyn Hatfield? How would you feel about any involvement on the part of the royal family?'

'It's an academic and mischievous question. I can't imagine for one moment that Her Majesty would wish to be involved in this matter in any way whatsoever.'

*

'Dr Shelby to see you, sir.' The security guard held the door while Eugenie Shelby walked through into Ogilvy's office. Unusually for him, he was wearing a sports jacket and no tie. Because he was so nervous, he was trying hard to look relaxed.

'Sorry to bring you in on a Sunday but, as you'll see, it's necessary.'

Eugenie Shelby sat on the upright leather chair in front of the director's desk and tidied her skirt around her legs. She was brown-haired, not tall, and had an attractive – but rather masculine – face, a strong brow and fairly prominent teeth. Lovely skin. 'What's all this about?'

Ogilvy took his time. He wasn't a good liar and did not look forward to the next few minutes. So far as he was concerned, Dr Eugenie Shelby was what she had always been: a very good stone conservator. He had telephoned her the afternoon before and invited her to come to the museum now. 'How's the new lab?' he asked. The museum had a new conservators' laboratory, in the basement.

'Fine. No daylight down there but the new equipment is a big help.'

Ogilvy nodded sympathetically. 'Would it disrupt you if I pulled you out of there for a while?'

Eugenie Shelby sat up straight. 'What? Why should you? I haven't even mastered the software yet.'

The director bit his lip. 'Answer my question first. Would it disrupt you?'

'Yes, it would disrupt me – and not only me. We're planning to clean the Rosetta Stone – you know that. We're nearly ready to go. I was looking forward to it. But why do you want to pull me off? What else do you want me to do?'

'Something else, more important, has cropped up.' Ogilvy looked out of his window. There were still protestors with placards at the gateway to Great Russell Street.

Eugenie Shelby said nothing, waiting.

'Where do you stand on the Marbles business?'

'What do you mean – "Where do I stand?"?'

'I mean . . . do you approve of what the Prime Minister has been doing, do you think it's right they should have been returned? Do you think the Greeks have a case?'

'Does it matter what I think?'

'For the job I have in mind it matters very much.'

Eugenie Shelby hesitated.

Ogilvy reflected darkly that she was trying to assess which answer he wanted.

'Lockwood is a fool. The Marbles have been here for nearly two hundred years. They should stay here.'

Ogilvy smiled. With luck, Eugenie Shelby would think he was delighted by her answer. In fact, he was relieved she had deceived him. Now it would be easier to deceive her. 'Before I tell you what I'm about to tell you, Dr Shelby, I must remind you that when you first came here you signed the Official Secrets Act.' He reached into a drawer and took from it several sheets of printed paper. 'Would you like to reacquaint yourself with the Act? What I'm about to tell you comes under this Act, very much so. I'm asking you to work on a top secret matter and I want your prior agreement that it will stay secret.'

'It concerns the Parthenon Marbles?'

Interesting, thought Ogilvy, she doesn't think of them as the Elgin Marbles. 'Yes . . . yes it does.'

Eugenie Shelby shrugged. 'What would you like me to say? I've never worked on anything truly secret before . . . I don't know how I can convince you I'm trustworthy.'

Ogilvy smiled again. 'And I have never had to ask this of anyone in the museum before . . . so I am as inexperienced as you.' He tapped the papers. 'Your promise will be sufficient. A promise to keep to yourself whatever I may tell you.'

He put the papers away again. Was he making too much of this encounter?

She stared back and shrugged again. 'I promise.'

Ogilvy nodded. 'Thank you.' He brushed his fingers through his hair. 'I saw the Prime Minister yesterday. At Chequers. He asked to see me specially.' Ogilvy rocked back in his chair. 'He told me a great deal about this . . . Elgin affair that I didn't know – and this is where the Official Secrets Act begins to bite. I'm not at liberty to tell you everything – I don't know everything myself – but what I can say is that . . . behind all this . . . behind the government's apparent desire to return the Marbles, there is . . . there is blackmail. Apparently the government is being blackmailed – Lockwood wouldn't tell me what exactly but it's very embarrassing, so he said.'

'What sort of blackmail?'

'I don't know and even if I did I wouldn't be able to tell you.

But the important thing is this: the dispatch of the Marbles on HMS *Anglesey* was a bluff – '

Ogilvy noticed a very slight constriction at Eugenie Shelby's throat but, in general, she kept very calm. He too had to press on in the most natural way.

'– a bluff in that its journey was intended to buy time during which the government's security services could investigate, and perhaps capture, the blackmailers.'

'And did they? . . . Did they catch them, I mean?'

She was cool, this Shelby woman. 'No, not a whiff, so far as I am told. But in any case that's not our concern. The point of this meeting, the point about my questions to you earlier, is that . . . some time tomorrow – I am not allowed to know when exactly – the *Anglesey* will be recalled. She will change course and head for home. The blackmailers' terrible story will come out, but the Greeks won't get their Marbles. And that's where you come in. By the time they get back to London, the Marbles will have had more than a week at sea. They have been decently enough packed but there's been rough weather off Malta and who knows what damage may have been done to them? Your job is twofold. The Marbles will be back here in four or five days. I want you to get your work on the Rosetta Stone orderly enough to leave it for a while. I'd like you to be ready forty-eight hours before the Marbles and I want you ready to carry out a survey of their condition as soon as they come back, so that they can go on public display as soon as possible. Ideally, I'd like the Duveen Galleries reopened within a week, ten days at the most. Don't worry about budgets . . . leave that to me. The Prime Minister won't stint us on this one. Get whatever help you need and have everybody working all hours until it is done.' Ogilvy rocked back on his chair again. 'Do you think you can handle it? I, not to mention the Prime Minister, will be very grateful if you do a good job.'

Eugenie Shelby sat very still but her eyes glowed. She couldn't help that.

'Now you know as much as I do, Dr Shelby. And you and I are the only people in this building who know as much as that. For the next twenty-four, or forty-eight, or seventy-two hours, it has to remain that way, until Downing Street gives us our release.' His eyes bored into hers.

She smiled. 'I'm glad you asked me to help.'

*

The lights on the bridge of the *Anglesey* had just gone on. It would be fully dark in thirty minutes. For the past hour, Victoria and Edward had watched the crew enjoying itself – water-skiing in the distance, a makeshift game of water polo nearer the ship. On board, the rows of 'dressing lights' had been hung over the superstructure and, ten minutes before, had been tried out. That had been the signal for the skiers and polo players to come back aboard.

Earlier that day, exactly on schedule, they had passed Kithira. Potamos they had seen as a huddle of white walls to the port side. Radar had duly picked up a large ship which had left its moorings off Kithira about half an hour behind them. It had pursued a more easterly course than the *Anglesey* but then, about eight miles further out from the Greek coast, it had turned north. This was entirely in order if the boat intended to head east of the Greek mainland in due course and proceed up the Aegean towards Thessaloniki and Istanbul. But of course it was the *Strabo*. When the *Anglesey* had stopped, the *Strabo* had carried on for a while, until she was about fifteen miles to the north-east. Then she had headed more or less due west, towards Idhra, where to judge from the radar she had berthed a mile offshore. She was keeping a radar watch.

There were just the three of them on the bridge. Lynn kept his eye on the radar while Victoria and Edward waited for the phone call from London. Their conversation was desultory. 'Dare I ask what time we have dinner?' Edward grinned sheepishly. 'I'm famished.'

Lynn grinned back. 'Seven-thirty for the ratings, an hour later in the senior mess. Two more hours, I'm afraid. Feel like a drink?'

'That might help, I suppose.'

Lynn reached for the phone but as he did so it rang anyway. They all stared at it. He picked up the receiver. 'Bridge.' There was a pause before he held it out to Victoria. 'For you.'

She listened, absently biting her lip. She looked across to Edward, then to the captain. After several minutes she put down the phone. 'Eugenie Shelby was briefed by the director of the British Museum at around three p.m., London time, five o'clock here. She was followed from the museum in Great Russell Street. She went straight to a public payphone at King's Cross station. Her call was not overheard but she may have called the *Strabo* or . . .' Victoria looked at Edward. 'Or she may have called Nancy

Tucker. Either way, the next move should be a call from the *Strabo* to the man in Basle, at ten o'clock Swiss time tonight as usual. That's eleven here. Assuming it goes to plan, and they tell him to stand by, pending our change of course, we need to get him to go to the bank as early as possible. The bank opens at nine-thirty, ten-thirty here. So we need to start heading north before that – say, seven o'clock. If we head north for about an hour, that should be time enough to make sure the *Strabo* is following us again – yes?'

Lynn nodded.

'At eight, we change course, decisively, away from Piraeus. Then it gets tricky. They might follow us for a bit, or they might head somewhere else, Piraeus itself perhaps. Either way we have to maintain our new course but at such a speed that we keep the *Strabo* on our radar. It will take them perhaps half an hour to contact Basle on the ship-to-shore, call it eight-thirty to nine o'clock our time, seven-thirty to eight o'clock in Basle. To arrive at the bank at nine-thirty, the Greek needs to leave his house around nine. The arrest, if it goes to plan, should take place around ten-thirty Basle time, eleven-thirty here. So, after changing course at eight, we shall need to maintain radar contact with the *Strabo* for three and a half hours. The question is: can it be done?'

Lynn raised his eyebrows. 'Impossible to answer. It depends on the *Strabo*.'

'Not good enough, captain. We mustn't lose her! If we do, the whole thing goes up the shoot.'

Lynn bit a nail. 'Hmm. There might be a way . . . Let me think about it for a bit.'

'This van feels quite like home.' Riley had parked the van in Gerbergasse, on a parking meter, so as to be sure of a good vantage point in the morning. They were planning to be back next day, at eight, when they would have to start feeding the meter with money. Riley locked the driver's door and stepped back. He looked up and down the street. 'Good view of the bank, room enough to turn, in case we need to make a quick exit in either direction, well out of the way of the trams, a full tank of petrol, lead-free and environment-friendly. We'll bring the purple Ford tomorrow and park it nearby. I think we are all set – yes?'

312

'Not quite,' whispered O'Day. He took something from his raincoat pocket and handed it across. In the dark, Riley couldn't make out what it was. As he took hold of it, however, its weight told him exactly what it was. He should have realized. It was a gun.

Lockwood's black Jaguar swept east along the A40, past Northolt Airport. In all his time as Prime Minister, this was the one perk he had never come to take for granted, the one privilege he was still thrilled by. Not the car itself, though that was nice enough, but the four police outriders, motorcyclists whose split-second timing, leapfrogging activities and diligence with their official radios meant that the Prime Minister never had to trouble with a red traffic light. Officially, of course, 'security' was given as the reason for this piece of showing off – the IRA, certain Arabs (though no longer the KGB) were an ever-present threat. No matter. The sheer speed and slickness of the operation never failed to excite Lockwood. In his heart of hearts, he knew that if he lost the vote tomorrow this was one of the things he would miss most. Except for his driver, Patrick, and his bodyguard, also sitting in the front, Lockwood was alone in the car. Sally, his wife, was spending another night at Great Ormond Street. Little Tommy was improving, apparently, but was still poorly, and the strain was beginning to tell on their daughter. Sally also knew her husband would be preoccupied both tonight and tomorrow and that he would prefer to be alone. She would come across to Number Ten tomorrow, for the vote. She would be needed only if he lost. She wouldn't really mind if he lost. She would see more of him. Patrick was a different matter. He took a fierce pride in his job and, if Lockwood was ousted, so would he be, at least from the number one slot in the civil service car pool.

'It's just coming up to midnight, Paddy. Let's have the news on.' The atmosphere in the car was thick and the chatter of the radio would help.

'. . . thousand Athenians have tonight crowded the slopes of the Acropolis in what eyewitnesses are describing as one of the most moving pieces of natural theatre ever seen. All those who attended what was dubbed a "vigil" carried a candle or torch, so that the entire hillside, lit in this way, could be seen as far away as Sounion, some thirty miles to the south. The vigil, of course, had been called to prepare for the arrival tomorrow of the Elgin Marbles, which left Greece almost two hundred years ago. Meanwhile, here in Britain the latest calculation on tomorrow's vote, taken from tomorrow's newspapers, predicts that – '

'Enough, Paddy. Turn it off.'

The driver did as he was told. The car turned off Westway and raced down Addison Road. The outriders kept the way clear as they turned into Kensington High Street, past the Commonwealth Institute, Kensington Palace and the Albert Hall. The convoy reached Hyde Park Corner, sped down Grosvenor Place and into the Mall. How many more times will I be doing this? thought Lockwood. Next time I drive up the Mall, maybe it will be to see the Queen . . . Horse Guards Parade, Birdcage Walk, Whitehall. Beside the Cenotaph, Patrick slowed. The outriders had already reached the gate into Downing Street, the elaborate filigree that had been erected when Margaret Thatcher was Prime Minister and had never been taken down again. The gate was opened and the car turned in. As it did so, a shout went up from a small posse of people on the pavement opposite Number Ten. At the same time, a television arc light went on. Some television crews, desperate for footage, were filming the Prime Minister's late return and the rump demonstration that still hung on. As the car drew up, the chanting started. It matched the placards: 'What a carve-up: save our stones'; 'Don't bear gifts to Greeks'; 'Lock up Lockwood; he's lost his marbles'.

The bodyguard had opened the door of the Jaguar and, wearily, Lockwood got out. As he did so, a television reporter, using a megaphone, shouted across the street, 'Prime Minister, do you expect still to be Prime Minister this time tomorrow?' Lockwood was about to wave and smile – the only response that was really called for at that hour – when he noticed Patrick standing in front of him.

'Paddy – what is it? What have you got there?'

'It's for you, sir. All those candles in Athens, sir, they don't mean a thing. I'm a Catholic. We light candles for good people. So this is for you.' And he handed Lockwood a small, lighted, wax candle. 'I'll be keeping a vigil for you tomorrow, sir.'

Lockwood took the candle and, without looking back or speaking, stepped inside the front door. He didn't say anything because he couldn't. There was a lump in his throat.

WEEK FIVE

The Vote in the Commons

27

Monday

Victoria stumbled on to the bridge. She was not yet fully awake and it was still dark. Edward was already there; he had not shaved.

'Something wrong? What time is it?'

'Nearly three,' said Lynn. 'No, nothing wrong. In fact, I wouldn't have wakened you but I've had an idea. Look at this.' He led them to the radar screen. 'Look at these blips on the screen. They are enormous. There are two of them and they are about eight miles south, heading our way.'

'So?'

'I can't be sure but my guess is that they are two tankers heading for Piraeus. In about forty minutes they are going to be abreast of us and, more important, they will pass between us and the *Strabo*. Now, the only thing that worries me about our plan of action tomorrow is that we might easily lose the *Strabo* after we change course. She doesn't have to follow us, and the plan you gave me includes a period of around three and a half hours – maybe more – when I can't give chase without giving the game away. During that time, the *Strabo* could easily stray off the radar and, once she does that, we will never know where she has gone.'

The others stared at him.

'Now, my idea is this. Just as the *Strabo* is on my radar, so this ship is on theirs. Any direct approach from us to them is therefore out of the question. However, if we were to slip one of our launches just as the tankers were passing, then we would be in radar shadow and the *Strabo* wouldn't be able to tell what had happened. Then, if the launch kept in the shadow of the tankers as they headed north, it would remain an unknown. It would take about three hours for the tankers to pass through the range of the *Strabo*'s radar – say at about six-thirty, quarter to seven. Once the launch had left the *Strabo*'s radar screen along with the tankers, she would then be free to part company from them and head back towards the *Strabo* from the north-east. They will never connect the blip they will see with this ship. A launch can do over twenty knots and so could get back to the *Strabo*'s position within an hour. If that position changes from where it is now, we shall know from the radar on this ship, which will be in touch with the launch by radio.'

He looked at them anxiously. 'What do you think? I thought that one or both of you might like to go with the launch. Otherwise, I'd have to brief at least one of the crew on the reason for the rather roundabout journey.'

Victoria grinned. 'Clever. Bloody good. I'll go.'

'Me too,' said Edward.

'Is that wise? Shouldn't one of us stay -?'

'I'm coming.'

Forty-three minutes later, Lynn signalled from the bridge to the launch riding on his starboard side that the *Strabo* was now in radar shadow of the passing tankers.

The launch cast off, and Lynn strained his eyes to watch as Victoria and Edward disappeared into the darkness. He hoped the Greeks had not sent out any of their naval ships to welcome the *Anglesey*. If they had, and they came across the launch, alone, in the early hours of daylight, they would be within their rights to arrest the entire crew.

'Riley, I think you and me should get married after all this. Days together, all alone, and not a single argument.'

'I've a better idea. We should set up as burglars. It's got to be better paid than this job. Half past six in the morning for Christ's sake and we've already been on the go for half an hour. A decent burglar would be tucked up in bed now. With a woman. Give me that flask of coffee.'

They lapsed into silence again. They were both used to that. A gentle rain fell on the roof of the van. The bank didn't open for three hours – but they were taking no chances.

'We are about five miles from the *Strabo*,' Victoria yelled into the radio phone. During the night the Greeks' yacht had moved, steaming slowly to the south and west of Idhra. She was now much closer to the Greek mainland.

318

The launch was a lot less stable than the frigate and Victoria wasn't feeling as well as she might. 'She's put down her dinghy, as if someone is preparing to leave. When are you going to change course?'

'At precisely eight o'clock, in seven minutes' time.' Lynn's voice came over clearly, if not very loudly. 'The horizons are clear and I've been thinking . . . I reckon that, if I change course right on the button of eight o'clock, it will look to them much more like part of a plot, as if I'm turning back once and for all. They will be less inclined to suspect that I might turn yet again. So stand by.'

Victoria was exhausted, Edward too. Not only had they been awakened in the middle of the night but they had spent the last four and a half hours in an open boat zigzagging across the Mediterranean, or the Mirtoan Sea as it was referred to on the Admiralty charts in the launch. Coffee had been produced by the crew after they had been at sea for an hour, and again at seven o'clock, that time with biscuits. The biscuits had helped but the constant rise and fall of the waves, for hours on end, was wearing. The seats, such as they were, were uncomfortable too and now the glare of the sun on the water strained the eyes. Edward was beginning to wish he had stayed aboard the frigate.

'This is the *Anglesey*. Come in – over. This is *Anglesey*. Come in – over.'

'Yes. Receiving. Go ahead.'

'I'm going about now. Repeat, I'm going about now. New course will be one hundred and eight-seven degrees, repeat one eight seven, at a speed of nine knots, repeat zero nine knots.'

'We copy, we copy.' Victoria trained her glasses on the *Strabo*.

Edward was also looking, with a pair of glasses loaned to him by the launch's bosun. 'How long does a change of course take to show on the radar?'

'A minute, minute and a half,' said the bosun. 'It's more obvious, of course, if you make a right-angled turn. If you turn on a sixpence and retrace your steps the only thing to see on the radar is an increasing gap between you and the blip. That can take three or four minutes to become clear.'

'Except that the people on the *Strabo* are expecting a change,' said Victoria. 'Ah – there she goes!'

Edward too had called out. 'Turning!'

'She's altered course!' Victoria cried into the radio phone. 'Did you hear that? The *Strabo* is turning. Keep your fingers crossed. It looks as though they have swallowed the bait.'

'Good morning. It is just after seven a.m. and this is Robert Onslow with the BBC Breakfast News and Comment. In the programme this morning we concentrate on this afternoon's historic censure debate in the House of Commons. But first the news, which is read today by Harriet Ottery.'

'. . . Later today, the debate takes place in the House of Commons which will decide the future of William Lockwood, the Prime Minister. The opposition's censure motion over Mr Lockwood's handling of the Elgin Marbles affair will be proposed by Frank Whiteman, deputy leader of the party. Mr Arthur Page, leader of the opposition, will wind up the debate at about nine o'clock tonight. The Prime Minister is expected to speak at about nine-thirty/ten o'clock after which the vote will be taken. The debate takes place against the resignation, four days ago, of the Defence Secretary, Mr George Keld. Overnight, the Prime Minister's position did not improve with the announcement that one of the British tourists attacked in Athens on Friday night has died of a heart attack. Already this morning, in a statement released through the Press Association, Mr Michael Sidey, Member of Parliament for Bridport, Dorset, in whose constituency the tourist lived, has said that Mr Lockwood's government "appears increasingly accident-prone" and that it is time to call a halt to what he called "a mad episode" in British foreign policy. Mr Sidey was believed to be wavering in his support for the government but this statement suggests that he will now vote against Mr Lockwood . . . And in Athens last night over twenty thousand people converged on the Acropolis, each of them carrying a candle or a flaming torch. The vigil has been described as one of the most moving pieces of natural theatre ever seen . . . Elsewhere in the news, two off-duty policemen were killed last night when the car they were driving near Londonderry was fired on. In a phone call to a Dublin newspaper, the IRA later claimed responsibility. One of the policemen was married with a young daughter . . . The fishing war continues in the waters off New Zealand: during the night a Royal New Zealand gunship fired on a Japanese trawler, which dropped its nets and made off . . . The Pope is in Russia again for the canonization of St

Fyodor at Kiev. Among those present in the celebration of High Mass was Olga Litov, wife of the Russian President. Now back to Robert Onslow.'

'William Lockwood has been a Member of Parliament for forty-two of his sixty-nine years, yet today he faces the most testing time of that long and distinguished career. It comes, it should be said, after one of the most mysterious episodes during his time as Prime Minister. Only a matter of days ago, the political world's attention, in Britain at any rate, was given over to the date of the next general election. With a majority of thirty-four, the government's position was never unassailable, but then it was never so exposed as it is now. Following a sudden decision to return the so-called Elgin Marbles to Greece – an action which, incidentally, may well culminate today while the censure motion on the Prime Minister is actually taking place – Mr Lockwood has mismanaged the situation, or been overtaken by unforeseen events, to the point where deaths in New York – and now in London and Athens – have been blamed on him. Buildings have been defaced around the country. The Board of Trustees has resigned from the British Museum, demonstrations have clogged the capital's streets, the Reading Room of the British Museum has been closed, the only time this has happened since it opened in 1857. We have seen small boats drawn up on the Thames, trying to prevent the departure of a Royal Naval frigate. And of course the Aghia Sophia, the Greek Orthodox cathedral in London, has been torched, provoking reprisals against the Anglican church in Athens, the British Embassy and the British School. Now, Lockwood is paying the price of all that, with this afternoon's debate.

'With me in the studio to discuss the issue I have Hilary Stockton, chairwoman of the Commons Select Committee on Arts and Education, who is also a trustee of the V & A, and Colin Raine, political editor of the *Daily Tribune*. Colin, if we may start with you, we heard in the news there about Michael Sidey's press release this morning . . . Is that typical, do you think? Are people detaching themselves from the Prime Minister at the moment?'

'Well, in my view Michael Sidey was never going to support Mr Lockwood anyway. He is the member for Bridport and, whatever he says about his constituent who was killed, Sidey believes he has been overlooked by Lockwood for a place in the government. There are several backbenchers in Mr Lockwood's party who dislike him heartily for his blindness to what they consider to be their talents. No, to get a truer picture of what will happen tonight you have to consider a different matter, which is this: if Lockwood loses tonight, he will come under very strong pressure to resign as party leader and fight a leadership contest as soon as one can be arranged. His resignation would probably take place tomorrow, after he had been to see the Queen. Then a new leader would have to be elected. At the moment, over breakfast at their clubs, or in their flats around Westminster, MPs are trying to work out whether their party has more chance of winning the general election if it survives tonight and fights the election with Lockwood at its head, or whether its chances would be better if another leader was in place, that leader almost certainly being George Keld.'

'All right, but the crucial question is: how will the vote go?'

'According to my soundings, there will be about thirty to thirty-one abstentions so far – '

'Leaving Lockwood with a majority of about three?'

'Leaving Lockwood with a majority of about three.'

'Now, Mrs Stockton, if we can come to you. Is there anything the Prime Minister can say in today's debate which will cause the troops to rally to his support? What do the party faithful want him to say?'

'We would like him to say two things.' Hilary Stockton had vivid purple hair, or so it seemed under the studio lights, and an immense chest. She also wore spectacles with bright-red frames. 'We want him to put this Elgin Marbles business behind us. It is utterly confusing to the parliamentary party, as it is to people in the rest of the country. Why did we get into this mess to begin with? Why has it all been cloaked in such confusion and secrecy? We want a full explanation and then we want to let it go. Most of us would not have wished the Marbles to leave in the first place but, now that they have, let's put them behind us. Second, we need a lead from the Prime Minister, he needs to take an initiative . . . There's an election due very soon now, and it's time the government started taking the fight to the opposition, showing up the weaknesses in *their* policies rather than allowing this Elgin Marbles issue to concentrate minds on our faults all the time.'

'Do you think the Prime Minister will survive tonight?'

'My own soundings are pretty close to Colin Raine's. It will be very close. I don't know if this Athens vigil or the new death will affect the vote in any way.'

'Now, we talk about the vote being pretty close but of course no one in your party will actually be voting against Mr Lockwood. And even if those thirty-one abstentions are counted as votes against him, that still leaves him with some two hundred and seventy MPs who support him. Doesn't that still make him a convincing leader of the party?'

'Of course not. If William Lockwood loses the vote tonight, there will be many in the party, both inside and outside Parliament, who will not forgive him for exposing us to such a drubbing so close to a general election. There are some who believe we should call an election straight away, to remove the uncertainty that will then exist. There is no doubt in my mind that, if the Prime Minister loses tonight, he will have to resign as leader of the party. As I say, some of my fellow backbenchers believe he should dissolve Parliament at the same time and call an election. The alternative would be for us to hold a very quick election for leader, and then have George Keld, say, as PM for a few weeks before we are forced to call an election under the law.'

'But would George Keld command any more support than William Lockwood? Couldn't the opposition call another debate in, say, a fortnight's time? Would Keld survive that?'

'It would depend what he did in the interim. If, for example, he cleared the air over the Elgin Marbles, and showed himself capable in other ways . . . if the opinion polls were to show that the party's fortunes were reviving after this damaging time, then no, I don't think the opposition would be wise to call another debate. If they secure Lockwood's demise, they would probably rather go into an election with that in people's memories than have a second debate and risk Keld being unanimously supported.'

'So, it all depends on tonight. Colin Raine, that was a backbench politician's answer. You're a lobby correspondent . . . what do you think will happen tonight?'

'The one thing we can say with certainty is that it will be one of those debates which will be affected by the performances of the major players. It all comes down to the Prime Minister's own performance. If he can really explain the Elgin Marbles affair, then I think he might rally one or two people to his side, and survive. But if he can't, if he persists with the style that has so far governed this whole crazy business, then I think it's a different matter. I think another five or six MPs could turn against him and he will lose.'

'Someone is leaving the *Strabo*!' hissed Victoria, pressing the binoculars closer to her eyes.

'Got it!' said Edward almost straight away. 'Five people in all – yes?'

'Yes . . . Four men – Kofas, the Leondaris brothers and Kolettis? – and a younger man? Who's the younger man?'

'Crew, probably. Yes, there they go. The younger man is steering the dinghy . . . in a circle . . .'

'They're going ashore. Look, they're heading for that town over there – see all that white.'

'That's Leonidhion,' said the bosun. He had a map open on his knees.

'Okay,' said Victoria, 'let's follow. But be careful . . . zigzag behind them as they did behind the *Anglesey*. We don't want them to notice us at this stage. Keep a distance to begin with but try to close on them as they get near to the harbour. We don't want them to notice us but we can't afford to lose them.'

For forty minutes they bucked on the waves swinging to the north of the *Strabo*'s dinghy as if they were headed towards somewhere else. Victoria used the time to raise Lynn on the radio phone, to explain what they were doing.

He had no news. He had heard from his admiral but London had not yet heard anything from Basle. 'But it's early, don't forget. If it's half past nine here, it's eight-thirty in Basle, seven-thirty in London.'

'Well, our people are on the move and you'd better tell London. I'm wondering whether the Basle contingent and the Greek contingent are planning a rendezvous? But where?'

'Yes, that had occurred to me. I'll relay that to London and get back to you.'

The *Strabo* dinghy was now approaching Leonidhion harbour. Through his binoculars Edward could see that the town was quite large, with several churches and a number of modern apartment blocks ten or twelve storeys high. The two fingers of the jetty stuck out crookedly, overlapping slightly so that the dinghy had to turn to get inside. As it did so, Edward got a much clearer view of the people in the boat. 'Yes,' he breathed, 'it's Kolettis, all right, and the others. What are they doing here?'

With the jetty wall barring the view, the bosun felt safe in turning towards Leonidhion and accelerating over the last mile, so that they too were soon slipping in between the crooked fingers of the harbour. Once in calmer water, Victoria and Edward sat in the well of the launch. Kolettis and the others might just recognize them from the amount of time they had spent 'sketching' near the *Strabo* at Datça. On their behalf the bosun found where the *Strabo*'s dinghy had tied up. 'In fact,' he said, 'it hasn't tied up. It's just putting them ashore. The crew man is going back out again, taking the dinghy back to the *Strabo* straight away.' Another *Anglesey* crew member guided the launch into a berth as the bosun continued his commentary. 'The four people who have gone ashore are walking along the jetty . . . They keep craning their necks as if they're looking for someone or something – ah! I think I've found what it is they're looking for.'

'What is it?'

'A big black taxi. They've obviously arranged to meet it over the ship's phone.'

'Christ! Now what? We've got to keep in touch. How on earth are we going to do that?'

'Waiting is always worse than anything else.' Riley sniffed. 'Eight-thirty. Two and a half hours and I'm stiff as stubble.'

'It's my birthday next week,' replied O'Day. 'We could still be here then. If only Lockwood wasn't so paranoid about security . . . a couple more bodies would make it a lot easier.'

Riley nodded. 'Let's hope our Greek friend doesn't have any hidden reinforcements of his own.'

'I wonder what the other side has in mind? What I mean is: just how many pictures are there? Is Zakros waiting while all the others go to ground? After all, they have people in Greece, the American in London and that conservator woman at the British – '

'That's it! That's the delay. We're stupid! We should have thought of it! What they did before.'

'What?'

'He's waiting for the Tucker woman to come from London,

325

like he did before. What time did they meet then? Twelvish, wasn't it? It will be the same today, I'd lay money on it.'

'You could be right.'

'You wait here. I'm going to phone London. It will help them to know. I'll come back as soon as I can. If the Greek arrives and leaves again before I get back, follow him. But I'd lay money the rendezvous is here, at twelve.'

Opposite the Savoy Hotel, the wind on the Embankment was bracing. Arthur Page stood for a moment. He looked downriver, to the totems of the City, the cranes of Dockland, the white stone of the Tower. He looked across to the National Theatre and Waterloo Station – not all of London's river was beautiful. And then he looked upriver, for the best view of all, the fine bronze lines of Parliament herself. He checked his watch: just after eight. Tonight, this time tomorrow certainly, the place should be his. So far, the arithmetic of the voting was close but the mood was shifting his way: he could feel it.

This breakfast he was about to join, for instance – that was a sign. The chairman and editor-in-chief of 3Ns, the National News Network. They had asked to see him. Some time ago, of course, but they had been assiduous in their attentions lately, confirming and reconfirming the appointment.

He had stepped out of his car at the Temple. He needed a dose of cool air to clear his head. The news this morning was good, very good, from his point of view. He would send flowers to the widow of the tourist who had suffered the heart attack. But from his – Page's – point of view, the man had died right on cue. These broadcasting people would want to talk about the Censure debate, of course, but he would have to be on his guard, for they would be testing him, gauging his attitude. He had to be careful not to give any hostages to fortune which they could hold up to him when he was Prime Minister.

Prime Minister Page. It had a ring to it, one had to admit. It could happen in February, it really could. It could happen sooner if Lockwood panicked – and went to the country. Page was ready for that too. Lockwood had lost his touch. It happened. For Page a fight couldn't come soon enough.

He had reached the Savoy. His driver had already parked the car. Page took a last deep breath of cool air and strode across the dual carriageway. His bodyguard was just behind him. Ahead, at the entrance to the hotel, he saw a doorman and, next to him, Harold Swale, his press officer.

'Harold? What are you doing here? Nothing wrong is there?'

Swale had a round face and salt-and-pepper hair. The frames of his spectacles were perfectly round. 'I don't know Arthur – but it may be that Buckingham Palace think you are going to form the next government. You're to call Sir Francis Mordaunt, the Queen's equerry. He says it's urgent.'

'No! Choose the other one! It's a Mercedes. They have a fast car. We'll need a big one if we are to catch them.' Victoria argued with the man in the garage near the harbour. The garage also had the local car rental agency. There had been no other taxis in Leonidhion and the garage was their only hope.

'Bribe him!' hissed Edward. 'And bribe him quick!'

A fifty-dollar note was flashed. The keys to the Mercedes were found. The forms produced. Victoria brandished her driving licence. It was fifteen minutes since they had put ashore.

As they got into the Mercedes, Edward was inspecting his watch. 'They must be ten or twenty miles away by now. And we don't even know where they are headed.'

Victoria was speaking in Greek to the garage owner. After a moment, she said, 'There's only one road out of here in the direction they set off. It goes north towards Argos and Athens. And, don't forget, they don't know they are being followed, so there's no need for them to hurry on our account.'

Edward, who was driving, manoeuvred between bicyclists, children, a few animals. No one, save them, appeared to be in a hurry. Out on the main road they drove up behind an old bus belching black diesel smoke. Its smell began to fill the car and Victoria soon felt sick. 'Can't we overtake this damn thing? It's slowing us down, too.'

Edward was also feeling ill but there was too much traffic coming towards them to attempt overtaking.

They rumbled on for about a mile until they came to a hill. The road was clear now but there was a bend a hundred and fifty yards away. Edward pulled out. Immediately he did so, a lorry appeared from around the bend. It bore down on them but Edward still accelerated and moved alongside the bus. All the passengers turned to see the Mercedes overtake but Edward and Victoria could not take their eyes off the lorry coming towards them. Edward, with just one hand on the wheel and the other on the gear lever, kept looking to his right to see how soon he could pull over, in front of the bus and out of the way of the oncoming lorry. The lorry driver was now flashing his lights, leaning on his horn. The big, bright-red vehicle was sixty, maybe seventy yards away. Edward was too frightened to feel sick but Victoria urged him to go faster. Then, at the last minute, the old bus seemed to drop quickly behind. Whether the driver of the bus had suddenly braked, it was impossible to say, but in no time Edward had pulled over and the lorry had screamed past, horn still blaring. The Mercedes accelerated away from the bus.

The road wound up the side of a range of hills, which sloped away from the coast. Looking back, Victoria could see across the water to the *Strabo*. The *Anglesey* could not be seen. Both Victoria and Edward were silent to begin with, scanning the road ahead for the black taxi.

They passed a small village, barely slowing. People kept out of the way but one or two animals had near misses, very near misses. They were losing sight of the sea now. Victoria looked over her shoulder in time to see the blue expanse disappear as it dropped behind the brow of a brown hill.

They came to another sharp bend. Half-way round it, a black car swept past in the opposite direction.

'The taxi!' yelled Victoria.

'And empty!' shouted Edward almost at the same time.

For a moment Edward took his eyes off the road to look at Victoria. They were both perplexed and worried. Then they heard a noise, above and to the left. A small twin-engined Cessna, like the one in which they had flown from Crete to Kithira, was descending out of the sky, ready to land. The road was straighter now, the land being flatter hereabouts.

Suddenly Edward slapped his hand against the steering wheel.

Victoria turned round in her seat. 'What's the matter?'

'Look, that plane! That's why the taxi was empty. They've turned off this road – they are going to fly to . . . Athens or wherever they are going to fly to. There's an airfield somewhere – there *must* be! See, where the plane is landing.' He pointed.

Victoria went to say something but changed her mind. Edward drove more slowly for about three miles until they did indeed come to a road sign with an aeroplane on it and an arrow pointing right. He turned on to a track and the car began to buck along it. They saw a windsock ahead of them.

'Stop the car here,' said Victoria. 'We don't want to announce our arrival.'

Edward brought the car to a halt. They got out. Up here on the plain there was a slight wind, enough to raise the windsock. But it was still warm. Ahead of them there was a line of olive trees and a drystone wall. The trees were close enough to hide them from the airfield to begin with, and Edward and Victoria hurried along as quietly as they could. About fifty yards from the windsock, however, they were forced to bend down and crouch behind the stone wall. They edged forward until the wall gave out. Here there was an open gate and a length of rusty chain that had once been used to keep the gate closed.

Edward twisted and whispered to Victoria. 'We've got to take them on here – '

'We can't! That might alert the others in Basle, it might spoil the entire – '

'If they get away from here, in that plane, we will never find them again. It has to be – ' Above the breeze, they suddenly heard the throaty roar of a propellor coming to life. 'They're already aboard!' hissed Edward. 'Jesus.'

He poked his head around the edge of the wall. As he did so another engine whined into life. He could see the plane easily enough. It was not sixty yards away. And it was certainly within seconds of taxiing to the dusty runway, for its navigation lights were already illuminated and rotating. The airfield was just that – a barren, dry expanse that could have been on Mars or the moon for all the life there was. Not even a small dilapidated building like there had been on Kithira. The noise of the aircraft engines rose, and then immediately fell, as the aircraft started to wheel left, back to the runway. As the plane turned, the wind from its propellors swept back in Edward's direction.

He ran towards the plane but then stopped. The field was deserted but for himself, Victoria and the Cessna. The strip was hard earth, a light brown line about three hundred yards away.

'They're too far,' gasped Victoria. 'We've lost them.'

Edward groaned.

The plane had reached the end of the runway and was beginning to turn. Edward's heart was thumping as he grew angry at the thought of the Greeks getting away. Then he began running. At first he ran away from the runway, to the old gate. He retrieved the length of rusty chain. Then he turned towards the runway. The plane had to be stopped. He had one idea and one only. But he had to be on the runway, as far down it as possible. The plane had now completed its turn and was waiting at the end, perhaps while the pilot completed his checks, or perhaps while he sought permission for take-off on his radio from some central air traffic control. Edward kept running. Perhaps they would think he was the taxi driver, come back to tell them something . . . in which case they might stop completely. He kept running. On the other hand, they might have seen that they were being followed, in which case they would be doubly anxious to take off. He kept running.

He was fifty yards from the runway. The Cessna began to move, about three hundred yards to his left. He covered half the distance. The plane was moving faster now but still had to pick up real speed before it could leave the ground. Edward had nearly reached the runway when his foot landed in a hole and a pain shot through his ankle. He gasped but still pressed on. The plane was gathering speed now; he could hear the thrust of its engines. His ankle was red hot with an agonising pain. He tried to ignore it. In agony, he reached the runway. The plane was a hundred yards away, its engines roaring. His ankle throbbed and he groaned out loud. Sweat from his forehead slid into his eyes. He could barely hear himself cry out as the engines roared closer. He positioned himself not in the centre of the runway but to one side. He knelt. He fingered the chain. Now he needed luck.

The plane was fifty yards away. Edward judged he should move a yard to his left. The plane was twenty-five yards away. He could see the pilot staring at him. He could see mouths moving as those inside discussed him. They had obviously decided he was not the taxi driver and were leaving the ground as quickly as possible. Would the plane lift?

The Cessna was ten yards away and the roaring of the propellors was upon him. Edward raised the chain. He held it as a mass, a bundle of iron links. He had to get the timing right or . . .

He crouched, his ankle throbbing. He knew the pilot had no choice; he had to keep a straight course. The plane screamed abreast of him, or nearly so. Just before it did so, Edward leaned into the plane and, almost gently, threw the chain up into the air in front of the aircraft's starboard propellor. No sooner had he done this than he himself hit the ground and rolled over and over, till he reached the edge of the dusty strip.

The Cessna had roared past him . . . except that it was no longer simply a roar. Edward looked up from his position in the dust on the ground. The air around him appeared to have been slapped hard as, first, two propellors from the plane's starboard engine snapped off. Edward watched, silently, as the chain was wrapped around the engine. The aircraft was just off the ground by now. But then the starboard engine seized up, black fuel appeared on the casing and burst into flames. The Cessna reached perhaps ten feet, fifteen – but then started to wheel to the right; the starboard wing dipped and the plane lost altitude. Moments later the tip of the starboard wing clipped the ground and the Cessna cartwheeled once, twice, three times, diving into its own flames.

Still on the ground, Edward watched the plane flop on to its back. In no time a silence settled over the field. All was still, save for the black smoke rising into the sky and the crackle of flames that engulfed the fuselage.

Riley had to hand it to O'Day. The Irishman had got it bang on the button. The Greek had arrived at the Gerbergasse at a few minutes before noon. Almost immediately a taxi drove up and stopped outside the bank: Nancy Tucker was right on time. The taxi drove off, she and Zakros embraced, exchanged a few words, and then the two of them disappeared into the bank.

O'Day fingered his weapon. He was required to 'keep warm', as they put it in the Service, every six months on a course at Didcot. But it had been years since he had fired in anger. It didn't feel natural.

The rain had started again. Christ, but it rained in Switzerland! He had never expected that. None the less, today he liked the feel of Basle, what he had seen of it. It wasn't an exciting city, far from it. But the city fathers had made the most of the river; the place had some unexpected vistas, and that counted for a lot in his book. He pressed his eye to the drill-hole in the back of the van and looked up the Gerbergasse to –

'Ssshhhit!' he hissed under his breath. 'Look at that.'

Riley applied his eye to the other drill-hole. About two hundred yards away, almost opposite the entrance to the bank, and walking towards the van, were two policemen.

Edward held his shirt to his face to shield it from the flames. With his free hand he gripped a fist-sized rock and aimed it at the glass of the cockpit. The impact cracked the glass but didn't shatter it.

'Edward! It's hopeless. They're dead. Let's leave before anyone arrives.'

But Edward couldn't leave. The flames and the thick black smoke of the burning Cessna held him there. Even if the people inside were dead, he had to rescue their bodies. But the heat . . . He moved around the wing, pointing pathetically into the sky. He was still limping, from the pain in his ankle. The nose of the plane was the only section unaffected by the flames. He noticed a catch and remembered from their own flight, from Crete to Kithira, that these Cessnas had luggage compartments in the nose. Maybe that was a way in.

He approached the nose. The heat was certainly more bearable here. Less unbearable.

'Edward! Come away! What if it explodes?'

But he had the catch undone. Inside there were two or three canvas bags and a leather briefcase, all unscathed. He took them out and threw them towards Victoria. He peered inside the luggage compartment. He felt the partition that divided the compartment from the footwell of the cockpit. It was fairly flimsy and he might be able to –

'Edward!'

But he had heard it: a sound, somewhere between a whoosh and a growl, which indicated that the Cessna's fuel reserve in its port wing had caught fire. He could feel the heat down the side of his body and he pulled himself back.

'Jeeesus!'

'We can't do anything, Edward. Really.'

'You never know Victoria, one of them might be – '

'Look at this!' She had the briefcase open, the one Edward had taken from the nose of the plane.

'What is it?'

She waved some papers at him. 'Airline tickets. Now we know where they planned to go.'

Riley was sweating and cursing, cursing and sweating. The Greek and Nancy Tucker had now been inside the bank for more than an hour. They must emerge soon – but he didn't want them to: the policemen were still on the street. They had strolled along Gerbergasse in one direction, disappeared into the market place and then, after only a few minutes, reappeared. Now they had found someone to talk to, a young blonde woman, and seemed in no hurry. They were both dressed in similar long grey rain-coats, with white peaked caps, so they were well insulated against the weather. O'Day was going through the same agonies as Riley. They had even considered getting out of the van, approaching the policemen and asking for a light, in the hope that that would dislodge them from their talk and they would move on. But they didn't want the police to get too good a look at their faces.

The rain had worsened. Smells of cooking reached them from a nearby café and that didn't improve matters. Riley had developed a raging hunger, in contrast to the night before. Until now he had felt no real anger against the Greek, but now, now that he was being kept waiting, Riley was starting to get very raw indeed. It was the frying he could smell, of course. Fried steak, maybe, fried potatoes. Smells were very evocative and he suddenly had an image of a fried halibut steak he'd once eaten on holiday in Vancouver. Funny, he even remembered the wait-ress, a tiny blonde not unlike the woman now talking to the –

He saw Nancy Tucker first. He tapped O'Day's shoulder.

'Yes!' the other man replied, meaning he had seen her, too.

Her white raincoat was buttoned against the rain and Riley immediately registered that she was carrying two long holdalls. She descended the steps of the bank and set them down on the pavement. She stood up and rubbed her hands: the holdalls were clearly very heavy. She looked back up the stairs as Zakros appeared. Under one arm he carried a large black portfolio case; under the other there were four or five cardboard tubes. Did those tubes contain rolled canvases? Were there more in the holdalls? Zakros set the portfolio down on the pavement. Riley looked across to O'Day but as he did so he was conscious of a large Mercedes taxi turning into Gerbergasse. Riley pressed his eye to the drill-hole. Nancy Tucker was handing one of the holdalls to the taxi driver. The cardboard tubes were put on the front seat next to the driver and Zakros got into the back with yet another holdall. Nancy Tucker joined him and the taxi accelerated away.

Immediately it was level with the van, Riley opened the doors. He didn't dare hurry. The police were not far away and two men getting down from inside a parked van would look odd enough without adding to it. They moved round from the back of the van and got into the driving cab but then had to wait, agonizingly, as a tram clanged past. Finally, Riley let in the clutch and they moved off. They sped down Gerbergasse, sending sprays of dirty water everywhere. The two policemen stared after them.

The van reached the market place, where Riley braked so that they could decide which way to turn. They both searched the square for the white Mercedes. No such car.

'There!' commanded O'Day, pointing to the street which led to the airport.

Riley again let in the clutch and accelerated, causing the van to skid once or twice as it crossed over the wet tramlines. They reached Mittlerestrasse and zoomed along it until they came to the roundabout at the far end. There they had to turn left for the railway station, or go straight on for the airport. Riley stopped the car at the roundabout. They stared down both roads.

'Which way?' O'Day asked.

'I don't know,' replied Riley. 'We've lost them.'

'How far is Athens?' Edward pulled the Mercedes' wheel and the car moved to overtake a very old motorcycle and sidecar.

Victoria inspected the map on her knees. 'About seventy miles.'

'So the airport will be a bit more.' Without slowing down, he pulled the Mercedes out again, this time to pass a truck loaded with fruit. 'If it's two o'clock now, we should be there by four-ish, just in time, maybe.'

Edward had eventually given up trying to rescue the occupants of the Cessna. The flames and the smoke were still several feet high when they had left the airfield and it was still too hot to get anywhere near the cockpit. And when Victoria had shown

Edward the air tickets in the briefcase that had made a dash to Athens the main priority. There had been ten airline tickets, four for Athens–Geneva and six for Geneva–New York. And there were six American passports. The names on the passports had been strange – Hassam, Lassiter, Kimball, Stanfield, Quincy and Dearing. But the photographs had been very familiar. The Apollo Brigade. The Athens–Geneva tickets were for a flight that afternoon, at four-thirty.

Edward had been sick twice on the airfield but, eventually, Victoria had dragged him away.

'Obviously they are rendezvousing in Geneva, then on to New York, where they will go public. It makes sense. But, if we can make the plane they would have been on, we still stand a chance.'

'Surely not – '

'We don't know, do we? If Kolettis and the others were supposed to check in with Basle, or Geneva, from Athens, then the whole thing is blown. But timing was tight and they may simply have arranged a rendezvous. If Zakros is expecting the rest of the Brigade and we show up – he may be so shocked it could just do the trick. They might be so surprised . . . But we must make that plane. Can you do it?'

'Seventy miles in a hundred and twenty minutes. It all depends on whether we see any police.'

Sir Francis Mordaunt was sweating and that didn't often happen. His left hand, which gripped the phone, was especially sticky. He was standing by his desk, staring down at the seated figure in front of him. Outside in the palace grounds a light wind rippled the surface of the pond.

'No, Mr Page,' said Mordaunt. His voice was quiet, controlled but as cold and as sharp as a stalactite. 'I made it clear, crystal clear, that I wished to speak to you. Alone.'

'I can't get away from the House. You must see that. Today of all days.'

'It is the debate I wish to talk about.'

'Then why can't you tell Swale? That's why I sent him – he has my full confidence.'

'Well, he doesn't have mine!' Mordaunt's tone grew, if anything, more glacial. 'It is a delicate matter. I must speak with you.'

'Then come to the House – '

'No! How many more times must I say it? It is too delicate, much too delicate, for me to risk being seen in your company.'

'What's wrong with my company?'

For a moment, Mordaunt was wrong-footed. 'No, no – I didn't mean it like that.' His hand on the phone grew even more sticky. 'It needn't take long – twenty minutes, but I must – '

'Sir Francis! It is half past one. In less that two hours one of the most important debates the House of Commons has seen is due to begin. The most important debate in the Prime Minister's career and the most important debate in *my* career. I have arrangements to make, people to see. I have to polish my own speech and reassure my own side. I am party leader and I have to lead . . . Part of me is dismayed and worried that the Palace would even hint at getting involved in this issue. And I am not sure I want to be seen entering Buckingham Palace on today of all days. People might draw the wrong conclusions, and government backbenchers could make a lot of it in the debate. In other circumstances, then of course I would respect your wishes and come to you. In these circumstances, today, the rules are different. Now, I am very busy and must go. If you decide to change your mind and come to the House, I will see you. Otherwise . . .'

'No.'

'Very well.' And Page put down the phone.

'I don't like it. I don't like it one bit,' growled Riley. They had opted for the airport, after they had lost Zakros and Nancy Tucker outside the bank. But although they had lost them they were only two or three minutes behind them, which was why, in the end, they had decided to make for the airport. Zakros and Tucker could not have checked in for any flight, even a domestic one, in that time. And Basle was not a large airport: if the Greek and the American woman were there, they would have been very obvious. But they weren't there.

'Okay, so you don't like it.' O'Day slapped the dashboard with the palm of his hand. 'Now what? The border with France? The border with Germany? Or the train station?'

'It has to be the station. No one would take a taxi into France or Germany.'

'Good enough for me,' said O'Day. 'Make for the Bahnhof.'

It took them twenty-five minutes to get to the railway station. They ran into the forecourt, not caring now if Nancy Tucker or Zakros should recognize them. The forecourt was crowded but it should have been possible to see immediately a couple with such prominent luggage. No couple and no luggage. Riley saw O'Day turn on his heel and march back to the forecourt. He followed. He found the other man studying the timetable. 'What are you doing?'

O'Day looked at his watch. 'They came out of the bank at about one-forty. It would have taken them . . . oh, four to six minutes to get here. Another three or four minutes to pay the taxi, buy their tickets and get on to the platform. So they couldn't have got to a platform before one-fifty at the absolute earliest. It's now two-thirty-nine. Between one-fifty and now only two trains have left this station: one to Lucerne and Como, one to Berne and Brig. There's a third, to Geneva, in two minutes. It has to be Geneva.'

'Why?'

'These people are intending to go public. For that they need a major newspaper. That means a major city. The only major cities in Switzerland are Basle itself, Zurich, Berne and Geneva. Also, Geneva has a bigger airport than Basle. From there they could fly anywhere – Athens, Rome, Melbourne – '

'Melbourne!'

'No, probably not. But you see my point. Platform eight!' He was already running.

A passage led under the railway lines and the platforms, with staircases leading off every so often. The third staircase was the one they wanted and O'Day bounded up the steps two or three at a time. Riley wheezed along behind.

At the top, platform eight was to their left. Blue and cream coaches were waiting in place.

O'Day halted and examined his watch. 'It must be about to leave,' he gasped and pointed to the rear of the train. 'I'll get on and work my way forward. You stay on the platform and keep abreast of me. That way we can't miss them and they can't escape.'

He ran to the last coach and, without pausing or looking back, climbed the steps.

Riley kept pace as O'Day moved through the train, looking hard into each compartment. They covered the first coach, the second, the third. There were about seven more. The train seemed fairly empty.

Suddenly, Riley noticed that the train was moving – these electric Swiss trains started so silently. He grabbed at a door and pulled. Someone shouted at him. He heard footsteps behind him, running. The train was picking up speed.

He pulled on the door handle. It was a big door. Whoever was behind him shouted again. The train was going faster. But now he had the door open and he jumped on to the lowest step. Others were shouting now as the door swung wide. The train was already travelling at about fifteen miles per hour. But Riley was inside now, wheezing hard. He pulled the door shut and then stood for a moment, to regain his breath. He moved across the carriage so that he could look down the corridor.

O'Day was at the far end, with his back to Riley. Riley started to move towards him, the train swaying as it picked up speed and rattled over some points. O'Day had disappeared by now, through the doors which connected the carriages. Riley followed. He opened the first connecting door, steadying himself as he crossed the divide. The doors were heavy and stiff but he had the second one open.

At that moment he heard a cracking sound, loud but very brief. At first Riley thought the train had cracked a wheel, or slipped a rail. But he didn't think that for long. The train was still bucking along at twenty or more miles an hour. He rushed through the second door, reaching into his pocket as he did so. The train went into a tunnel and for a moment everything went dark. But then they were in daylight again and he moved across the carriage so that he could again look along the corridor. His heart seemed to expand in his chest and the blood rushed up his neck.

At the far end of the corridor, a figure was slumped on its back, blocking the corridor. It was moving, but not of its own accord. It was being dragged into the lavatory.

Riley took in the scene immediately. The Greek must be inside the lavatory, pulling O'Day, because Tucker was standing over the body.

She saw Riley and raised her arm. He fumbled again in his jacket pocket and brought out his own gun. As he did so, he felt a massive force bounce him on the right shoulder and a hot pain zipped down his right side. He dropped his gun as his body was spun by the force of the bullet that had passed through his shoulder, splintering the blade. He cried out as he fell – and he cried again as his shattered shoulder hit the floor of the carriage.

The train rattled over another series of points, louder now as the train gathered speed. Then another crack rang out as a second bullet from Tucker zipped into the floor near Riley's head. He knew he had to move. The train swayed – and he swayed with it, grunting in pain, sweating in fear. He rolled across the carriage and out of the line of sight of the Tucker woman.

She would come for him, of course she would. She had dispatched O'Day without hesitation or a moment's reflection: she had been ready. And she had very nearly dispatched him equally efficiently. This time, when she reached the end of the corridor . . .

Riley sat up. The door-handle of the carriage was virtually level with his head. He reached out. But the train was moving at twenty-five or thirty miles an hour. Could he survive that?

He heard a movement in the corridor. She would appear any moment and he knew he couldn't survive that.

The pain was making him feel sick and he was beginning to retch. The burning sensation throbbed in his shoulder, sweat ran into his eyes, and the fingers of his right hand appeared dead already. With his left hand he leaned on the door-handle. The door clicked half open and then caught on a safety latch. He heard another sound in the corridor. Again he leaned against the carriage door.

Suddenly the door swung open and cool outside air and noise from the wheels rushed in. The Tucker woman would surely notice the change in noise level and realize what Riley planned. The pain in his shoulder was making him dizzy now, as well as sick. The American woman must appear any moment. Expecting another punch of pain in his back, Riley shifted forward and placed both feet on the bottom step of the doorway. In the wind generated by the train, the door swung back, trying to close itself. It swung against his right shoulder and he screamed in pain. With his knee he forced it open again. He heard someone behind him and, without waiting to turn, he half jumped and half fell from the step.

*

A cheer rang out on the government side as Lockwood stepped from behind the Speaker's chair, ready to take his seat on the green Commons benches. The House was packed. The vote was a three-line whip but whipping in was unnecessary – the House of Commons offered few dramas like the one to be enacted this day and every member who was not in a hospital bed, or abroad, was present.

As Lockwood picked his way around the various members who had not found seats, he was conscious that all eyes were on him. His back was patted by loyal friends and colleagues but there were painful silences too. The opposition parties weighed in with noises of their own. Catcalls, laughs of derision intended to imply that Lockwood had already lost the debate. Other ministers – Lessor, Hatfield, Scylde – had arrived already. However, a space had been left for Lockwood opposite the dispatch box. As he sat down, Lockwood looked around the House. Although most eyes were on him, one set that were not belonged to George Keld. Now that he was no longer a minister, Keld had taken – and been granted by others – the first seat below the aisle, on the government side. This was the traditional spot for the chief critic of the day from within a government's own party.

While the Speaker was conducting prayers and the opening business of the day, Lockwood leaned towards Hatfield, who was seated next to him. 'Any change in the arithmetic?'

Hatfield sucked his teeth. 'A lot of people are being very cagey. They say they will make up their minds, depending on the debate. That may be true of some of them but I suspect others have already decided to go against you but don't have the guts to tell me. I'd say there are twenty-nine who are definitely going to abstain, four are against you while pretending to wait and see, and another six or seven are genuine in that they will be swayed by the debate.'

'So there's everything to play for.'

Hatfield sighed. 'I suppose. With a fighting performance, as you are well capable of in normal circumstances, you could win by one or two votes. But I'm bound to say, Bill . . . unless you can come clean on the . . . matter we cannot come clean on . . . it's going to be very difficult.'

Lockwood patted the Chief Whip's thigh. 'Courage, Joss. Don't you fail me now. We only need one little word from Basle and this whole thing will be turned upside-down.' He looked at his watch. 'The vote is more than six hours away. If we get word from Basle, nothing anyone says in this debate is going to matter.'

'Leave the car here!' Victoria pointed to a space marked, in English, 'Airport Security'. She had her own door open before Edward brought the car to a stop. He was out from behind the wheel and not far behind her as she ran into the departures terminal. His ankle was easing now.

The place was crowded, thronged with people. She stopped, craning her neck.

'Swissair, right!' Victoria saw it first and led the way.

The Swissair desk was empty. 'The flight must have closed,' she breathed. 'It's quarter past four.' But Victoria had already turned away. She ran across the hall but then stopped. In the car they had decided they had to use two of the tickets they had found in the nose of the Cessna: there wasn't time to buy new ones. They just had to pray no one noticed the tickets and passports didn't match. But now they might not even get that far: the queue for security stretched nearly half-way through the building. It would take half an hour to get through.

'There!' Edward said, urgently but softly, and pointed to a row of three wheelchairs. When he reached them, however, they were locked together. 'Damn!'

'No. Stand in front of me. I can manage this sort of thing.'

Edward stood in front of Victoria as she kneeled down. He didn't look, not wanting to draw attention to what she was doing. Thirty seconds passed. Forty. Fifty. 'We'll never – '

Suddenly he felt something pushing at the back of his legs and Victoria hissed: 'Sit down.'

She pushed again and he almost collapsed into the chair.

She wheeled him to the front of the line where other passengers immediately gave way. The security guard spoke to her in Greek and she answered. What sounded to Edward like a quarrel then ensued and he began to sweat. But then the guard and Victoria were joking and they were allowed through. Victoria pushed the chair as fast as she could without looking suspicious.

'What was all that about?'

'He wanted to know why I didn't have my airport pass and you didn't have a boarding card. You need special clearance to escort disabled passengers.'

'And what did you say?'

'I said the lamination machine, the thing that covers the security pass with clear plastic, had broken down and eaten my card.'

'And he believed you?'

'He had a northern accent. I asked him if he was from Kavalla or Xanthi. He was from Drama, nearby. We got on very well. And he could see that the Swissair desk was already closed.'

Edward grunted. He showed his passport and they were through.

'Gate seventeen,' said Victoria, looking at the signs. 'We turn right here.' She pushed the chair round a corner. 'Okay . . . *run!*'

Edward leaped from the chair and together they ran down the corridor. Gate eleven was ahead.

'It's miles!' gasped Victoria.

'Run!'

Gate thirteen, gate fifteen. A long line of baggage trolleys barred their way. They skidded around them. A gaggle of schoolchildren filled the passage. Edward, in front now, pushed gently through them. He lifted one child bodily out of the way. She, and some others, protested. But Edward and Victoria were through.

Gate seventeen, when they reached it, was peopled by just two women and a man. Victoria slapped down the tickets. 'The flight is closed,' said one of the women. Her accent was German. She was Swiss.

'The plane is still here!' cried Victoria, pointing.

'It is leaving now.'

'Please!'

'The flight is – '

Edward held up his passport. 'I'm a doctor,' he said quietly and calmly. 'I am a liver specialist. I must get to Annecy tomorrow morning. I must operate on a young boy, who may die if I don't. Are you a mother?'

The woman stared at him. She looked hard at his passport, which Edward held on to but which did indeed say 'Dr Edward Andover' on the front. 'If you are British, why are you operating in France?'

'I'm well-known in my field.'

Victoria said something in Greek to the man standing next to the Swiss woman. He nodded and spoke to her. She picked up a phone and punched some buttons. After a short delay she spoke in German. Then, without smiling, she said, 'Very well.

You may go on board. The door will be opened for you. You are very lucky. Swissair is always punctual.'

Edward and Victoria marched down the jetway before there could be any second thoughts. As they reached the plane, the door was being opened. They stepped aboard and were given seats in the front row. Everyone else on board stared at them, but they just flopped down, exhausted.

Not until they were taxiing to the runway, a glass of champagne in their hands, did Edward think to ask Victoria what she had said to the Greek man standing next to the Swissair woman. 'It seemed to do the trick. What on earth did you say?'

'I said you'd been working in Greece too. And that you had just operated on a famous Greek: George Kofas.'

'Some of the newspaper comments prior to this afternoon's proceedings have been such as to suggest that the precipitating issue today is a slight one, that a few marble sculptures do not really amount to a row of beans in the scheme of things.' Frank Whiteman looked around the crowded benches. 'I am bound to say that I do not see it like that. Not like that at all. And I know that many of my colleagues agree.' Murmurs of 'Hear, hear' rustled around the chamber.

Frank Whiteman was an excellent choice to open the debate. He had a good speaking voice, deep, warm, easy to listen to. He was tall, with a full head of white hair, like a fresh fall of snow, and an open face, given to smiling. More than that, however, he was, if not exactly liked on the government benches, then certainly respected. He was not a cheap politician, out for quick points. He even thought that on occasions the other side had a case. Government supporters never gave him credit for this in public, but in the House they paid him the compliment of listening to what he said. As deputy leader of his party, he commanded respect on all sides.

'As we approach the end of the twentieth century, we in this country live – whether we like it or not – in a post-industrial world. Religion has declined massively. Political allegiances are no longer set in cement; they change. Technology, in the form of travel, computers, communications, changes our lives time and again, literally from month to month. In such a world, a world where freedoms are growing at an alarming rate, there is an important role for governments but, in a sense, a new one. As the old frontiers of government recede, as the state grows smaller, so – in my humble view – the new role expands. People are confused by the pace of change, they are alarmed when the old certainties, the old ways of doing things and, more important, of thinking, are changed. Governments therefore have to give a lead here. They – and only they – are in a position to shape the world we choose to have. They – and only they – are in a position to set the values a country wishes to espouse.'

He lowered his voice, for effect. 'And it is here, in this sense, that I believe the government has gone wrong. It is here, and in this sense, that the Elgin Marbles are so important.' Now he raised his voice. 'Art, the role of art, the place of beauty in our lives, has never been more important. The signs are there for us all to see. Not just in the enormous prices fetched at auction for masterpieces by Van Gogh or Picasso or Renoir, but in the millions who go to museums, art galleries, who go to the theatre, the ballet or the opera. In the simple fact that thousands and thousands of people turned out last night in a candlelit vigil on the Acropolis in Athens. We have arrived at a point in the evolution of the west where many of us, perhaps most, can do these things. We want to do these things, we enjoy them. In an ever-uglier world, the arts enrich our lives as no other aspect of it, save love and family life, can. I may regret the fact that religion no longer plays as important a part, but I cannot deny that, nowadays, for many people, for most people, art is the greater pleasure. It is, if I may speak grandiloquently for a moment, man at his best.

'This is my first point – and, don't worry, I'm only going to make two.' He smiled as the rest of the House chuckled. 'Hear, hear.'

'So I am saying, firstly, that the newspapers – not for the first time – are wrong. The arts are not a small issue, a side issue, an irrelevant issue in the grand scheme of things. In the late twentieth century they are among the most important issues of the day, in some ways the most important, and I think the government has underestimated that. Of course governments have miscalculated before. But this has been no ordinary miscalculation. This miscalculation has been insulting. I have said that the arts, in the late twentieth century, are the very vitals of the nation. All the more reason therefore for the Prime Minister to have come to this House with his plan for these sculptures and to have laid before Parliament his ideas, his policies, for open discussion. Nothing would have been lost had the Prime Minister brought this issue to the House – and a lot may have been gained.' Whiteman shifted another sheet of paper from the dispatch box. He raised his voice to show that he was winding up. 'We shall never know, Mr Speaker, for the matter did not come to Parliament. Instead, the Prime Minister put himself above this House. With the mother of parliaments he behaved in the most unparliamentary fashion. In one of the oldest democracies, he behaved as an arrogant authoritarian, disdainful of others, rivals and colleagues alike. On an important issue, a matter on which almost everyone in this House, in this country, has a view, no one was consulted. The Prime Minister acted alone. Therefore, he alone bears responsibility for all that has followed – I will not delay the House with the details, we all know them, the Prime Minister better than anyone and he has to live with his conscience. But I repeat: he alone is responsible for the mismanagement that has led to this censure motion being put today – a grave charge. Alone! That is the key word here. If nothing else, he alone should go.'

Whiteman picked up his remaining sheet of paper, retrieved the others from the table at the side of the dispatch box and slumped on to the bench behind him. A chorus of roars burst about him on the opposition benches. Lockwood kept his eyes closed. He was more interested in the noise behind him on the government's own benches. It was muted but not, he noticed, all that hostile to Whiteman.

'What do you think?' whispered Hatfield, in the short few seconds before the next speaker was called.

'Not bad. He didn't need to convince his side . . . it's our side he's got to win over. Saying I have neglected the House was good tactics. Anyone on our side who is thinking of abstaining can convince himself he's acting in the interests of democracy. And of course it's true; I *did* neglect the House. I had no choice.' He opened his eyes and sat up, smiling at Hatfield so that others could see he was still in the land of the living and still able to smile. 'But, if we get the news we want, I shall still be able to bring them round. Ah! Maybe this is it.'

A steward, wearing the tailcoat and chain of his office, was approaching the Prime Minister with a note. Lockwood took the envelope and thanked the man. He tore it open and studied the sheet inside in such a way that only he could see. He smiled again at Hatfield. Only the Chief Whip could see the look in the Prime Minister's eyes as he whispered, 'Riley and O'Day have had an accident. O'Day is dead and Riley has a broken shoulder and a broken leg. The Brigade in Basle got away.' Only Hatfield could see Lockwood's lower lip tremble. 'Whiteman was right to lament the decline of religion. We need a miracle now.'

'Ladies and gentlemen, this is the captain. Owing to air traffic congestion, we will have to hold for a few minutes, before landing at Geneva airport. I apologize for the delay but there is nothing we can do about it. However, we shall have you on the ground just as soon as we can. Thank you.'

Victoria looked at Edward and squeezed his arm. Half-way through the flight his brain had seized up as the realization of what he had done to the Cessna hit him. He had killed five people, including its pilot. Five? He couldn't even be certain how many people were – had been – in the plane. Maybe there had been two pilots. He had gone cold with the shock, and put a blanket around his shoulders. Victoria had talked to him the whole way, trying to keep his mind off what he had done. She squeezed his arm again. 'A few minutes, Edward. You'll feel better when we land. It's sitting still that's frustrating. Don't forget, we are on the very plane that Kofas, Kolettis and the others would have taken. Maybe Zakros – even Nancy – will be here to meet us.'

Sir Francis Mordaunt was familiar with the layout of the Houses of Parliament. If he were to be pushed, then he supposed that he knew the Lords better than the Commons. It was in the Lords, after all, that Her Majesty delivered the Queen's Speech. But the Commons was hardly less familiar.

Mordaunt would have much preferred to have talked to Page at Buckingham Palace, and he couldn't risk being seen anywhere near the leader of the opposition's room in Parliament. Too many questions might be asked and Lockwood might get to hear of it. But he could, quite legitimately, watch the debate from the Distinguished Strangers' Gallery, where he could keep an eye on Page in case he left the debate at any time. Mordaunt looked down into the chamber now. A steward was standing over the leader of the opposition, handing him a piece of paper. Page glanced at it, read it more closely and then stood up. He walked down the chamber, away from the Speaker's chair, turned and bowed, and then sauntered out.

Mordaunt was already on his feet. This was exactly what he was waiting for and he thought he knew where Page was headed: the central lobby, where MPs met visitors who were not allowed into the more exclusive precincts of Westminster. Mordaunt nodded to the steward in the Strangers' Gallery and hurried down the steps at the back. Parliament was full of little mazes of corridors and he threaded his way through one of these now, before emerging into the central lobby. His steps rang out on the marble floor.

He saw Page immediately. He was talking to a figure Mordaunt recognized, a well-known journalist from a national newspaper. The journalist appeared to be giving Page a piece of paper.

Mordaunt found a bench and sat down, trying to make himself as inconspicuous as possible. He would wait till Page had finished with the journalist and then approach him. If he could just warn Page . . . as to why this débâcle had occurred . . . a vote – a damaging vote – might be averted.

The lobby was busy, as was bound to be the case for such an important debate. A long line of ordinary members of the public, waiting for seats in the gallery, various Lords crossing the lobby from their end of the palace, constituents who had fixed meetings with their MPs a long time ago, well before today had turned out to be so important.

Page and the journalist seemed to be winding up. They were shaking hands.

'Sir Francis? What are you doing here?'

Mordaunt nearly fell off the bench. He looked up. It was Jocelyn Hatfield. Across the lobby, Page was turning away from the journalist, back towards the chamber.

'The debate, of course. What else?'

'But this is the lobby. You can't see much from here.'

Page's footsteps rang out as he crossed the lobby.

'It was stuffy where I was seated,' said Mordaunt. 'I needed some some air and to use the phones.'

Page had reached the edge of the lobby but had stopped to talk to someone else.

'How do you think it's going?' asked Hatfield.

'What?' Mordaunt kept Page in view out of the corner of his eye.

'The debate!'

'Oh . . . Whiteman was effective, I think.' He faltered as he watched Page break off his conversation.

But Hatfield still stood over the equerry. 'Bad news from Basle. Have you heard?'

Mordaunt didn't reply. He was concentrating on Page, who at that moment was leaving the lobby and disappearing through the door that led back into the chamber.

As they shuffled forward, Edward offered a silent prayer for the compactness of Geneva airport. Once outside, he looked around. He didn't know Zakros but he did know Nancy. There was no sign of her.

'They can't have known immediately what happened to the others,' Victoria said softly. 'They were supposed to be on our flight.'

'Someone in Greece must have been in touch by now.'

Victoria shook her head. 'Don't forget, Riley and O'Day overheard Nancy say the Brigade was seven-strong. There's no one to alert them.'

'They must have a rendezvous point. They were highly organized – the car at the harbour, the plane arriving so promptly, the airline tickets. All within hours. Until last night, they must have thought that everything was going according to plan.'

'Kofas. He has a big organization. His own travel agency, even.'

'All that surely means *someone* must have been in touch with Zakros and Nancy by now.'

'No. Not at all. The Brigade was as secretive as our own side has been.'

'I can't believe it. And the crash will have been on the news by now.'

'Maybe. But we have no choice anyway. If Riley and O'Day have kept a tail on Zakros, they may need our help. And we still have one advantage: they don't know they are being followed.'

It had been some time since Edward last visited Geneva airport but he remembered it well enough. He knew there were some phones by the bar. Victoria ordered some coffees. She was happy for Edward to do the phoning – it would help keep his mind off the Cessna. The bar was crowded but not, it seemed, with travellers. International airports were modern communities in their own right and this bar was the meeting place, the piazza, of the airport.

Victoria was glad when the coffee arrived. It had been a wearing day and it wasn't over yet. She sipped her coffee and closed her eyes in pleasure. When she opened them again, Edward was standing next to her.

'You look dreadful!' she cried. 'What's wrong? Drink your coffee.'

He did. He drained his cup at one go. Then he said: 'O'Day's dead, killed by Nancy. Riley is in hospital with multiple fractures. Nancy and Zakros were followed, after they left the bank carrying holdalls and several tubes – pictures presumably. They took a train from Basle to Geneva, non-stop. O'Day was killed on the train and Riley had to jump for it. So Zakros and Nancy reached Geneva but they knew they were being followed. That changes everything.'

'As the House may be aware, Mr Speaker, my wife is – or was, until very recently – chairman of the Friends of the British Museum. In common with many of her colleagues she has resigned her position over this matter. The House may wish to hear, through me, why she did so and what went on inside the museum which led so many professional colleagues to protest.' With these words, Anthony Rolfe, the leader of the Liberal Democrats, had the immediate attention of the entire House. It was coming up for seven-thirty. Soon the chamber would thin, as members went for dinner. But tonight it wouldn't thin very much or for very long. The vote was at ten, so the summings up would begin some time before nine and members would want a good look at Page and Lockwood in the final locking of horns.

Lockwood was still in his place. He had been there throughout the debate but the grim look on his face was now set. To many members, and to those in the gallery, which included Lord Renfrew, Sir Henry Misco, the Greek ambassador and Madeleine Rolfe in addition to Sir Francis Mordaunt, this must have seemed as though he hated what he was hearing in the chamber. In fact, it had more to do with what he'd heard from Basle and from Greece. The whole plan seemed to be falling apart.

Anthony Rolfe half turned so that the backbenchers on the opposition side of the House could hear what he had to say. 'The most surprising, and the most disturbing thing – '

'Let the Marbles go!' A deep voice rang out from the public gallery. All eyes left Rolfe and looked upward.

'They belong in Greece!' cried a second voice, a woman's this time.

Stewards converged on the demonstrators from both directions. In common with all the other MPs, Lockwood scanned the gallery. The stewards had now reached the three people, who, the Prime Minister could see, were Indians. 'The British are cultural imperialists!' the woman shouted as she was pulled from her seat. 'Send back the Hindu throne!' cried a third figure, and he too was pulled into the aisle. 'Lockwood has the right idea!' yelled the first man. 'Give back to Greece what is Greek! Give to India what is ours. This debate is – ' and he was pushed through the double doors by the steward, with the other two behind him.

The House had been disconcerted. Lockwood certainly had not counted on support from such an unlikely quarter and he was far from certain what good it had done him. Not much, he fancied.

Anthony Rolfe still stood, he still had possession of the House, but for a moment he too seemed flummoxed.

Now Hatfield slid into his seat by Lockwood. He leaned close and whispered in his ear. 'Keld isn't going to speak.'

Lockwood glanced at him sharply. 'Why on earth not?'

'Think, Bill! If he doesn't speak and you lose, his hands are clean. He's played no direct role in your downfall and therefore his case to take over after you will be that much stronger. He'll be the white knight.'

'But Keld is a pro. He'd want his say, to make sure I lose.'

'You're missing the point. The point is: he is not speaking because, in his view, the arithmetic is against you. He doesn't *need* to speak.'

'The Rhône Hotel? Good evening, this is the American Airlines office here, at Geneva airport. Someone has left some fairly valuable jewellery on one of our aircraft and we believe it may have been one of a party of Americans who travelled together. We're anxious to trace them, so that we may return it. I wonder . . . if I give you the names, could you check if they are staying at your hotel?'

'But of course. What are the names, please?'

'Hassam, Lassiter, Kimball, Stanfield, Quincy, Dearing.'

'Just a moment.'

During the pause, Edward looked across the lake to the lights on the far bank. It had been a risk, coming into Geneva and checking into this hotel, La Paix. The trouble was, neither he nor Victoria, nor anyone, knew how much Nancy and Zakros knew. Yes, they now knew they were being followed, in Switzerland. But they couldn't know what had happened in Greece, not until they got to Geneva and maybe not even then. The question was: what had Nancy and Zakros done when they got to Geneva?

'Given what happened to them on the train,' Victoria had said, 'they would have called Greece immediately.'

'But who would they have called? By the time Zakros and Nancy reached Geneva the others should have been on the plane.'

'But they killed someone. They would have left the country immediately.'

'If that's true, we've had it. But, don't forget, they wanted to go to America. Presumably that's where they were planning to go public – for maximum impact. And they thought that Kolettis and the others were bringing the false passports. There's a good chance, therefore, that they checked into a hotel under a false name. Not until the others don't arrive on our flight, not until they don't turn up at the hotel, will Nancy and Zakros know for certain that the whole thing is blown. Even then, when they check with Greece, if they can check with Greece, they will only find that the Cessna exploded on take-off. They will still think that their aliases are safe.'

'It works on paper, Edward. Very neat and tidy. But this isn't art history, and we're not in a library. Your friend Nancy killed someone today. She may be a hard-faced bitch, for all I know, but not even she can be used to killing. Think how she feels. She's probably panicking, wants to go to ground – fast. Hide out for a month, or a year. And what are they going to do once it's confirmed the others are dead? Panic all over again.'

'All right. Think about this. When we reached Geneva, Nancy and Zakros still thought Kolettis and the others were alive. Kofas is rich, powerful – probably the best hope Nancy has of hiding. On that boat of his, for a start. You yourself talk about a second panic – but that can't take place until they contact someone who knows about the Cessna crash – and that brings us back to my earlier argument. They had to go to the hotel where they were all intending to stay. Then think of this. No one, so far as we know, saw the crash. At some point a crash investigator will find the chain – but, as of now, the crash could have been an accident – '

'Edward! That's ridiculous.'

'Maybe. But it's just as much human nature to continue in a set groove as it is to panic and behave wildly. And in any case, why argue? If they did fly off, we've lost them. If they didn't, and I'm right, we're wasting valuable time while we could be looking for them.'

Reluctantly, Victoria had agreed and they had checked into the Paix Hotel. Two rooms, but with an interconnecting door, which gave them the use of two telephones.

The woman at the Rhône came back on the line. 'Are you sure this party is staying in the hotel, sir?'

'No, we're checking all the major hotels in the city. Have you no reservation in those names?'

'No, sir.'

'Very well. I'm sorry to have bothered you. Thank you.' He rang off and put a line through the Rhône in the Geneva Yellow Pages. He had already crossed off the Richemond and the Hilton. Victoria had tried the Angleterre, the Bristol, the Beau Rivage and the Ambassador.

Edward next tried the President and Les Bergues. 'Have you tried the Warwick?' he shouted through the interconnecting door, which was open.

'Yes!' replied Victoria. 'No go. Try the Berne and the Alba.'

Edward looked out of the window again. An old woman with a dog walked into the arc of light spread across the quay by one of the streetlamps. What sort of life would he lead when he was old, he thought. He had no family, no children, not even any dogs. Would he ever be old? he asked himself. Would he get to know Victoria any better? How long would it take to get over Nancy?

Wearily, he turned back to the phone and began to dial.

'Mr Speaker, my honourable friend, the Member for Thornhill, showed at the beginning of this debate just how unusual these proceedings are. The House has not seen a debate like this one for many a year. It has certainly not seen a Prime Minister who has behaved like this one, ever.' Arthur Page gripped the dispatch box with both hands. His blond-grey hair was swept straight back. His skin looked shiny with health. The only sign of nervousness was that he kept licking his lips with his tongue.

He used no notes. He knew as much as anyone that, if he won tonight's vote, he could be Prime Minister within months, maybe much sooner. He needed to show the House that he was Prime Minister material. He knew, as Whiteman had known before him, that he must speak to the government's backbenchers. His own side would vote with him, come what may. True, he needed a strong speech so that, should there be a general election, he could send them off with a spring in their step. But, before that, he had to win tonight and that depended on enough government backbenchers abstaining. His had to be a careful speech, not too party political. He had to move those government backbenchers, despite themselves and despite the fact that he was on the other side of the House. He had to appeal to them as parliamentarians above all else.

'We have heard from all sides in the debate tonight, and I am bound to say that it is not just this side of the House that objects to the Prime Minister's behaviour. The right honourable gentleman, the leader of the Liberals Democrats, the Scottish Nationalists – even a few Ulster Unionists – have expressed grave reservations. It has been a debate filled with feeling – and not just down here, but up there.' He smiled in the general direction of the government backbenches and pointed to the gallery. 'At the end of the day, however, and it *is* now the end of the day, the issue is not feeling, however important feeling is; it is not art, however important art is in our lives . . . No, the issue is democracy, the very operation of this House and the administration of the country. The Prime Minister has been attacked on many fronts in this House today, and shortly he will defend himself. To me, however, as leader of the opposition, the loyal opposition, as I will remind members, his chief sin, his important sin in this matter, has been his neglect of, and contempt for, Parliament. Like every other member in this House I am utterly perplexed by the way this issue came to prominence, like everyone else I have been astounded at what has come to pass. Astounded, angered, humiliated and – yes – shamed. Like everyone else, I have views about art and its place in our lives. I have been angered and shamed by the attack on the Greek Cathedral here in London, angered and shamed by the vigil in Athens, angered and shamed by the demonstration of the Nigerian athletes at Crystal Palace on Saturday. But all that has been well put by others, put better than I could hope to do. As leader of the opposition, I see it as my duty tonight to defend above all else the traditions of this House. And I do so, Mr Speaker, not simply on behalf of this side of the House, but on behalf of all sides.'

Murmurs of 'Hear, hear' rang out. Page was sure that some of them came from the government benches.

'It is tempting to say that, by themselves, these Elgin Marbles are just so many pieces of stone. But history, life, is made up of such episodes. It is tempting to argue that these Marbles are just museum pieces, two thousand years old and without relevance today. Well, the whole history of this sorry episode shows just how wrong that reasoning is. The whole history of this episode shows just how wrong the Prime Minister is.' Page drew a finger across his lips. 'That he should not bring this matter to the House is, to my way of thinking, Mr Speaker, incredible. To undertake such a contentious and controversial programme shows a deep cynicism on the Prime Minister's part so far as this House is concerned. And, given what has happened since the matter was first leaked to the press, it also shows that he has miscalculated on a gigantic scale. The Marbles are on their way back to Greece, despite the fact that the vast majority of people in this country want no such thing. As a result of the Prime Minister's unilateral action, people have died, and been injured, a police horse has had to be put down, churches and other fine buildings have been attacked. The House does not need me to remind it of what has happened – suffice it to say that the list is long.'

Page thumped the dispatch box with the palm of his hand. 'What I also find incredible is that, even after this whole thing started, even after it started to go wrong, to backfire, the Prime Minister *still* did not bring it to the House for discussion. His arrogance continued, his insulting attitude to this House continued, even as the evidence mounted that what he was doing was wrong.

'Now, I don't deny that governments sometimes have to pursue unpopular measures. That is a fact of life. But this was and is no ordinary unpopular measure. It was a single individual pursuing an act of folly. It was a Prime Minister foisting on a nation a whim of his own. And, worse, he did it in secret. That is how ashamed, how guilty, he was about what he was doing.

'Mr Speaker, there are no parallels with this action of the Prime Minister. It is in a class by itself. Most people in public life hope, in their heart of hearts, that somehow events will conspire so that some aspect of the country, some law, some practice, some institution, will become a monument to their achievements, to their memory. Some are even paid the very great compliment of having a stone monument sculpted in their honour. I ask the House to consider what the Prime Minister's monument will be. It will certainly be extraordinary, will it not? Every time we go to the British Museum, we shall find entire rooms empty. Perhaps on the door to an empty room there will be a sign: "These rooms are empty, courtesy of William Lockwood MP." Or on a wall there will be a notice: "Thanks to William Lockwood MP, the exhibits that once occupied this space can never be seen here again." '

Opposition MPs cheered, cackled coldly. Backbenchers on the government side sat unmoving. But Page's imagery had a ring to it. He had hit home.

He thumped the dispatch box again. 'What kind of person is it whose monument is an empty space? What kind of person is it whose contribution to our cultural life is to give it away? What kind of politician is it whose definition of the national interest is to put the concerns of a foreign country above this one?' Page half turned to face the rest of the House. 'This, surely, is topsy-turvy land. This is the world turned upside-down.' He turned back to the dispatch box and thumped it again. 'It is certainly a world that has got to stop! This way of treating the House has got to stop. This way of shrouding in secrecy anything and everything has got to stop. Government by one individual has got to stop.'

Page allowed his shoulder to sag a little, to show that, after that crescendo, he was quietening down a little. But he hadn't finished. He was now moving on to fresh fields. 'I take it that some of the Prime Minister's colleagues in his own party share this view of his behaviour. That is the only interpretation I can place on the resignation, at last week's Cabinet, of the right honourable gentleman, the Member for Rothesay, as Defence Secretary. I am sure the right honourable member had more than one motive for resigning but that need not concern us tonight. What should concern us is that he could not, he would not, continue in a government led by the Prime Minister in the way that he is leading it at the moment. The right honourable member at least had the courage to resign. It is an example that many of us would like the Prime Minister himself to follow. This debate need not proceed to a vote tonight, if he will resign ahead of it. I do not need to remind the House of the damaging consequences of a vote. If the Prime Minister is censured, we on our side shall be prepared to fight an election, should the Prime Minister choose that course, but that does not mean we are unmindful of the consequences, consequences in terms of the economy, of the country's political standing, of the "commotion", if I may use a nineteenth-century word, that will be caused. The Prime Minister's resignation could avoid all that – and I ask him to heed that warning, and to behave responsibly. Of course, I do not expect him to listen. Given the way he has been behaving recently, he listens to no one but himself and his narrow coterie of advisers. And it is perhaps foolish to expect him to behave responsibly when, for days and weeks past, he has been doing the very opposite.'

At this point, opposition front bench members could be seen passing a slip of paper from one to the other. Finally, it reached Whiteman, who took it, looked at it, then leaned forward and placed it in front of Page. Page opened it and scanned the contents. He alone knew what they contained, for this was a stage-managed job. He again gripped the sides of the dispatch box. 'Although I have said that the Prime Minister's authoritarian and high-handed disregard for this House has been, and still is, his chief offence, it is of course not the only one. The extent of his miscalculation on this issue is so gross as to constitute an entirely separate reason why he should now resign. For he miscalculated not once but many times. He has vacillated and wavered, he has contradicted himself and shilly-shallied to the point where his performance, on behalf of this country, has been embarrassing and shaming. Moreover, his behaviour has contrasted markedly with that of the United States of America, which was thrust into this issue largely as a result of the Prime Minister's mishandling of this affair.

'The United States government, so unlike our own, has behaved throughout with candour and above all with firmness. And, I can now tell the House, this firmness has paid off.' He held aloft the piece of paper Whiteman had handed to him. 'I can reveal that, as we speak, as this debate takes place, the eight statues stolen from the Metropolitan Museum have been recovered. As a result of prompting by the United States government, which, as the House knows, has suspended aid to India, the Madras Regiment today attacked the holy Hindu shrine at Hindupur. Eight Hindus were killed in the raid, and three soldiers. Nineteen, from both sides, were injured. The stolen statues have been recovered but not . . . ' Page looked directly at Lockwood '. . . not without more blood on the Prime Minister's hands.'

A rustle of interest zipped along the Commons benches. This was luck on a spectacular scale, or a masterly stroke of Page's, to have hot news and to deliver it in this fashion. Either way, the Commons admired it. In the Strangers' Gallery, Sir Francis Mordaunt now realized what the journalist had been handing to Page in the central lobby.

'And so, Mr Speaker, the American involvement in this whole shameful episode, this shabby charade played with the culture of this country, the American involvement is over. Honour has been satisfied, and both the Indian and American governments can hold their heads up in international company. Sadly, the same cannot be said of the British government. But in any case, so far as the British government is concerned, the issue is not yet over. In its final act, perhaps, but not over. That may come later tonight. I urge the House to bring this matter to a fitting close. This shabby matter has sullied the good name of Britain for too long.'

Page sat down as roars of approval rang out around him. Feet were stamped on the ground, order papers rustled in the air. On the government side, no one was actually going to applaud the opposition leader openly but there were some, there were definitely some, who stamped their feet. Everyone could feel it.

'Wicked touch about Hindupur,' Lessor mumbled into the Prime Minister's ear.

Lockwood nodded. He looked pensive, sucking his lower lip. It was his turn now, when the clamour died down. He looked up. Hatfield was approaching again. He slumped into the space beside the Prime Minister. 'How much are you planning to say?'

Lockwood looked up at the Commons clock. 'It's twenty five past nine. Not much. Why?'

'Talk for as long as you can. We've found where Zakros and Nancy Tucker are staying in Geneva.'

All it had taken was a phone call. As Victoria had instructed, Edward had called the Berne Hotel, then the Alba. No luck. Then they had started calling the hotels in the old city of Geneva, across the Rhône, by the cathedral. He started with the Helvétique. When the receptionist answered he repeated the patter he had used with the other hotels.

'Just a moment, I'll see.' A pause. Then: 'Well, I don't think we have the entire party here but we do have a Mrs Kimball and a Dr Quincy. Shall I put you through?'

'No, no! Don't do that. You've been very helpful but my job is to locate the people. Our customer liaison officer will visit the hotel in person. Goodnight.'

'As you wish. Goodnight, sir.'

He called Victoria through into his room. Excitedly they pored over the map of Geneva provided by the car rental company when they had hired a car at the airport. They found the hotel easily enough on the map. It was on the Rue Saint-Léger. 'What's the number?' Victoria asked, picking up the phone. She then called the hotel herself and, to Edward's great surprise, booked a room in the Helvétique.

'Is that wise?' Edward asked. 'What if Nancy sees me?'

'You don't have to stay there. But if we want to get hold of the stuff they brought from the bank we're going to have to break into their room, if we get the chance. For that, we need a room of our own, in the same hotel.'

While Edward stayed in the car, Victoria checked into the Helvétique. She returned after about fifteen minutes and leaned into the car through the open window.

'Well,' asked Edward.

'The room's fine. But I don't quite know what to do about Nancy and Zakros, or Kimball and Quincy. The one advantage we may possess is that, at the moment, they are unsure that they're being followed. If I start asking at the reception desk, our questions may just get back to them – '

'Get in!' hissed Edward. 'Over there, by the taxis. It's Nancy.'

Victoria got into the car. Nancy was wearing a white raincoat with a vivid green scarf.

'So that's Nancy Tucker,' murmured Victoria, looking from her to Edward and back again. 'Striking.'

Edward's emotions were finding it hard-going. Nancy certainly did look striking – Victoria was right there. He could imagine all too well her flesh, her breasts, her movements under the raincoat. But then . . . what she had done, the deception, the lies, and now the killing. He would never have believed he could have been so wrong about someone.

As they watched, a man held the taxi door open for Nancy and she got in. Then he got in beside her. The taxi made a U-turn, and as it sped off down the Rue Saint-Léger both Edward and Victoria saw the man lean across and kiss Nancy.

Victoria gripped Edward's arm. He put his hand on hers. 'That must be Zakros. I'm glad I saw that.' He looked at Victoria.

'They seem very relaxed,' she said. 'I wonder why?'

'Yes, it's worrying. They must know everything by now.'

'Can they really think they are safe? Surely not.'

'What about this? They've had a . . . well, unusual day. But . . . Zakros and Nancy are lovers. They've been apart for weeks, maybe months, plotting this thing and hardly ever seeing each other. At last, tonight, they are together. That would be one cause for happiness.'

'Yes, but come on! They killed O'Day and nearly killed Riley.'

'And got away with it, so far as they can tell. Riley was the only witness to the killing, and I assume he's not saying anything, at least not to the Swiss police. He'll have claimed diplomatic privilege, so the Swiss police probably don't have a clue who to look for – what age, sex or name.'

'It doesn't make sense, Edward. Why shouldn't Riley tell the police? He doesn't have to tell them everything.'

'But say the police *catch* Nancy and Zakros first. What's to stop them telling the Swiss police everything? And who's to say one of the police won't earn himself a decent dinner with a call to a newspaper?'

'Hmm. If you say so. But *I* think they should be panicking.

But let's stop nattering. They are out of their room and they didn't have any briefcases with them when they left. That means the stuff is in the hotel – so this is it. One of us ought to follow them but I need you for what I have in mind.'

'And what do you have in mind?'

'Follow me.' She got out of the car and led the way into the hotel. Inside the lobby, she said, 'Borrow the Michelin Guide from the concierge. Pretend you're looking for a place to eat. I'll be back in a moment.'

Feeling rather jittery, in case Nancy should return, Edward did as he was told. Victoria was gone a few minutes but when she returned she was carrying an envelope, a hotel envelope.

'Now, take the Michelin,' she said to Edward, 'and return it to the concierge. Get a good conversation going with him about a restaurant to eat in. I shall interrupt you but your job is to watch where he puts this envelope I'm going to leave with him. It's addressed to Quincy. When you've finished, come up to my room – number thirty-eight. Okay?'

Edward nodded, picked up the book and sauntered over to the front desk. The receptionist was a tall, rather lugubrious man with a Mexican-style moustache. Edward had the Michelin book open at the Geneva pages. 'Excuse me,' he said softly. 'Last time I was in Geneva I tried Le Cygne and the Amphitryon. Quite frankly they were a bit rich . . . I prefer plainer food. Can you suggest somewhere?' He smiled at the concierge and thrust the book towards him.

The concierge took the book but didn't look at it straight away. 'You like Swiss food? French food? Italian? There's a good German restaurant in Geneva and a fish place. What you like?'

Edward shrugged. 'French, I suppose, or Swiss – '

'Excuse me.' Victoria leaned over the desk and held the envelope under the receptionist's nose. 'Today is Dr Quincy's birthday and I'd like him to have this. It's a surprise. Can you put it in his pigeon-hole, please, so he gets it as soon as he returns?' Victoria left it by the Michelin Guide and disappeared back up to the room. Edward watched as the concierge absently picked up the envelope and tapped the Michelin Guide with it. 'I would recommend L'Or du Rhône, or, if that's too expensive, or you can't get in, the Buffet Cornavin.' He looked up, smiled, then turned and placed the envelope in pigeon-hole number sixteen.

'Thank you,' said Edward. 'I'll try the Buffet first, I think. I'll call from the room.' He retreated up the stairs.

The hotel was made for burglary, as Victoria put it. Short corridors, tiny cul-de-sacs which gave on to the staircase. This meant that Edward could keep watch while she went about breaking and entering.

They found room sixteen at the back of the hotel where it probably overlooked the Petit Palais Museum. 'Ready?' whispered Victoria. She took a set of skeleton keys from her pocket and twirled them in her fingers. 'We're given a course on these at Didcot. They're the American Express Card of the security services: we never leave home without them.' She grinned. 'This shouldn't be too difficult.'

Edward nodded. 'You seem confident.'

'I've been trained. The British government believes women make just as good burglars as men. My aunt would have approved.'

She bent to the lock. Edward heard a click, then a deeper click, then a rattle, still louder. Then he heard Victoria whisper again, 'Voilà!' – and the door swung open.

'A great deal has been heard about morality in this House today. But maybe we should take a look at the morality of this debate.' Lockwood leaned his elbows on the dispatch box. The chamber was perfectly still. He had stopped sweating. As his time to speak had approached, the Prime Minister had been more nervous than he had let on to any of his close colleagues. Normally he was not at all nervous and he knew that, other things being equal, he performed well. But other things were not equal. Andover and Tatton in Geneva had located the blackmailers again, but what exactly did that mean? Did it mean that he would get some news in the next fifteen minutes? News which would mean that the complexion of this whole debate would change? The closeness of the timing had wrong-footed him, he had to admit it, so that now, in this the most important speech of his political career, he was not giving his best. He knew it, and that made his performance even worse. People would conclude that he really was losing his grip.

'I would like to ask the House a question. A set of questions. The first is this: Is not the return of the Elgin Marbles, so-called, a moral issue? Should governments not lead on moral issues? I seem to remember being lectured, earlier today, on that very subject, when it was said emphatically that governments should give such a lead.' He hunched further forward over the dispatch box. 'Here is another question: what would have happened if I had announced to this House that the government was thinking of returning the Elgin Marbles? I will tell you what would have happened. A great deal more hot air than has been generated even in the past few days. And maybe much more than hot air. A great deal has been made of the demonstrations, the arson attacks and – yes – the death of the security guard in New York. You may even throw in the deaths at Hindupur if you wish. The collision of those tankers in the Thames. The vigil in Athens. These arguments have been paraded through the newspapers and throughout this debate. But I say to the House: had the government simply announced that it was *thinking* of sending back the Marbles then the troubles might have been far worse. There would have been debate, yes, but there could easily have been demonstrations, there could have been – '

'Rubbish!' yelled a voice from the opposition backbenches. 'Rubbish!'

Taken aback, Lockwood faltered. Seeing him falter, weaker souls now joined in the catcalls. Cries of 'Rubbish!' sailed around the benches, accompanied by foot-stamping and even a cry of 'Resign!'

Lockwood knew he had to get a grip on the House. He stood up straight. He raised his voice. 'This House cackles about morality, yet won't even stop to listen to the argument.'

'You didn't stop to listen, Lockwood,' someone shouted. 'You just stormed ahead. We had nothing to listen to!'

'I *will* be heard,' Lockwood shouted. 'I will be heard.'

The Speaker now stood, meaning that all other members, Lockwood included, had to be seated. 'Order! Order!' the Speaker shouted. 'The House will come to order.'

Complete silence did not return but the din subsided. Before he sat down again, the Speaker cried, 'The Prime Minister will continue.'

'But not for long,' someone else shouted, earning a wave of laughter.

'Order! Order!' The Speaker stood again.

This time the noise subsided more quickly and as it did so

Lockwood got to his feet and approached the dispatch box. He waited for a moment so that he might better be heard but also for effect. 'I will not be lectured on morality in this House by the honourable gentleman opposite. Contrary to what he has claimed, this government, my government, has done nothing to be ashamed of. The fact that our action was unilateral does not make it unnatural as he implies, or humiliating. On the contrary, it shows that some people in Britain, some people who, fortunately, are in government, can act from the best of motives, where immediate personal gain is not the only measure by which they lead their lives. I cannot be the only one in this House who has been disgusted to hear the self-righteous self-interest shown in this debate, by weasels who – '

'Withdraw! Withdraw!' The cry was immediately taken up by many backbenchers, and the opposition front bench too.

Lockwood was sweating now. That remark had been a mistake.

'Withdraw! Withdraw!' They would not be silenced.

The Speaker was on his feet again and the Prime Minister gave way. 'Order! Order!'

Arthur Page was on his feet too, as the noise subsided. 'Mr Speaker, it ill behoves the Prime Minister, who is the subject of this debate, to use words such as "weasel" about honourable members. I accept that he is more familiar with weasel behaviour than any of us. Yet he should withdraw the remark. It is yet another example of the way he is losing his grip on events.'

'Withdraw! Withdraw!'

Lockwood stood and approached the dispatch box. He had recovered some of his composure. 'I am grateful to the right honourable member for his advice,' he said in a sarcastic tone. 'I have sat here all day and heard myself described as a coward – '

'Hear, hear' rang out from the opposition benches.

'– as inept – '

'Hear, hear.'

'– as a shilly-shallyer and an authoritarian at the same time – '

'Hear, hear.'

'It therefore seems to me, Mr Speaker, that "weasel" is only too appropriate. The honourable gentlemen on the other side spend most of their time underground and only emerge when they sense a kill.'

This time cries of 'Withdraw!' mingled with 'Resign!', 'Disgrace!', 'Shame!'. The foot-stamping started again, combined with a general din. The Speaker, knowing he couldn't stop it, at least for the time being, remained seated and Lockwood still stood at the dispatch box. He looked up to the Distinguished Strangers' Gallery where Mordaunt sat, his legs crossed in elegant fashion. He returned Lockwood's stare without blinking.

The hubbub died down.

'Honourable gentlemen opposite have their tails up now. Like many beasts of prey they hunt in packs – and only in packs.' He rushed on before they could interrupt again. 'But I ask the rest of the House, the more reasonable and intelligent parts of it – '

More cries of 'Withdraw' but he pressed on anyway.

'– I ask them to place this whole episode in its proper perspective. This country is in the process of returning to another country one work of art, one set of stone sculptures. That country – Greece – is, let us not forget, the cradle of democracy, one of the founding fathers of Western culture as we know it and as we enjoy it, day in and day out.' He spread his arms wide. 'And that is all the episode is about. Nothing more. To see in it some wider conspiracy is to stretch the opposition's admittedly limited imagination beyond breaking point. This is no major issue of defence, of health expenditure, of educational priorities. Honourable members have made much of the fact that these objects, these sculptures, have a great beauty. We have been told that the arts have a special place in our lives, a place that can only grow in importance as religion declines. I must say that I agree with that view but I wonder if, in this debate, it has not been overstated. I wonder when the right honourable gentleman opposite,' and Lockwood waved dismissively at Page, 'I wonder when he last went to a museum, or to the opera. When did he last buy a painting or visit the theatre?'

Lockwood could see Page looking uncomfortable and he smiled. 'Yes, I see from the guilty look on his face that it must have been some time ago. As someone else said in another context, "Make me good, Lord – but not just yet." ' That got the Prime Minister a few laughs from his own side. But not many. 'So I say to the House: don't get this matter out of perspective, don't lose your sense of priorities. This is an issue which has been blown up out of all proportion by an opposition that is, despite all its high-flown talk, more interested in bringing down a government than in anything else. More interested in its own welfare than in the welfare of this nation. More corrupted by its

364

own selfishness than it is willing to admit and is therefore blind to the merits of any case other than its own.' He raised his voice, till he was nearly shouting. 'This is a mean opposition – '

'Mean and lean,' someone shouted and there was a ripple of laughter.

'Mean-spirited, mean-minded, small and inward-looking – '

The roar was growing on the opposition benches now.

Lockwood opened his mouth to shout them down, but then he noticed that a small envelope had been slid on to the dispatch box in front of him. The House watched as he picked it up. He seemed excited, but was this a similar ploy to Page's – with a similar dramatic intent? Lockwood turned and looked at Hatfield. The Chief Whip shrugged, meaning he didn't know the contents. Lockwood tore at the envelope. Maybe this was what he had been waiting for all day.

The House watched, more or less in silence. What was going on?

Lockwood seized the paper inside the envelope and opened it flat. The note was hand-written and read:

Our side broke into the Greeks' hotel room in Geneva less than ninety minutes ago. The room was empty. Don't expect any more news tonight. Sorry.

Midwinter

Lockwood crumpled the paper in the palm of his hand but to the others in the House, watching him, it was the Prime Minister who seemed to crumple. His shoulders suddenly sagged and he seemed to grow physically smaller. He took a handerkerchief from his pocket and wiped his forehead. 'Mr Speaker, the House has heard the honourable gentlemen on the opposite side do their worst. They are not very good when it comes to doing their worst and, I can assure the House, they would be no better if they had a chance to work at something more positive – like occupying the government benches. This has all been a diversion, Mr Speaker, diverting for those with nothing better to do but no more than that. I reject the criticisms implicit in this debate and I accept the challenge thrown down by the other side.'

He sat down. There was a short-lived roar of approval from the government's own backbenches but it was soon overtaken by the rustle and bustle of chatter as the House now looked forward to the vote, or asked itself what had been inside the last-minute note the Prime Minister had received, or assessed his performance in relation to Page's.

As the division bells rang people stood, to stretch their legs. One or two gambling members were quietly arranging their wagers on the outcome of the vote. The tellers were being marshalled into place.

'What was in the note?' Hatfield whispered.

Lockwood passed him the wrinkled paper. Hatfield opened it and read the message for himself. 'Oh,' he breathed. 'Oh dear.'

'I wasn't at my best, Joss. I know that. But what does the arithmetic look like now?'

'Not more than three or four in it either way. You must understand, Bill, that on occasions like this there will always be some backbenchers who refuse – on principle, they say – to tell the whips what they are going to do. It is the only time when they have real power over us and there are always some who want to rub it in.'

They both watched as members moved towards the lobbies, for the count. Seeing them looking, an opposition backbencher grinned and shouted to his colleagues. 'This way to the weasels' den. Come on, weasels . . . Remember, we hunt in packs. This way to the kill.' There was laughter, and other members surged after him.

'When I think of that large, spongy bed up there I could weep.'

'Don't think about it. Count my freckles instead.'

Victoria groaned. It had been a shock to discover that the room used by Nancy and Zakros was empty. At first neither she nor Edward had been able to believe it and had searched the room again. But it was empty all right.

And it had been a shock for Edward to see Nancy's things in the room, next to the Greek's.

They had gone back to Victoria's room to call London and confer with Leith. As a result of that, they had decided they had no choice but to keep watch on the hotel from their rented car, all night if necessary. On their way out, Victoria had reclaimed the envelope she had given the receptionist for 'Dr Quincy'. She explained that she now preferred to give it to him in person.

Twenty minutes before, they had watched Nancy and Zakros

return from – where? The all-important luggage was either in the hotel safe or somewhere else – the left-luggage compartments at the railway station, for example. There was an anonymous safety in that.

'Where do you think they went?'

Victoria shook her head. 'Search me. There's something that worries me more.'

Edward stroked her shoulder. 'What's that?'

'Why are they so relaxed? You saw them when they came back just now – very lovey-dovey . . .'

Yes. Edward had seen that.

'Smiling and kissing. It's unnatural in these circumstances. I tell you, Edward, there's more to this than we know.'

The benches were filling again, as members filed out of the lobbies. One thing was immediately clear: the amount of people entering and leaving each lobby was more or less the same – it was going to be very close.

The Prime Minister returned to his place, with Hatfield and Lessor behind him. George Keld had remained in his seat below the gangway, with one or two others on the backbenches. What neither Hatfield nor the junior whips knew was how many more cowardly rebels had left the chamber altogether, so as not to be seen to be abstaining.

They all sat and waited as the Speaker resumed his seat. As the last members returned to the benches, the four tellers, two from either side, approached the Speaker's chair. A cough rang out somewhere in the chamber – it was the only sound. One of the tellers was holding a slip of paper with the count on it.

'The Ayes to the right, two hundred and ninety-eight votes. The Noes to the left, two hundred and ninety-four – '

Before the teller could finish a great roar swept around the Commons, and Page and his colleagues were on their feet. Lockwood felt a cold tide rise up his spine and the hair at his temples was damp with sweat.

He had lost.

28

Tuesday

'Do you think we could risk one of us going off for coffee?'

'No,' said Edward. 'The New York flight – assuming they are still going – is at eleven. Check-in by nine-thirty to ten o'clock. In normal circumstances that means leaving here around eight forty-five, nine o'clock. But if they did leave the stuff at the railway station, say, they will have to leave the hotel even earlier.'

'But it's only just seven now. That gives us an hour, just to buy a measly cup of coffee and – '

'We can't risk losing them. Lockwood would skin us alive.'

'You do realize that, for all we know, Lockwood may no longer be Prime Minister? Shouldn't we check in with London? Our orders may have changed.'

'We're staying put. I'd rather be chewed out for being over-zealous than for letting these two slip away from us. Nancy's not getting away with anything.'

Seven-thirty came, eight o'clock.

At nine-thirty Victoria voiced what they were both thinking. 'They're going to miss their plane unless they get a move on.'

'Change of plan?'

'Oh yes. A change of plan. But . . . to what?'

'Good morning if you have just joined us and welcome to BBC Radio's Breakfast News. Late last night in the House of Commons Mr William Lockwood was defeated in a censure motion on his handling of the Elgin Marbles affair. So far there have been calls for the Prime Minister to resign from Mr Arthur Page, leader of the opposition, and from two daily newspapers, *The Times* and the *Guardian*. But there has been no word from Downing Street. In the studio with me I have our chief political correspondent, James Nickerson. James, what is the form from here on in, in a case like this? Is the Prime Minister's resignation automatic? How does he go about resigning and what happens then?'

'Well, of course, Britain is a country which is famous for not having a written constitution. Therefore nothing is certain, even in a serious situation like this. To my way of thinking, there is no question but that William Lockwood will have to resign as leader of his party very soon, if not today. He would remain as Prime Minister while a leadership contest was arranged. Alternatively, he could call a general election if he thought he was more popular in the country than in the House. However, the opinion polls do not bear that out. My understanding is that he is to lunch with the Queen – an unusual move that, but then these are unusual days. In normal circumstances, he would pay the Queen a short visit, to tender his resignation and then drive straight to Parliament to make a statement. I am assuming that he will go to the Commons after his lunch with Her Majesty. In the Commons, he will make his statement and I assume, resign. Once he resigned as party leader, if that is the course he adopts, he would remain as caretaker Prime Minister until a leadership contest either re-elected him or produced a new one. But, as I keep saying, these are not ordinary times and this course of events may be varied in a number of ways.'

'Such as?'

'Well, this is where it gets truly intriguing. Since we have no constitution, there is nothing in principle to stop the Prime Minister from calling a general election, *without* resigning. The Prime Minister is not popular at Westminster after the last few weeks but no one really knows how this whole Elgin Marbles business is going down in the country at large. Now, if Lockwood simply called a general election, he would in all probability remain as leader of the party throughout the campaign – there simply would not be time to organize a leadership contest and it would clearly be suicidal from the party's point of view to even attempt to do so in the middle of a three-week general election campaign. It would be a hell of a gamble for Lockwood, and the party would not forgive him if he lost. But it would deny Keld a crack at the leadership, at least for the time being. And, as a result, either Lockwood would get back, or Page would. But not Keld.'

'As you say, these are intriguing possibilities, James, but which path do you expect Lockwood to follow?'

'He looked pretty shattered to me when the debate finished last night. It may be that he has lost the capacity to fight, which you need if you are to remain as Prime Minister. I suspect he will be visited by some of the party chiefs this morning, who will tell him that he no longer has the automatic support and loyalty of the majority of the parliamentary party. Remember, a lot of people who voted for the government last night did so only because there was a three-line whip. They weren't disaffected enough to defy the whips, but that doesn't mean they liked what was happening, or what has been happening over this Marbles business.'

'James Nickerson, thank you very much. That's all from us for the moment – except for this late news flash. The Elgin Marbles have still not arrived in Greece but, according to news from Piraeus, a Greek tanker passed HMS *Anglesey* in the Aegean Sea two nights ago and reports that she was "dressed" for an official arrival. In anticipation of this, the Greek government have announced that they are to give Mr William Lockwood a national honour. Now, here is the weather.'

The weather in Geneva at last gave signs that summer was about to break after all. In between the fluffy clouds, the sun shone bright and clear.

'Now, what's this?' Edward rubbed his chin. The stubble was a familiar feel these days. Both he and Victoria watched as a blue Renault drew up outside the Helvétique. A man got out, locked the doors and went into the hotel. 'Relax,' said Edward. 'Nothing to do with us.'

The Rue Saint-Léger was busy without being congested. They had watched as the shops opened up one by one. An electrician's, a charcuterie, a shop selling dolls and toys. There was a café further along the street but Edward was still saying it was too far away to risk going.

'Look!' he suddenly whispered. 'Here they are.'

They both sat up in their seats as Nancy and Zakros came out of the hotel. Each carried an overnight bag and Zakros had some papers in his hands. The man who had arrived in the blue Renault came out with them and stood on the pavement. 'It's a rented car. They had it delivered.' Edward's fingers drummed the wheel as they watched Zakros open the driver's door and then throw the bags on to the back seat. 'So they're not going to the airport. No one would bother to hire a car for a twenty-minute journey. There *has* been a change of plan.'

They watched as Nancy got into the passenger seat. The engine was switched on and the car moved off. The man who had delivered the car disappeared back inside the hotel. Edward let the Renault get about three hundred yards away and then followed. The blue car turned right, down a hill, then left on to the Rue Jacques Delcroze which led under two bridges to a large roundabout. At the roundabout the Renault went straight ahead, before turning left on to the Avenue Pictet de Rochemont. This led to the bridge which crossed the Rhône, where it drained out of the lake.

'They're going towards the airport,' breathed Edward.

'And lots of other places too.'

Across the bridge, the blue car went straight up the Rue Mont Blanc into the Rue Chantepoulet. It turned right at Notre-Dame. 'The station!' breathed Edward. 'We were right all along. They left the stuff here.' He stopped the red Audi at the edge of the square, facing the station. Nancy and Zakros got out of the Renault, leaving it with its amber hazard lights flashing. They entered the station under a sign which said 'Livraison des Baggages' – left luggage.

The square was busy. Buses, cars, taxis and trams all circled slowly, dropping off or picking up. Five minutes passed. 'Bit of a while, aren't they?' Edward bit his lip.

'Maybe there's a queue. Shall I look?'

'I don't want to show our faces unless we have to. Give it a while longer.'

Five more minutes passed.

'Okay,' said Edward. 'You go, my face is known. Check out the baggage counter. But try not to be obvious.'

Victoria got out of the car and sauntered across the square. There were puddles from the previous day's rain but they were vanishing rapidly in the sunshine. Edward watched as Victoria hovered outside the left luggage and then, gingerly, went inside. Edward kept his gaze fixed on the doors.

Less than a minute had elapsed when Victoria reappeared. She waved frantically for Edward to hurry over and there was no attempt to be discreet. He put the car in gear, dodged a bus that was entering the square and drove across to the station. He switched off, put on the handbrake and opened the door. He went to speak but Victoria got in first. 'They're not here. I asked

371

at the counter – no one like them has picked up any bags in the last half-hour.'

Edward was already running into the main lobby of the station, which opened off the left luggage department. He stood in front of the 'Arrivals and Departures' board. Victoria followed him. 'Nothing has left in the last ten minutes – '

'The next train is for Zurich – platform three.'

'Watch the taxis, in case they try to trick us.' Edward ran along the underpass and up the steps to platform three. He scanned the people waiting. Neither Nancy nor Zakros was among them. He ran back to the front of the station where Victoria was waiting. She shook her head. 'No sign of them.'

'Ssshhhugar!' hissed Edward. 'They were clever. We thought they were relaxed last night. It was an act! They left the hotel as a lure, to see if someone broke into their room. They probably left the room arranged in such a way that we were bound to disturb something. That told them they were being followed, watched. And it gave them all night to work out a plan to deceive us. They obviously didn't have time to pick up any of the Blunt stuff – but used the left luggage counter as a delaying device. But if they didn't take a train, or taxi, what did they do?'

'Look!' said Victoria, and pointed.

Edward followed her gaze. At the far end of the station building was a red sign. In white letters it said 'Alpine', and then, underneath, 'Car hire'.

He was already running. He skidded to a halt outside the door of the Alpine office and then walked slowly across to the desk. 'Has my brother-in-law picked up his car yet?' he said casually to the woman behind the desk. He gave Zakros's name. She smiled and said, 'Oh, you've just missed him. They left – oh, five or six minutes ago.'

Edward groaned – but then his manner changed abruptly. He dipped into his inside pocket and took out his wallet. He fished out a hundred-franc note. 'What sort of car was it and what was the registration number?' The girl stared at him. This was not brother-in-law behaviour. Edward took another note from his wallet. 'Quickly!'

A man sitting at a desk overheard this exchange and came towards them. 'What is it, Monica?'

'This person wants information about a client.'

The man looked at Edward, then at the notes. He smiled and

took the money from the counter. 'I'll deal with this.' He bent to delve in the records. After a moment, he took out a sheet and handed it across to Edward.

Edward scanned the paper. Zakros had rented a Mercedes, white. Edward scribbled down the registration number.

'They didn't say where they were going, did they?'

Monica looked across and shrugged. 'No. Few people do – though they did ask where they might buy maps of France.'

Victoria and Edward hurried back to their car. 'But where in France?' she asked of the air in general.

'First things first,' said Edward. 'I've just realized – last night, when they reached their hotel, they didn't know they were being followed, so they must have had the Blunt stuff with them. They probably left it in the hotel strong-room while they went out, just to be on the safe side.' He started the car and they drove off. 'They confirmed when they got back that they were being followed – which is why they worked out the plan to drop us.' He turned left into the Rue Chantepoulet, past the church and back down towards the lake. 'But they abandoned the bags they took in the blue Renault – they needed to do that to convince anyone following that they were just stopping off at the left luggage.' The Audi reached the crossroads before the bridge. 'Therefore they have to go back to the hotel first, to collect the Blunt stuff, before going on anywhere else.'

Edward pulled rapidly away, across the bridge, retracing their route of a few minutes earlier. He was as nippy as he could be but the traffic was heavy and they were trapped several times. When they did reach the Helvétique, it was immediately clear that there was no white Mercedes in the vicinity. Edward stopped the Audi and marched into the hotel lobby. He buttonholed the receptionist they had talked with the night before. 'Has Dr Quincy left yet?'

'I believe so – let me ask.' The man turned and spoke with his colleague.

'Yes,' said the colleague. 'They were shopping, they said, and didn't want to leave their luggage in the car. But they collected it oh, about fifteen minutes ago. And they paid their bill earlier this morning, of course.'

'Of course,' said Edward forcing a smile on to his face. He stepped outside with Victoria and got back into the Audi. He was not given to swearing but there was a word Nancy had been fond of. 'Sonsabitches!' he hissed.

Victoria opened out the map and spread it over her knees. 'France! Jesus, there must be five or six ways out of Geneva into France. The place is *surrounded* by France.'

Edward looked at her, then snatched at the map. He studied it for a few moments.

'What is it?'

'You don't know what you just said.'

'I don't?'

Edward handed back the map and started the car. He accelerated up the Rue Saint-Léger and turned right, hurrying back down the hill to the Boulevard Jacques Delcroze. 'I'm sure I'm right but I'll explain as we go.' He turned right at the Rue F. Hodler. 'Nancy and Zakros couldn't know they had been rumbled until yesterday evening, when they got back to their room. They couldn't have known we would get on to them when we did, so they would have had to work out a completely new plan during the night. Even now they may be in the dark about all the details. They must have contacted someone in Greece by now – someone in Kofas's organization, Stamatis Leondaris's wife, even if there are no other members of the Brigade. So they found out about the Cessna. As a result of that, perhaps, they set a trap for us. Now they will have put two and two together. They successfully lured us away – and gave us the slip. But they had to come back here, I mean to the hotel. We have confirmed that.' He slowed at the Boulevard des Tranchées, then accelerated into the Route de Malagnou. 'Now, the fact that they behaved the way that they did at the railway station proves that they thought they were being followed – '

'Well, of course – '

'If you're being followed, you don't leave clues as to where you are going.'

'But they didn't. Not really. As I said, there are six or seven ways into France from here.'

'They're not going to France.'

'What? How do you know?'

'I don't know. I'm guessing. But it's a good guess. That's why they asked the woman at the Alpine car rental about maps for France. They wanted to wrong-foot us but in a not too obvious way. There was always the chance that whoever was following them would eventually find their way to Alpine, as we did. So they spread a little gentle confusion.'

'Then where –?'

'There are two possibilities. Either they could stay in Switzerland. They could go to ground, here in Geneva, sit still for a few days. But they need to get to a good newspaper and Geneva doesn't have one. So that means Zurich. The *Neue Zürcher Zeitung*.' He pulled out, to pass an enormous Dutch coach. 'But think about that for a moment. This story isn't exactly flattering to the Swiss. It reflects badly on Swiss banking laws and on Swiss banks. All that Nazi loot secreted away. Knowing the Swiss, there's a good chance that the newspaper Nancy and Zakros went to would turn them in, rather than publish anything damaging to their precious banks.'

'So?'

'So . . . that leaves the second alternative.' Edward pointed ahead, at the road sign they were approaching.

'Chamonix?' said Victoria. 'That's France, too.'

'Mont Blanc,' said Edward. 'The tunnel. It leads to Italy. Italy has plenty of good papers – in Milan, Florence, Rome, Naples. For that matter they can sail to Greece or fly to America from there.'

'But how can we be so certain?'

'We can't. We've just got to risk it.'

'Why not alert the French or Italian police – get them to close the border?'

'How are we going to convince them over the phone? And without telling them everything? And how long would it take? Chamonix is eighty kilometres away, fifty miles. Motorway for most of it. Thirty-five, forty minutes at the most. We couldn't even get a helicopter in time – and once they are in Italy they can take any number of roads, abandon their Mercedes and hire something else.'

Victoria lapsed into silence as Edward manoeuvred the car through the Geneva suburbs. In a few moments they reached the border with France. They sailed through. Victoria remarked gloomily, 'They probably got the same treatment, too.'

Edward pushed the Audi to 190 kilometres per hour, close to a 120 miles an hour, and held it there. Neither spoke. The Mercedes ahead of them was easily capable of the same speed and more. If Nancy and Zakros were worried about being followed – and they must have been apprehensive, at the least – they would certainly have pushed the Merc as fast as it would go. Which meant Edward and Victoria had no chance of catching them. They passed Vetraz and Arenthon. By now the day had cleared gloriously and the sun shone from almost directly in front of them. They passed Bonneville, where the road crossed the river Arve, according to the sign. The valley sides began to close in about them. Towards Cluses the road began to rise, lifted on huge stilts. A temporary roadworks sign loomed.

'Jesus!' groaned Victoria. 'Just what we need.'

'With luck, it might be exactly what we need,' replied Edward. 'Keep your fingers crossed. How far ahead do you think they are? If they are ahead.'

'Ten, fifteen minutes. Maybe a bit more.'

The temporary road signs showed that the traffic in their direction was crossing to the other side of the divide and that for six kilometres the traffic was two-way. Small plastic poles were inserted in the carriageway every twenty yards or so and overtaking was forbidden. Edward drove fast right behind a lorry labouring up the incline. He was forced to slow to around 40 kilometres an hour, barely 25 mph. Two trucks rumbled past in the opposite direction, then a coach. Immediately afterwards, Edward pulled out. The Audi moved into the other lane, between two of the poles, and Edward changed down. He accelerated past the truck that had been ahead of him, then past another. The driver sounded his horn and flashed his lights. Ahead, a car coming towards them was flashing its lights. Edward pulled back in between two poles and accelerated away from the forward truck.

The next traffic was about half a mile ahead and again he raced up to it, changed down, and pulled out as soon as there was a chance to do so. He passed two coaches, their occupants goggle-eyed as the Audi raced past them. Edward pulled in again when he had to, this time snicking one of the poles which sounded tougher than it was. Looking in the rear-view mirror he could see he had left it bent and bouncing around the road. The forward coach of the two blared its horn. But Edward was accelerating away again. 'If Nancy and her lover got behind a slow truck we could be making up minutes,' he breathed grimly. Twice more he slipped the Audi into the oncoming lane. Twice more the other traffic – in both directions – flashed their lights and blared their horns. Once more he hit a pole and sent it careering across the roadway and underneath an oncoming lorry. Had the driver of the lorry braked there might have been the most almighty collision but he had the sense simply to run over the pole and crush it.

Then the roadworks were over and they were crossing the divide, back on to a clear carriageway. Edward edged the Audi close to 200 kilometres per hour but he could feel it growing less stable; the wheel had a slight tremble. He didn't let up. They passed Magland and Sallanches. 'What's the time?'

'Quarter to twelve.'

'How long since Geneva?'

'Twenty-one minutes, since you ask.'

'We might have saved . . . four, five minutes on that incline? That still leaves them three or four minutes ahead, a long way on a motorway.'

'If they came this way in the first place.'

Edward didn't respond, except to press his foot harder on the accelerator pedal, even though it was already flat against the footwell. They passed Le Fayet and then Servoz. Then a sign which said, 'Mont Blanc tunnel, 12 km'.

'Seven miles.'

The valley sides were now very close to the road and the air felt cooler all of a sudden. Both scanned the road ahead. A sign told them they were coming to the toll area, where they had to pay for the autoroute. 'Lie back, close your eyes,' said Edward.

'What –?'

'Do it!' At the same time he switched his headlights full on. Ahead of him was a row of seven or eight toll booths and leading back from each of these were lines of cars and caravans, nine or ten vehicles long. Edward pulled over to one side and drove past the lines. He pulled up very close to the right-hand booth and, at the same time, rolled down his window. To the irate driver of the car next to him he gesticulated to Victoria and shouted: 'Hôpital! Crise de coeur! Hôpital!'

The driver looked, then beckoned Edward forward.

Waving his thanks, he eased the car in front and stopped by the cashier. As he handed some money to the woman, he said quietly to Victoria. 'There's a white Mercedes just gone through. I don't know whether it's them or, if it is, whether they've seen us.'

The woman gave them their change and Edward sped off. He

accelerated, but now the autoroute came down to two lanes and they were blocked behind a caravan. The driver of that took several seconds to pass another, very similar caravan. By the time Edward was free, the traffic was slowing for the border control as they left France.

'Got it!' said Victoria. 'White Mercedes, five cars ahead.'

One by one the cars were waved through the border control without being stopped. As the Audi approached the uniformed passport control officer, however, he waved Edward to a stop.

'Now what?' Victoria groaned.

The man was pointing. Edward opened the door and looked back. Part of the chrome flashing of the Audi had come away and was hanging down. It had been dislodged by one of the plastic poles he had hit. Edward put on the handbrake, got out and twisted the strip back and forth, back and forth, until it snapped off. 'Merci,' he cried to the passport officer and got back into the Audi. He threw the chrome strip on to the back seat, eased off the handbrake and moved the car forward.

The tunnel mouth loomed ahead, a dark cylinder illuminated by amber lights. The first part had two lanes going in each direction but that soon narrowed to one. Overtaking was again forbidden and for the first kilometre there were yet more short poles in the centre of the road – sturdy metal ones this time. Again Edward pulled up behind the caravan in front of him and, when he could, when the dividing poles stopped, he pulled out and passed it. A coach coming towards them flashed its head-lights. For a few moments the oncoming traffic was too heavy to do any more overtaking.

'How long is the tunnel?' asked Victoria.

'Seventeen kilometres, end to end, ten and a half miles. Four-teen kilometres to go.' Suddenly the road cleared and Edward was able to pull out again. He passed two cars and a van. As he pulled in again, there was a Volvo shooting-brake immediately in front and, ahead of that, a white Mercedes.

'It's them!' said Victoria. 'Nancy just looked back.'

'Yes – they've seen us.'

The oncoming traffic cleared again, and now the Mercedes moved out too, overtaking a BMW. Edward pulled out and passed the Volvo but was forced to pull in behind the BMW. An articulated truck went past in the opposite direction. More traffic – coaches mainly – was bearing down on them.

'Nancy is leaning over to the back seat,' Victoria said. 'She's pulling at something, a bag I think.'

They watched as she turned back in her seat. Since there was a car in between them, it wasn't easy for Victoria or Edward to see clearly what was going on in the Merc. The headlights of the oncoming traffic didn't help either. The Mercedes accelerated, to about 80 kilometres per hour, 50 mph. The BMW, with a Turin number plate, accelerated to keep pace. Edward gave silent thanks for the competitiveness of Italian drivers. He too accelerated, and so did the Volvo, which was still behind him.

'She's raising her arm. A lot of activity. I wonder – '

Suddenly an object shot up through the open sun-roof of the Mercedes. It was a bag, a Vuitton-type holdall, soft, without a frame but sturdy and full of soft things by the look of it. As they watched, it flopped on to the boot of the Mercedes and rolled backwards to the road.

'Watch out!' shouted Victoria as the BMW struck the bag and braked fiercely. Cars, caravans and a truck raced towards them on the other side of the road. Edward stood on his brake and Victoria put her hands on the dashboard to avoid being thrown against the windscreen. The tyres of the Audi – along with others, squealed under the pressure, the high pitch ricocheting around the tunnel gallery. By dint of pressure, and skill, Edward managed to keep the Audi fairly straight and he avoided hitting the BMW. Just a fraction of a second after he had stopped, however, the Volvo slammed the Audi from behind. The thud was felt in their backs as the car was shunted forward, so far forward in fact that the Audi was forced against the BMW, which was badly dented but shot forward a few yards under the impact. Behind them the sounds of battered metal told Edward that four, five or more vehicles had piled into one another. The white Mercedes was already fifty yards away and accelerating.

'Ssshit!'

One or more of the cars behind must have slewed across the road because the traffic coming in the opposite direction was now braking hard.

Edward and Victoria got out of the Audi and looked back. Yes, half a dozen cars were mangled together. They walked forward to where the driver of the BMW was trying to extract the Vuitton bag from under his vehicle. Edward and Victoria bent to give him a hand.

'Who were those people?' the Italian asked. 'Crazy – and I didn't even get the number.'

'Don't worry,' said Edward. 'I did. Here, let's pull together.'

The bag, oily, dirty and now torn, yielded when they all pulled – but it cracked the BMW's number plate as it came out. Edward threw it to one side. 'I shunted you rather badly, I'm afraid. You'd better have a look.' They walked back to begin examining the damage. 'The man in the Volvo is bleeding,' said Edward, pointing. The BMW driver set off to look, but Edward tapped Victoria on the shoulder and pointed to the Italian-registered car. She grasped his intention immediately.

As the Italian bent to examine the Volvo driver, Edward and Victoria quickly opened the BMW doors and slid inside. The engine hadn't even been turned off. Edward put it into gear and accelerated away. The Italian looked up, shouted and started to run towards them. But it was too late. The BMW was badly dented in the rear but it was otherwise undamaged. As Edward accelerated away, they passed the sign which announced they were crossing the mid-point of the tunnel. Just over eight kilometres to Italy, a shade over five miles. Edward accelerated past 50 kilometres per hour, 80, 100. The limit was 70. He reached 130 kph. Now there were tail-lights ahead. Heavy traffic was coming towards them but Edward didn't slow down. He assumed no one else would take the sort of risks he took.

The BMW closed on the tail-lights fast. As they reached the Mercedes, they saw – in the headlights – Nancy turn and look back. Edward switched the BMW's headlights fully on so that they dazzled her and Zakros. The bag incident had snapped something inside Edward. Nancy was unnatural, evil. He was at last beginning to hate her. Nancy turned back again and they saw her shouting something at Zakros. Edward drove right up behind the Mercedes, as he had done behind other cars and trucks on the autoroute, but this time he didn't stop. He shunted the Mercedes, trying to force Zakros to wobble and brake at the same time. That might provoke him into a skid.

Nancy looked back again. Edward shunted the back of the Mercedes a second time. There was a loud clanging but nothing else happened. He cursed the fact that Mercedes were very tough cars.

Suddenly, the Merc swung out into the oncoming lane and accelerated past a long Citroën that was in front. A truck that was bearing down blared its horn and flashed its lights. Edward was forced to stay behind the Citroën.

'Watch out in case they try the bag trick again,' said Victoria.

'You think I'd forget that easily?'

But it didn't happen.

'They must have run out of bags,' said Victoria. 'Only the Blunt stuff left.'

Seconds later the Merc moved out again, but so did Edward. The Merc overtook a small truck, the BMW overtook the Citroën. Another kilometre sign went by. The Merc moved out and overtook a caravan, the BMW overtook the small truck. A further sign announced that the 'Dogana', customs, was six kilometres away. Heavy oncoming traffic kept anyone from overtaking before another two kilometre signs had passed. Four to go; two and a half miles. The Mercedes moved out again, and so did Edward. He passed the caravan but the Merc had passed two trucks and there was no more time – Edward had to dip back in behind the second of the trucks. The cars and buses bearing down on them were blaring their horns and flashing their headlights. The three-kilometre sign went by. Edward changed down. The engine raced but it gave him the acceleration he needed for when the traffic thinned.

If it thinned.

They passed two huge cylindrical fans hanging from the roof of the tunnel, the machinery which kept the air circulating. The Mercedes moved out and Edward hit the floor with his accelerator foot, pulling on the wheel at the same time. As the car surged forward he noticed, out of the corner of his eye, the two-kilometre sign flash past. Just over a mile to daylight and Italy.

The BMW kept going faster – he was catching the Merc.

Edward overtook the first of the trucks. A bus was coming towards them, three hundred yards away. The Merc, seventy yards ahead, swung back on to the proper side of the roadway. Edward held the BMW steady. The forward truck was very long. The bus was blaring its horn, flashing its lights. The BMW was abreast of the cab of the truck. It was ahead. Edward heaved on the wheel and slid the BMW in front of the truck. The bus, its horn still blaring, whistled by.

The road behind the bus was clear and Edward heaved the wheel to the left again. The Merc was overtaking too. But Edward's car still had its revs and momentum from the near escape and he was gaining on the Merc. The one-kilometre sign went by and daylight could be seen at the end of the tunnel. An articulated tanker was coming towards them but it was two or three hundred yards away. The Merc was overtaking a coach while the BMW was abreast of yet another caravan. The Mercedes was now about thirty yards in front of the BMW but Edward and Victoria were no longer closing on Zakros. If anything, he was pulling away.

Edward hit his headlamp switch and they shot on again, dazzling Zakros and Nancy. They also must have annoyed the tanker driver for he put his on too. Now the Merc was surrounded on both sides with light. In the light Edward saw something that made his heart lurch and he hauled the wheel to the right. He made it just in time.

To mark the end of the tunnel, as at the French end, a continuous row of heavy-duty, red and white metal poles had been inserted into the central gully of the roadway. There was little space – a few inches maybe – between the poles. The Merc was now on the wrong side of the road, with the poles between it and safety. The tanker was seventy yards away.

Zakros drove into the poles. They buckled under the force of the Mercedes and one or two snapped off and shot into the air. Still others, however, wedged themselves between the tyres of the car and the bodywork or the chassis. One must have interfered with the steering mechanism for Zakros found that he could not correct the wheel. The Merc broached the row of poles but then hit the nearside wall of the tunnel. The rear end slewed round and the car bounced back into the middle of the roadway.

'Brake!' screamed Victoria. 'For God's sake!'

But Edward was already braking. He had also punched the hazard warning lights, so that the car behind him would also stop, or try to. The Mercedes was about seventy yards ahead of them now but moving backwards on the other side of the tunnel roadway.

The BMW had slowed to about 15 kilometres per hour when the tanker hit the Merc. The tanker driver was doing his level best to stop but he didn't have the space. The cab of the truck rose up above the Mercedes' boot. The first half of the articulated section slewed across the road, propelled by the back half. The metal tank slammed into the Merc a second time and Victoria saw petrol seeping from a crack that had formed.

'Out!' she yelled.

Edward wasn't much behind her. Behind the BMW the traffic was screeching to a halt and they heard two collisions. But the collisions didn't register, for the pair of them were running down the tunnel, away from the tanker but on the tanker's side of the road. They had gone perhaps thirty yards when the felt a warm blast of air sweep over them. They kept running. A klaxon sounded as the smoke detectors went off and the big fans above them in the roof of the tunnel suddenly switched into double time. Sweeping the air towards the fire so that it blew out of the tunnel.

Edward and Victoria kept running, but less and less fast as they felt they were escaping the fire and the asphyxiation that went with it. Suddenly a cooler draft of air hit them and Victoria gasped, 'This will do. The fresh air comes in here.'

Only now did they stop, breathing heavily. They looked back. A fire was burning fiercely. They could hear the whoosh of flames, the crackle of burning, the screams of dying. They had been closer than anybody and so they knew what was happening. They waited five minutes, ten, fifteen minutes. Every so often there was a fresh explosion, a soft whoosh! as another compartment in the tanker went up.

Other drivers left their cars and joined them, asking what had happened. They both just shook their heads, as if in shock. No 'as if' about it. They heard the klaxon of the fire service, and the machine which was kept at the end of the tunnel for emergencies raced down the wrong side of the road. By now the smell of burning petrol, burning paint and burning flesh had reached their nostrils. It made everyone cough.

The flames disappeared, to be replaced by dense black smoke. This made the coughing worse but the fans still kept the air flowing out of the tunnel so that there was no serious hazard of asphyxiation. Edward looked at his watch: 12.50, ten to noon in London. It was now half an hour since the collision. 'Come on,' he said.

They walked back to the BMW, and then on past it. The stench, and the heat, got worse, but the smoke was beginning to clear. Water ran everywhere.

The forward section of the tanker, they could now see, had fallen on the Mercedes. They bent to peer inside.

'Don't look!' said a fireman from behind a plume of smoke. 'It will horrify you for the rest of your lives.'

But Edward and Victoria had to look. They stared at what they saw, the remains of Nancy and Zakros, of the holdalls and the tubes and what had once been magnificent pictures.

There was really nothing to see, for nothing was left, the heat had been too intense. But no, they wouldn't forget.

The steward leaned forward and filled Lockwood's glass with wine. It was a deep-gold colour.

'My father bought this, Mr Lockwood. I am not a wine authority – or an authority on very much.' The Queen smiled a very relaxed smile. 'But I'm told this is one of the best there is.'

Indeed it was. It was a 1928 Château d'Yquem.

Lunch was being served in a part of the palace that neither Lockwood nor any Prime Minister had been admitted to before: the royal family's private quarters. The Duke of Edinburgh was there and the Princess Royal. Princess Margaret was still in Mustique, still ill apparently.

'I want to hear what happened this morning, Mr Lockwood. But first . . . how is your grandson? What is the latest news?'

'Slightly better, ma'am, thank you. The clot has not re-formed and the pressure has been relieved. Touch wood . . . the operation was a success.'

The Queen smiled.

'This morning . . . what happened was not very pleasant, I am afraid.'

'This is not a time to be squeamish.'

Lockwood told them about the 'accident' in the Mont Blanc tunnel. Some of the details he didn't know himself. But when he had finished the Queen said, 'The tanker driver . . . do we know his name?'

'He was Italian . . . I can find out.'

'I think we should offer discreet help to his family – and to the family of the pilot killed in Greece . . . I'm sorry for what happened.' There was a silence around the table. There was no escaping the fact that, in order to preserve the good name of the British royal family, innocent people had suffered and been killed.

'And . . .' The Queen looked embarrassed. 'The pictures? . . . The documents?'

'All destroyed, ma'am. There was an almighty fire, fanned by the extractors inside the tunnel. The cardboard tubes and the canvases rolled up in them, the holdalls with other pictures and the documents, the portfolio case – all were engulfed in the explosion. Andover and Tatton both checked. Dr Shelby, who is the only member of the Apollo Brigade to survive, is the most junior of all. She knew the aims of the plot, but she had never seen the Blunt pictures and did not know the details. She's no threat.'

There was silence around the table. Then the Queen said, 'As for yourself, Mr Lockwood, you face a difficult afternoon in the House of Commons.'

'Not as difficult as last evening, ma'am.'

The Queen smiled. 'Perhaps . . . but this time I think I can help.' She told him two things, both of which caused him to smile. He looked at the Princess Royal and then back to her mother.

'Thank you, ma'am. Thank you, very much.'

'The Prime Minister.' The Speaker pulled his gown around him and sat back in his seat. He crossed his legs. The House was again overflowing – with MPs, with distinguished strangers, with the general public in the gallery, with more than a hundred peers from the House of Lords.

Lockwood stood up and stepped forward. He looked up at the clock. It had just gone three-fifteen. He was wearing a double-breasted navy suit, a pale-blue shirt and a silk tie with a light-blue paisley pattern. He carried no notes. He turned to survey the House. He allowed his gaze to linger on George Keld, and then on Arthur Page. He looked up and found Francis Mordaunt in the Distinguished Strangers' Gallery.

'Mr Speaker,' he said loudly. 'I must begin by offering the House an apology.' A murmur, a rustle of movement, exploded softly along the Commons benches. This was not the Lockwood they expected. Hadn't the man just been to Buckingham Palace to see the Queen? Wasn't he about to resign? Silence again took over. 'I offer the House an apology because, in the debate yesterday, I misled honourable members. I misled them not because I wanted to but because I was forced to. I can explain best what I mean if I give the House an account of certain events which have taken place in the last days and weeks and of which this House had no cognisance. By the time I have finished I hope that the House will accept that I acted correctly in not divulging certain . . . secrets before today.' Lockwood paused and looked again at Keld and Page. Both men returned his stare.

'Just under three weeks ago, it was briefly noted in the "Court & Social" page of *The Times* that Princess Margaret was confined to her bed on the Caribbean island of Mustique, suffering from food poisoning. Members may not remember this item of information since it was overshadowed by the news that, on the very same day, Her Majesty herself was confined to bed through influenza. I have to tell the House that neither of these illnesses occurred. The day before, a group of seven terrorists, most of them Greek and calling themselves the Apollo Brigade had kidnapped the princess and were holding her hostage – '

There was another burst of movement along the benches of the Commons. It began to dawn on people that the game they had come to watch had changed. The Prime Minister, who should have been out cold by this stage, still had plenty of life left in him.

'The Queen's "influenza" was in fact a public sign to the kidnappers that we – the British government – were willing to negotiate with them.' Lockwood stared intently at Page. 'I need hardly add that the demands of this Apollo Brigade were . . . the return to Athens of the so-called Elgin Marbles. So began a very dangerous time. Days and weeks in which only I and a few very trusted aides knew the complete picture. Days and weeks in which the Queen was most anxious for the safety of her sister.' Lockwood looked up at Mordaunt again. The Princess Margaret idea had been the Queen's own – one of the two things she had broached at lunch. 'Days and weeks in which it appeared, as I was told several times in this House yesterday, that I was behaving in an unconstitutional and authoritarian way. Days and weeks during which it appeared that the government was losing its grip – "shilly-shallying" as it was described.' Lockwood beamed. 'None of that was true, of course. But I – we – could not tell the House any of what we knew. It was a condition of the kidnappers that nothing was made public. They had their own plans for announcing their end of the "deal" when the Marbles reached Greece.

'Naturally, the government did not sit idly by as these demands were made. The House will not expect me to go into details which might compromise our security forces in future operations. Likewise, I am sure the House *will* expect me to convey its good wishes to Her Royal Highness now that she has come through this ordeal successfully. As I say, the amount I can disclose publicly about this issue is limited, for the moment anyway, by security. However, I can say that we established fairly quickly that the Brigade, as it called itself, was composed of six Greeks and one American. One of the Brigade was a Greek based in Switzerland and the others all lived in Greece.' Lockwood had decided to leave out any reference to Shelby – it was safer for the Queen not to have it known that the conservator was on Fleet Street's doorstep. 'I say "was" and "were" because I can report to the House that the operation was brought to a successful conclusion at around noon today. Princess Margaret, as I have said, is safe – though all members of the Apollo Brigade are dead. A fuller statement will be issued from Downing Street later today, after the security services have examined what happened in detail and they have vetted the details that can be released without jeopardizing future operations of a similar nature. What I can tell the House is that HMS *Anglesey*, which was carrying the Elgin Marbles to Greece, has now changed course and is returning to Britain – '

A cheer erupted from the public gallery as Lockwood said this, soon taken up on the government benches. On the opposition's side of the House, members sat as if stunned. Lockwood waited for the noise to die down before even attempting to go on. He knew the House was hanging on his every word, that it was a complete reversal of the day before, and he did not intend to throw this moment away.

Eventually he felt able to make himself heard. 'I hope honourable members will concede that this news I bring casts a different light on the events of the past weeks – '

Cheering again now from the government benches.

'Far from being a "shilly-shallying" government, this has been one which has handled an unprecedented situation with determination, intelligence, tact – and has emerged successful. I need hardly add that both Her Majesty and Princess Margaret have been through a very difficult time. As honourable members may know, I have just returned from Buckingham Palace, where I had the good fortune to lunch with the Queen in her private apartments. She is naturally very relieved, but the Queen was also anxious to show her gratitude to the government. She has therefore told me she intends to honour it by bestowing personal knighthoods on Mr Bernard Midwinter, Press Secretary at Downing Street, on Mr Jocelyn Hatfield, Chief Whip, on Mr Tom Lessor, Home Secretary, and on Mr Eric Slocombe, my personal political adviser. I, too, am to receive a similar honour. I need hardly remind members that this honour enables a Commoner to still remain a member of this House.' Lockwood beamed at Page, now cowering on the opposition front bench. The knighthoods had been the second of the Queen's own ideas.

He turned again to face the Speaker. 'However, I do recognize that, although this country has no written constitution, some procedures do have the force of tradition if not the force of written law. And there can be no getting away from the fact that, last night, I as Prime Minister, lost a censure motion. In the circumstances, therefore, and in the face of so many opposition calls for my resignation, I now announce that Parliament is to be dissolved. I am resigning as Prime Minister but I am *not* resigning as leader of my party. Quite the reverse, in fact. I intend to fight the general election, in three weeks' time, with the same team as has just won through the difficult battle against the Apollo Brigade. The opposition and some members of my own party' – he looked at George Keld – 'wanted a fight. They shall have it!'

Epilogue

The mirror jigged up, down, up again, down. Edward's tie remained untied. He cursed.

'The taxi's here!'

'I'm nowhere near ready. Bloody houseboats! You never let on the river was so busy . . . All these waves, from the traffic – '

'You think I'm ready? Look.'

He turned. Victoria stood in the doorway to the bedroom. She wore high-heeled shoes, a big floppy hat, and nothing else.

'I'm not sure your aunt would have approved – but I do. You're overdressed.'

'And you're oversexed. If it hadn't been for you, we'd both've been ready.'

'It's only Buckingham Palace.'

'And I'm only coming because you can show me the pictures.'

She disappeared back into the bedroom and Edward faced the mirror again. He felt nervous, thrilled – and more than a trifle embarrassed. Everything had moved so swiftly since . . . since the episode in the tunnel. Back in Britain, there had been endless meetings, debriefings with the Queen, with Mordaunt, with the security services – and of course with Lockwood. Lockwood had offered Edward a job. In fact, a choice of jobs. He'd invited him out to Chequers – all by himself – for lunch. There, Lockwood had said, 'I've fixed Arran at the National Gallery, by the way – and that Ramsay chap. I've threatened them with the Official Secrets Act but I have also promised them more money to acquire pictures. They won't talk – or ask questions.'

Edward nodded, relieved.

'Now, you. You're wasted in the art world, my boy. Come into politics. It's more interesting, more important, more fun.'

'And more dangerous.'

'Of course! I want you to run a Number Ten research outfit. Think up new, imaginative ideas for the government.'

'You're convinced you're going to win, then?'

'Come on, Edward. You're not a naïve academic any more. If you ever were. Have you not been reading the polls?'

Edward had. Lockwood's coup, a week before election day, had been to put the Elgin Marbles back on display at the British Museum. 'The Elgin Marbles' was the term used by everyone now. The queues at the museum were immense, reaching to Southampton Row and creating traffic jams as far afield as Great Ormond Street Hospital.

'Well, if you won't come and work for me, what job do you want?'

'I . . . I'm not sure I'm old enough – experienced enough – for the job I really want. I haven't published enough – '

'Bah! Academics! You've got to take your chances in this life, Edward. Look around you. You're never again going to get a Prime Minister's invitation to lunch, one to one. No other Prime Minister is going to offer you such enormous patronage. Don't be such a bloody fool . . . In your wildest dreams, before this whole . . . Apollo Brigade business blew up . . . what was the job you coveted above everything else?'

Edward hadn't replied straight away. He knew that Lockwood spoke sense but he was embarrassed all the same.

'Come on! What is it? The National Gallery? The Tate?'

Another pause. 'The British Museum, sir.'

'Perfect. Perfect,' purred Lockwood. 'Ogilvy nearly jumped ship in the middle. Now he can walk the plank.'

'Could you be . . . discreet about it, sir?'

'All right, if that's how you want it. I'll kick him upstairs somewhere. Some arts commission maybe.' He had beamed. 'So that's settled.'

Mordaunt had been relieved by the news. 'Hillier is a bit miffed at missing all the excitement,' he had said over a glass of sherry in his office. 'It's probably for the best that you are leaving.'

'What about the three pictures?' Edward had asked. 'The Raphael, the Canaletto and the Poussin.'

'What pictures?' Mordaunt's cold stare had put in another appearance.

Edward had finished his sherry quickly, glad now that he was leaving the Palace.

His feelings about Nancy were quite under control now. Discreet enquiries by the security services seemed to confirm that her interest in sculpture had led her to Greece and given her a sympathy for Greek culture. That had been fanned into a political involvement after she had met Zakros. She had been steered to him by Kolettis, whom she met naturally through academic circles. Zakros was the link to Blunt. He had been an art dealer who had arranged introductions for the art historian on the Greek homosexual network. The security services had been able to find out little else in concrete terms, but Zakros and Kofas had always known each other well – the dealer had sold the businessman paintings and antiquities – and were on the same staunchly monarchist circuit, which included minor Greek royals among its number.

So presumably Zakros, or Kofas, was privy to the rumours about Blunt's pictures in Switzerland – and had finally been able to put the whole thing together after his death and thanks to the traitor's cunning co-operation, as Mordaunt had always suspected. It all dovetailed together, as elegantly and as coldly as the equerry's attire.

'You're going to be so important,' Victoria had said, when he told her about the British Museum job.

Edward had smiled. 'I'll lose my flat, of course. Leaving the Palace job.'

She had slipped her hand in his. 'Could you bear living on the river?'

It hadn't been mentioned directly again. They both knew they were taking a risk, moving too fast perhaps. But, at the same time, they were both ready. Though they had been invited to Hatfield's election night party, at 12 Downing Street, they had spent the time moving Edward's belongings from Kensington Palace to Chelsea Embankment. Victoria had solved the problem of Edward's untidy piles of paper by simply throwing them away. He hadn't missed them. His pictures had fitted well with the silver objects and the treen, and in any case, he told himself, his life was going to be a whole lot tidier from now on: the Director of the British Museum had three secretaries.

By five in the evening on election day, it had become clear from the exit polls that Lockwood's majority would be nearer seventy-five than thirty-five in the new Parliament. He had been photographed the next day on the steps of Number Ten with his wife and grandson, Tommy.

Edward finally had his tie knotted. He put on a black morning jacket and stood again in front of the mirror.

'Sir Edward Andover, unless I'm much mistaken.'

He turned. Victoria had left her hat and shoes where they were but between them had wrapped a black and white silk dress around her body. She looked very sexy. Edward gave a mock bow. 'As you said, this is the chic-est houseboat in history.'

Edward locked the door and they walked up the gangway. It was amazing how easily he had taken to living with someone. He had always looked upon himself as a solitary soul. Not lonely – far from it – but someone who enjoyed his own company. He had even believed that his disposition helped if you were a scholar. But all that had gone by the board after he had moved in with Victoria. Both had their jobs, their engrossing jobs, but Edward now found it easier to switch off when Victoria was around. Marriage had not been discussed, except by Samantha, who said she would only forgive Edward for his non-appearance for the concert if she could be a bridesmaid.

On the Embankment, the taxi – a white Mercedes almost identical to the one that had crashed in the tunnel – was waiting. Edward held the door open for Victoria as she got in. He went around to the other side and slipped in alongside her. 'Buckingham Palace,' he said to the driver.

The driver looked at him in the rear-view mirror. He had a dark complexion – Greek maybe.

'Buckingham Palace,' Edward repeated, and the driver grinned.

'Great,' he said. 'It's the first time I've ever been.'

Edward looked at Victoria and smiled. 'And it's probably my last.'